I0720962

A CURSE OF FATE

SHIFTER CITY FATED MATES
BOOK 1

JAYMIN EVE

Jaymin Eve
A Curse of Fate: Shifter City Fated Mates #1
Copyright © Jaymin Eve 2024

All rights reserved
First published in 2024
Eve, Jaymin
A Curse of Fate: Shifter City Fated Mates #1

No part of this book may be reproduced, stored in a retrieval system or transmitted in any form or by any means, without the prior permission in writing of the publisher, nor be otherwise circulated in any form of binding or cover other than that in which it is published and without a similar condition, including this condition, being imposed on the subsequent purchaser. All characters in this publication other than those clearly in the public domain are fictitious, and any resemblance to real persons, living or dead, is purely coincidental.

Cover and art: Tamara Kokic
Editing: Ocean's Edge Editing
Proofing: Jaymin Eve's Badass Team

TRIGGER WARNINGS

Your mental health is important to me! If you need any specific information about what might be included, please contact me at jaymineve@gmail.com

Triggers include:
  * Death of a parent.
  * Mild references to past abuse/trauma (not her mates and not detailed on page).
  * Scenes of a sexual nature (it's a series that will build in spice with each release) with dominant males.
  * Explosions and violence.
  * Alpha males with obsessive and possessive tendencies.

ABOUT THIS WORLD

This will contain some mild spoilers about the world and characters.

In this world shifters have evolved from living in isolated packs with a single alpha leader. Now they live in large shifter cities (five in USA) where multiple alphas lead smaller bonded groups of five (quintet).

Shifters fall under one of the following designations (in dominance order): Alpha, Beta, Delta, Omega.

These cities and bonded packs do have an Alpha Council which is made up of the 20 strongest alphas in the city.

The five cities are: Silver City (Vermont), Greenville (Louisiana), Durangille (Montana), Thorny Gardens (Kansas), and the largest of the cities is Golden Claw (Oregon).

Quintets are not always sexually involved with each other (all members) but usually some of the members are. Most of the time they choose to bond due to love, respect, and power. The strongest, true mate bonds though, come from a scent match. Where the shifters scent their mate in a strong connection, that is blessed by the goddess.

Scent matches form the strongest quintets.

To claim members in their quintet, shifters will bite while partially shifted (jaw), so the souls of their beasts can connect. This can happen before you have completed the quintet (generally for sexually involved shifters), or once you have a complete quintet, the entitled alpha of the five will create the bond.

This is dedicated to the "big boy" trend.

Need a big boy?

Want a big boy?

I'll give you four.

CHAPTER 1

Freedom. *An illusion that was about to shatter.*

"Stop! The council requires all shifters to be registered with a pack city."

Not bothering to look back, I sprinted down the alley, heading for the metal ladder I secured to the ground the day I moved into this apartment block. I never went into any situation without a plan B, C, and D in the works. These plans had kept me out of shifter cities for the past ten years, ever since Mom died.

"Fucking rogue! Stop!" he shouted again.

I felt the force of his dominance as he attempted to halt me in my tracks, but it rolled off me like it was never there. The fact that I was unaffected would clue him in to my designation, increasing the danger to me tenfold. Which I'd worry about *if* I got caught.

I'd never expected to encounter an alpha in Jacksonville, Florida. Alphas, as a rule, stuck to the main shifter cities, and I, as a rule, never went near those places.

Slamming against the ladder's metal rungs, I scaled it in seconds, my long legs and lithe frame giving me the assist needed to move quickly to the second floor. When I scrambled onto the metal balcony, I partially shifted and used my wolf claws to swipe through the rope binding the ladder.

I was gone before it even retracted. In these situations, the difference between freedom and finding myself at the mercy of the packs was a matter of seconds. This wasn't my first chase, but it was my first from an alpha.

"Unregistered shifters are required to face the Alpha Council in Golden Claw City," he repeated, his rage spilling so loudly that even inside the building I heard him. If there were weaker alphas—*or beta and delta shifters*—around, they'd be on their knees at his dominance. Thank fuck I didn't have to deal with that. There weren't a lot of positives to my designation within the packs, but this was one.

I heard a bang as he grabbed the railing to pull himself up, but I was already racing through the empty apartment hall. I'd lived in this rent-by-the-week craphole long enough to know the quickest path to the other side and into the alley where I'd stashed my bike.

Without my baby, a Yamaha YZF-R6, I'd already be dead ten times over.

Golden Claw City was the absolute worst place for me to end up. Or any of the pack cities. The moment I stepped foot in front of the council they'd figure out my designation and the alphas would fight to destroy me. I'd spent too many years avoiding my mom's fate to give in now.

Exiting the building through an open window, I dropped the full story down to the ground, my legs barely registering the impact as I scrambled for my bike. I hadn't even been here a month, and it was already time to move on. Farther from the pack cities. Farther from whatever destiny awaited me at the hands of the council.

Farther from turning into my mother.

Not that she hadn't deserved absolutely everything that happened to her, but that wasn't the point. The point was, I couldn't let the same happen to me.

My baby was exactly where I'd left her, tucked into a side street, already packed with a bag holding enough essentials to get me through a week. My getaway bag never left my bike, no matter how long I spent in a town.

The engine roared to life with a twist of my key and press of the button. There was a shout from behind. *Fuck a delta! He found me fast.* The alpha had my scent now, which would absolutely bite me on the ass, but I couldn't worry about it today.

I had to get out of Jacksonville.

Lifting the kickstand, I pulled the clutch and shifted it into gear, taking off into the darkening street. It was early evening, but the weather in Florida was far from cooling off, even as we approached Halloween. I had wondered about the weather changes here, but I wasn't going to find out; it was time to ditch the East Coast and head into a new territory.

Step one: avoid the main pack cities. There were five that I was aware of: Silver City in Vermont, Greenville in Louisiana, Durangille in Montana on the Canadian border, Thorny Gardens in Kansas, and the largest of all cities was Golden Claw. It sat on the West Coast in Oregon, right near the Californian border, taking up a large chunk of its forests and land.

Don't get me wrong, shifters could be anywhere—witch magic kept the humans out of shifter cities, but unfortunately it didn't keep shifters from human towns. But they never stayed long-term. If you weren't tied to one of the cities and their council, then you were considered a rogue.

And rogues got put down.

I'd been on the run for a long time, but the last eight

months had been particularly tough. It was almost as if I kept finding myself drawn to areas where shifters were visiting, which had forced me to run more than usual. It was freakin' exhausting.

My ride through the dense urban center started slow, then I was able to fully open her up on the highway. As I sped into the darkness, my pulse finally stopped hammering in my throat, and my wolf's growl simmered down in my chest. We weren't on the best of terms these days, my beast and I. We might share a soul but her instincts were ancient and didn't always align with human emotions. To her, we should be with other shifters, going on pack runs, protected from the human world.

A wolf's instinct knew that a strong pack was the greatest force on Earth, and she pushed me toward the shifter cities every time I was in wolf form. Hence why I hadn't shifted in weeks and would hold out until there was no other choice. *Pack*, she rumbled before settling down.

It's too dangerous, we're not like other shifters.

My wolf huffed, and I knew she thought I was an idiot ruled by a weak brain, but she left it with a derisive huff for now.

Forcing my thoughts away from another narrow escape, I let my mind calm, until there was nothing except the open road.

I rode for days, traveling across multiple state lines, only stopping to refuel and sleep beside my bike in pockets of forest.

Six days into my journey I crossed into New Mexico and pure exhaustion had me deciding to find a hotel. None of the larger pack towns were nearby, so it should be safe to rest for a few days. I reached Santa Fe by mid-day and parked my bike in a street lined with shops and market stalls.

After dismounting, I stretched my legs and eased the ache

in my back, desperate for a proper shower and bed. I'd never been here before, but I was captivated by the city's colorful buildings and unique architecture. Santa Fe held on to its history, and it echoed in the street until I could scent it in the cobbled stone paths and crumbling bricks.

No one paid attention to me as I explored, and I worked hard not to let my tourist show. Everyone noticed tourists, and I needed to blend. Eventually I headed back to my bike, thankful that I hadn't encountered any sign or scent of another shifter in the area.

For the first time in almost a week I was relaxed as I munched on the meatball sub I'd purchased from a nearby café, which was the freshest, tastiest meal I'd eaten in days.

Even better, the owners directed me to a reasonably priced hotel for the night.

With the sun setting and the air cooling, I rode a couple of blocks to park beside the hotel. It wasn't the best spot to stash my bike, but it'd do for a night. I planned on being gone early tomorrow.

Slinging my duffle bag over my shoulder, I procured a room easily enough and headed for "twenty-four," the number drawn on the weathered green door with a sharpie. It was an old building with a square, low-set design. Ugly as heck, but I didn't care. My only hope was for no roaches or rats. After days of sleeping on the hard ground, the rest I could deal with.

Inside, I was pleasantly surprised to find a dated but immaculate space. Cream walls highlighted simple furniture: two queen beds, a table with a lamp between them, and a desk in the corner. When I slid open the bathroom door, I discovered a shower-bath combo, and almost let loose my shriek of excitement.

I was going to soak my aching bones for an hour. Refusing to shift except when necessary had cost me over the years, but a good bath could fill some of the gaps left from my weaker healing abilities.

I locked the door and slid the deadbolt across—not that it'd stop a shifter, but it would give me a few seconds' notice. Leaving my bag on the bed, I entered the bathroom and cranked the water full blast. While it was heating, I retrieved my bag of toiletries. I only had a toothbrush and paste, facewash and moisturizer, along with mascara and lip gloss. Everything else was back in Florida.

My financial situation was tenuous, but I'd managed to stash a few grand over the last two years. Thank the moon goddess I had it on me when I'd run. It would hurt to dig into those funds to replace everything I left behind, but it was better than being dragged to the pack cities.

Ditching my clothes on the floor with plans to wash them in the sink later, I stepped into the shower and quickly scrubbed myself down using one of those complimentary soap packets. It smelled grossly of roses and chemicals. Usually shifters avoided anything lab-made, but for the last few years they'd come in handy to hide my natural scent.

It was my bad luck that I'd run into that alpha after finishing my shift at the diner, when I'd already sweated through the synthetic scent. He'd scented me as a shifter from across the street, and when his alpha growl hit me, I'd taken off. I wasn't about to wait around for him to ask for my pack affiliation.

Not if I wanted to live to see my twenty-sixth birthday.

CHAPTER 2

After the best bath in the history of baths, I crawled into bed naked. I didn't have enough clothes to waste on sleeping in them, especially when I was down to three shirts, a pair of denim shorts, and two pairs of jeans. I'd be living light until I could hit some thrift stores.

By the time my head hit the pillow, I was crashing so hard that I was out for almost twenty-four hours. Once or twice a month exhaustion forced me into a deep sleep. As a rogue, it wasn't safe to leave myself so vulnerable, but I hoped my wolf would alert me to any true danger.

When she piped up, just as I opened my eyes, screaming *danger danger danger* at me, I thought she was commenting on my trust in her, until I heard the scrape of shoes on the pavement.

I jumped off the bed and was hit with the earthy scent of shifters. Holding desperately to my panic, which would debilitate me, I yanked on athletic shorts and a tank with an inbuilt bra. With my duffle bag in hand, I raced on light feet toward the window, thanking the goddess when the flimsy screen lifted easily. On the breeze the musky scent grew stronger, indicating there was more than one shifter outside.

Fear and annoyance hit simultaneously as I cursed my rookie error in parking my bike beside the hotel and not out the back. Now I had no other option except to run and hope I found a bike to hijack on the way.

As I threw myself out of the window, my wolf stirred. *Stay with the pack.*

No! I cried in a panic. *Pack is not for us.*

After everything I'd done to remain out of the pack cities, my one encounter with that alpha in Florida had fucked it all up. I'd known he was a tracker, and he'd clearly followed my path, even as I fled across multiple state lines.

The hotel door was kicked open as I rolled across the loose gravel outside. I felt a few cuts and nicks from the fall, but even my weaker shifter healing would kick in soon, and I was no stranger to pain. It wouldn't slow me down.

Sprinting like my life depended on it, I took as many side roads as possible, while keeping an eye out for a bike. I managed to make it almost back to the street I'd first parked in, when a rumble echoed from behind me, growing in intensity until it filled my chest.

They'd sent a powerful alpha after me, but his dominance wouldn't stop me—provided I remained out of reach. Rough ground bit into my feet, which spurred me on harder.

It wasn't enough, though, as strong arms wrapped around me.

I was fighting before we hit the ground, but the much larger shifter didn't pull any punches, slamming the full force of his weight into me. I was tall for a woman, standing five-eleven in bare feet, but his frame completely engulfed mine as we went down together. "Stay the fuck down, rogue," he growled, slamming me against the ground again.

Twisting as I was taught when pinned by a larger opponent, I managed to get my hands under me only to be slammed down once more. My skull cracked the ground, and everything went dark.

Warmth surrounded me as my awareness returned, and I had a second to bask in the semi-conscious glow before I remembered exactly what had happened.

Shifters found me. I was truly in the hands of the packs for the first time.

I'd been on the run with mom until I was four, and even when she met the Rogers pack, we'd lived outside the cities. She'd died when I was fourteen, and although I'd managed to make it on my own for eleven extra years, that luck had come to an end.

Needing to assess the danger nearby, I kept my eyes closed and slowed my breathing. My skull throbbed faintly, but whatever damage was done by the alpha had almost healed.

I sensed at least two shifters in the room, giving off the faintest scents of citrus and soap bubbles. But the clean, non-chemical versions.

"Are you sure she's an omega?" The deep voice almost startled me into revealing I was awake.

They know my designation. Which was more terrifying than anything else happening in this room. "She ignored an alpha call twice," another, smoother toned male replied. "Does she feel strong enough to be more dominant than Alpha Brandon or Davison?"

As an omega, my dominance was all but nonexistent. My

strength lay in other areas, areas that made me valuable to a pack. *Just like Mom.*

A fact that had eventually destroyed her miserable life.

"How has she managed to stay off our radar?" the first shifter asked, sounding confused that anyone could outrun the big, bad pack cities. "Do we know how old she is?"

His question gave me a flicker of an idea. I looked younger than my twenty-five years, which could work to my advantage. Rogues were generally put to death—they didn't allow any shifter to remain unbonded from a pack, and my number of years on the run would squarely cement me as unsalvageable. Except if they offered leniency due to my *younger* age.

"It really doesn't matter," the smoother voice said. "She needs to go before the Alpha Council either way."

A firm hand pressed against my chest, and my eyes jerked open to bring a brawny male into view. He didn't look much taller than me, but he was twice the width with hard brown eyes and tousled brown hair. "Your heartrate changed a few seconds ago," he said in the gruff voice. His wolf shifted behind his eyes briefly, and I noted that he didn't carry alpha energy, but was a strong beta. "You're only delaying the inevitable."

Knocking his hand off me, I quickly pulled myself up to a sitting position. A glance around revealed that I was in what looked like a hospital with white walls and a twin bed.

"Where have you taken me? What city?" I rasped through a throat that felt drier than a desert.

The beta sat in a chair beside the bed, and never took his gaze off me. The other shifter remained near the door, and I didn't bother to glance his way.

The threat was right at my side.

"You're in Golden Claw, awaiting trial in front of the council."

Golden Claw... I'd been out for hours, maybe longer,

depending on how they'd transported me here from New Mexico.

"Why am I on trial?" I'd already decided to stick with my plan of playing young and dumb.

The beta shook his head, as if I'd disappointed him. Too fucking bad. "Rogues are outlawed. You're uncontrollable, and a danger to the human population. If you were unaware of that for a reason, you'll have a chance to plead your case to the council. Start working on your story now." When his lips twitched, it was clear he thought I was full of shit, and not for the first time I wished my face wasn't so expressive.

I wasn't a great liar, and in my line of work—running from the pack cities was a full-time job, ask anyone—it made for a difficult time. Today, though, would be my greatest challenge. I couldn't screw it up.

Step one was to convince them not to rip my heart out where I stood. Step two was to stay in the city just long enough to create a plan which would not only get me out of here but help me skip the country.

America wasn't safe for me any longer. Not now they'd scented and cataloged me as an omega. Nothing was safe for an omega. That was the legacy Mom left me with, and I'd sacrificed everything to change my fate and not end up like her.

"You have five minutes to freshen up," Mr. Gruff said, waving his hand toward a door on the right of the bed. "Bathroom is through there."

Without removing my focus from the two shifters guarding me, I slid out of bed, relieved to see I was still in the clothes I'd thrown on in the hotel. Shifters weren't the best with consent, and after living in the human world most of my life, I didn't have their casual approach toward nudity. If either of these assholes had touched me, I'd have lost control of my beast and tried to destroy them.

In the bathroom, I closed the door behind me, unsurprised to find no windows or means of escape. They'd never have let me in here alone if there was a chance I could make a break for it. After using the toilet, I washed my hands and splashed water onto my face, attempting to bring a touch of color back into my pale cheeks. My reflection flashed as I straightened, and lucky for me, I looked as terrible as I felt.

My strawberry blond hair was tangled in matted clumps around my head, my skin paler than usual, giving the spattering of freckles across my nose and cheeks a chance to stand out as the stars of the show. *The shit show.* My light blue eyes were dull, but that wasn't only due to today. Life had been beating me down for years, and never letting my wolf out had weakened my natural shifter healing and energy.

Come on, Emmeline. Get your shit together.

Yep, I was the queen of pep talks, and I'd never needed one more than I needed it today.

Gruff voice was waiting for me when I emerged from the bathroom; the other shifter had left. There was a split second when we eyed each other. He wore a stupid little smile as if daring me to try my luck.

As I took a step closer, he opened his palm, and I jerked to a halt at the piece of technology he held. I'd never seen this particular device before, but as it was in my best interest to keep up with the cities, I recognized the flame and lightning strike symbol on the side. Reeves Industries was the leading manufacturer of weapons in the shifter world, and if my guess was correct, Gruff held a state-of-the-art taser that would send me into a partial shift, leaving me stuck between wolf and human form, and completely at his mercy.

"I'm not going to run," I scoffed, my false bravado in the

face of such a weapon thin at best. "I'm not an idiot. I've accepted my fate." *Total lie.* But I had accepted it for now.

He twirled the small device in his hand, and I stopped breathing to keep my chest from expanding closer toward him. "Good to know you're not as stupid as first appearances suggested," he said, and I start praying he accidentally zapped himself. *Asshole.*

The door opened and another shifter stepped through, this one with strong alpha energy. The beta stopped fucking around, straightening to his full height of exactly one inch taller than me, as he pretended he hadn't just been juggling a very expensive weapon.

I hadn't gotten a lot of scent traces from any of the shifters so far, outside of faint citrus and wolf musk. One of the few shifter lores Mom ever bothered to teach me, was that I'd only ever *truly* scent my fated-match. *My mate.* Thank the goddess that wasn't happening here.

"Is she ready to go?" the new arrival said, his voice without inflection.

He was huge, like all alphas, with dark skin, buzzed hair, and a flinty stare. "Yes, sir," Gruff said, a very slight waver of nerves in his voice to indicate this newcomer was important enough to warrant respect. "Are you here to escort her?"

He ignored Gruff and turned to me. "I'm Alpha Warrick of the Annandale pack. And one of the council members who will be overseeing your trial today. Are you ready?"

My throat dried out fast and I almost vomited on his shoes. With a fraction of my dignity intact, I nodded and stepped closer to the imposing alpha. At a guess, he was a few decades older than me, but with shifters' extended lifespans, there was no obvious signs of aging, outside of a few wisps of gray visible in his buzz cut. "Ready," I choked out.

Without another word, he wrapped a huge palm around

my right biceps and pulled me from the room. He wasn't rough so much as impatient, and I forced my legs to move faster to keep up with him. I wasn't completely up to date with the structure of pack cities, but I knew there were multiple alphas who led smaller packs within the community.

A pack was a bonded group, sometimes sexually involved with each other, while other times a platonic family. If *Alpha* Warrick was an *entitled* alpha, then he was powerful enough to command other shifters. Maybe even other alphas. Add in that he was on the council, and they'd sent a VIP to escort me. Lucky me. Always the superstar.

"What's your name, shifter?" he asked as we exited the generic room and marched along a lengthy hallway with many closed doors.

I debated lying, but there wasn't much they could learn from my name. As far as I knew, Mom had ensured it was never recorded anywhere. For her own selfish reasons. "Emmeline Anders."

Warrick grunted, using the preferred method of communication amongst dominant males. "How old are you, Emmeline?"

Fuck. Now I did have to lie. "Eighteen." Another grunt, and I had no idea if he believed me or not.

"Where's your family?"

Wasn't that the question of the hour. "Dead. I've been an orphan since I was young. The streets raised me." I'd only ever known my mom, and when she died I didn't bother to search for anyone else in our fucked-up family tree.

"How did you survive on your own? What age did you shift for the first time?"

"Ten, and my wolf looked after me. She's always had my back." Except when she didn't, which was never about survival; it was about her instincts to be with her pack. But even when I'd refused, she'd always stepped up and kept me alive. We hunted, slept in the woods... did whatever it took to make it through until I was old enough to get a job and apartment.

We did what it took to survive and had no regrets about it.

"Sounds like a tough life," the alpha said, a sliver of sympathy in his tone, his dark eyes softer as he watched me. "Did no one ever tell you about the pack cities? Why have you kept running when you could have found shelter and support here, amongst your kind?"

I was well aware he questioned me to get a jump on the trial, and I chose my answers with that in mind. "Mom was killed by her pack, so it never felt safe to be around other shifters." The goddess honest truth.

"Your mom was an omega too." That wasn't a question as he arrived at the true heart of the issue. The reason I had to get out of the pack cities before it was too late. Omegas were pawns in powerful alphas' worlds, and I refused to end up with the same fate Mom had: destroyed by her pack.

CHAPTER 3

e exited the building via a short staircase. "That's the healing ward," the alpha said, his grip remaining firm around my arm. "It's next door to the main council chambers."

We emerged into a city, a cacophony of cars, horns, and other "city noises" crashing into me. It was extra-loud after the sensory deprivation of the silent hall. The council chamber and healing ward were two large buildings sat side by side. The healing ward was square and squat, with white walls and lots of windows. The council chambers were nothing like that. They stood at least four stories high, and were built from gorgeous red brick with green ivy trailing up the sides of the archways leading to the main entrance. I had no idea what style the architecture was, but I'd guess it wasn't built in this century.

Warrick walked us through the central doors, past a male and female shifter in a navy-blue uniform standing guard. They didn't stop us, but both lowered their heads respectfully to the council member.

Warrick glanced down at me. "We take care of our omegas

here. If they don't have a bonded pack, they're guarded and revered. They're never forced to bond. In fact, we have very strict laws against that in Golden Claw."

"Not everyone obeys laws, Alpha," I said with a huff of sad laughter. "And it's too late once it's *too late*. If you know what I mean."

Tension kept his broad shoulders rigid, and I wondered if I should suggest he take a weekend to enjoy a few cocktails and a massage. He was coiled tight. "I don't expect you to trust us straight away, but if everything goes your way today, I promise that we'll give you a reason to stop running."

The very thought almost sent me to my knees. The hardest part of the path I'd chosen was... *I didn't want it*. Secretly, deep in a place that I kept locked up tight and never visited, I craved this world. I wanted to be part of the packs with a bonded mate and family.

Yep, there was a sad and lonely little girl buried deep inside. I'd tried to burn her out, but like my wolf she wasn't quite ready to give up on the dream. We were all pathetic, and at this stage I couldn't be sure I wasn't suffering from multiple personality disorder.

Desperate for a distraction, I said, "I've got to survive the council first. I don't know much about your world, but it's clear that you don't take well to rogues. I didn't understand before that I wasn't just keeping my freedom, I was flouting your laws." Might as well get started on the lies necessary to build my *innocent* persona.

His gaze remained shrewd, and I wasn't sure he bought it. "Rogues are generally trouble. They lose control of their beasts due to a lack of pack stability. We're not designed to be on our own, it messes with the animal's mind and instinct. You, on the other hand, are about as far from unstable as I've ever seen a rogue shifter who's been without a pack since they were young. I think you'll do just fine."

There was no more time for conversation as we arrived at the trial room. Warrick led me through a set of double doors, where two more navy-clad shifters stood guard. Inside, there was a lot of chatter and mild scents, with dozens of shifters standing in groups looking very alpha-like with their arms crossed over broad chests. More shifters were seated to the sides—the spectators—with all those chairs already filled.

In short, the room was packed, and I was about to pee myself.

"Breathe, Emmeline," Warrick murmured. "You know we can scent your fear and hear your heartbeat. You're not prey. Remember that. *You are not prey.*"

My spine straightened, seemingly of its own volition, and I lifted my head to meet the gazes boring into me. A lot of their eyes were wild, as if their beasts peered through, and I assumed they were attempting to use dominance to test me. Which was never going to work. Omegas weren't part of the normal structure; our designation stood apart, even though technically we could be considered the least dominant. Depending on how you looked at it.

"Alpha Warrick!" a burly redheaded shifter greeted him with a small bow. When he turned his light, orange-tinted eyes on me, I was reminded of a tiger. With the faintest Scottish accent, he added, "And you must be our new omega. It's a pleasure to meet you. I'm Alpha Sorenson of Thenguard Pack."

Sorenson Thenguard was dynamic. There was no other way to describe him. And he was most definitely *not a wolf shifter*.

To my knowledge, the pack cities were made up of seventy percent wolves, with a decent array of other creatures scattered amongst their ranks. Sorenson, with his fair skin and arresting eye color, was a tiger shifter for sure, with his power falling mid-level for an alpha. Not that I was an expert, but omegas were good at reading the power of others.

Another *glorious* gift.

"Emmeline," I said, sounding calmer than I felt. "It's nice to meet you too, though it could be nicer. Under different circumstances."

Sorenson threw his head back and laughed like that was the funniest joke he'd ever heard. I mean, maybe being on trial for my life was a punchline around these parts. "You'll be just fine, lass," he finally said. His beefy hand landed on my shoulder, and I was surprised to feel such a gentle squeeze from this larger-than-life alpha.

"Soren, stop flirting with the rogue," another alpha growled. He was in the group standing near the door. "She's on trial."

Sorenson didn't look worried, flashing his broad smile and shooting me a wink. "I'll see you after the trial, Emmeline," he murmured. "I've got a proposition for you."

I stiffened in Warrick's hold, and before I could stop myself, I shot the older alpha a glare. He promised they were different here, and yet the first alpha I'd met outside of him already had a *proposition for me.* "You *are* safe here," Warrick repeated near my ear. "We can't stop the offers, but we can back you if you refuse. Now, let's get this trial over with."

The rest of the shifters took their seats, and I noted that the vast majority were male. There were alpha females of course, but not many who were both *entitled* and amongst the twenty strongest shifters in the city which made up the Alpha Council.

With a quick glance along the table, I started to calculate my odds of making it through alive. A few of the alphas were already glaring at me, and I knew they wouldn't care what was said here today. In their eyes, I needed to die for my crimes.

Others were better at concealing their emotions, and I couldn't get a clear reading on them.

There was a diverse range of ages, races, and faces seated before me, and I never imagined seeing such a display of power in one place. It was overwhelming, even for a shifter who stood outside normal dominance structures.

"We're still waiting on Reeves Pack," said a tall, blond female on the left side of the council table. She didn't look much older than me but was clearly powerful enough to sit amongst the strongest alphas. "There was an issue on the eastern border that Alpha Hunter wanted to personally deal with, but he'll be here soon."

She preened, as if to point out she had inside information, but I was stuck on hearing that pack name. *Reeves.* As in... Reeves Industries? I didn't know much about the company itself, but the name Hunter Reeves sounded familiar. It would explain why that guard had expensive, patented technology in his hands. I'd been dragged to the city where the genius inventor of weaponry made his home.

Warrick straightened at my side and nodded toward the female. "Thank you, Alpha Sissily. While we wait for the Reeves pack, we can get started with preliminaries." His hold on me loosened and I was moved to stand in front of him. "Here we have Emmeline Anders, aged eighteen, without a pack since she was young. Her mother was murdered by shifters and she ran right after, not realizing she was breaking the law. There's been no formal testing of her designation yet, but she shows signs of being a strong omega, able to withstand direct orders from dominant alphas."

Forcing myself not to fidget, I stared over the top of the long table toward the closed doors which represented my escape. While I daydreamed about *never standing on display like this again*, the doors to the council chambers slammed open.

Power reached us first, crashing into the room with the same force as the doors. Silence descended as a male shifter strode inside, and since I'd been staring longingly at my escape, I was the first to meet his dark as sin eyes.

There was no doubt in my mind who this was...

Alpha Hunter. *Holy shit.*

He was a giant of a shifter, standing at least six and a half feet, dressed in a dove-gray suit, his white button-down open at the collar with no tie. I might have hailed from the poorer side of life, but even I could tell his suit, stretched across broad shoulders and over heavily muscled arms, was custom made and no doubt cost a year of my wages.

As he moved forward, a tsunami of destruction in designer wear, I took in every part of him like he was a piece of art I wanted to buy—only I definitely couldn't afford him.

Hunter's ethnicity wasn't immediately clear, but he had the look and coloring of a Hawaiian guy who'd flirted with me during a shift at O'Malley's bar last year. His brown skin was flawless, his strong jawline covered in a five o'clock shadow, as if by the time he'd finished shaving there was already growth. He wore a look of impatience, running his hand over inky black hair, cut short on the sides and wavy on top where he'd let it grow longer. I could see his attempts to tame the loose curls with product, but rough hands had knocked a few wayward strands free.

As he stalked through the room, I remained locked in a gaze so dark his pupils and irises were almost indistinguishable from each other. *Sweet baby shifter gods.* Hunter Reeves was the most dominant, terrifying alpha I'd ever seen in my life, and considering I was in a room filled with the strongest in Golden Claw, that said a lot.

As he moved toward the remaining empty chair, I was hit

with the delicious scent of coffee laced in chocolate. A *strong* and perfectly noted scent.

NO! Unable to help myself I breathed deeply, and my wolf jerked inside as my entire world stopped. Hunter Reeves was my... scent-match. *What the hell?* My first day in a shifter city, a goddess blessed true mate had strolled into my life.

Hunter ground to a halt, his nostrils flaring as his energy sent more than half the shifters in the room down to the table, most of them barely avoiding a head-smack against the wooden surface. He threw dominance without trying, and even I felt the push against my wolf.

All the while he never took his eyes off me once.

His gaze grew harder, penetrating deeper into my soul.

A soul that screamed for him.

The need to run hit me and I took a step away, and then another, until my back landed against a wall. From my peripherals, I noticed Warrick turn with me, but I couldn't tear my gaze from Hunter to see him clearly.

The darkly enticing alpha, *who my wolf kept screaming* mate *at*, had me locked in his predatory stare. I felt rather than saw Warrick reach out to grab me, but he never got a chance. Hunter leapt across the table and slammed into the other alpha, sending him flying. When his rumble filled the room, utter chaos broke out.

CHAPTER 4

Hunter towered over me, and I mentally readjusted my assessment of his height. How freaking tall was this shifter? Not just height, but breadth and muscles. There was too much, including that sweet mocha scent which had me wanting to climb him like a tree and bury my face in his neck. Gah, scent matches were the worst; they completely clouded the mind and destroyed reasonable thought.

No! Fuck. No.

I had to get myself under control. I could not cave after all these years just because I'd stumbled across my scent match and true mate. An alpha this dominant would destroy me in a heartbeat. He made Mom's alpha pack look near powerless in comparison.

"Alpha Hunter, what are you doing? Stand down from the omega." Warrick was nearby, but he didn't move any closer to the heaving mountain of a male crowding me against the wall.

I couldn't see anything around his giant form, and no one else made any attempt to subdue Hunter Reeves, leaving me completely at his mercy. "Are you going to kill me?" I asked breathlessly, tilting my head all the way back to meet his gaze while bracing myself for his reaction.

His chest rumbled again, and it was clear his wolf was close to the surface. He held on to his control though, retaining a grasp on his beast. "What's your name?" he murmured, his deep rasp sending shivers down my spine.

There was no way I could resist if he touched me, but so far he maintained the smallest distance between us. "Emmeline Anders," I choked out.

Up close, his eyes weren't quite as dark as I'd thought. They were a gray so stormy it was almost charcoal. As I revealed my name, there was the smallest flash of gold around his pupils, and a predatory tilt to his head as he observed me. "Why would I kill you, Emmeline?"

Sissily, the blond alpha, with impeccable timing, piped up: "We don't care if you kill the rogue, Alpha Hunter. But, love, could you release us all from your dominance first?"

Love? Now I was the one who wanted to growl, which was wildly inappropriate considering he was *not my fucking alph*a. Nope. No matter how desperately this brutally beautiful shifter called to me, I could never have a mate or pack.

"Looks like you're being paged, *love*," I whispered, swallowing my snarl. "Might want to back up before your girlfriend gets angry and plucks my eyeballs out."

Even a whisper was heard in a room full of dominant shifters, and I wasn't surprised when Sissily lost her shit and started raving about how I was a mouthy cunt and all rogues should be put down.

"Shut the fuck up, Alpha Sissily," another council member snapped. I couldn't see him of course. I couldn't see anyone around the giant wall of dominance crowding me. Typical fucking alpha.

"Uh, hello?" I called, hoping someone out there could

control Hunter. "Is Alpha Hunter broken? What the hell is actually happening?"

My breath escaped in a harsh rush as Hunter snapped out of his rage, his dominance dying instantly as he took a step away from me. By the time I blinked again, he was gracefully lowering himself into his council seat at the table as if nothing had happened.

Meanwhile, I'd forgotten how to breathe, and why *for the love of all that was holy* did I feel cold now that his overpowering energy no longer encircled me like a gravitational force.

"Emmeline, please step back to the head of the table." Warrick sounded calm and unruffled, as if a hurricane hadn't just blown into the room. "Let's get this underway."

Hunter's appearance had me all but forgetting that I was literally in a fight for my life. The hurricane had blown every thought out of my head but his imposing presence, which was a giant kick-in-the-ass reminder of why I could never have a pack.

I managed not to stumble as I hurried back to the head of the table, and it took every ounce of the control I'd built over the past two and a half decades not to glance at Hunter. Especially when I felt his darkly penetrating gaze on me. My wolf whined for our mate, and I shoved her down. *We have to get through our trial first.* Please. I just needed her on my side this once.

With a huff, she settled, but her awareness remained solidly across that boardroom table with the most dominant shifter in the room.

Warrick picked up where he'd left off: "As I said, Emmeline Anders, eighteen years old, has been on her own since she was very young. Her mother was killed by shifters, which caused her to believe she was unsafe in the shifter cities. We have discerned no signs of instability, but as an omega wolf, that's to be expected."

"*Omega!*"

Despite my best efforts, my head snapped toward Hunter at his growl. He was half out of his chair like he couldn't help himself, and I swallowed roughly, searching for moisture in my mouth. With a strength of will I had no idea I possessed, I pulled my gaze from him and spent an inordinate amount of time staring at the grain of the wooden tabletop.

"Correct, Alpha Hunter," Warrick said, his tone as respectful as one entitled alpha would ever get with another.

"Which means she needs to join a pack," a male council member at the farthest end of the table stated.

Sorenson stood abruptly, and it was a testament to everything that had happened since I met him not ten minutes ago that I'd almost forgotten he was here. "Thenguard Pack is more than happy to speak for her and her safety, once she's cleared from the trial." A smile broke out across his face, his red hair disheveled in a cute, rumpled way. "You know we're a strong pack, and we already have one blessed omega in our ranks."

There are other omegas here?

I straightened. "How many omegas are in this city?"

Sissily scowled at me, and I wondered if she was aware of how she looked with that expression. Should I advise them not to get her wet or feed her after midnight? She snarled. "Prisoners don't get to ask questions, bitch. Shut the hell up."

Hunter slammed his closed fist on the table and half the room jumped. A low, creeping growl rumbled from his chest, catching us all in his vortex. "Emmeline Anders belongs to the Reeves pack. She'll be taken into our custody, and we'll ensure that whatever bad habits she picked up as a rogue are corrected. She *will* become a productive member of our society."

Excuse the fuck out of me? Was this asshole actually for real?

"Yeah, I'm going to pass on that generous offer, but thanks."

My flippant reply had the room falling so silent I could hear the dripping of a tap in a bathroom at least four rooms away.

Hunter slowly rose to his feet, and I wasn't the only one holding my breath. "I'm the true alpha of the strongest quintet in America," he said softly, but no one could miss the deadly intent. "We're a blessed-by-the-goddess pack of scent matches, and you are the fifth of our quintet."

My breaths came out faster as the truth of what I'd stumbled into here became very apparent. It was so much worse than I'd thought. It wasn't only Hunter I had to deal with in this scent match—there were *three more* waiting in the wings. Scent matches were the strongest match a shifter could find.

True freaking mates. Praise the goddess.

Except four alpha males with one omega was the exact situation my mother found herself in, and it got her killed before she even turned forty.

"We're missing the final of our quintet, too," Sorenson called, still upbeat. "I mean, we're not all alphas, because you fuckers have to be overachievers, but we have two betas and an omega."

Quintets were the top tier of the common five-bonded-pack within shifter cities. And *scent-bonded quintets* were considered the Holy Grail. The fact that Sorenson's pack had an omega they hadn't killed yet was a great review, while Hunter was my absolute worst option here. Not only was he my scent match, already driving my wolf crazy, but he was scent matched to other alphas.

Outside of my mom's former quintet, I'd never heard of another with that many alphas. Reeves Pack was my death waiting to happen.

An alpha snarled at Sorenson from down the table. "Most of the alphas at this table are powerful and part of an incomplete quintet or pack. That's why we're all on the council."

Hunter pointed his finger at Sorenson. "Sit the fuck down, Soren."

Despite the room being filled with the strongest alphas in Golden Claw, most of them exhibited fear and deference toward Hunter. Sorenson, on the other hand, acted as if they were old friends. He flipped him off as he grumbled, "Cranky bastard."

But he also did as he was told and sat.

"Is anyone against keeping Emmeline alive and part of Golden Claw shifters at this stage?" Warrick called to get everyone back on track.

Sissily raised her hand along with four other council members, but the majority appeared fine to let me keep my heart beating in my chest.

An older, blond alpha beside Sorenson said, "We have so few true omegas, it would be the greatest crime to execute her. I'm excited to see what dynamic this adds to the pack structure."

Warrick smiled, flashing his perfect teeth. "Excellent. That's part one settled. Part two is going to be more complicated, but we can all agree that Emmeline cannot be allowed to roam freely without security. I've promised her that no harm will befall her from the shifters in our city, and I stand by that promise."

Hunter, who had remained on his feet after the last outburst, didn't interrupt. But I could feel his wolf's dominance simmering through the room.

Warrick glanced down at me with an apologetic stare. "The Reeves pack is the strongest in our city. You will be safest with them. Do you have a good reason for not taking up Alpha Hunter's offer?"

Yes. An exceptionally good reason. A reason I was never going to reveal because I wasn't sure it was common knowledge that a pack of alphas could destroy an omega in the way my mom's pack destroyed her.

Instead, I said, "I'm used to freedom and Alpha Hunter clearly enjoys control and dominance. I think we'll end up coming to blows if I stay in his pack."

"But we're a scent match," he boomed, his scowl infinitely more attractive than Sissily's.

Warrick jerked like I'd used a Reeves Industries' Taser on him. "Scent match? Why didn't you say so before?"

I was confused by what they thought his behavior before had been about. Was I not the only female he'd ever acted this way around? The very idea made me angry enough to snarl into a lie. "Not on my end you're not. I won't be forced to bond no matter how many times you blow into a room and throw your power around, *Alpha Hurricane.* I'll take my chances with literally any other pack."

Several of the alphas lifted their hands, but Hunter's glare shut them down fast. All except Sorenson, who smiled and waved his arm like he was having the time of his freaking life. *Weirdo.*

"Are you saying you reject our offer and pack?" Hunter asked in a softly dangerous tone.

I was too pissed off to care as I replied with the falsest chuckle I could muster. "Wow, not just a pretty face. I don't need or want your protection, but thanks for the offer. I really hope you have the day you deserve."

His eyes grew wilder. I was sure a shifter like him had never been rejected before.

Get used to it, asshole.

"At least she thinks you have a pretty face," Sorenson called with a laugh. "Never thought I'd see the day you found a shifter immune to your charms and power, Hunt." Hunter's face went blank, which only amused Sorenson further as he laughed again and shot a wink my way. "I like you, sweetheart. You're a fun addition to the city."

I wanted to join him in laughing, but I was currently working on *not* vomiting across the council table. Finding a scent match on my first day in a shifter city was not on my to-do list. I mean, *what the actual fuck?* Mom had told me scent matches weren't even common, with most packs bonding out of love or friendship. Was that another one of her lies?

Before I made an even bigger fool of myself, Warrick came to my rescue. "Why don't we give Emmeline a few days to get her bearings," he suggested in a calm tone. "She could stay with my pack, as we're fully bonded in a solid power structure and not looking to add any others to our ranks. I'm sure all of this has been very overwhelming for her after being in the human world. I'll provide some basic training on what to expect in Golden Claw, and when she decides on her path forward, I'll inform the Reeves pack and the council." His smile was gentle, and I found myself calming enough to stave off a full-blown panic attack. "Is that agreeable with you?"

I nodded disjointedly, my head feeling weird and floaty. "Yes, perfect. Thank you."

A few days or a few weeks would make no difference; I'd never agree to live with the Reeves pack. But I did need time to figure out how I would escape *and never* get caught again.

CHAPTER 5

The spectators were the first to leave. After all the commotion with my entrance, and then Hurricane Hunter, everything was calm as the room emptied. The council members were mostly silent as they exited; only a few threw lingering stares my way—including Sorenson—before it was just Warrick and me.

And a tropical storm set to blow us all away.

"We need to talk, Alpha Warrick," Hunter said through gritted teeth, his strikingly handsome face set in hard lines. He didn't look at me, which grated on my wolf. Though only her; I was personally grateful not to be on his radar. Well, *well*. They might make a decent liar out of me yet.

It wasn't my fault that my awareness of the giant shifter was distracting to the point of danger. Scent matches were as destructive as mind-altering drugs.

Not. My. Fault.

Warrick squeezed my shoulder gently, both of us ignoring the low rumble from the other alpha. "Give me a second to speak with Alpha Hunter, then we'll get you settled."

My senses were not as strong as other shifters, so I couldn't hear a word of their hushed, five-minute discussion. Neither of them looked my way, but Warrick's expression grew progressively more annoyed as he listened to whatever Hunter was saying. *All good things, I'm sure.*

It was clear that this alpha had no plans of letting me stroll off into the sunset, and the fact that I was on his intense radar was only going to make my plans to eventually ditch America for greener countries all that much harder. But not impossible.

Nothing was impossible when you had no other choice *but* to succeed.

The conversation wrapped up with grim faces and shifter dominance filling the room, and as Hunter strode past me it appeared as if he was going to keep ignoring me until...

His head snapped toward me and as our gazes clashed I gasped. Gold heavily threaded his dark irises, and the air crackled between us with an unspoken energy. He held me with nothing more than his gaze, but thankfully before I made a fool of myself and stepped toward him, he was gone, leaving my legs so weak I almost collapsed into a nearby chair. Pure strength of will kept me standing, and by the time Hunter was out of the room and Warrick had returned to my side, I'd gotten myself together. *Sorta.*

Okay, not at all. But fake it till you make it and all that jazz.

"Come on, Emmeline." Warrick's voice was gentle. "Let's get you to your new, temporary home."

"Emme," I said softly. "If I had friends, I'd tell you that's what my friends call me."

"You've got friends now, kid."

Dammit. I was already out of sorts after meeting a scent-match, which left me vulnerable to softer emotions. The last thing I needed was to grow attached to shifters or this whole pack life.

The loneliness of my life had never felt so soul withering as it did today. "Well, in the spirit of friendship, and the fact I'm no longer on death row, I'm actually twenty-five years old. So, not technically a kid."

Warrick snorted out a laugh, and I was relieved he didn't appear upset by my lie. "When you get to my age, everyone younger is a kid." He paused briefly. "Also, in the spirit of friendship, let's keep your actual age between you, me, and your scent-matched pack. At least for a while."

"I'd really rather keep them out of it completely. It's none of their business."

Hello, denial, my old friend.

Warrick hid his confusion fast and didn't push me for a reason, making him my new favorite shifter in Golden Claw. He led me down to a basement where a black Range Rover was the only car still parked. I was a bike wolf through and through, but that didn't mean I couldn't appreciate a four wheeler. "Nice, Alpha Warrick," I said as I glided my palm just above the shiny paint and curved lines. "This model isn't supposed to be released in America until next month."

Surprise flashed across his face, followed by a genuine smile. "You know your cars. I'm a collector. My pack indulges me because I'm the one who makes the most money."

I smothered my laughter with my hand. "That sounds like a fair exchange."

He unlocked the door and gestured for me to enter. "What did you drive out in the human world?"

My heart panged as I think of my baby. "I had a black Yamaha YZF-R6. Nothing fancy, but she was very good to me. I assume it's still at the hotel where they took me down."

Dwelling on her loss would only make it worse so I changed the subject as I buckled myself in. "Is being on the council your job? The one that pays all the money?"

Warrick shook his head and started the engine; the first

throaty thrum calmed me in a way I hadn't felt since before Florida. "I head up an enforcer squad of twenty shifters. We're like... SWAT or black-ops in the human world. There's ten of these squads in Golden Claw, and we're the security and law enforcement here. Interestingly enough, one of your mates heads up another squad."

My insides twisted and squirmed at the usage of *mate* in such a casual way. I replied stiffly, "*Interestingly enough*, I don't have mates."

Warrick wore an infuriating smirk as he exited the parking lot. "Right, kid. Keep telling yourself that."

Smug bastard. I was tempted to retract my *spirit of friendship*.

For the rest of the drive, as Warrick weaved through bustling city streets that reminded me of a few of the mid-sized cities I'd lived in over the years, he filled me in on Golden Claw.

"We've moved past the days of one alpha controlling a large pack, with the rest considered betas and deltas beneath them." His gruff voice filled the car. "With the number of dominant wolves across the five cities, we had challenges and fights constantly, until we decided to try a different way. So, in Golden Claw for example, the twenty thousand shifters are now governed by the council of twenty alphas you met today. We're considered the strongest and most dominant alphas here. With one stipulation..."

Despite my lack of plans to ever integrate into this world, I found myself listening closely, barely resisting asking questions to sate my many curiosities.

"Only one alpha per quintet or smaller bonded pack can hold a council seat. Hence why Hunter was the only one of your mates there. All of them would slot into the top twenty strongest... *right at the top*."

He was persisting with the mate thing, and I was very aware he'd revealed this information for a reason... or more likely a warning. This pack was filled with powerful alphas, and I could try to deny them all I wanted, but they were used to getting their own way.

"What did Hunter say to you just before he left?" I asked. I wasn't sure I could mentally handle the answer, but I needed more information on this pack. Especially if *ignoring them* out of my life wasn't going to be an option.

"He threatened me," Alpha Warrick said casually, taking a right turn that brought us out of the downtown and into a more suburban housing estate. I waited for him to expand on that cryptic and worrying statement, but he just started whistling a fucking tune like we were about to head into a diamond mine while a girl as white as snow slept in our cottage.

With a huff I finally said, "Okay, what did he threaten you over?"

Warrick eased off the gas as we turned into another neighborhood where the houses were larger and the estates farther apart. He was not kidding about earning luxury car money.

He pulled the Range Rover up to a white metal gate, and while we waited for it to open, he turned and faced me. His expression was neutral, but his eyes called me a fucking idiot. "You're not that naive, kid. What would any man threaten another man over when they're close to their mate. I'm lucky he didn't attempt to rip my head off in the council chambers."

"Why didn't he?" *Wait...* The fact that I even asked that question told me I was in serious need of therapy.

Warrick drove through the open gate and up the long driveway before he answered. "You're skittish and he's trying not to scare you off, but he's not known for his patience. That's my only warning. Oh, and don't let any males touch you if you want them to keep breathing. That's a backup to the first warning."

I was totally screwed in a way I had no skills to fight against.

"If the alphas in Reeves Pack are scent matched, are they sexually involved with each other?" Maybe I had read their whole pack situation wrong, and they were satisfied in their current bond.

Warrick shook his head. "No. They're brothers in the true sense of the word, and they've always known their fifth would be a female that they share."

Fantastic. My vagina wept at the very thought. *Just don't ask me in what way.*

We approached Warrick's Tudor style home, which was a nice distraction from my impending doom. Despite its grand size and layout, it retained a perfectly adorable cottage facade with white walls and dark wood accents.

"This is all my mate Cora," he said, watching me gawk over his pretty home. "Her family is English. They moved to America when she was a teenager, thank the goddess, and this was the style of her home back there. She's my scent match, and I'd have moved England here for her if she asked me too. Thankfully, this appears to be enough to keep the homesickness away." He parked in the circular drive, near the front door.

"How many are in your pack?"

"Five." A perfect quintet. "But Cora is my only scent and romantic match. The other three include my brother and his two mates. We're loyal and strong as a pack, and there's more than enough love between us all, even though we're technically not all bonded in the same way."

From the little I knew, the dynamics of a pack varied with

everyone. There were no hard and fast rules, and it sounded as if these five found the perfect balance. "I'm not supposed to like shifters or being in a pack city," I grumped, unsure why I had such strong feelings of home and safety when I had literally never been less safe. "Shifters are dangerous, and you're making it hard not to get attached."

Warrick didn't dispel me of my *shifters are dangerous* notion, and I wondered if he was thinking about the pack of alphas waiting out there for me. "That's tomorrow's worry," he finally said, opening his door. "Enjoy these few days of reprieve before the real world comes calling."

As I jumped from the car, I took a second to consider if Warrick might turn out to be an ally when I decided to escape the country. Right now, he wasn't going to help me, but maybe if we built real trust between us, I could reveal what happened to my mom.

I'd never had an ally. I'd never relied on anyone before, not even when Mom was alive, and it grated against every instinct I possessed to ask for help.

But there was no way I could do this alone, not now that the packs knew about me.

It was a wait-and-see plan, so I decided to take his advice and enjoy a few days insulated from the real world.

CHAPTER 6

By the time Warrick opened the front door and stepped inside, a female was throwing herself into his arms. *Cora.* Warmth oozed from her as she murmured how much she had missed him, before she finally noticed me standing awkwardly in the doorway, trying not to look like I was soaking up all the love and happiness they exuded.

I'd never been hugged like that before.

Even when she was alive, my mom was cold and cruel, and I grew very used to a life without physical contact. My skin itched as I stared at the couple, emotions warring inside me as I was torn between annoyance and envy.

I hadn't asked to be here, witnessing shit I couldn't have in my life. I'd been okay with my existence before the packs dragged me off the streets. I'd been fucking okay.

This didn't feel okay.

Cora pulled away from Warrick, and her expression remained warm when she faced me. I took in her light skin, dark hair pulled up high in a bun displaying her slender shoulders and neck, along with her claiming bite mark. She was all grace and beauty as she moved toward me. "Hello, I'm

Cora, it's so lovely to meet you." Her accent was light and faintly British.

When she held out her hand, I fidgeted, wishing I wasn't dressed in crappy gym shorts and a beat-up shirt. She wore an exquisite pink and purple bohemian skirt, swishing around her ankles, along with a white, ruffled midriff top that showed off her curves and gorgeous skin. She didn't look as old as Warrick, but I got the feeling she was just aging well, because there was a sense of maturity around her deep blue eyes.

Taking her proffered hand, my return smile was genuine. Cora was instantly likeable. "I'm Emme, and it's nice to meet you as well. I'm sorry Alpha Warrick brought me around without notice, and I promise not to stay more than a couple of days."

I had no idea if he'd told her why I was here yet, but I assumed she had some idea when nothing in my ramble changed her open expression. "You're welcome to stay as long as you need." She released me with a gentle squeeze. "We have plenty of room, and I can't imagine how it must feel to have your life completely upended this way. Let us help you get back on your feet."

These shifters were completely blowing any pre-conceived notions I'd had of being part of pack life. They were weirdly lovely, which of course, only made me retreat further into myself. "Please don't do anything extra. I don't need it."

Warrick took pity on me and wrapped his mate in his arms, half carrying her through the entrance. "Come on, let's go find the others."

The downstairs of their house was dreamy, with comfortable furniture, plush cushions and rugs, lamps with warming light, and the general feel of a real home. Everything was high quality and lush, but also practical and lived in.

"They're out on the patio preparing dinner," Cora called as

I followed them past two living areas and a pretty white kitchen to a set of double doors opening onto a large, paved patio.

Out here the sound of conversation and the scent of steak on the grill hit me, and I was filled with a desperate urge to escape before I grew accustomed to this life.

This is not yours to keep. It was a reminder I knew I'd have to keep delivering the longer I was here.

I focused on the trio sitting on a large outdoor couch, all squished together and wrapped around each other. A male who could pass as Warrick's twin, just with longer hair, jumped to his feet. "Brother!" He greeted the alpha. "We were hoping you wouldn't miss supper."

I followed slowly behind, and Warrick whispered a few low words to him before they both turned to me. "This is Richard, my younger brother."

Richard chuckled as he confirmed my previous assessment. "By two minutes, asshole." His curious gaze shifted to me. "It's a pleasure to meet you, Emme. We're happy to have you here." He turned and waved over the other two shifters. "These are my mates, Sierra and Marcus."

Richard's shifter energy didn't pack the same punch as his brother's, but he was still a strong beta. His mates were deltas through and through. Sierra stood no taller than five feet, a delicate female with bright red hair, skin much paler than mine, and startling hazel eyes. The green in them was biting, even as the brown pigments calmed the color.

She smiled as she grasped Richard's hand, twining herself around his side. He dropped a kiss right on the scarred bite on the junction of her shoulder and neck. Marcus moved forward next; he was about my height with Mediterranean coloring. His skin was a nice brown, his dark hair perfectly coiffed, and when he wrapped himself around

Richard's other side, the beta dropped a kiss on his claiming bite also.

I wasn't sure if they were testing how I'd handle the dynamics of this threesome, but my only thought was of how adorable they were, along with a mild case of jealousy at the obvious bond and love they shared. "It's really nice to meet you all," I said, surprised to find I truly meant it. "Sorry to crash your pack life, but I promise not to stick around for too long, no matter how tempted I am by your beautiful home."

They laughed and waved me off as the five of them assured me I was more than welcome. Cora led me to the outdoor lounge sectional and I ended up seated on thick blue cushions, a glass of wine placed in my hand, as she and Sierra perched on either side of me. The men wandered off to do the cooking, leaving me with their mates.

"Warrick warned us that we should keep male scents away from you," Sierra said, her voice light and breathy. "And I've been dying to add another girl to our dynamics. We're outnumbered here in Pack Annandale."

Cora threw her head back and laughed. "Girl, you've never complained about being outnumbered in your little trio. I'd say you are *more than satisfied* with the arrangement."

A cough of laughter escaped me, and I almost choked on my sip of wine. Which set Cora and Sierra off again. I found myself strangely relaxed considering where I was and everything that had happened in the past twenty-four hours.

The girls chatted about random gossip in their local friendship group and made me promise I'd be at their next book club. I didn't have the heart to tell them I'd never read a book in my life, and due to reasons I wouldn't be disclosing, couldn't imagine ever reading for fun. But it was nice to be included.

After a while, Cora moved on to my scent match. "Is it true

that Hunter Reeves claimed you in the council chambers today?"

I sensed that she'd been sitting on that question for a while, and due to my own innate need to sate my curiosity, I nodded. "Yes, and I'm not sure what to make of it. Everyone in the room acted very deferential toward him, but no one forced me to go to his pack."

Sierra jerked beside me. "Oh my goddess! That would never happen in Golden Claw. Some of the other cities are less liberal than us, but we don't allow the forcing of mate bonds any longer."

Cora chimed in with her own horrified expression. "It's law here. About fifteen years ago there was an incident that brought about new laws carved into the shifter stones. No one will make you join their pack, Emme. You're safe."

I had no idea what shifter stones were, but I was relieved to hear about the laws.

Sierra propped herself up from where she'd been slouched, gulping more wine as she examined me closer. "Just for clarity's sake, what is it you have against Alpha Hunter, and the Reeves pack as a whole? I mean, we are talking about the hottest, richest, most powerful quad of alphas this city has ever seen."

"I heard that, mate," Richard growled as he wandered over with a stack of plates and cutlery in his hands.

I tensed, wondering if we were about to see a shifter fight as Sierra shot him a cheeky smile. "No one compares to you and Marcus, my love, but I mean... I've got a point."

Richard attempted to hold his annoyance, before exhaling loudly through his nose. "Yeah, you've got a point. If Hunter Reeves propositioned me, I'd be tempted."

Everyone laughed then, and I had no fucking idea what to do with these dynamics. My experience was limited, of course, but the little I'd experienced in my earlier years had been packs filled with anger and destruction.

These five were downright domesticated. I found it hard to believe they were shifters.

"Sorry, mate. The Reeves pack doesn't swing that way." Marcus slapped Richard a nice love tap on his ass. "You're stuck with us."

Richard dropped a kiss on his lips and removed the large dish from his hands. "No shifters I'd rather be stuck with."

Gah, they were delightfully non-toxic in their relationships, and I was reassessing everything I thought I knew about shifters and pack dynamics. The guys hurried off again, finishing preparations for dinner, and as Sierra refilled my wine, I had to ask, "Who else is in the Reeves pack?"

There was a flash of a smile from both ladies before I threw my hands in the air. "No, wait! Don't tell me. I don't want to know, I'm already too curious about them."

Cora started to respond, but Warrick interrupted by popping over carrying a tray piled high with seared steak. The thick, juicy cuts distracted us all, and we spent the next hour eating and chatting about everything *except* the Reeves pack. I'd never had a night like it before, and by the time Cora showed me to the spare room, handing me a stack of clothes and toiletries, I was both confused and *a little* suspicious. This pack was far too good to be true.

Not once through the whole dinner had they even mentioned my designation as an omega. As if it didn't even matter to them. While there were no real benefits of an omega unless I was bonded into their pack, I still held value to others. I had to keep my guard up until I knew for sure they could be trusted. No one hid their true colors forever.

The room they'd given me had an attached bathroom, and I took a long, glorious shower, scrubbing every inch of my body.

Whatever injuries I'd sustained in New Mexico were fully healed, and when I emerged into the steamy room, I felt like a new wolf.

After towel drying my long hair, I brushed my teeth with the toothbrush they'd included and dressed in a pair of soft, gray PJ shorts and matching tank top. I was much taller than both females here, so the shorts flashed a lot of my booty, but since I generally slept naked it was more than enough coverage.

I'd have to get a job as soon as possible to replace everything I'd left behind. It was frustrating that when they'd grabbed me I lost the cash I'd spent two painstaking years saving. I wouldn't have years here to rebuild, but I'd do the best I could.

Their spare room was sparsely decorated, with white walls and a soft burgundy rug, but the bed was as soft as a cloud when I crawled in and slipped under the thick duvet. No scents surrounded me; this pack had the financial means to wash with high-quality detergents, free from scents.

It was heaven, and I was almost asleep when I felt a tingle of energy down my spine, just the slightest pulse, and despite my exhaustion I pried an eye open to find a shadow stalking closer to the bed. Alpha energy slammed into me, along with a familiar mocha scent: *Hunter*.

There was a brush of his hand along my cheek, and in my dazed state I didn't fight the touch. If anything, as his power and heat infiltrated into me, I sank deeper into the darkness of my subconscious. "Sleep, little omega," he whispered. "You're going to need your strength."

My wolf whimpered but not in pain or worry. Horny bitch wanted to drag him into bed with us and roll around in his scent and power. The heat of his touch vanished, and by the time I forced my eyes open, the room was empty.

There was no sign Hunter had been here, and I wondered if I imagined it. Did I fall asleep and dream an alpha into my room?

After lying awake for an hour in mild panic, I finally gave in to my exhaustion and let sleep claim me. Hunter was quite possibly the greatest threat I'd ever faced, and I could not go up against him fatigued. I refused to let him destroy me, no matter what it took to keep fighting.

CHAPTER 7

When I woke the next morning, I felt surprisingly well rested and calm. I wandered down to the living room to find Cora and Warrick in the middle of organizing a decent array of new clothes for me. All in my size, and in the style I would have chosen myself.

Even in the short time I'd known them, it was abundantly clear that when Annandale Pack set their minds to a task, it was done quickly and with great proficiency.

Staring between the multiple bags, I shook my head. "This is too much, and I won't be able to pay you back for a couple of months. Even if I start looking for a job today." Which was absolutely the plan.

I'd worked pretty much every day for at least the last eight years, and the thought of sitting around felt weird and lazy.

"You don't need to pay us back," Cora huffed with a firm shake of her head. Today she wore a floaty teal dress that made her look like an ethereal fairy. I was still in borrowed PJ's with my butt hanging out, so... same same. "Firstly, it's a dozen pieces of clothing. Secondly, the council has an allowance for newcomers to help them integrate into Golden

Claw and we're taking full advantage of it. This is all yours, free and clear."

Warrick backed her with a nod, and I had no idea where all of this good luck was coming from, but for once, I decided not to question it. "Well... thank you," I said feeling awkward but grateful.

As I leaned down to grab the bags of clothes, Warrick cleared his throat. "Richard, Sierra, and Marcus have already headed off to their jobs. They all work for the Celtic Wolves, our hockey team. They run the hospitality sector but will be back for dinner. Do you have any food requests tonight?"

I shook my head as I straightened with two bags on either arm. "Nope, I'm not picky at all. Whatever you have is perfect, and I could even help cook if needed." In truth, I wasn't the best cook but could whip up a mean chocolate chip cookie.

Cora chuckled as she leaned against her mate. Warrick shot her a warm smile as he brushed his hand over her silky hair. "Richard's a qualified chef," Cora told me, "and we all take advantage of his skills. Though I'm sure he'd be more than happy for you to hang around."

A chef in the pack was my idea of perfection. Minus the pack of course.

"Sounds like a plan." I jerked my head toward the stairs. "I'll just take these up to my room and get ready for the day. Thanks again."

Feeling like a kid sneaking around a stranger's house, I walked away, only to find Cora falling into step with me. "If you didn't have to look for a job today, what else would you want to do?"

Her question caught me off guard, so I gave it a little thought. "Maybe let my wolf out for a run. I've had to keep her so locked down over the past ten years, that it'd be nice to run safe in pack lands."

Cora clapped her hands together and every part of her face lit up until I found myself smiling in response. "That's what we're doing, then! We'll shift in the pack forests. Warrick has today free, and I manage my own business from home, so we could take you out and show you the stomping grounds."

I was tempted. So very tempted. My wolf whined and clawed at my insides, reminding me that if I didn't release her soon she would force the issue. She might be weak, but her wild soul remained. "I really need to find a job," I said with a sigh, forcing myself to be responsible.

Cora patted my arm. "We'll get you one, don't worry. My mate knows everyone in this city. But it's important to take a second for self-care as well. When you're ready, meet us downstairs and we'll head out for a run."

Before I could protest again, she was flitting back down the stairs toward Warrick, leaving me to get ready. Wasting no time, I took a quick shower and brushed my teeth and hair. Cora had left a few hair ties for me, so I parted the thick strands of my strawberry blond locks and braided them into two Dutch braids hanging halfway down my back. I'd always called myself a strawberry blond, but it was quite pink, with shades of gold interwoven.

Truth be told, my hair was my one vanity, and it pleased me to see that after using Annandale Pack's shampoo and conditioner last night, it already showed more shine and volume.

My skin was a rosy tan, a color I held naturally all year, and the smattering of freckles across my cheeks and nose never went anywhere. The arctic blue of my eyes were the only real reminder of my mom, while the rest of my features must have been from *father-unknown*, who fled the moment Mom fell pregnant. Not that I blamed him, after living with her for the first fourteen years of my life. If I'd had the means to escape her, I'd have been gone in a flash.

I considered myself an orphan now. Family-less. Alone.

Perpetually fucking alone.

Pawing through the clothes in the bags, I found a loose pair of shorts and matching tank. It was warm out today, and we'd be ditching the clothes soon enough, so I didn't bother with underwear or shoes.

Moving faster because I'd already left them waiting too long, I hurried into the living room to find Warrick dressed in a loose pair of basketball shorts and nothing else. He was fit, with corded muscles across his shoulders and down his abdomen. I wasn't surprised that he led one of their enforcer groups. He had that badass *could snap your neck with one hand* look about him.

Yet he'd still been cowed by Hunter Reeves.

"Ready for a run?" he said, glancing over as I entered the living room. "My wolf is clawing at my insides like a fucking pup right now. Nothing like a good pack run to get the blood pumping."

I shrugged, even though I was thrilled to be taking part in a run. "I'll take your word for it."

He prowled closer, observing me like I was a particularly perplexing science experiment. "You've never run with a pack before? Not even when your mom was alive?"

Mom refused to allow my wolf out when she was alive, so I'd been forced to change in my room and run in circles until I'd thought I would both puke and lose my mind. "Nope." That was all I'd say since there was no need for my pathetic past to ruin our run.

"That all ends today," Cora said as she breezed in, dressed in an almost identical set of my shorts and tank. Only hers were pink. "Let's get moving."

The black Range Rover was still parked out front, and I hopped into the back, trying not to bounce in excitement. My wolf didn't have the same reticence; she howled and scratched inside me.

"I've called in a few of my enforcers to give us security while we're out here," Warrick said as he exited through their gate. "Not that I'm worried, but you are an unbonded omega, and I promised you safety. I take my word very seriously."

Leaning forward, I went to pat his arm before remembering it was safer for me not to touch another alpha. "Thank you."

Warrick and Cora exchanged a glance and smiled back at me. "It's our pleasure," he replied simply.

I settled in for the drive, and it was less than ten minutes until he parked in a spot at the edge of what looked like a national park. The trees were so huge that I could barely see the top of some.

As Warrick opened his door, the scent of dirt, leaves, and decaying foliage lingered in the air—along with a sweet scent I couldn't quite identify but had me craving candy.

There were a couple of other cars parked in the lot. "Enforcers are already patrolling," Warrick said, casing the area. He paused when he noticed a blue and black Bugatti Veyron, in a model that I was fairly sure was one of only fifty in the world.

Just sitting here in a Golden Claw parking lot.

I let out a low whistle. "Not the only car enthusiast with money in this town I see."

I meant it as a joke, but Warrick didn't look amused. "There are a few of us," he muttered, shaking his head and turning away. "Come on, let's take that run and hope for minimal surprises."

I swore his gaze darted to the Bugatti once more before he

got ready to shift. Cora moved to his side and the bonded pair shed their clothes quickly. I averted my eyes while I stepped out of mine.

My hangups with nudity would hopefully ease over time, especially if I remained in Golden Claw for a while. For now, though, I wished we weren't standing out here in the open. Exposed.

When I was naked, I closed my eyes and handed the reins over to my beast. She burst from me with ease. The pain was minimal these days as the magic of my body did the rest.

Mom's pack taught me that shifters were originally cursed by the first-blooded witches, long before we had a peace treaty with them, forcing us to share our souls with a *hideous creature.* Their *punishment* turned out to be a beautiful symbiotic relationship between man and beast, giving us strength and longevity over humans. Giving us packs and bonding and a lot of amazing abilities. There was truth to the saying that from shit the best flowers grew.

Shaking off the shift, I rose to my full height, finding I was bigger than Cora's wolf. Her mahogany-colored pelt was thick and shiny as she bounded toward me, while the blue of her eyes remained the same. She nuzzled against my neck, and I marveled at the sensation.

Warrick joined us and he was massive, towering over me. He was easily large enough to double as a small horse if needed, and unlike his mate, he didn't bound... he prowled.

This was a predator through and through, despite the generally gentle nature of the alpha in his human form.

My wolf gave zero fucks that the alpha wolf was a beast, she was just elated to be here. We were about to run with a pack, which was all of her dreams colliding in one perfect moment.

Warrick got closer to me but didn't nuzzle in like Cora,

remembering to keep his male scent away. *Find mates*, my wolf whined, and in this form I couldn't recall why we stayed away from Hunter and his pack. *So close.*

Thankfully, before I did something quite stupid like make a break for the Reeves pack, Warrick let out a low bark and turned to head deeper into the forest. Cora nudged me, and with a sense of real freedom I released my worries and followed along. There were many scents as we ran, and one with a lingering caramel sweetness caught my attention over and over.

At first it freaked me out, as I'd trained my entire adult life to avoid shifters, but once I wrapped my head around being in pack lands, it felt soothing to be amongst our kind.

Warrick initially set quite a brutal pace, and I enjoyed stretching my legs, despite not being the strongest shifter. When he finally slowed down and let us just frolic and play, I was almost consumed by my happiness. Cora pounced on me and I rolled, my white pelt picking up sticks and rocks from the undergrowth.

From what I knew, omegas were always white wolves, the only shifters with a pure white pelt. The white teamed with my eyes always reminded me of the Arctic. It was fitting because I loved winter, even though I wouldn't want to live in constant snow.

After we'd been out for about an hour, we took a breather near a picturesque creek, beside a section where water trickled over rocks. Our wolves drank and then we rested near the bank with Cora pressed against my right flank, and Warrick on her other side.

It was the sort of contentment I'd never known was possible.

Her warmth against me, and the thudding of their hearts

beating with my wolf's, felt like family and home. Even if it wasn't quite right, because it was *not quite my family*.

My eyes closed as a cool breeze drifted through my fur, and with it, the sweet scent I'd been chasing all morning grew strong enough for me to make out the strong, individual notes of caramel and cinnamon.

It seeped into my essence and wrapped around me, and my wolf was suddenly alert, springing up to take off after that enticing scent.

Warrick leapt in front of me, growls ripping from his chest.

I wasn't experienced enough to understand an alpha command in wolf form, but instinct told me that he wasn't attacking... he was warning me not to chase the scent.

A much louder growl echoed around us, vibrating with menacing intensity, and Warrick turned to face the threat. I flinched at the dominance of this new shifter as it stalked toward us, flashes of a tan pelt visible when the beast emerged between the trees.

His scent grew stronger and tugged at my wolf in the same way Hunter's had yesterday.

Another scent match! A scent match who was stalking toward me with singular intent. His beast was larger than Warrick's as he stepped out of the shadows, his tan pelt streaked with gold in the sunlight. His eyes were a dark blue, piercing and locked on me as if I were the prey and he was most definitely the predator.

Warrick remained in his protective stance, and I almost shifted back until I realized I'd be naked in front of my scent match. Which was frankly *a terrible* fucking idea.

Leaving my wolf in control was also a worry, since she was already pissed about another alpha standing between us and our mate. She released a few low growls at Warrick, and only pure respect for what he'd done kept her from attacking.

Dominance poured from the tan wolf, and Warrick backed up a step until I felt the whoosh of his energy as he shifted back to his human form. "Kellan Jackson," he snarled. "What the hell do you think you're doing?"

I kept my gaze straight on so as not to catch a glimpse of Warrick's bare ass and balls hanging between his legs. It wasn't really difficult when my wolf was firmly locked on the most predatory predator in the forest. Kellan Jackson, apparently.

There was another whoosh of energy and the giant tanned beast was replaced by a giant... uh, tanned man. Lifting my head to keep his face and defined chest in focus, I noted that Kellan was a golden boy through and through.

His skin was a glorious caramel-gold shade, his hair blond, short, and tousled around his forehead, and the dark blue of his eyes leaned toward violet in their intensity. Kellan's piercing gaze was locked on my wolf, but he didn't move closer, allowing a respectful distance to remain between us.

He was beautiful.

Not in the hard masculine lines of Hunter, but in a square jaw, straight nose, perfect white teeth, all-American hero way. Everything about him screamed handsome and virile. Of course the goddess would bless me with a pack of gorgeous alpha males.

No way she'd make it easy not to fall into all their overt masculinity.

"She's my scent match," Kellan said softly, and despite his threatening rumbles from before, his tone was filled with awe. "Hunter told us last night, but... fuck, it's so much stronger than he described. That first punch in the gut when her scent hits..."

He crouched down until we were eye level, and so far I'd managed not to sneak a peek any lower than his broad shoulders and nicely muscled arms. The self-control that took almost did me in. "You smell like chocolate and honey, omega. And your wolf is such a pretty girl. You're both the sweetest, most delicious treat I've ever experienced."

Hunter was all growl, and this alpha was all heart. He wore it on his face as he stared at me, and I wished I could shift back to speak with him. "Let's head to the cars," Warrick suggested. "Allow Emmeline to get dressed so she's more comfortable chatting to you. She's not used to pack life. This is her first run with other wolves."

I swore a flicker of hurt flashed across Kellan's face, but he schooled himself quickly. "I didn't mean to make her uncomfortable, it's just impossible to ignore the draw of a scent mate. I'll meet you back at the parking lot."

He shifted back to his wolf in the fastest, most seamless change from man to beast I'd ever seen. Kellan might not be the entitled alpha of the Reeves pack, but he would have been one in another pack. He was stronger than Warrick, and I was starting to see that my chances of surviving all four alphas in my scent match were slim to *not a fucking chance.*

CHAPTER 8

By the time we made it back to the Range Rover, Kellan was dressed in jeans and a fitted white shirt. He leaned against the side of the Bugatti, and Warrick's reaction earlier when he saw the car, now made perfect sense. The other car fanatics in Golden Claw were of course my scent-matched pack.

Why wouldn't they be? Who else would have the money for that sort of hobby?

Stepping around the Range Rover, I shifted back and yanked on the shirt and shorts, running a hand over my braids to ensure they'd survived the shift. Outside of a few loose strands, they were intact.

There was no way to avoid this meeting, so I straightened my spine and pushed my wolf's influence down as I headed toward the Bugatti. Kellan hadn't moved, continuing to give me space as he waited against the side of his million-dollar supercar. Nodding toward the beauty, I asked, "Do you ever get to open her up?"

He uncurled in a movement of predatory grace. I hadn't really had a chance to assess his height back near the creek, but he had a good five-plus inches on me. He wasn't as bulky as Hunter, but his athletic frame was far from small.

I'd never been around so many males who made me feel positively petite.

"We have a track right out the back of Golden Claw," he said in his smooth rumble. "Even Alpha Warrick has been known to take his ride around there a time or two."

Warrick laughed roughly from behind us. "If you mean get my ass kicked by you and your brothers a *time or two*. Then, sure, I take it around."

Kellan didn't remove his piercing gaze from my face, not even to acknowledge the other alpha. "Do you race, pretty girl?"

Goddess... Hunter's bossy dominance filled me with rage, but I was helpless to fight against Kellan's sweet intensity. "Moto," I rasped around a sudden dry throat. "I had to leave my bike behind, but I prefer two to four wheels, if we're being honest."

His lips twitched. "You sound like Slade. You might have to test yourself against him."

I had no idea who Slade was, but odds were he was another in my pack. "I'm not sure that's a great idea." It felt wrong to deny this perfect golden man anything, but I had to be honest. "I'm not sure what Hunter told you, but I'm not interested in having a pack. For many personal reasons. I—" The words lodged in my throat, and I really wished Kellan would look away. I was drowning in his blue eyes, and there was no mistaking the hurt this time when I rejected him.

Why was this so painful?

I'd never intended to meet my pack and know them as living, breathing shifters with real emotions. The intensity of my feelings after meeting Kellan for less than two minutes was hard to explain. Was it this all-consuming draw to her mates that got Mom killed? This incessant need to crawl into your pack and lose yourself.

Kellan's expression softened as he took a step closer, and I swore our scents started to mingle like long-lost friends. "Hunter can be hardheaded and controlling, I'll give you that, but I promise the rest of us—" he hesitated "—okay, not Slade, but Fin and I won't let them do whatever it is you're afraid of. None of us would ever hurt you, Emmeline. We couldn't even if we wanted to... you're our scent match."

Truth in theory, but I was an omega. A designation they apparently knew very little about.

"Just come home with me and meet the rest of the pack," he continued in a low, soothing tone, as if he knew I was on the edge of a breakdown. "Get to know us before you make a decision that will change the course of all our lives."

He held out a hand and there was no sense of pressure about it. My fingers twitched and I physically fought myself not to touch him. If I did, I'd lose a piece of myself that I was desperate to keep safe. Every relationship started good, otherwise people wouldn't fall into them, but it was the next part that defined it all.

I couldn't get to the next part.

"No," I choked out. "I can't. I'm sorry, Kellan. I'm so fucking sorry."

Spinning, I raced toward Warrick and Cora, who had been giving us a moment alone. My vision blurred as I yanked open the door and dove into the back seat.

"Emme, are you okay?" Warrick said, glancing back at me.

"Just drive, please," I bit out, tucking my trembling hands under my legs. "Please."

Cora's expression was full of sympathy, but she remained silent as her mate pulled out of the parking lot. Kellan hadn't moved, and his face was harder as he watched us leave.

"They won't just let you go," Warrick warned as we headed toward the city. "You need to figure out your plan moving forward, because that pack is relentless in their pursuit of what they want."

I'd only met two of them, which was more than enough for me to know exactly what they were capable of. The worst part was my desperate need to take what they offered: pack, security, and four sexy alphas who'd no doubt destroy any concept I'd ever had of decent sex.

Even worse than all of that was the possibility of love I saw shining in Kellan's eyes.

As a poor little orphan girl, I'd kill for a fraction of the devotion that burned in the depths of his blue-violet gaze. As an omega though, it would quickly turn into a toxic, deadly obsession that would strip me of everything and leave me wishing for death. Or worse.

The ride back to Annandale Pack house was quiet, and while the tension was my fault, I couldn't bring myself to say anything. There was a very real possibility that if I opened my mouth, I'd just start screaming and never stop.

The rest of the afternoon was spent in my room pacing and planning, working out how long I could safely stay in Golden Claw before I got in too deep with these shifters. I wondered if they allowed city transfers. If I could at least get out of Golden Claw, I'd have some breathing room.

When I brought it up at dinner that night, Warrick shot me down fast. "We're not enemies per se," he started, "but it's a big deal to transfer cities. You're now a member of Golden

Claw. You were added yesterday after the trial. Your paperwork and identification should arrive in the next few days."

My dejection must have shown, as Sierra leaned forward and patted my hand. "You're not a prisoner. You can absolutely leave our borders and travel to other cities, but you need to inform the council of the three W's. Why, where, and when you'll be back. They keep an eye on their shifters, but it's for our safety."

Right... I'd been alone since I was a young teen and had never had a reason to need the packs, but *now* I required their control to keep me safe.

Conversation shifted to other topics, and I stayed quiet, eating slices of my meat loaded pizza, handmade by Richard. He was a top-notch chef, and I'd miss this cooking when I was gone.

After dinner, the pack invited me to watch movies with them, but I wasn't sure I'd be decent company, so I pled exhaustion and hurried off to bed. In my room I showered and changed into soft mauve PJ's, but, unable to settle, I wandered to the huge double windows. I pushed open the blinds and shutters to let in fresh air, and there was a hint of bonfire on the breeze, washing around me as I admired Annandale Pack's nicely manicured yard.

It wasn't huge but they had enough space for the illusion of privacy from their neighbors. The pool, which sat off the back porch, sparkled in the lights from nearby lanterns, giving it a very resort-like feel. I'd never learned to swim; it wasn't a priority for my mom, even before she found her pack, but I had always found water calming. I hoped there'd be a chance to try swimming before the weather got too cold.

After an hour of night watching, listening to the packs calling their kids inside, I was just about to close the shutters when movement in the back corner of the yard caught my attention. Stilling, I squinted until the shadows parted to reveal a massive black wolf. Well, at least its snout and two piercing eyes.

My fingers tightened on the windowsill to the point of pain as I examined him. He was the size of a bear, looking near my height even in his four-legged form. I was about to scream for Warrick when a tugging in my center stopped me.

Mate.

My wolf piped up to confirm what I'd suspected from the second the shadows moved—suspected but refused to admit to myself. The black beast was one of my pack, though I had no idea which one, except it wasn't Kellan. Judging on his size and pelt color, it was fairly safe to assume Hunter, but until I met the others, I wouldn't know for sure.

Nailing him with a glare, I waved my hands in an outward *fuck off* motion.

This light stalking they were currently into wasn't working for me.

I swear he shot me a wolfish grin, lethal canines coming into focus as his lip lifted. He didn't *fuck off* as requested though, and with a huff I closed the shutters and blinds, hoping that I wouldn't wake tomorrow with an alpha in my room.

There had to be a way to keep them out of this house... Surely a shifter of Warrick's power level would scent another alpha sneaking into his territory. Which meant he was allowing this to happen.

That threat delivered by Hunter in the council chambers could have been more than just a warning not to get close to me. Maybe they'd struck a deal where Hunter could enter *this* property to keep an eye on *his* property.

The thought of Warrick and the others agreeing to that sent a trill of unease down my spine. I'd been wary of trusting them from the start for this very reason; I didn't know their true intentions.

It was too late now to ask, so I just doublechecked the locks on doors and windows and crawled into the bed that only smelled like me. No other shifter had been in this room since I left, which was a small reassurance.

Wake me if anyone sneaks into the room. It was a sleepy murmur to my wolf and she just grumbled in agreement, though I wasn't sure I could trust her either.

Not if the one who snuck in was our pack.

Traitor.

CHAPTER 9

"My word for the day is job. I've got to find a *job*," I said to Cora the next morning.

She was the only shifter in the house today, and I hoped she'd help me get my life moving in the right direction. "Also, do you know how one goes about renting a house or apartment in Golden Claw? I assume there are investment properties for rentals, or does every pack just own their own house?"

Before answering, she handed me a plate of already sliced fruit, and I reminded myself not to get used to princess treatment. "Thank you," I said, clutching the plate closer.

"You're welcome. Now, there are two large apartment buildings that are literally rented to singles and new packs. We could stop by there on our way into town today and inquire as to what is available. You have that stipend from the council to get you established, which should cover the initial rent requirements. Provided you find a job in the next month, you're pretty much good to go."

I had just bitten into a ripe berry, and it almost fell out of my mouth at how perfectly that would work out. At least for the short term. "Amazing. I didn't know the councils had enough money to be splashing it around like that."

Cora chuckled and ran a hand through her long hair, which she'd left down in soft waves today. "We're the richest pack city in America. Everyone here lives very well because even minimum wage jobs pay *well above standard*. You don't have to worry about your future, Emme. This is the perfect city to establish yourself in."

If my scent-matched pack hadn't been part of this beautiful dream, I might have even considered staying here for a few years.

"They mentioned in the trial that there's another omega here. Is she the only one?"

"Yep. Chelsea is part of the Thenguard pack led by Alpha Sorenson."

The Scottish tiger shifter sprang to mind. "Oh right. We met at my trial. I'd love to chat with their omega too, if you think she'd be okay with it."

"I don't see why she wouldn't be. She runs a little bakery called Chelsea's Sweets on Bond Street, which is the main junction for cafes and eateries. We can stop in there today, and I'll pick up a few pastries for dessert tonight."

With our plans for the day settled, I dressed quickly in denim shorts, a cropped white shirt, and white sneakers. I took a minute to run a brush through my hair, leaving it out and wavy.

Cora waited for me near the door, and we walked side by side to where a white Mercedes AMG GT was parked out front. "*Nice* ride," I said, stepping back to take in all of the sleek car. "I see that Alpha Warrick isn't the only one in your pack with great taste in cars."

Cora rolled her eyes hard, and it was the oddest gesture from such a refined shifter. "War is a big fan of buying all the cars he enjoys and pretending they're for other members of the pack. Mostly so we stop calling him a hoarder."

I busted out laughing, and she joined me a beat later. "I admire and fear that alpha," I finally choked out. Even with my unease over him possibly allowing the Reeves pack to stalk me, I genuinely liked Alpha Warrick and his pack. Hopefully that wouldn't change after we talked about Hunter.

The car beeped as Cora unlocked it. "He's one of a kind, that's for sure." Her gaze ran over the sporty lines of her fancy car. "And look, don't ever tell him I said this, but I love my car. He chose well."

He really did, and that stood for more than just the cars in his life.

Cora drove just below the speed limit the entire way into the downtown, where multiple shiny high-rises made up the skyline. It took us a while to get there, mostly because Cora traveled the very scenic route, pointing out lots of sights including the Reeves pack family estate, which was hidden behind huge black gates.

She didn't bother to be discreet as she showed them off to me, but I found that I didn't mind. They were an annoyingly impressive pack.

If material stuff mattered to me, I'd be jumping at the opportunity to claim them. Unfortunately, my priorities were skewed more toward living a long life and not just a luxurious, short one.

Cora parked downtown in the shadow of the two largest, shiniest, most impressive buildings I'd seen in Golden Claw so far. They were twins of each other, standing a full block in size with a three-story parking structure between them. "This is Reeves Pack offices," Cora said, pointing toward the silver and black tower. "And the one beside it belongs to Thenguard Pack.

Hunter and Soren are best friends. Not that you'd always know with the way they talk to each other."

That explained Sorenson's lack of deferential treatment during my trial in the council chambers.

Examining the two structures, I noted that Thenguard's building was just as impressive as the Reeves', and I had to ask, "What does Thenguard Pack do to warrant such an extravagant office building?"

Cora's lips quirked into a smile. "Shipping. They control the import and export of all goods through the shifter cities."

I was immediately hit by my own stupidity; I absolutely should have known that. "Thenguard Shipping is even in the human world," I said faintly.

She nodded. "Yep, and so is Reeves Industries. Those two packs have more money than they know what to do with, so it's no real surprise that they're always competing."

Despite our scent match, I wondered if there was a part of Hunter Reeves that wanted an omega to even the score with his best friend. "How do Thenguard treat their omega? Has she been bonded into the pack for long?"

Cora's face went all dreamy as she sighed. "Oh, you should see them, Emme. *They're so sweet.* Soren and Chelsea are childhood best friends, and you just know that he'd die for her without thought. There's never been a safer place for an omega in all the packs."

Chelsea lucked out, then. To have bonded to an alpha without him abusing the gifts she could offer was rarer than dragon shifters. And I was fairly sure they were extinct.

Maybe the years of friendship kept him in line, because simply being a *decent guy* wouldn't be enough once the power exchange started. From what I remembered, my mom's pack treated her well at the start too. Until they'd all bonded.

Cora was once again staring up at the Reeves building, so I

asked, "Is there a reason you've brought me here, to this particular building?"

Her smile turned sheepish as she met my gaze. "Uh, I might have forgotten to mention that the main place to inquire about rentals, and even jobs to some degree, is with one of these two packs. One rental building is owned by Reeves. The other by Thenguard. And…" Her cheeks pinkened. "In regard to a job, you mentioned the other night wanting restaurant, cafe, or bar work, and that industry is mostly controlled by them as well. It makes sense to start here. Do you have a preference which pack you want to check with first?"

Her *forgetting* to mention it was clearly deliberate, and I understood why. After my little breakdown yesterday, it made sense that she'd be cautious of bringing me this close to my pack.

"Let's try Reeves," I said, deciding I was strong enough to handle it. "If I can't leave Golden Claw, there's no point letting them scare me into hiding forever. That's not feasible, which means I need to deal with them like an adult."

Cora hurried to add, "You can stay with us as long as you need, but eventually it would bother your wolf to not have your own space and territory. Which I totally understand. I wouldn't change my pack or home for anything, but there's a reason we also have two separate wings to our house with guests in the center. All of us enjoy space with our romantically bonded mates."

My smile was brief while the ache in my chest lingered much longer. "If I had what you do, I'd never want to leave either. I don't have much experience with love or friendship, but you're all teaching me that there's great joy in the family we choose. I hope, even after I move out, I'll be there for *some* family dinners."

Cora's hug was unexpected as she wrapped her arms

around me, and my insides twisted at the odd sensation. "Always. You have a standing invitation. Now, come on, let's get you settled into your new life. And can I just say, I really admire your courage in facing your pack to ask for independence."

Standing there, after a perfect hug, and her affirmative words, I found myself just a touch *destroyed*. She'd given me the same sort of hug as the one Warrick received when he'd walked through the door. The sort of hug I'd stood on the outside and admired, wondering if it felt as good as it looked. Spoiler alert: it did.

I wiped my hand across my eyes to hide my sadness. It turned out hugs were as addictive as pack life, and I was in grave danger of falling victim to both.

Fighting this life was much easier when I had no idea what I was missing.

"Come on," I said roughly, clearing my throat as I marched toward the row of stairs leading up to the automatic doors of the office block. There was a fancy sign across the top that read *Reeves Industries*. It listed two of the four pack members: Hunter Reeves, CEO; and Slade Riverson, CFO and Securities.

Slade. Kellan had mentioned him when we talked, and I pondered on possibly meeting him today. Not that I was interested in getting to know the last two members of this pack, when the two I'd met already occupied far too much of my mental space.

Inside, cool air surrounded us as we crossed the light marble floors. The reception and security desk were in the middle of the entrance, and as we approached one of the ladies behind the counter, I hoped to get this sorted without having to see Hunter or... anyone else.

"Good morning, welcome to Reeves Industries," she said,

lifting her head to grace us with a practiced smile. In her white blouse with one button open to showcase a hint of cleavage, she was the epitome of professional. Her dark hair was slicked back into a low bun, her makeup completely on point with just enough color to enhance her brown skin and natural beauty, and her minty scent gave off delta bear vibes. From what I knew, bears and big cats were second to wolves in both numbers and power.

"Hi, Fee, how are you?"

She noticed Cora after the greeting, and the aloofness melted from her smile. "Cores, what are you doing here in the middle of the day? Aren't you setting up the Norman pack's new games room?"

Cora was an interior designer and in great demand from what I could tell. "I'm heading over tomorrow to get the preliminary setup done," she said. "Today I'm here to help a new friend. This is Emme. She's recently moved to Golden Claw. We need information on available jobs and rentals in the singles building with the higher level security."

Fee relaxed as she looked me over. "You've come to the right place, Emme. If you'll take a seat, I'll call up and see if our divisions that deal in career opportunities and rentals are free to see you."

"Thank you," I said, hoping my nerves weren't showing.

Cora and I relocated to their waiting area, and as I sank into a soft beige couch I tried to ignore the slight pounding behind my temples. Being here was harder than I'd expected, especially with the knowledge that my mate sat somewhere above my head.

King of the world.

I reassured myself that a CEO would never oversee rentals or career opportunities, so there was no reason to suspect he'd even know I was here.

"You shouldn't see Hunter or Slade," Cora said softly, as if having similar thoughts.

I didn't reply, too busy watching Fee chat on the phone. When she dropped the handset, it rang not even ten seconds later, and whatever the other person said had her gaze landing right on me. She nodded a couple of times and got to her feet, placing the phone back down once more. She hurried over as fast as she could in her tight suit skirt and black heels. "I'm so sorry about the wait," she said breathlessly. "If you'll come with me, Emme, I'll get you sent up to the correct floor."

Cora got to her feet as well, but Fee waved her off. "If you could wait here, that would be amazing. I've got some paperwork that needs to be filled in while Emme is going over her options."

My stomach dropped but I forced a smile across my face. "Absolutely no issue. I can handle this on my own."

"I'll be right here if you need me," Cora said, eyeing Fee like she wasn't quite sure she trusted her. "You have security on every floor, correct?"

"Every floor," Fee confirmed. "Emme's safe here, I promise." She muttered a few words that sounded like, *She's safer here than anywhere else.*

Cora's gaze remained on me as I was led to the elevator, and when I stepped inside, floor twenty was already lit up. The highest level, and I knew exactly who was waiting for me at the top.

My wolf whined as we ascended the floors. It was partly that we'd never been comfortable in enclosed metal boxes shooting into the sky, but it was also the awareness that with each floor, we moved closer to our mate.

Hunter Reeves.

How did that arrogant, dominant asshole even find out I was here?

Glancing up, I noticed the camera and blinking red light, which left my skin itching.

He was watching me.

Narrowing my gaze into a glare, I hoped he knew what he was in for when the elevator doors opened. I swore I heard a dark chuckle, so for good measure I flipped him off and then crossed my arms, leaning back against the rails in the corner of the box.

We reached the top floor fast, and when the doors opened I didn't move except to press floor one again. As expected, nothing happened.

I was trapped in the sky with a domineering, psychopath of an alpha.

"Well, well, what do we have here? Who'd have thought the lamb would voluntarily wander into the wolf's den."

His deep voice felt far too intimate and familiar, considering I'd only heard it on two previous occasions. It was hard to keep my reply from spilling free—*Who the fuck is he to call me a lamb?* But I forced myself to remain silent.

I had a feeling nothing would annoy him more than being ignored.

No one ignored a powerful alpha.

"I can understand why you'd be scared to face me," he continued, appearing in the elevator doorway. The box shrank around his massive frame as he ducked his head and stepped inside. I swear it bounced in protest at the ten tons of muscle and power entering its domain.

I really hoped this elevator was triple reinforced to withstand an alpha.

CHAPTER 10

Hunter moved closer to me, and I realized my mistake in not leaving when the doors opened. I was completely trapped here with him, but at least he didn't crowd me, stopping a few feet away and crossing his arms over his chest. He was dressed in black suit pants, a white button-down shirt—no tie at the open collar—with both sleeves rolled up to expose thickly muscled forearms.

Swirls of black tattoos peeked out from under those sleeves, but I forced myself not to spend longer than two seconds staring. I'd love to know what he inked on his skin, since I'd heard it was quite the process for shifters to get a tattoo to stick around. With our natural healing, you had to want them badly, and he appeared to be covered under his designer suits.

"I've been waiting for you to come to me, little omega," he said in a soft, dangerous tone. "Hiding with the Annandale pack doesn't seem to be your style."

"How would you know my style?" Instead of snappy, my words come out tired. A little broken. Navigating conversations with Hunter Reeves felt like navigating landmines. You couldn't ever let your guard down, and there was still an excellent chance you'd get blown up.

"Instinct. Trust in fate's design. Whatever you want to call it, I possess it in abundance, and I know that my scent match would never cower under the strength of another."

He had far more faith in me than I'd ever had in myself. "I've never had a choice but to stand on my own. Pack Annandale is a nice reprieve from battling everything alone."

Hunter's chest rumbled in a light, barely discernible sound. "You shouldn't have had to battle alone. That's why we have packs and quintets. That's why we aren't human out there stepping on each other to get to the top. We're shifters, and we bond in ways that means *you never battle alone.*"

I repeated, with more force this time: "I *had* no choice."

Hunter regarded me more closely, his brow furrowed, and I wasn't sure what he thought as his lips thinned. "Let's make a deal," he finally said. "There's no single housing available right now, and it's not safe for you to live alone anyway. Come and live in our pack house while you're getting yourself settled here. We have a lot of room. You won't be crowded or forced into any of our lives."

Horror flooded my system until I felt nauseated, leaving me unable to reply for fear of vomiting.

"You can have your pick of jobs across our businesses. Save all of the money for your plan to run away." He stated it so matter-of-factly it was clear he was well aware of my intentions to run again. "But you *will not* live by yourself or with another pack." His expression darkened as he morphed from businessman to hurricane in a split second. When he stepped into my space, I had to tilt my head back to keep his face in view. "If a male shifter gets too close to you, Emmeline, I will kill them."

There was nothing in his expression to suggest he was kidding.

Finally finding my voice, I scoffed weakly: "Kill them? Feels a touch extreme." And psychotic.

He shrugged, unconcerned. "Extreme or not, it's the truth." He brushed a strand of my hair back behind my ear, sending energy tingling across my skin.

"Stay with us," he murmured. "It's our job to keep you safe, and I promise, none of us will force any sort of bond on you. We're willing to swear it to the council and the goddess herself, if that's what you need."

He was a dangerous shifter, and I should be running for my life, but strangely I no longer felt fear as I stood before him.

"Live in our pack house," he repeated. "Let us keep you safe."

His scent surrounded me, and being this close to him while trying to make a life and death decision was a bad freaking idea.

Hunter's gaze dragged over my skin as he leaned against the sidewall. "Kellan said you are absolutely exquisite in your wolf form. All white fur and arctic eyes." As a powerful alpha, it was possible he could sense her energy, bouncing around inside me. "Which isn't surprising. You're exquisite in all ways."

I was lost for words. All my refusals of living with them died on my tongue. "I want it in writing before the council that no one will force my bond, and you'll give me fair pay if I work for you."

As I said those words, I knew it was a terrible mistake, but it was too late to take it back. Hunter would never let me take it back.

"Deal!" His growled reply had me wanting to take a step back, but I was already pressed to the wall. "We'll have everything moved over to the compound this afternoon. Now, let's go over your job options, if you're brave enough to leave the elevator."

He stepped to the side, giving me room to move past him. "Tomorrow," I bit out as I finally moved. His scent grew stronger, and I fought the urge to close my eyes and inhale deeply. Being this close to him was intoxicating.

"Tomorrow?" Hunter questioned, narrowing his eyes and tilting his head to the side.

"You can move my stuff out tomorrow. I'll be with my friends tonight to say goodbye."

He'd already gotten his way far too easily, using alpha wiles to cloud my brain. Now I needed to double down on keeping as much distance between them and me as I could while living in their pack house.

I internally snarled at my beast, knowing she had a lot to do with this. *I hope you're happy with yourself. When they're murdering us, I'll be sure to say I told you so.*

Her snort was filled with annoyed derisiveness; she thought I was an idiot, and she might be right. Just not for the reason she suspected.

From the elevator we headed toward a large reception desk where Hunter's assistants sat. There were two blond women behind the computers, as polished and perfect as Fee. Both eyed me closely as I followed their boss past the shiny white desk and through to a massive office near the back of the floor. I noticed at least three other closed office doors on this level, and I wondered if everyone in the pack had space here.

Inside his office I crossed toward his desk while Hunter closed the door. Everything in here was massive, starting with the room itself, and followed by the dark timber desk that dominated the center of the space. His high-backed, black leather chair was as custom-made as his suits.

To my right was a whole wall of windows, giving him a royal view of Golden Claw. It was no surprise Hunter Reeves was used to getting exactly what he wanted. The world sat at his fingertips, along with all the power and control he commanded.

"Take a seat," he said, gesturing to the chair on the opposite side of his impressive desk. I found myself sinking into pure luxury, the leather soft as it cupped my body like a lover's caress, padded in all the right places for maximum comfort.

Hunter sat across from me and let the silence extend between us. As hard as it was, I didn't squirm, letting him look his fill. Neither of us appeared to be in a rush to break the tension, even as the air crackled between us.

"You're not what I expected," he finally said, and I congratulated myself on waiting him out. Yeah, it was a stupid dominance game, but I had very little power in this situation, so I'd take what I could get.

"What did you expect?"

He leaned onto his forearms, still observing me in that unblinking way of a predator. "I expected a delta shifter. One with softer edges to temper our dominance."

My forehead wrinkled as I tried to figure out if he was disappointed by me or not. "I'm an omega though. There's no shifter with less dominance."

"You are," he confirmed, "and while I have glimpsed softness from you, most of your edges are sharp and biting. Omega or not, you have alpha energy."

Your edges are sharp and biting. Sad but true. "I was tempered in fire," I said, too truthful again. "I'm the product of my past and future."

He probably wondered what I'd meant by being a product

of a future that hadn't come to pass yet, but I'd known how my life would play out long before I lived it.

I was surprised when he said, "We need your fire, little omega. Four alphas would have destroyed a delta, especially if she had the sweet, soft nature I envisioned. Now that I've met you, I can't imagine anyone more perfect for us."

My hands shook as I pressed them to the edge of the table. "You promised that there'd be no forced bonding."

Hunter's intensity faded, and he leaned back in his chair. "And I always keep my promises. Let's talk about what you're looking for in a job?"

It was a rapid subject change, but I welcomed it. I might have screwed up in agreeing to live in their pack house, but I couldn't forget why I'd come here in the first place. A job was my ticket to freedom, and since he'd agreed to let me keep all my earnings, I'd be able to work hard and save even harder.

"I have experience with bar and diner work mostly."

"You don't want to work here in the office?" he asked, not looking all that surprised. "Better hours, pay, and less time lugging around heavy trays."

The thought of being stuck behind a desk for eight hours had me wanting to throw myself from those impressive windows. "I know my strengths, and trust me when I tell you I'll be most useful in the service industry."

He gave in without an argument, which was very un-alpha of him. "We own two nightclubs and four restaurants in Golden Claw. All of them could use more staff."

"I'll take one club and one restaurant, and I'm happy with a mix of day and night shifts. Whichever is the busiest and needs the most staff."

He didn't show it, but I got the feeling my response had surprised him. "Okay, I'll get a schedule to you tomorrow when you move in. Is there anything else you need, Emmeline?"

He drawled my name, dragging it out slowly, and I almost gave in to the need to squirm in my seat. The overload of sensation he created was a lot, and I was ill-equipped to deal with it.

"Nope, I think that covers everything." I jumped to my feet. "You've done more than enough, and... thank you."

It pained me to say those two words, because I didn't ask to be here at this pack's mercy. But here I was anyway, and he was being surprisingly reasonable.

Not that I planned on letting my guard down any time soon. Hunter was an alpha with a plan, and I looked to be squarely set in his sights. This reasonable face he presented was no doubt a ploy to lower my defenses and allow Reeves Pack to infiltrate my life until they were indispensable.

Which could never happen.

My time in Golden Claw was no more than a small reprieve from a life on the run.

Pack life couldn't be mine. No matter how attractive it appeared in its designer suits.

CHAPTER 11

HUNTER

I'd never been a shifter who enjoyed sweets.

My brothers would inhale our chef's desserts growing up, while most of the time I was satisfied with the main meal. But from the second I scented my mate across the council chamber, I'd been craving chocolate and honey in a way that was driving me out of my mind.

Being trapped in an elevator with her, surrounded in her sweetness, was enough to bring a shifter to his knees. Not that I'd ever kneeled for another, but fuck… to have a taste of Emmeline, I might make an exception.

I followed her to the first floor of my building, feeling the thrumming of satisfaction that she had agreed to live with us. Followed by annoyance that I had to let her go re-join her friend. I wanted to claim her. To drag her back here, strip her clothes away, and lose myself in my mate.

To seal our scent-matched bond with my bite.

It was a primal need, driven by my beast.

I tempered my rage as she stepped out the door, leaving behind her tempting scent. Her rejection that first day almost drove me to lose control of my beast. I hadn't lost control since I was a fucking pup, but she had a way of getting under my skin. The knowledge that she'd be in my house tomorrow, under my command, calmed me for the first time since we scent matched.

When I returned to my office, Slade's energy filtered through the hall, and I was unsurprised to find him standing against the bank of windows, staring out into the city below.

"Why was she here?" he rumbled, his annoyance spilling freely in those four harsh words. "I told you not to bring her around me."

The grumpiest shifter in our pack never minced words, when he bothered to speak at all. "She's our scent match," I reminded him, settling into my chair. With anyone else, I'd have had to stand, but we were long past playing dominance games. Even if the grumpy asshole was the only shifter I'd ever had to look up at. "She'll be living in our house tomorrow, so you need to get used to her presence."

His beast made a guttural rumble from deep in his chest, and I was reminded that just because he conceded to me taking the mantle of entitled alpha in our quintet didn't mean I was the strongest. Slade had no time or patience for politics, leaving me to play our role with the city council, but he'd destroy me if it ever came to a fight. Hence why there was no need for games.

Second strongest shifter in America would have to satisfy me, because I was never taking him down. "Just don't kill her," I said with a sigh. Managing alphas was a full-time fucking job, and I already had a ton of other work to do.

Slade made no promises, leaving in a cloud of dominant energy. His office was next door, where he lorded over our tech and security footage. My brother had a skill with hacking that was beyond any I'd ever come across. He was second to none in the shifter, witch, or human world. If it was stored online, Slade could find it. If there was a camera or electronic device in the vicinity, he'd own you.

I'd be surprised if he wasn't already keeping close tabs on Emmeline, even with his dismissiveness toward her. Knowledge was power, and he was powerful in ways greater than just his dominance. I'd need to keep an eye on him while she lived with us, in case he decided our little omega was more trouble than she was worth.

My phone rang and I knew it was Kellan before I even glanced at it. "Brother," I snapped, "You've got to stop fucking calling me. It's the fifth time this morning."

"Good morning to you too, asshole," he chuckled down the line, his good nature both endearing and annoying. "I'm just calling to see if you have any updates on our delicious mate. I'm wearing my fucking hand out thinking about her."

Curse the damn goddess, I did not ask for this shit. "She agreed to move into the pack house tomorrow—" He let out a whoop which I ignored "—but you cannot be all over her. Get used to your fucking hand, Kel. If you spook her, she'll run for the hills."

Our mate *was* delicious, no arguments there. In more ways than just her sweet scent. The fire in her arctic eyes when she had glared me down earlier had me harder than a fucking baseball bat, and worried my dick was about to punch through my damn pants.

She was tall and curvy with miles of golden skin on display beneath her denim shorts and cropped shirt. And those fucking freckles. If I had one more dream about freckles, I'd lose my mind.

"She is skittish," Kellan agreed with a sigh. "But when she lives with us, she'll see that we're not a threat to her. From the little she shared with Warrick, it seems she's under the impression that bonding into a pack will get her killed like it did her mom. We can't scare her."

"Better keep Slade away from her, then," I rumbled, shaking my head as tension pain sliced through my temples, "and I doubt Finley is going to be much better. After everything with his family, rejection is his Achilles heel. That stubborn bastard would rather slice his own balls off than give her any concessions."

Kellan was silent for a beat as he considered our other brother and his teammate. "I'm going to talk to him at training this afternoon." Hope still threaded his tone. *Poor bastard.* Even if I did occasionally envy him his unjaded outlook on life. "I'll get him to at least agree to ignore her and not make life harder while she's getting to know us."

"Yep, you try and smooth him over before she arrives. I'll do my best to keep Slade from accidentally murdering her." No one controlled Slade, but he could be persuaded. Occasionally.

Kellan might have a chance at getting Finley to agree to ignore her, or I could use dominance on him and force the issue. It had to be a last resort though—our pack of alphas only worked because I didn't overstep my control.

To force them over Emmeline would only create more animosity between them and her.

Kellan recovered his upbeat tone quickly. "I know you've been putting in solid hours stalking her at night, in your control-freak obsessive ways. But tomorrow... I'm picking her up."

Control-freak and obsessed was accurate. Emmeline had cast a spell over me, and I'd be pissed about it, but I was too busy obsessing. "You sound like an overgrown puppy, Kellan. All I can picture is you bouncing around with your tail wagging."

His snort of laughter filtered down the line. "You're half

right. Parts of me are definitely wagging. I'm just so fucking excited that we finally found her. Years I've dreamed of a scent match, and she's so pretty and snarky and smart. And those freckles, broooo. I just want to kiss a path across them."

Fucking freckles. "You need to pull yourself together. Do not slobber on her when you pick her up from Annandale Pack house tomorrow. I don't have time to chase her down when she tries to skip town again."

"No slobbering," he promised. "I'll be a good boy."

This asshole and his praise kink. I hung up the phone before he could say anything else, and turned toward the pile of work I should be getting to. But fuck, all I could think about was Emmeline, and that crackle of intensity anytime she was in the room with me.

My new craving for chocolate would not be satisfied with anything less than a taste of a cagey, smartass, strawberry blond shifter.

Pushing to stand, I wandered toward Slade's closed office door and knocked. Only a fool would enter his domain without permission—many of us had learned that the hard, extremely painful way.

"Enter," his arrogant ass called.

Pushing the door open, I found him sprawled back in his chair, eyes locked on me as he tracked my movements. The first time I'd seen him do that, I'd prepared to be attacked, but it was just his way. We were all prey to his beast.

"Have you dug up any more information on her background? Who were her parents? Where the fuck did she come from? At this stage we only know she's twenty-five because Warrick updated us."

Slade almost smiled. "You only know that because you threatened to burn his house to the ground with his pack inside if he didn't disclose all pertinent information."

I shrugged. That wasn't even the worst threat I leveled against the other entitled alpha. He had my mate; he was lucky to be alive. "What else have you dug up?"

Slade crossed his arms, letting the silence extend until it was almost uncomfortable. But I was used to his ornery ass by now, and my wolf barely reacted. "What makes you think I've been digging into that insignificant shifter?"

Alphas didn't roll their fucking eyes, but I was close. "Because you would never let a person into our pack house without a thorough investigation."

And because a part of you is just as curious about her as the rest of us.

He'd never admit it, but we both knew the truth.

As always, I appreciated Slade's lack of time for lies or sugarcoating the truth, even when he used that gift to rip you a new asshole in less than ten words. "She's a ghost. There's no paper trail. There's no social media. There's no sign she exists at all, except for the fact that she's standing here in Golden Claw, a physical person."

"How is that possible?"

"I don't know," he grumbled slowly, "but I'm going to figure it out."

Great, he'd be an even bigger pain in my ass until he got to the bottom of our mysterious mate.

Leaving him to it, I returned to my office, throwing myself into work, pausing only to call my managers at Luxuria, our high-end nightclub, and Golden Fin, our seafood restaurant. By the end of the calls, I had a schedule worked out for Emmeline, with a mix of day and night shifts. All except Sunday, which was reserved for family bonding time.

Emmeline Anders was about to learn what living under my roof entailed. I'd be subtle about it in the beginning, but she was already under surveillance whenever she left her temporary accommodations, and I was there every single night.

Watching my prey.

Once she came home to us, I'd have her exactly where I wanted her.

CHAPTER 12

When I left his office, Hunter remained a silent shadow all the way down to the first floor. He didn't follow me over to Cora, who waited by the couches, but I felt his gaze burning into the back of my head until after I'd left his building. "I'm guessing you didn't end up on the floor for rentals and job opportunities," Cora whispered as we hurried down the steps.

"Not unless that's part of the CEO's duties," I replied dryly.

Cora's shoulders hunched as she sighed. "I'm so sorry. It's hard to avoid your pack in Golden Claw, and I figured it'd be easier to deal with them straight up. But I never expected you'd get dragged right up to Alpha Hunter."

She was starting to fidget so I took pity on her. "It's not your fault. Hunter and I reached an agreement that I'm happy with." *Bleh.* "You don't need to feel any guilt. Your pack's kindness has meant everything to me."

The strain in her features eased but it didn't completely disappear until we were in the car and driving. I filled her in on what happened between Hunter and me as she navigated through the city, bringing us to a stop in front of a bakery. It was only when I saw the *Chelsea's Sweets* sign that I remembered the other omega in Golden Claw.

Our designation was so rare that I'd never known another outside of Mom, so meeting Chelsea felt almost as nerve-racking as being stuck in that fancy office, twenty stories above the ground, with Hunter Reeves.

The scent of pastry and sugar hit me long before we stepped inside the adorable shop. It was painted in light teal with pink accents, and the glass cabinets that ran the full length of the counter were stacked with more delicious pastries than I'd ever seen in one place. "Welcome to Chelsea's Sweets, how can I help you?" The young woman behind the counter had delta energy, so she couldn't be Chelsea.

Cora confirmed that: "Hi, Macey, we're here for pastries and to have a quick chat with Chels, if she's available."

Macey's smile lessened as she turned her curious gaze on me and then back to Cora. "She's at the Thenguard building having brunch with her pack. I expect her back in an hour or so."

Disappointment hit me, but I shook it off. I'd be in Golden Claw for at least a few weeks, giving me plenty of time to meet the omega and learn of her experiences.

"No worries, just let her know Cora from Annandale Pack stopped by. We'll grab some of your delicious treats, then."

I followed Cora as she moved along the display, pointing at everything she wanted, and when we walked out with the massive white box, I huffed in the delicious aroma.

Surely Cora would encourage a sneaky treat before dinner.

"You're drooling." She chuckled as she balanced the box with one hand. "Since you'll have to hold the box while I drive, if one or two of those sweets disappear during that job, I'll be none the wiser."

"And this is why we're going to be best friends," I said,

before wondering if that was completely creepy and weird. I was so far out of my league with this friend thing that I felt like an alien species trying to navigate a new planet. But despite my initial lack of trust, there was something about Cora that put me at ease.

Relief slammed into me when she laughed again and patted my cheek. "Girl, you know it. You had bestie vibes written all over you from the first moment we met."

A trill of warmth shot through me, and I knew my cheeks were pink. I'd never been a bestie before, and I found I quite enjoyed the concept.

When I was seated in the passenger side, she handed me the box, and by the time she'd made her way to her seat, I'd already picked out one of the apple strudels. I inhaled the cinnamon and sugar, mixed with the slightly tart green apples.

The first bite was better than sex. Swear to the goddess.

My sex life might be nothing to brag about, but this pastry was worth all the bragging.

"When I start work, I'm going to spend all of my money in Chelsea's Sweets," I mumbled around a bite. "And it'll totally be worth it."

Cora held up her right hand like she was giving an oath. "Can confirm, absolutely worth it."

The rest of the ride was filled with conversation about dinner and plans of how to handle living with the Reeves pack. "I'm going to work as much as possible, be home as little as possible, and ignore the four of them at every possible opportunity."

She side-eyed me. "You're a stronger shifter than me to ignore four scent-matched alphas." I sensed that she wanted to ask for the real reason *why* I was ignoring them, but she left it be. So far no one had pushed me for more information than I'd already given regarding my worries over losing myself to such a strong pack.

Warrick's SUV was out the front when we returned, and Cora called out for him as we entered the house. I was right behind her balancing the pastry box.

"Welcome home, love," he shouted back, already striding out to meet her.

They hugged and kissed like it had been days since they were together, and I had to turn away. Apparently, you could be both *happy for* and *envious of* a shifter all at the same time.

Warrick dropped another gentle kiss on Cora's forehead before he tucked her under his arm and met my gaze with a smile. "So, I received a call from one Alpha Hunter this afternoon." He quirked an eyebrow. "He was talking a lot of nonsense about you agreeing to move into Reeves Pack house tomorrow."

There was no judgment in his expression, and I tried not to let defensiveness seep out in my tone. "I know, I know. Somehow, I agreed before I knew what I was saying. Hunter is a freakin' bulldozer, I swear. He promised that there'll be no forcing of any pack bond, and... he's giving me a job at least."

Warrick stepped away from Cora, his hands ghosting over my shoulders. "Don't ever think you have no other choices, Emme. You're always welcome here, and if that pack steps one foot out of line, I'll bring the full force of the council down on them. You're not alone in this."

"But it is a great opportunity to get to know them," Cora added quickly, shooting him a frown. She'd been on team Reeves all day, starting with her scenic route into town. "You should enjoy your time with them, living under the banner of their protection."

Warrick backed her with a swift nod. "Right. Laws or not, you're still an omega, and living with a powerful pack will go a long way to deterring others from stepping over the line. No one wants to piss off those four."

"Not even Kellan?" I asked, thinking of the sunshiny, golden retriever alpha.

"Not even Kellan," Warrick confirmed. "It might take a lot to rile his gentler nature, but when you do... Don't underestimate him."

I filed that away with all the other information and advice I'd received so far about the pack, and hoped I had enough knowledge to stay safe during my time in their house.

My last night with Annandale Pack was a celebration with tacos and pastries filling their outdoor table. The wine and beer flowed, and while it normally took copious amounts of alcohol to override our rapid metabolisms and get us drunk, they added shots of shifter serum, a natural additive which cranked the booze factor a hundred times.

The room spun when I crawled into bed, and I hoped this wasn't my last night filled with laughter and friendship. Their consistent support and kind natures had melted most of my suspicions over their intentions. They'd remained as genuine as they'd appeared the first time I met them, even as they made me promise to come around for family dinners at least twice a month.

Frankly, I couldn't wait for my next hangout at their place.

Early the next morning, light stabbed me in the face like a vicious beast, and if I had the ability to reach out and pluck the sun from the sky, I'd have done so without regret.

I groaned as my tender stomach reminded me that I'd overindulged last night.

In reply, I received a low chuckle. "Rise and shine, sweetheart."

That deep rumble had me blinking rapidly to bring the room into focus, and I found Kellan Jackson perched on the edge of my bed, his perfect sun-kissed face staring down at me. Caramel and cinnamon filled the room—he smelled even better than Chelsea's Sweets, and that was saying something.

"What are you doing here?" I rasped in confusion, looking around as I pulled myself up to sit. Thankfully there was no sign of Hurricane Hunter; I was far too out of it this morning to deal with him.

Kellan's face swam in my blurry gaze, and I shook my head to clear it, swiping a hand over my mouth in case I'd drooled or dribbled snot in my sleep. His sudden appearance had me out of sorts, like he'd stumbled in on me naked, even though I'd fallen into bed in my shorts and shirt last night.

"It's moving day!" His enthusiasm should offend me in my current ragged state, but his good looks upped the charming factor. "I'm here to pack you up and bring you home."

Home. Such a simple four-letter word. Simple and gut-wrenchingly painful.

"Temporary home," I corrected dully.

Kellan's smile didn't slip as he stood and offered me a hand. "Why don't you go and shower, and I'll get started on packing your room up."

I hesitated briefly, before placing my hand in his, the spark between us jolting my system into full-awake mode. The last of the fatigue and alcohol was swept from my system, only to be replaced with a new aching need inside. "I'll be out in a minute," I said in a rush, grabbing the first clean clothes I got my hands on and escaping into the bathroom.

Cranking the shower to cover my panic attack, I spent two long minutes gripping the side of the vanity and forcing myself not to return to the bedroom. The knowledge that Kellan was out there packing up my meager belongings had me fifty percent panicked, fifty percent nauseous, and one hundred percent losing my mind.

Agreeing to live with them was possibly the stupidest decision I had ever made, and I was fairly certain I wouldn't come out the other side unscathed. If I was already struggling to remain impartial after five minutes in his presence, how in the fuck would I handle weeks in their house, drowning in their scents? Fighting the tugging in my gut to seal that mate bond?

I was afraid that I'd vastly underestimated my control and strength here.

Mom.

I needed to remember Mom and the last time I'd seen her face and broken body.

The last time I'd felt her lifeless aura after her pack destroyed her.

That was the memory I'd bring forth whenever it got too hard to fight fate, and I prayed it would be enough. I was scared that after a few months of living with this pack I'd forget that bonding with them meant my inevitable death. Or worse, I'd no longer care.

I couldn't let that happen.

I made a promise long ago that I'd choose a different path to my mom.

A promise I could not break.

CHAPTER 13

By the time I left the bathroom clean, dressed, and mostly calm, Kellan had me completely packed up. "Grab your bathroom shit and we're good to go," he said, standing next to four brand new suitcases that I knew for certain were not mine.

"Where did they come from?" I asked, eyeing the matching set of gold and pink bags.

Kellan's smile was sheepish as he ruffled his blond hair until it sat in attractive disarray. "I picked them up for you. I thought you might need luggage, and these... matched your hair." He mumbled the last few words as his cheeks pinkened.

Damn this alpha.

He was both thoughtful and sweet, and I refused to be the asshole who crushed him in the middle of a nice gesture. "Thank you, Kellan." Somehow, I managed to keep my voice even. "But you don't have to buy me stuff. *I promise*. I'm really low maintenance."

He glanced down at the bags. "I'm starting to see that. I mean, I only filled one and a half with your clothes, and—" He peered over the top of me into the bathroom. "—it doesn't look like you have any extras."

"Most of my personal items were left behind when I had to run from Florida, and then again when they knocked me out in New Mexico and dragged me here."

His sunny disposition darkened as I felt a wash of powerful dominance. The rapid change reminded me of Warrick's comment that while Kellan contained more sunshine than others in his pack, if you riled him, you'd get the summer storm of your life.

"I'm sorry that you were brought here under those circumstances." His voice grew even deeper. "Who was there? *Who touched you?* Do you know their names?"

A smile tugged at the corners of my lips. "You're my favorite, Kellan... I hope you know that. But for real, you don't need to murder them for me. They were just doing their jobs." A job that had fucked my entire life, and I was ready and willing to kick their asses myself if I ever saw them again. But I refused to let these alphas fight my battles.

Relying on them could be my downfall.

Needing a distraction, I grabbed the small toiletries bag, and filled it with my few items from the bathroom. "Okay, we're good to go," I said, heading for the suitcases to help him haul them downstairs.

Kellan got to them first, and barely let me take one of the small empty ones, while his massive paws gripped the other three. Deciding that I would choose my battles wisely with this pack, I didn't argue, and made my way down the stairs to find the entire Annandale pack waiting near the entrance.

"We're going to miss your gorgeous face," Cora cried as she wrapped her arms around me and yanked me into one of her full-bodied hugs.

Nope. *No freakin' crying.* Now was not the time to fall apart. "I'll see you all for a family dinner soon, okay?"

Sierra hugged me quickly, but the three male shifters kept their distance thanks to the giant alpha standing at my back. "It was a pleasure to have you here, darlin' girl," Marcus said, blowing me a kiss. Richard nodded in his stoic way, and then there was Warrick.

"I can't thank you enough, Alpha Warrick." I placed my hand on his arm and ignored the scowl boring into the side of my head. "I'll never forget the kindness you so freely offered."

I might have only known them for days, and there was still the whole Hunter-stalking-me-in-their-territory to deal with, but my wolf didn't care. She considered them allies, and we were grateful for their freely offered support.

Warrick's eyes softened and I got the feeling he wanted to say more, but ended with, "I'll contact you about our next family dinner. I can go through one of the Reeves pack until you get a phone."

He glanced over my head toward my towering alpha shadow. "Any night except Sunday," Kellan said shortly. "That's our family bonfire night."

Tilting my head back to take in his tense features, I wondered if they'd truly expect me at their *family* bonfire when I'd made it very clear that I wasn't family and never would be.

Kellan's gaze settled on my face, and I could see in the depths of his blue eyes that I would absolutely be there. No excuses. Not wanting to argue in front of the other pack, I filed that topic away to speak with Hunter about later. For now, I'd continue to choose my battles wisely.

When we exited their Tudor house, there was a blue Range Rover parked outside. It was the model up from Warrick's fancy ride, and I did a quick walk around while Kellan loaded the suitcases in the back. "Do you own shares in Land Rover?" I asked in a tone that conveyed my shock. "Because you all are driving models that aren't even released yet."

Kellan laughed, looking more relaxed now we were out of the Annandale pack house. "Reeves Industries probably does. Fin and I stay out of the company stuff most of the time, but we're happy to reap the benefits. Getting early models not yet released to the public is one of those benefits."

"That they occasionally pass on," Warrick called from where he stood near his front door.

I narrowed my eyes because he'd conveniently forgotten to add that part when we were discussing his Range Rover the other day. It made sense that the strongest alphas would all be tied in financial ways, but it irritated me all the same.

Kellan opened the door for me, and a scent I could only associate with leather and wads of cash drifted from the interior. I made a rapid decision to enjoy this aspect of living with Reeves Pack, even if it was the only benefit I got from the four powerful alphas.

Kellan closed the door behind me and hurried to the driver's side. When he jumped in, I kicked myself for not taking that seat first. Hunter had forced me to live at their house, and for that reason alone I should get to drive this glorious baby.

As the engine fired up, Kellan shot me a cocky grin. "Ready to go, freckles?"

"Freckles," I said with a disappointed shake of my head. "Very original."

Kellan's brows furrowed. "No good? Okay, I'll keep working on the nickname."

"I really wish you wouldn't," I muttered.

He ignored me as he pulled out of their driveway, and the quintet standing on the front porch waved their goodbyes. A part of me wanted to dive from the moving car and return to their warmth and security. With Annandale, there were no worries that I'd slip and lose myself in a bond, forsaking my life to turn my scent matches into the most powerful alphas in existence. *Nope.* There was only food, laughter, and safety.

Three things I had sorely lacked in my life.

"You'll see them again, sweetheart," Kellan said, unexpectedly gentle in his approach considering I'd stayed with them after rejecting his pack. "I promise, we'll keep you just as safe as they did. I don't know what you're running from, or what spooked you as a child to prevent you from even giving pack life a chance, but I'm going to change your mind about it. I never back down from a challenge."

I forced myself to keep breathing evenly to hide my sudden tension. "It's not a game to win, Kel. It's my life, and I made this choice *for a very good reason* long ago."

Please believe me. Please take my word for it.

Kellan fell silent and I was afraid to catch his expression, so I kept my gaze firmly out the window. Hurting him felt like stabbing myself with a blunt knife, and I had never wished so hard that my life was different. Or at least my designation.

As he smoothly navigated us through the town, he finally said, "If your past was different, and you weren't fighting a lifetime of pain and fear, would you want us? Our pack?"

I sensed how badly he was hanging on this answer, and for a second I was tempted to break his heart and damage his need to *change my mind*, but I just couldn't. "Yes."

I want you. Every part of you.

The air was electric, and I couldn't look away from him any longer.

His eyes blazed until they were almost a dark purple. "That's enough for now."

We didn't speak again until he pulled up in front of a large, wrought iron fence that I recognized from Cora's *extended* tour yesterday. We were at the Reeves family compound.

Two shifter guards, wearing the same navy uniform as the ones in the council chambers, stood on either side of the gate. When Kellan glided to a halt, he powered his window down and a male with a shaved head, huge muscles, and a no-nonsense attitude hurried over. "Alpha Kellan," he said with a brief nod. "Is everything okay, sir?"

Kellan might not be the entitled alpha in the Reeves pack, but he was powerful enough to be addressed similarly by the beta guard. "This is Emmeline," he said, leaning back to allow the shifter a brief glimpse of me. "I wanted you to meet her so that no one reacts if she wanders around the compound."

The security guard nodded, and his gaze momentarily took me in before it returned to Kellan. "Anything else?"

Kellan briefly hesitated. "Hunter has the full details to pass on. Emmeline is to be treated with respect and protected the same as you would for us. That's all you need to know for now."

The guard continued to avoid meeting my gaze, even as I leaned forward and said, "It's nice to meet you. What's your name?"

"Dave," he replied with a snap, staring at a spot beside my ear. "If you ever have any trouble, head for our security hut right there." He turned and pointed toward a small wooden hut beside the gate.

"Thanks, Dave." I shot a smile in his direction *that he didn't see.*

Kellan and Dave exchanged a few more words, and then we drove through the now open gate and onto a paved, double-laned private road. "Our main pack house sits at the end of the street in the family compound," Kellan told me as he idled slowly along.

The term *family compound* wasn't familiar, so I turned in my chair to take it all in as Kellan played tour guide. "My brother Tyson lives there with Ben, his mate," he said as we passed the first house on the right of the road, a small rustic cabin sitting on a large parcel of green grass. "They refused a quintet and settled into mated bliss as a couple. They're both accountants for Reeves Industries. Almost everyone in our extended families works for us."

I was surprised by how close-knit they were with their extended family, but I schooled my features to keep it from showing.

"Over there is Hunter's sister." Kellan nodded toward the next house we passed on the left side. It was a cute cottage, painted in shades of pink, purple, and yellow. Bright and simple in design with another large plot of land around it. "Kassidy lives alone. Has no interest in finding a pack and refuses to participate in any scent-matching events. You'd probably like her a lot."

I coughed to cover my laughter. With that as her introduction, I was more than looking forward to meeting Hunter's sister. Maybe she'd give me a few pointers on how to torment her brother without getting myself killed. He deserved it after all but tricking me into living with them.

"My other brother, Julien, and his quintet live there." Kellan pointed toward another house on the left. It was a single-level log cabin, expanding across half their fenced land. "He's the entitled alpha," he said with a fond smile. "The rest of his pack consists of two betas: Jemma and Gordon, and two deltas: Chastity and Lucas. Some of them are scent matches, others are just love matches, but they're all together."

That arrangement of designations was normal for quintets. One alpha, and a mix of betas and deltas.

The next house we passed was a two-story farmhouse, with light yellow walls and white trim, accentuating its huge wraparound porches. "Finley's brother Kenzo lives in this beauty, with his two mates, Ness and Luce. They're a lot of fun, actually. They have this massive teppanyaki grill out the back, and you haven't lived until you've tried Kenzo's cooking. His dad was a teppanyaki chef back in Japan before they moved out here."

"I've never had Japanese food," I admitted, without adding that I'd always wanted to try it but could never justify the price of takeout.

Kellan's stare was probing, and I was relieved when he finally returned his gaze to the front windshield. "You're in for a treat if Kenz is your first. You might as well start with the best."

We continued the tour, moving past the rest of the houses which belonged to an array of aunts, uncles, and cousins. I was assured that I'd meet them all at Sunday bonfire night, and I wasn't sure if that excited or terrified me. Either way, it would definitely be interesting.

The Reeves pack house at the end of the street was the largest and grandest. "Hunter and Slade are snobby bastards," Kellan chuckled, the deep, rich sound sending shivers down my spine. "They like the best of the best."

I cleared my throat. "I think they nailed it, then."

I'd never seen anything as beautiful as the three-story residence, which was a perfect mix of white cladding and gray natural stone. Windows lined every wall, and I could already imagine the abundance of natural light inside.

Kellan parked near the front porch, and I found myself mesmerized by the sheer size of the entrance—the front door had to be at least ten feet tall.

"Welcome home," he said, shocking me to a standstill.

Rubbing a hand over my chest, I wondered if it would have hurt less to be punched in the boob. This wasn't my home. It would never be my home.

Shifters like me don't get pretty homes on amazing, picturesque streets where all my family lived. We got neglectful, cruel mothers, who ended up getting themselves killed because they couldn't control their omega urges.

It hurt though, because if I'd ever allowed myself to dream of my perfect life, this was it in spades. The reality of knowing what I'd be leaving behind when I ran tasted like ashes on my tongue.

Bitter and dead.

CHAPTER 14

Inside the pack mansion—calling it a house was ridiculous—everything looked exactly as I'd expected. Open, airy, and filled with natural light. The furniture, oddly, reminded me of Annandale Pack house. Expensive but comfortable. It was cozy and oversized, as to be expected when four massive alphas occupied the space, but none of it felt showhouse-ish. This was a lived-in home, and I hadn't expected to find it so… comfortable.

"We've given you a room on the second floor near me and Finley," Kellan said, throwing back a quick smile as he hauled the suitcases up the stairs.

I only carried the toiletries bag, and even that he eyed as if trying to figure out how he'd fit a fifth handle in his grip. "Slade and Hunter are on the third floor. Slade has the largest space, and if you take any advice about living here, please take this piece: don't ever go into his room uninvited. He doesn't allow any of us to enter his dominion alone, and half the time not even when he's there."

"He sounds worse than Hunter," I mumbled, wondering what I'd gotten myself into.

Kellan's reply held the slightest hesitancy: "Just stay out of his way and you'll be absolutely fine."

I cleared my throat and tried not to roll my eyes. "Very reassuring, thank you."

It was no surprise that these alphas were a threat to my life, but I expected it to come *after* bonding. It felt weird that I hadn't even met two of them and I found myself with questions I never expected to have. Like... were they both wolves too? What did they look like? Why did Kellan speak about Slade in hushed, fearful tones? I had no idea if any of my questions would be answered considering this house was huge enough to possibly avoid them for my entire stay.

When we reached the second floor, Kellan pointed out his room right by the stairs. "You're always welcome inside, even if I'm not there. I have nothing to hide."

I had no idea what to say to that, but he didn't appear to require a response as he continued along the lovely hallway, with its blue walls and white wainscoting. "This is your room." He clicked open the next door we reached and waved me inside.

I followed him in and forced myself not to visibly react to the striking space. In my mind, though, I was squealing like a stupid girl over how perfect it all was.

Filmy white curtains framed a wall of windows, all which were open to allow in the fall breeze, showering us in scents of grass, citrus, and wood smoke. The floors were dark wood boards covered by fluffy white wool rugs. Shucking my shoes at the entrance, I enjoyed my bare feet sinking into the soft depths as I moved toward the bed.

It was straight out of a dream with the four posts holding up the same white curtains that lined the windows. The bedding was checkered in mauve and cream, and looked so comfortable I barely restrained myself from diving into those cushy depths.

"Is this room okay?" I was shocked by the waver in Kellan's tone, as I turned to where he'd perched near the doorway, my four bags stacked neatly against the wall.

"Are you kidding me! It's gorgeous. I'm about two seconds from a princess twirl, flying hair and all. This room is just perfect. Thank you."

He cleared his throat, and I caught a glimpse of his soft smile. "We wanted you to feel at home here. Anything you need or want, just let me know and I'll make it happen."

Anything except my freedom, but that was a worry for another day.

He straightened and pushed off the doorframe. "Okay, the wardrobe is through that door, and the bathroom is there." He pointed out the two attached rooms. "I'll leave you to unpack and settle in. Come down to the kitchen when you're ready and we can have breakfast."

It was all so normal, and I was mentally scheduling in a panic attack for when he left the room. Sure enough, as soon as he was gone, closing the door behind him, my breaths turned rapid and shallow. My wolf whined in my chest, and for the first time in a long time I almost lost control of her.

The house smelled like my pack. More than just the cinnamon-caramel of Kellan and the mocha of Hunter, there were another two interwoven: vanilla and cherries and ashy roasted marshmallows.

I had no idea which belonged to Finley or Slade, who was already a terrifying visage in my head, but I craved this knowledge, and it near drove my beast out of her mind.

It took an embarrassing number of minutes to get myself under control, and it was only through sheer force of will that I managed to pull myself together. Needing to stay busy, I wheeled the suitcases into a massive walk-in wardrobe which was already outfitted with hangers and drawers. I unpacked to find my clothes took up a small fraction of the available space.

Next, I placed my toiletries in the bathroom, which was a white and mauve dream like the bedroom. I paused at the large clawfoot bathtub, in a style I thought only existed in movies and my daydreams.

Did they know about my love of baths?

Goddess, they even had jars lining the shelf, filled with oils and salts. Baths were the secret love of my life and my place of respite, but I'd rarely been lucky enough to rent an apartment with one. This pack had stepped up and showed me a glimpse of perfection.

How hard would it be to return to purgatory after being this close to heaven?

With nothing else to keep me occupied, I checked my reflection one last time to find I mostly looked put together. My face was slightly flushed, but otherwise the rest of me appeared as per normal. If only my insides felt the same.

Kellan's scent was easy enough to follow as I left my room and headed downstairs. "Wow," I said as I entered the large and sunlit kitchen, with its white Shaker cabinetry and marbled counters. "I'm jealous of your house."

Kellan's head popped out from behind the doors of their white fridge, a glass jar filled with strawberries in his hand. "No need to be jealous, pretty girl. It's your house too."

Ugh. I'd walked right into that one.

Choosing not to argue, I focused on the spread of food he'd assembled across the white island counter. There were only two place settings but enough food to feed an army. "Uh, how many shifters are you feeding this morning?"

He shrugged as he added the strawberries to the other fruit

already sliced in a bowl. "I had no idea what you liked to eat and wanted to cover all bases."

His words created the tiniest crack in my chest, as if the protective shell I'd kept around my heart since I was a young girl had fractured. No one had ever cared what I wanted before. Not in food or life or love. This simple gesture from Kellan was almost too much for me to handle.

In my overwhelmed state I started to babble, "Oh my goddess, you really didn't have to go to any trouble. I'm super unfussy. Everything looks amazing, though, and outside of hating avocado and tuna, there's no other foods I won't give a try. You didn't have to bring out everything in the fridge and pantry..."

Holy shit. Shut up, Emme.

Kellan watched me with a fascinated expression that felt far too familiar for a pair of strangers, but he never interrupted, leaving me to continue making an absolute tool of myself.

When I finally ran out of words, collapsing into one of the stools under the counter, he pulled out the chair beside me. "I'm not a fan of tuna either," he said casually, "but avo on toast is a gift from the gods. You just need to season it properly."

Breathe. Just breathe. "I'll take your word for it, but I can't imagine changing my mind. If I was supposed to eat mushy grass, I'd be an herbivore."

A burst of genuine amusement escaped him as he shook his head. "You sound just like Slade."

I had no idea what to say to that, so I grabbed a plate to start loading it with food. If I was eating, then I wouldn't be talking, which was better for everyone.

Kellan had set out fruit, cereal, pastries, perfect crispy bacon, fluffy scrambled eggs, and piles of toast. Not wanting to offend him, I took a little of everything, along with a heap of bacon because I was a growing wolf who needed her protein.

Kellan didn't touch anything until my plate was filled *and* I'd started eating. When he looked satisfied that I had enough, he added a heap of eggs and fruit to his plate, leaving the bacon mostly untouched.

"I need to up my clean proteins for training," he said, digging into his eggs after seasoning them with pepper. "The season starts soon, and then we'll spend our time getting pummeled on the ice. Can't lose any of my bulk."

While he chatted, he added extra bacon to my plate, and even poured me a glass of orange juice. I found myself losing interest in the food, more focused on this fascinating shifter beside me. He was so unlike the few alphas I'd known in the past, fitting none of their stereotypes.

Kellan was open and friendly, rarely spoke in grunts, and never threw his substantial dominance around like he was in an unending pissing contest. It was refreshing.

When I stopped eating for a few minutes to watch him, he nudged my plate closer as if to remind me that I needed sustenance. I took another bite of the perfect eggs. "I don't think you need to worry about losing bulk. You and Hunter are two of the biggest males I've ever seen in real life."

Kellan looked pleased by my observation. "I'm six feet four and the smallest of the pack. Wait until you see Slade."

Great. With each new revelation about Slade, I grew more terrified of meeting him.

"What season are you talking about," I asked, picking through the fruit to find the nicest piece of melon.

He let out a loud whoop. "Hockey season, baby! I can't fucking wait to be back out there pummeling the shit out of the other teams."

Ice hockey. I'd been vaguely aware of the NSHL, the *National*

Shifter Hockey League, but had never seen a game. Not even in the human world. "You play ice hockey professionally?"

Kellan smirked, and I was drawn to the strong muscles in his throat as his head tilted back. "You really haven't bothered to find out one thing about us, have you?"

He didn't appear upset by my lack of knowledge, but I felt judged all the same. "If I want to learn about someone, I prefer to talk directly to them. I didn't want to have preconceived ideas about your pack." It was also safer for me to know less, because Kellan already felt far too real.

"Finley is also on the team," he added, as if it was a casual afterthought. "I know you didn't learn that from him, but I don't want you to be blindsided if you ever watch us train. Or come to a game."

Of course he was, why would I have expected anything less. "So, Hunter and Slade work in your billion-dollar company, while you and Finley are professional hockey superstars. Meanwhile, I'm a homeless, jobless runaway who has skills in waiting tables and mixing cocktails. Yeah, I totally see why the goddess scent-bonded us." There was literally not an ordinary quality about my larger-than-life, hotter-than-the-sun, and highly successful pack members. Leaving me feeling pathetic and insignificant in return. Not that I wanted to fit in with them but come on... *make it make sense.*

Kellan stilled. Predatory still. The room felt smaller as tension grew, and I gasped when he reached out and jerked my chair around to face him. He slid me closer, slotting my body between his open legs, and I found myself holding my breath.

Whether out of panic or to keep his scent from clouding my mind, I was too far gone to know.

His chest rumbled, barely discernible but I felt the vibrations. His voice was a slow, deep rasp tingling over my skin. "I don't want to *ever* hear you talk badly about yourself again, Emmeline Anders. You're perfect for us. You're strong and resilient, surviving in the human world for years without a pack or support. Despite all of that, you came back to us whole and in control of your beast. Very few could have done what you have, and I'm proud to have you as a mate."

I was ripped underwater by his words, and overwhelming emotions crashed inside until I drowned in Kellan. "My friends call me Emme," I finally choked out, feeling the previous crack Kellan had punctured through my protective shell growing wider.

"Emme," he murmured, leaning in so close that our lips almost touched. My wolf clawed for our mate, and I wanted to do the same, but he didn't breach that final distance between us.

"Good morning."

I jumped about a foot in the air, my heart slamming against my chest as I almost fell from the chair. Hunter strode into the kitchen, having clearly seen how close Kellan and I were, but he didn't say a word as he grabbed a mug and poured coffee.

"Late morning into the office," Kellan commented as he resumed eating like nothing had happened between us. Meanwhile, I had to discreetly check to make sure I hadn't peed myself.

"Yes," Hunter replied shortly. He leaned back on the counter and gave me his focus. "We'll both be out of the house for most of the day today." He sipped his coffee, which he took like his soul. Dark. No sweetness. "Will you be okay here alone?"

I nodded. "Of course. I've been alone most of my life." It was a relief to sound somewhat normal. "It's actually my preference." At this point, I wasn't even sure what the truth was any longer; this entire situation had completely thrown me.

Hunter's lip curled, but he didn't call me out on my declaration. "Excellent. When I get back from the office tonight, we can discuss your work schedule. Until then, I ask that you don't leave the family compound—"

"Excuse the fuck out of you!"

"—only for your own safety. If you need to leave for any reason, there's a phone on your bed that's yours. Our numbers are already programmed in, and I expect you to use it. Keep in touch with us."

My breaths grew harder as he proceeded to address me like one of his employees. Kellan looked between us both but didn't interrupt.

"Fine," I gritted out, because I couldn't argue safety when I was an omega. "Should I expect your other two pack mates to lose their shit when they find me here?"

Was I the only one who found it weird that I would be living here and hadn't met them?

"Slade is already at the office," Hunter said dismissively. "And Finley is already training at the rink. Neither will be home before us." It didn't escape my attention that he hadn't confirmed or denied the *losing their shit* part. Not that I was surprised.

Them not being here was a fairly large indication that Slade and Finley had no interest in meeting me, and I should be grateful for their distance.

I am grateful.

It made it easier to separate myself from the pack, even as a part of me ached to know them. A part I needed to destroy before it was too late.

CHAPTER 15

FINLEY

When I slammed the door of my locker closed, voices filtered through the outer hallway and into the room. My team was finally showing up.

I was always the first to practice. I liked to get out on the ice while it was smooth and fresh, leaving the others to fuck around and talk shit while I glided. Throwing on skates and racing across that silky surface was the best form of therapy; it had been saving me since I could walk. And I'd never needed a reprieve from my thoughts more than I did today. *The omega* was moving into our pack house.

The omega who had rejected our pack before she even gave us a chance.

I hadn't officially met her, but I'd caught a glimpse the day she'd wandered into our company offices, all long legs and strawberry hair. She was gorgeous but fucking toxic, and as badly as I'd wanted a complete quintet, *a completed family,* now I mostly wished she'd go away.

She smelled like sweet chocolate, and for a moment as I'd watched her I almost lost control of my bear. He'd wanted to drag her out by her hair into our cave and hibernate the hell out of her all winter.

I'd barely managed to pull myself away, and now I was determined to avoid her at all costs. The ice had always been my escape from my family, and it would be again for this bitch of a shifter who believed she was too good for us.

I got fifteen glorious minutes alone, the chilled air soothing as I moved with mindless intent. Power skating up and down the rink didn't tire me out, instead I found it invigorating.

"Fin!"

Kellan's shout had my back teeth clenching, but despite his annoying ways I loved my pack brother. He didn't deserve to get his head ripped off because I was in a foul mood.

"Finley Thornton!" he called again, flashing a grin as he skated closer. "Are you ignoring me, brother?"

He slid to a stop, blocking me unless I plowed or dodged him. I debated both, and almost decided on the former, knowing the big bastard could take it.

"Not ignoring. Practicing," I gritted out, hoping he'd take the fucking hint that I wanted to be left alone.

Kellan, being a cheery sort of asshole, didn't remotely take the hint. "She's in the house, bro." He was bouncing on his skates, ripping up my perfect ice. "Her scent is everywhere and it's glorious. I barely stopped myself from getting naked and rolling on all the surfaces she touched."

Yep, that was fucking it... he was getting pummeled.

I slammed my hands against his chest, but he was too athletic to go down from a shove. It did at least move him out of my way. His laughter followed me as I took off again, skating faster to outrun my demons.

By the time the rest of our teammates made it onto the ice, I was calmer. Coach demanded a lot from us, and he was a huge part of the reason we won the Shifter Cup last year. None of us had any plans to relinquish the title, and I was ready for the season to start. We were training almost every day, and next week was the pre-season Summit game.

I couldn't fucking wait.

"Alright, assholes. Let's get this practice going." Coach Manuel Gerrado played for our team, the Celtic Wolves, for two decades before he'd hung up his skates and took on the coaching role. He was a tough old bastard, and like me, not even a wolf.

But we both bled in teal, gold and white on the ice.

"Prepare to puke your fucking guts up," Coach roared as his lion peeked out. "We're at the pointy end of the skate before the season starts, and there's to be no more screwing around. If I see any of you fuck around, I'll rip your balls off and use them as pucks."

"Fucking hell," moaned Kenz, who'd just slid to a stop beside me. It took a lot for his brown skin to pale, but the visual of our balls as a bloody mess under hockey sticks did the job.

Kenzo Yamamoto and I went through the juniors together, and outside of my pack he was the only shifter I considered family. His parents were a godsend when mine were a nightmare, and for that I'd always owe him. "Just don't fuck around," I said with a smirk, smacking him on the shoulder.

He moaned lightly again, and I took a step to the side in case he yacked. He was infamous for his tender stomach—everyone knew to never sit in front of him during a slasher flick. He could handle a little blood, but when a bone had embedded in the face of a murder victim, he'd power-chucked everywhere.

The next couple of hours were spent in drills, scrimmage, and skating until half the team were sprawled on the ice, heaving and trying to keep the contents of their guts *inside* their bodies.

Kellan, of course, had the stamina of ten wolves, cheerily gliding around everyone. He played center and was the most agile player on the ice. At six foot four, he stood a little smaller than me and the other defensemen, and we were never more aware of it than when he skated rings around us.

I was a right defenseman, and I enjoyed my position immensely. The crowd called me *The Eliminator*, because I never left anyone standing when I was on a warpath.

After Coach gave up on torturing us for the day, we limped and groaned our way into the locker room. There was a beat of silence as half the team collapsed onto the benches, and the rest looked like they'd just come from battle. All except Kellan. Our captain strode in with a fucking pep in his step and stupid grin on his face. "Great training today, boys."

"Shut the fuck up, Kel," groaned Christian, who was his closest friend on the team after me. "I don't have the energy to murder you right now, but if you give me ten or fifteen minutes to refractory myself, I'm going to rip your throat out." Christian's family immigrated here from Australia ten years ago, and he was the black cat to Kellan's golden retriever. He called him on his shit whenever possible, but would take a bullet for him. He was a solid wolf.

Kellan wagged his finger at him, his lips curling into a satisfied smirk. "I don't think you can use refractory like that. Take it from a wolf with *zero* refractory period."

Someone threw a sweaty old towel at him, but Kellan batted it away, whistling as he walked toward the showers. "I can't wait for this season to start," he called back.

A ton more towels and curses headed in his direction, and the happy fucker just laughed in response. Kenz dropped his head back against the wall and grunted. "He's even cheerier than usual. What's going on? Did he get laid?"

His question brought the omega's face to mind, and I decided then and there that I hated freckles. They were as annoying as she was, and I didn't need that shit in my life.

"He moved the omega in this morning." I lowered my voice in an attempt to keep this between us. It wouldn't take long for the rest of the shifter city to hear the news though, and then I'd never escape their scrutiny.

Kenz snapped his gaze to mine, eyes wide and concerned. "Are you doing okay, man? I don't even have to guess that this might be somewhat triggering for you."

The fact that I wanted to remove my skin along with my training gear to wash the irritation away told me he was right on the mark. "Makes no difference to me," I scoffed, desperate to believe the lie. "It's a big house, and I plan on ignoring her until she runs away again. We know it's inevitable."

She was weak and pathetic, and I'd had enough of that in my life to hope that this time the trash would take itself out.

After I was showered and dressed, I found Kellan sprawled in front of my locker. His bag was at his feet, and he held a small package. "No!" I growled, pointing my finger at him. "Don't even start."

His lips twitched as he peered up from under his blond locks. This pretty asshole used his looks far too often to get his own way, but it didn't work on me. "I mean it, Kel. I will release spiders through your entire room while you're asleep."

His eyes grew super wide, turning the blue even darker against all the surrounding white. "You wouldn't dare?"

"Try me," I snapped back.

He slapped a hand against his chest, a feigned look of hurt on his face. "How could you use my greatest fear against me? I thought we were brothers."

I covered up a laugh with a cough, rubbing my hand over my face. He looked so indignant that I couldn't even stay mad. "We are brothers. You know that."

A scent-bonded pack was the strongest bond outside of blood relations. It was everything. I'd die for this fucker in a heartbeat.

I knew he'd do the same for me.

Kellan, sensing my weakening, held out the package. "For the new season," he told me, like we weren't both aware of what was inside. He did this every season, and while it had never let me down before, I remained suspicious of his surprises. He'd used my superstitions against me far too often.

With a resigned sigh, I opened the package and pulled out the expected pair of socks. They were the teal, gold, and white of our team logo, but instead of the snarling wolf's head with crossed sticks, there were tiny bears printed across them and *The Eliminator* stitched around the top elastic. "You can't start the season without your lucky socks," Kellan crowed, looking pleased with himself.

Grateful that his gift had nothing to do with the omega, I slapped a hand on his shoulder. "I love them, asshole. Want to grab some drinks and a bite to eat before we head home?"

His expression softened. "I know you promised you wouldn't go out of your way to torment her, but I didn't expect you'd do that by never seeing her at all. You can't avoid her forever."

I could and I would. "You're going home to make sure she's okay, aren't you?"

She'd only been in our house for half a day and was already stealing my pack. "Come with me," he said, begging with his eyes.

I shook my head. "You know that shit won't work on me when it comes to her."

Turning toward the showers, I called out to Kenzo to see if he could make dinner. He was bonded to two betas, but he always had time for a quick meal and a few drinks.

"Fuck yeah, bro," he called back, rubbing a towel over his short dark curls as he emerged from the showers.

Kellan landed his meaty hand on my shoulder, giving it a squeeze. "I'll see you later," he said. "Don't get too fucked up tonight. Coach might be giving us a day off tomorrow, but we'll be right back into it the next day."

"You got it, Dad."

Kellan smirked as he flipped me off, then strolled out of the locker room like the golden child he was. No one would ever challenge him for that title.

Kenzo got dressed fast, and when he was ready I hauled my bag over my shoulder and led the way to my black RAM 1500 TRX. My brother lived in the compound too, so we usually drove in together.

"Where do you want to eat?" he asked as we jumped into the truck.

The supercharged V8 roared to life and I enjoyed the calming sound. If skating was my first escape, working on cars was my second. I loved the way this beast of a truck fit my height and muscles comfortably, but tonight I almost wished I'd brought my custom Ferrari SF90. A little speed went a long way to easing stress... it was science.

And if I couldn't have the speed, there was only one other solution.

"Marty's."

Kenzo let out a choked hoot. "Oh man. It's that sort of night, is it? Well... I haven't had good makeup sex for a while. Might as well start a fight with my girls."

His mate, Luce, was a fiery beta wolf who *did not* take any of my friend's shit. Vanessa was the peaceful center between them, and I shouldn't be screwing up his day just because mine had gone to hell.

"Fuck," I groaned, dropping my forehead against the wheel. "This is a bad idea, isn't it?"

Kenzo remained silent until I lifted my head and met his dark gaze. He was good at letting me mull my life choices over, while only offering advice after I'd sorted my thoughts out. "I'll never ask you to be in a situation that hurts you. If you need cheap booze and my company tonight, that's what you're getting. My girls will understand. We're blood brothers. Now and fucking always."

My chest grew tight, but I was nothing if not an expert at compartmentalizing my emotions. "I hated fate for a long time for not making us a scent match, but I think the universe already knew our bond was strong enough. In return, we got my brothers and your girls. A real family who'll have our backs no matter what."

"For life," he agreed, and for a fraction of a second his demons—which he hid better than me—spilled into his features, before a loose grin replaced his darkness. I wasn't the only one able to compartmentalize like a champ. "Now, let's go and get you proper fucked up."

Shifting into drive, I released all thoughts of the toxic omega from my mind.

I already had an amazing family and pack, and enough puck shifters to keep me satisfied when I needed a release. There was nothing this omega could offer me except heartache, and I was full up on that to last a fucking lifetime.

CHAPTER 16

After Kellan left for hockey training, I spent an hour exploring their mansion, and it wasn't an exaggeration to say that these alphas had everything. Including more bedrooms than they could ever need, unless they planned on having a dozen children.

My favorite part of the house was their gorgeous library, with a stone fireplace and row after row of wooden shelves filled with at least ten thousand books that I'd never read. It felt strangely calming just sitting amongst them though.

Next, I found their massive cinema, outfitted with a popcorn machine and candy bar. It was connected to a games room with a pool table and a bar, and farther on was a gym, jacuzzi, and sauna. Outside, there was a huge pool with a waterfall feature, and lots of couches to laze around and enjoy the luxury.

Reeves Pack house had more amenities than a resort, and I found myself wondering how they felt living amongst this opulence. Did they have a clue how lucky they were, or was it all taken for granted?

"Excuse me, Ms. Anders."

Turning from the pool, I found a blond delta shifter standing a few feet away. She was older than me, wearing jeans and a black shirt, holding a cloth against her hip. "Sorry to disturb you, but the alphas asked me to ensure that you have everything you need. I'm Florence, their head housekeeper. I don't live on-site, but I'm here most mornings and can assist with shopping, cooking, and cleaning needs."

I wanted to joke and ask her about my need *not* to be in Golden Claw, but I got the feeling she wouldn't find it funny. "I'm just exploring," I said with a shrug toward the pool. "That's okay, right? I made sure not to go up to the third floor, or inside any of the occupied bedrooms or offices."

Florence nodded vigorously. "Oh, yes. Alpha Hunter told me that you are to treat this as your home. There's nothing off limits except Alpha Slade's domain. We don't even clean in there."

Kellan had already mentioned he was on the third floor, hence why I hadn't set foot up there.

"Can I use the pool and sauna? I'd like to paddle while it's still warm out."

Florence's face lit up. "Of course! The pool is heated all year, but it's the perfect day to swim. There are towels in that large cupboard over there." She pointed out a set of cane doors behind an outdoor lounge. "I'll bring out snacks and drinks for when you finish."

"No, you don't need—"

She was gone before I could finish, moving fast for a shifter so tiny. I'd never been waited on in my life, and my immediate urge was to follow her and help make the food. Fighting against that instinct, I faced the pool again, searching for calm in the clear, blue depths.

I had no swimsuit, but I was wearing black cotton underwear which covered as much as a bikini, so I stripped off where I stood and dropped my jeans and shirt on a lounger.

When I dipped my toe in, I was unsurprised to find the water cool but not freezing. *Heated all year* was most definitely a rich person perk. Along with having a pool in the first place.

Without further thought, I dove in from the side and enjoyed the sensation of water sliding across my skin. I moved from the shallows to the deeper end, without a worry that I'd no longer be able to touch with only minimal swimming experience behind me. I just needed this mindless release.

When my lungs screamed for air, I surfaced near the middle, and awkwardly doggy-paddled my way over to the rocky outcrop of the waterfall. It was like having the largest bath and shower combo in the world, and only the faint hint of salt and chemicals on my skin reminded me I was in a pool.

Tilting my head back and closing my eyes, I let the water run over me. Their backyard was massive, going far beyond the pool area. From my bedroom window this morning I'd seen pockets of forest, fruit trees, and flowering gardens.

Add in the chirping song of birds this afternoon and it was the complete picture of tranquility.

It took a while for unease to filter through my serenity. A strong dominance caressed my wolf, and as my eyes flew open, I met the gaze of an unfamiliar alpha on the side of the pool.

Swallowing roughly, I pressed myself harder against the rocks and took him in, starting with a pair of massive, black biker boots and up long, jeans clad legs, to... *sweet mercy above.* He was the biggest shifter I'd ever seen.

His broad chest and heavy muscles were visible through a long-sleeved Henley, and his body just went on and on. He had to be near a foot taller than me.

A hint of a tattoo showed above the neckline on his left arm, and even though I shouldn't care, there was a cursory thought of how much of his skin under those clothes was covered in ink.

He moved forward until his boots hit the edge of the pool, and I was completely locked in his energy. The alpha didn't look much older than me, but his features were built of hard lines that reminded me of the ancients. There was a sense of godlike beauty about him as I took in his bronze skin, midnight black hair, and eyes a deep, forest green.

But if he was a god, it was a god of nightmares.

He remained expressionless as he watched me closely, but I sensed a hint of fire in those jewel-like eyes.

I can't look away.

Even as an omega, his dominance held me in place, and I was very aware that if he wanted to rip my throat out, there was nothing I could do but die at his feet.

This is no wolf. He was absolutely not a wolf, but I didn't have a single clue what his creature could be, as he held no signs of the usual suspects.

I was so caught in his thrall that I failed to notice Florence approaching until she stood at the side of the pool with a tray in her hands. She eyed the massive god-man warily, keeping a large distance between them.

"Alpha Slade," she said in a polite whisper, bowing her head. "Can I get you anything sir?"

Slade. Of course it was fucking Slade.

Who else could be this terrifying without uttering a single word?

Slade ignored Florence. His penetrating gaze remained firmly on me. When his stance shifted minutely again, he sent a waft of fire-roasted marshmallows my way, giving me my last two scent connections. Finley had to be the vanilla cherries.

Goddess save me.

As if the deity heard my plea, Slade blinked and released me from his stare, striding back into the house.

Sparks of unease and confusion crashed into me with force, sending my system into overdrive. My wolf had remained strangely quiet in the presence of the alpha, but not because she lacked interest. *Oh no.* She very much wanted to roll around in Slade's scent. But there was also a healthy dose of fear. She'd be cautious until he showed his true intentions, and I was doubly sure we had to be very careful with that alpha.

"Here's your food, Ms. Anders." Florence placed the tray on the table between two of the white loungers. "Is there anything else?"

I laboriously swam over to the steps at the shallow end, and by the time I'd pulled myself from the water, she held two fluffy yellow towels. "Thank you," I said, wrapping one around my body and the other around my hair. "Does Alpha Slade do that often?"

Fear briefly tightened her features and her mildly floral scent turned acrid. "He uses the pool, but not when anyone is here."

I nodded, unsure what I should make of his presence. Hunter had said the other alphas wouldn't be home before him, which meant Slade's appearance in the middle of the day wasn't a regular occurrence. "I'll leave you to your lunch, miss." Florence gave me a similar bow to the one she'd bestowed on Slade.

"Thank you," I called after her rapidly retreating form.

It took a while for my heart rate to slow, and when it did the growl of my stomach kicked back in. I picked through the tray of sandwiches and cold cuts, eating until I was full. Florence had also brought water, juice, and a carafe of wine that had me deciding to indulge on my day of luxury.

By the afternoon I was half sloshed, and Florence kept me

company as she refilled my wine. "You grew up in Greenville," I said with fascination. "You don't have a Southern accent though. And how did you end up in Golden Claw?"

She shrugged. "I've been here for many years, but I never forget my Southern roots, even if I don't always sound the part. I moved here because I got a job with the Reeves pack. They pay amazing and treat me really well... it's a dream job."

Kellan chose that moment to return home from training, bursting through the back door with his usual exuberance. Florence jumped to her feet like she'd been shot in the ass, and I covered by exclaiming loudly, "Thanks for bringing those drinks out, Flo. You've been such an amazing help today."

She bowed quickly, while still looking faintly panicked. "Of course, Ms. Anders. Just let me know if you need anything else."

When Kellan passed her, she bowed to him also, and then she was gone. His lips twitched as he approached me, taking in my towel-wrapped body, along with the almost empty glass of wine in my hand. "Having fun, pretty girl?"

"Are you giving up on the nickname caper?" I snickered, the alcohol sending me silly. Or maybe it was how delicious Kellan looked in his jeans and black shirt, hair slightly damp after training. There was a faint bruise along his cheekbone that must have been bad if it wasn't fully healed, and I almost reached out and brushed my fingers across the mark. "Tough practice?"

He groaned and fell into the lounger next to me. "Coach is trying to kill us in preparation for the new season. Apparently, you have to hit rock bottom before you can rise as superstars. And you should know that I never give up. I'll find the perfect nickname, sunshine, even if you'll also always be a pretty girl. From the moment I saw your white wolf, that was a given."

This alpha was a smooth operator, and his charm was

absolutely working on me. As my cheeks pinkened, I quickly said, "You're the sunshine one, golden boy. That's not going to work on me."

He wrinkled his nose and then shrugged. "You're probably right. I'll cross it off the list." He lifted his hand and made an imaginary strikethrough on an imaginary piece of paper.

It was far too easy hanging out with Kellan, and I found myself asking questions, despite my desire to remain detached. "What position do you play in hockey? I mean, I know absolutely nothing about the sport except that you use a stick to hit a black disc looking thing, but I assume you have positions."

He chuckled, snatching up some of the fruit I hadn't eaten yet. "I play center. I like to hit the *black disc* and score as many goals as possible. I'm actually the leading scorer of the league." He popped a piece of apple in his mouth, and never lost his confident grin even as he chewed.

"If you're waiting for my shock to show, it'll be a while," I told him dryly. Kellan had *head jock* written all over him. "Outside of your scoring prowess, is your team any good?"

His handsome features brightened, and I was really regretting all the wine. I needed my wits about me to fight the overwhelming attraction I felt toward Kellan. Even worse, how much I genuinely enjoyed his company. "The Celtic Wolves are the best. We've won the Shifter Cup for the last three years straight."

Shit, they were good. "Hopefully I'll get to see you play."

No, Emme! What in the fricking frack is wrong with you? The more I tangled us together, the harder it would be to leave with all parts of me intact.

Kellan looked so happy, though, that my regret over that slip of tongue faded. "I can't wait to see you in the stands, wearing my jersey. Finley will lose his shit, and I tell you, riling that bear is one of my favorite pastimes.”

Finley was a bear. The final alpha I hadn't had a chance to meet yet. I briefly debated asking what Slade's beast was, before deciding it was better not to know.

“Speaking of,” Kellan continued, “why didn't you answer the group chat?”

I tilted my head, wondering if I'd misheard him. “The what?”

His smile grew wider, flashing a lot of white teeth until he looked like the Big Bad Wolf come to eat me. “Where's your phone?”

Oh shit. After Hunter told me about the phone this morning, it had completely fled my mind. “I never went anywhere,” I said quickly, half-panicked. “He said to contact him only if I was going somewhere.”

Kellan shook his head like I was a weirdo. “You might want to grab it and chime in so that Daddy Alpha doesn't lose his shit. He's a little overprotective. Of all of us, but you... yeah, fair warning. He's going to be all over you in a way that will have you questioning your morals.”

“Because I'll want to murder him?” I suggested sweetly.

An odd expression tugged at his features. “Well, that's one way to look at it.”

“Are you suggesting I might be into his domineering, stalking ways?”

Kellan shrugged, and I was starting to think he'd lost his mind. Sure, I'd never really had the opportunity to explore my sexual preferences or kinks, but after what happened to Mom, there was no way I'd be into any sort of control or dominance.

After being alone most of my life, I had no desire to be controlled, in or out of the bedroom. Not even by powerful, sexy alphas.

No, *especially not* by powerful sexy alphas.

CHAPTER 17

I stared at the sleek, black phone which looked like it belonged in a sci-fi movie set a hundred years in the future. There weren't even any buttons, and I had no idea how to work it. After a few minutes of pressing the screen, it turned on, and I found it was already fully charged with five apps on the main screen.

One of which was for messages, with a tiny *thirteen* next to the curved symbol.

Thirteen messages already?

I opened it and immediately found the group chat titled:

ALPHA QUADS UNITE TO WOO OUR OMEGA

It took me a few seconds to read the title, which clearly had Kellan written all over it. Further confirmed by the first message in the thread, which I also deciphered slowly.

> Golden Boy: Welcome to the family chat. I'll be your host this evening, so buckle in and enjoy the ride.

I secretly loved that he'd used my nickname for him.

Daddy Alpha: Kellan, what the actual fuck are
you doing?

My lips twitched as I imagined Hunter's face when he wrote that message. Kellan had called him Daddy Alpha before, which I'd wisely ignored, but it was apparently no secret.

DADDY ALPHA HAS CHANGED HIS NAME

Alpha Hunter: Stop messaging me during
work hours unless the omega is in trouble.

Golden Boy: Uh, Emme is in this group chat,
asshole. Try not to fuck it up for us.

GROUCHY BEAR HAS LEFT THE CONVERSATION
SLADE HAS LEFT THE CONVERSATION

Ouch. Well, it'd be easier without them in here by the sounds of it.

Daddy Alpha: Emmeline, is everything to your
liking at the pack house?

Daddy Alpha: What the hell, Kellan? How did
you change my name again?

Golden Boy: A magician never reveals his
secrets.

GROUCHY BEAR WAS ADDED TO THE CHAT

It hadn't escaped my notice that not even Kellan fucked with Slade, which had me itching to add him back to the chat myself. I mean, yes, he was legitimately terrifying, but I refused to let anyone scare me *that much*.

Grouchy Bear: Spiders.

GROUCHY BEAR HAS LEFT THE CHAT

Golden Boy: Fin might be out for a while. For my safety's sake.

Daddy Alpha: Emmeline. You haven't answered me.

Golden Boy: She probably doesn't even have the phone on her. Give her a minute.

The time symbol indicated that Hunter had waited exactly one minute before he'd messaged again.

Daddy Alpha: Get your ass home right after practice, Kellan. Check on our omega.

Golden Boy: Yes, sir, alpha sir. Not like we don't all know you're stalking her via the security cameras anyway. She's fine.

DADDY ALPHA HAS CHANGED GOLDEN BOY'S NAME

That was the last message in the thread, and I glanced up in search of a camera, but couldn't find one in the bedroom. Apparently other rooms in the house weren't so safe.

Hitting the message thread, I started to type, grinning when my input name popped up.

Pretty Girl: Thanks for your concern, Alpha Hunter, but I'm perfectly fine. Your house is ridiculous, and I appreciate the mini vacation at Reeves resort. P.S your housekeeper is a freakin' gem. I'm stealing her. P.P.S Stop watching me via the security cameras. It's creepy.

I was thankful for autocorrect and voice-to-text to help with spelling, and after I got my message done, I managed to change my name to Emme. Mostly to fuck around with Kellan.

While I was doing that, three dots appeared as someone typed.

> Daddy Alpha: Answer your phone when I message, and I won't have to watch.

This bossy asshole...

> Emme: Should I bark when you call too? Would you like me to get a custom leash with your name on it, so everyone knows who I belong to?

> Annoying Pup: LOLOLOLOLLLOOLOLLOL. *skull emoji* *drool face emoji* Pretty girl, now you're just giving him ideas.

> Annoying Pup: Awww, Daddy Alpha, that name change is mean.

> *DADDY ALPHA HAS CHANGED HIS NAME*
> *ANNOYING PUP HAS CHANGED HIS NAME*

> Alpha Hunter: I'll be home in two hours for dinner. I'll have the leash ready for you.

I swear my body flushed in twenty different shades of red, and I regretted my need to act nonchalant in the group chat. I'd made it so much worse for myself.

> *EMME HAS LEFT THE GROUP CHAT*

I dropped the phone on the bed and forced myself to breathe in and out, *in and out*, until eventually my pulse steadied and my lungs stopped heaving. These alphas were too much, and dealing with more than one at once had me so far out of my league it wasn't funny. If all four ended up in the same room as me, I'd probably have a cardiac episode and die.

At least Hunter wouldn't be home for a couple of hours, so I decided to take a quick nap, and see if I could find the strength to erect that damn shield around my emotions once more. I had to harden my heart before one of them tore it from my chest.

Bringing Mom's face to mind didn't work quite as well as before, but it was enough to halt me from leaving my room to find Kellan and start up a conversation.

I wanted to learn about him. About all of them.

How old were they? Where did they grow up? What was their favorite color? Did they have demons just like me?

The problem with indulging in these curiosities, though, was it allowed me to truly know the alphas. What if they were actually good guys?

The odds were that good guys or not, if we bonded and shared power, it would corrupt their beasts until everything decent bled away. Though, I only had my mom's pack to base this off, and they'd never been good guys. Not even before they bonded her into their quintet.

Was there another omega in our world with a different experience bonding into a pack of alphas? If so, how the hell did I find her? I still needed to speak with Chelsea, but her experience in a mixed dominance pack wouldn't be the same.

My reading skills were too poor for me to comprehend any books on the subject—not only did I receive minimal schooling, but letters jumbled on the page, making it near impossible to both read and comprehend complicated texts.

If I trusted the alphas, I'd ask them for help, but it was too great a risk. I'd have to reveal what happened to my mother, which would also reveal the energy exchange possible between an omega and a pack of alphas. Maybe they were already aware, but if not, I sure as shit wouldn't be the one to tell them.

Maybe Chelsea... or Cora knew of other omegas across the cities.

Cora, I trusted as much as I'd ever trusted anybody, despite my doubts over Warrick allowing Hunter Reeves to stalk me.

Not that I fully blamed him—I was their scent match, and according to Pack City Law, I belonged to my mates. We might have evolved over the years, but at heart, shifters were still ruled by our beast and instincts.

Unable to nap around all my chaotic thoughts, I picked up the phone and scrolled through the numbers already listed. To my surprise, Cora was there with BFF in brackets next to her name. *Awww.* Kellan made me hope for impossible things.

When I pressed her number, it rang twice before she picked up. "Annandale Interiors, Cora speaking."

Just hearing her gentle tone lifted my spirits. "Cora, it's Emme."

Her professionalism faded as her voice grew more excited. "Emme, I was just thinking about you. How's your first day in Reeves Pack house going?"

"It's been great actually. They left me alone and I swam and ate all their delicious food. Basically, a free vacation."

Cora laughed delicately. "Next girl's night has to be there. I've been dying to see inside their space. No one gets in unless they're family, or friends of the family, and we've never made the cut."

"Well, you have now." I dropped back on my bed and pressed the phone harder to my ear.

"I assume you called for a reason?" Cora sounded like she was wandering through her house, as I picked up other voices. "Is everything okay?"

"Totally fine," I rushed to reassure her. "I was just wondering if you've ever heard of an omega being bonded into a full pack of alphas before. In Golden Claw, or any of the other pack cities?"

There was a brief pause. "You know... I don't think I've ever heard of that specific scenario before. I mean, a quintet with four alphas is almost unheard of by itself, but add in an omega and you've got one rare goddess-blessed combination."

My sigh escaped as she confirmed what I suspected. "That's what I figured, but I wanted to ask anyway."

"I'll do some research," she added quickly. "If this quintet is out there, or has been out there in the past, I'll find out about it."

I almost told her about Mom but decided at the last minute not to mention it. She shouldn't find out on her own; in the pack world we never existed. And Mom's story would be no help anyway—I already knew that tragic ending.

"I would appreciate that a lot," I said, my eyes closing as I attempted to release the tension from my muscles. "Let's organize that girls' night soon. I think I'm going to need a little break from all the alpha-ness around here."

Cora's laughter was soothing, and I relaxed just a touch. "I'll see you at the track on Sunday morning. We can plan it then."

"Perfect."

When we hung up, I knew there was no way I'd sleep now, so I headed into the bathroom. Filling the clawfoot tub was therapeutic on its own, as I sniffed the different oils and salts. Everything was fairly neutral, so I just tossed a handful of each one in, pinned my hair up to keep it off my neck, and sank into the warm water.

Bliss. Absolute bliss engulfed me as I bathed in temperatures just shy of a hell pit. I mean, was it even a bath if you weren't bright red and half-baked?

As the water cooled, I finally drifted off into the nap I'd wanted, waking wrinkled and disoriented, with just enough time to get dressed and race down the stairs for dinner.

To my relief, when I reached the kitchen, Kellan was the only alpha there, chatting with Florence and a male shifter I hadn't met before. The golden shifter turned as I entered the room, the blue of his eyes darkening as he took in the damp tendrils of my hair curling around my face.

He looked amazing, having changed into a fitted, dark blue Henley that was an almost perfect match for his eyes. *Gorgeous.* This alpha was distractingly gorgeous.

"Hey there, Shortcake," he said, and I blinked at him, not hating his choice for once but needing to point out the facts.

"Shortcake? I'm five feet eleven, I'll have you know."

A broader smile appeared, and I forced myself to look away. It was that or step into him, which was dangerous. "You're short in this house, Emme, but I actually chose that one from *Strawberry Shortcake.* As a tribute to all your glorious hair and those adorable as fuck freckles."

He tapped me gently on the nose, and my breath caught as his thumb scraped along my right cheek, leaving a tingling path of heat in its wake.

"Why not Strawberry?" I huffed out, my brain unable to come up with anything better through the haze he'd created.

Another stroke of his thumb and I was relieved when he removed his hand before I irrevocably fucked up my life. "Wouldn't want to be predictable, pretty girl."

Just kill me now. Take my damned life and throw me into the trash because Kellan had shattered every protective barrier around my emotions in less than twenty-four hours. He'd worn me down so quickly that I wondered if he was an actual magician.

"Dinner will be ready in ten minutes."

I jumped at the reminder that we weren't alone.

Kellan placed a hand on my back and nudged me forward. "Gerald, meet the fifth of our quintet: Emmeline. She's part of Reeves Pack and will be joining us for meals from now on." He tilted his warm smile toward me. "Emme, if you have any allergies, or specific requests for food, you can go through Gerry here. Or Florence."

The housekeeper nodded enthusiastically, and I couldn't help but shoot her a genuine smile. I had thoroughly enjoyed hanging out with her today, and hoped she felt the same way about me.

"It's really nice to meet you," I said to Gerald, who was a short, plump shifter giving delta wolf vibes. "I have no allergies, and I'm not super fussy as long as the meal is eighty percent meat."

Kellan's hand on my back flexed, his fingers brushing along a sliver of bare skin between my jeans and shirt.

"Easily done." Gerald let out a huff, looking relieved. "Alpha Slade would end my family line if I didn't serve a majority of meat in the dishes."

"Well, scary shifter and I have that in common," I replied, my smile a touch more forced at the mention of Slade.

Kellan threw back his head and laughed, his hand sliding higher on my bare skin, and I needed to move out of his hold before I begged him to strip my shirt off completely.

If only I could find the strength to step away.

"You nailed his nickname," he said, "and I might even be brave enough to use it in the group chat."

"Please don't," I choked out with a grimace. "I like you too much to watch you get torn to pieces."

Kellan released me to flex his impressive biceps, the striations visible even though his long sleeves. "I'd hold out for longer than you think," he said, with all the stupid confidence of an alpha. "Don't you worry about me, Shortcake. I wouldn't let you down."

Of that I had no doubts. "So, where do we eat?" My voice was breathless, but I felt too flustered to care. "I really can't see

Hunter perching at the kitchen counter like we did this morning."

Gerald cracked a smile while Kellan nodded. "You're correct. We eat in the dining room of course. *We're not savage beasts.*" He mimicked Hunter's gruff tones for the last four words.

We ended up in an adjoining dining room, and I was relieved to see the table—which could easily seat ten alphas—was only set with three places.

Looked like I'd get a reprieve from Finley the *Grouchy Bear* and Slade the *Scary Shifter* tonight.

Thank the goddess.

CHAPTER 18

Hunter strode in a few minutes later looking as perfectly pressed as when he'd left this morning, though his expression was harried. "Apologies. There was a slight disaster just as I was about to leave the office, but we got it handled." He rubbed his right hand over his face in a tired gesture, and I noticed a white bandage on top, stark against his olive skin tone.

There weren't many injuries an alpha couldn't heal within a few minutes, and as my annoyance rose at seeing him wounded, I was about to ask what happened, before remembering that it was *none of my fucking business.*

It would just have to be added to the list of questions on a constant loop in my mind.

Hunter shrugged off his navy suit jacket, and Florence was there to take it from him before he said a word. He sat, and I noticed the slightly tousled strands of his dark hair, as if he'd been running his hands through it. It was a good look on him, especially when he loosened his tie and released his cufflinks to roll up the sleeves of his dress shirt.

It took all my willpower to focus on the crispy white

tablecloth in front of me. There was no woman strong enough to watch Hunter Reeves relax after a hard day of work and not want to strip the rest of his clothes from him.

I never imagined how fucking sexy it was to watch him go from perfectly pressed and professional to this slightly ruffled alpha, his tattoos peeking out from his sleeves as he unwound from a long day.

Now I wanted to know how he looked in the morning after a night of running my hands through that glorious hair. *Wait! What?*

No. Emme. Immediately no. I was in desperate need of some therapy because my mental thoughts were getting out of control.

These alphas could literally kill me with almost no effort, and yet my body—*and wolf*—was ready to sign up for whatever they offered. I'd be ashamed of myself, but I was too busy being pissed off.

"What was the disaster?" Kellan leaned forward, uncharacteristically serious. In the short time I'd known him, he'd never given the impression that he was at all business minded, but as Hunter launched into an explanation about production and testing issues, Kellan understood it all, and even offered what sounded like practical and intelligent suggestions in return.

Hunter might be the genius inventor behind their gadgets, but if Kellan was any indication, the rest of the pack had plenty of input into their company as well.

"Enough about work," Hunter finally said as Florence appeared. She carried a tray in her hands, and the scent of roast meats and vegetables filled the room until my stomach rumbled in response.

"How was the rest of your day, Emmeline?"

Hunter drew my attention from the food, and since I'd

never liked my full name, I said, "Call me Emme, please. My mom thought Emmeline would class us up, but it's never suited me."

Hunter observed me in his focused way, and I waited for further questions, but none came. "Emme it is," he said gruffly.

Kellan pressed his huge hands to his chest. "Aw, Shortcake. Look at you and Hunter playing all nice with each other."

"Shut up, Kellan," he growled.

"Yes, Daddy."

The growls grew louder, and Hunter's wolf flashed in his stormy eyes as gold flecked brightly near the irises. I swallowed at the dominance in the room until Kellan threw both hands up, his face contrite. "Don't attack. I'll shut up. Sorry, I get annoying when I'm nervous."

Unable to help myself, I reached out and patted his hand. "You're not annoying, Golden Boy. You're exactly what I needed to keep from losing my shit. So... thank you."

He all but preened under my touch, his eyes bright and shiny.

"If you call him a good boy, he'll make a mess in his pants," Hunter added dryly, sounding calmer as he took a sip of what looked like whiskey in a crystal glass.

I'd missed Florence dropping off drinks, and I could have kissed her when I saw the wine in front of me. Clutching the glass, I took a gulp, worried that after a few weeks of alpha tension I'd be right on my way to regular day-drinking.

Kellan's cheeks flushed, but he didn't deny Hunter's statement. I filed his praise kink away, *for absolutely no reason*, because I'd never get to use it.

When my stomach growled again, I couldn't wait any longer, reaching out to take a serve of meat from the tray in the middle of the table. When I'd selected some of the seasoned chicken, beef, and pork, I also added one head of broccoli and two potatoes. Wouldn't want them to think I was uncivilized.

Neither Hunter nor Kellan touched the food until I'd filled my plate, and their consideration once again heated a place in my chest I thought was long dead. After I started to eat, they both selected from what remained. Kellan piled his veg and meat together, cutting everything into a mess and eating it all mixed like a psychopath.

Hunter, to no one's surprise, was methodical. He took an even mix of meat and veg, and while each dish sat close on his plate, a slight gap remained between them. When he ate, he started with his potatoes, and moved clockwise around the plate, one food at a time.

The alphas continued to discuss work while I ate the deliciously seasoned meat, drank crisp white wine, and enjoyed a chance to listen but not have to participate. It was as if they knew today had already been overwhelming and were letting me just float along in the deep hum of their voices. Voices that should not be soothing, and yet I'd never felt quite so relaxed as I did tonight.

These two, for all their alpha tendencies, were treating me with more kindness than I'd ever expected. Well, Kellan was anyway, and his personality went a long way toward softening Hunter's controlling nature.

"Do you think you'll be ready to start work tomorrow?"

I jumped and sloshed my wine over the side of the glass. Florence, bless her beautiful soul, filled right to the brim, which was great in all situations except when startled. "Sorry, what?"

Hunter's jaw twitched, but he didn't call me out on my absentmindedness or complete lack of coordination. "Work, do you think you can start tomorrow?"

"Yes!" I said too loudly, leaning down to lick up a few drops of wine off my hand. "I can start whenever you need."

The silence after my statement had me lifting my head to find both alphas staring into my soul. Their dominance was heavy in the air, and as unease and arousal trickled into my gut, I realized I had set them off by licking my hand. *Damn wine went to my head.*

Gently placing my glass on the table, I attempted to deescalate the situation. "I'm ready to start work and am free every single day."

Kellan recovered first, shaking his head. "Not on Sunday. I want her at the racetrack, and then we have family bonfire night."

Hunter's chest rumbled into a deep guttural sound, and while he didn't look away from me to acknowledge Kellan, he did at least speak. "You will train at our restaurant, Golden Fin, tomorrow, and our club, Luxuria, the next day."

Tomorrow was Thursday. "So, that's two training shifts and then a proper shift on Saturday?"

Hunter's nod was rough, his dominance finally fading.

"It's a relief to start working," I admitted, hoping to keep pushing these *normal* conversations. "Oh, and I'd like to be paid in cash."

Kellan's face shut down, giving nothing away, and while I hated to see his sunshiny personality dim, this wasn't a situation I could compromise on. Cash meant freedom.

Hunter, on the other hand, showed no outward reaction as he pushed to his feet. "That's fine, Emme. Now, if you'll excuse me, I've got some business to attend to. I'll see you in the morning with your schedule."

After he left, I felt like an absolute piece of crap, but there was no point in having money if it could be controlled or tracked. These alphas might not be a risk to me today, but they could in the future, and I had to plan for all situations.

To keep myself busy, I stacked the empty plates onto the platter, but before I could cart it into the kitchen, Kellan grabbed it first. "I've got it," he said, heading out, with me right behind him. We left the tray with Florence, who was fussing because *that was her job.*

She shooed us out of her dominion, and when we reached the entrance hall, Kellan paused as if debating with himself. "The night is still young," he finally said. "Want to watch a movie with me?"

Refusing to dull his shine again, I nodded. "I'd love to."

This had his smile broadening, and I could feel his warmth returning as I tried to ignore the rapid beat of my heart. "Any movies you've been looking forward to? We get access to all the theater releases."

"I've never actually been to a movie theater," I admitted. "I don't think I've watched a movie in years, so everything is new and exciting for me. Just no Westerns, war movies, or super gory horror."

I was stupidly relieved to hear his deep chuckle. "You sound like Kenzo, Finley's brother. He once puked on the row in front of him in the cinema after watching a slasher flick. He still can't talk about it without going green."

Ugh. I felt a little green just hearing about it.

Kellan didn't touch me as we walked to the theater, and once we were inside he told me to choose a seat while he got the popcorn going. There were five rows of four reclining chairs, each with a small table between them.

I chose the middle of the second row, deciding it had the best view. I sank into the soft depth and stared around the room with its dark, padded walls. The screen was massive, spanning high into the ceiling, and almost wrapping around to the side walls.

Within five minutes, the scent of popcorn, butter, and salt permeated the air, and I was relaxing again as I snuggled into the soft cushions. Kellan handed me a small remote. "You choose the film while I bring the snacks."

We'd only just eaten dinner, and I was pleasantly full, but as the popcorn smell grew stronger, I had no doubt there was always room for snacks.

Sliding my thumb across the touch button on the remote, I found row after row of movies, recognizing maybe ten percent of them. I finally settled on a superhero flick that looked interesting, right as Kellan returned with two bags of popcorn, chocolate bars, Twizzlers, and two bottles of water.

"I wasn't sure what sweets you liked," he said, handing half across to me. "But there's a ton of other options over in the kiosk."

"This is perfect." I clutched my goodies and tried to ignore the giddy shot of exhilaration blasting my stomach. I knew it was lame, but I was truly excited to watch this movie with him. It almost felt like a normal date with my alpha.

When the movie started, Kellan settled in close enough for me to feel his heat and energy down my right side. For once, I didn't fight the moment as I rested my weight against him. There was a heady, fizzing feeling inside my chest, and to distract myself I shoveled handfuls of popcorn into my mouth.

"Oh wow," I groaned as flavor burst across my tongue. "Why does this taste so damn good?" I'd bought popcorn from fairs before, but it had never tasted like this.

Kellan nodded in enthusiastic agreement. "Oh yeah, freshly popped is the only way to eat it. Along with a ton of butter."

He'd get no argument from me.

When the opening credits of the movie finished, sound wrapped around us as if there were speakers in every panel of the wall and ceiling. It felt so immersive; I could barely keep from bouncing in my seat.

"This is incredible," I squeaked, sounding like a freaking kid at Christmas. "I'm so excited."

It was lame, I was well aware of that, but... whatever. Kellan wouldn't judge me, and luckily the meaner alphas were nowhere to be found.

Kellan threw his arm over the top of my shoulders and pulled me to his side, sending my heart into splatters against my ribcage. My mind went blank as he pressed me into his muscles, dropping a brief kiss on the top of my head. "You're adorable, pretty girl. Fucking adorable."

Adorable wouldn't normally feel like a compliment, but there was no way to miss the catch of desire in his voice. Adorable or not, he wasn't currently thinking of me in a cute, platonic way.

Being plastered against his side left me floundering and unable to focus on the plot of the movie, even with intense action kicking off in the opening scene. My popcorn remained forgotten at my side, and Kellan's scent surrounded me until I was drowning in his sweetness.

"Relax, Shortcake," he murmured, the nickname apparently stuck now. His breath brushed over my ear. "Or do you need a little help with that?"

Oh, *fuck my life*. HALP! Abort mission. I was going down with this ship and there was no lifeboat in sight.

Kellan's scent grew stronger, and I tilted my head back to find his deep blue eyes staring into the deepest parts of me. His head moved closer, and I was frozen, unable to form any coherent thoughts. When our lips were a hairsbreadth apart, there was a bang as the cinema doors slammed open. Kellan growled and I leapt about a foot in the air right as an alpha stormed into the room.

CHAPTER 19

The shifter swayed in the doorway, hitting me with an overpowering scent of whiskey and florals, which itched my nose.

"What are you doing, Finley?" Kellan launched to his feet and put himself between me and the drunk-off-his-ass alpha.

I tilted to the side to see what Finley did next, because there was no way to leave while he blocked the exit. Kellan didn't move from his protective stance, but he did make a small shuffle to the side, allowing me to stare right at the final alpha in my scent match.

I gritted my teeth.

The bear might be wasted, but he was also rugged and handsome. He gave me *woodsman in the forest* vibes, and at this point I couldn't act surprised by his good looks. I just had to shake my head once more at fate's fucked up sense of humor.

Finley ran a hand over his thick, shiny chestnut hair, which was longer than the other guys', hanging to his jawline. His skin was light brown, and he rocked a short, dark beard that enhanced his bear slash mountain man persona.

Even from a distance the whiskey gold of his eyes, ringed

with thick sooty lashes, were tantalizing. He was massive, at least as big as Hunter, with shoulders so broad that I found myself staring at their breadth.

He finally noticed my observations and the scowl on his face deepened. "The entire fucking house smells like you." The deep, raspy timbre of his voice sent shivers down my spine. "Chocolate and honey. Sweet, deadly temptation."

Kellan shook his head and took a step closer. "Brother, you're drunk. You need to sleep this shit off before you say something you can't take back."

I remained quiet, understanding that anything I added here would only fuel his anger. But no matter how many times I told myself to get it together, I couldn't look away.

I was drowning in his whiskey gaze and the screaming chasm of pain in their depths. One look at Finley had me wanting to crawl into him and never leave. His pain called to my pain, but we were not kindred spirits. We couldn't be.

He didn't fight when Kellan strode over to grasp his shoulder, leading him from the room. As they left, a hint of vanilla and cherry reached me, clean and sweet, hidden under the alcohol and floral toxicity.

My heart clenched at the knowledge of where that cloying, flowery scent most likely came from, but since I had no right to care or let the hurt show, I forced myself to turn away and stare at the screen. The movie still played, but I no longer had any interest in watching it.

The joy and excitement I'd felt was long gone, leaving me flat and broken. I hated how life kept kicking me in the teeth, happiness so brief and fleeting, while the disappointments remained deep and consistent.

I decided to leave before Kellan returned, and I raced through the house and up the stairs to lock myself in my room.

My first day hadn't been as bad as I'd expected, but it had ended on a low note. Still, I was alive and unbonded.

In my situation, I really couldn't ask for more than that.

Finley had interrupted Kellan before he could kiss me, which was... *really lucky*. Yep, even if all I could imagine was tasting the alpha, wondering if he'd be as sweet as his caramel-cinnamon scent... *It's better not to know*. The second I kissed one of them, it'd all be over. No way to resist once I'd had a taste.

Dragging myself into the bathroom, I drowned myself in the fancy shower with its three different showerheads and steam bar. Like with the bath, there was already an array of bodywashes and shampoos lined up on the shelf, the fancy kind without lab-made scents, leaving my nose unbothered as I lathered up.

When I ran my hands between my legs, my clit pulsed at me, reminding me of the needs I'd been neglecting since I ran from Florida. Spending time with these alphas and their enticing scents had left a hollow ache pulsing in my core, and there was no way I'd sleep while this wound up.

Releasing a resigned breath, I slid a finger into my damp heat, using my arousal to rub against my clit. My breaths came out faster, and I bit my lip to keep the sounds from growing any louder. In a house full of shifters, it wouldn't take much for one of them to hear me.

The pulse strengthened with each stroke of my finger, and when I closed my eyes I didn't imagine my hand touching me. It was an alpha's touch, thick fingers pushing into the tight muscles of my pussy.

"Goddess be damned," I sobbed under my breath as the intensity grew and my orgasm ripped through me. I silently rocked against my fingers, drawing out the pleasure until my knees weakened and I had to use the tiled wall to remain upright.

It took me a few minutes to recover as I sucked in silent, ragged breaths. When I was finished, I stepped out feeling exhausted and ready for the day to be done. Grabbing two of the soft, teal towels, I proceeded to dry my hair and then body, skin extra sensitive to the touch.

The pack had provided me with essentials, so I brushed my teeth and lathered on face cream, before wandering out into my room with the towel still wrapped around me.

"Holy fuck," I gasped, sliding to a halt at the sight of Kellan's big body draped across my bed. Clutching the towel to ensure it didn't unravel, I said, "What the hell are you doing in here?"

He pushed himself up on his elbows, using what were surely impressive abdominal muscles to hold himself in place. When he leveled his gaze at me, I almost took a step back at how dark his eyes were. "I came to check and make sure you were okay after Fin's drunken tantrum."

My first instinct was to defend the stupid bear, which was ridiculous because he'd done nothing to warrant that, and clearly hated my guts. It was just that pain in his eyes. I couldn't forget it.

Swallowing hard, I attempted to sound more normal than I felt. "Haven't you heard of knocking?"

Kellan swung his legs off the side of the bed and stood, and my gaze was immediately drawn to his gray sweats. Or more accurately the clear outline of his massive erection in *gray sweats*.

Oh my.

I jerked my gaze up, but short of a sharp blow to the head resulting in amnesia, there was no way I'd ever forget what I saw.

He prowled toward me, and I tucked the joined sections of my towel tighter, anticipating that he was going to touch me.

Kellan grabbed my hand and lifted it to his nose, taking a deep breath as he groaned. "What were you doing in the shower, pretty girl, that has this room smelling like a candy factory?"

I understood his tension now, and why his beast flickered in his eyes. He'd heard me in the shower finger-fucking myself.

He'd scented my arousal.

Not that I hadn't been aroused around them before, but not to the extent of tonight where I'd brought myself to orgasm.

Caramel strongly scented the air, and I barely resisted the urge to drop my towel and climb him. "I... I need you to leave."

As my body thrummed, I decided that I absolutely deserved a medal for that statement.

Kellan's features were shadowed, matching the inky sheen coating his blue eyes. He released me and clenched his hands at his sides, sucking in a breath he didn't release, before turning to stride from the room. My door slammed shut as I collapsed to the floor, once again clutching my towel.

Thank the goddess I didn't just prance out here naked— the towel had been the sole barrier stopping me from making a terrible mistake. If I'd thought kissing Kellan would be a point of no return, then sex would irreversibly seal the bond. In the thrall of our first time, I'd be desperate for his claiming bite, and there'd be no chance either of us would have the rational thought to refuse.

When my legs worked again, I hurried into the closet and grabbed a set of the PJ's Cora had given me in a cream color, having no desire to get caught naked again.

Once dressed, I crawled between the soft sheets, and collapsed into the even softer mattress, which helped soothe my ragged edges. There was no real sense of accomplishment over surviving my first day with Reeves Pack, because in reality I'd barely fucking survived. Tomorrow, I had to do better.

To my surprise, sleep claimed me almost instantly, the

stress too much for my exhausted brain to handle, and when I woke the next morning, weak rays of sunlight were filtering around the edges of the blinds.

I rolled over to find the faintest wisps of mocha wafting up from the bed. *Hunter.* Even in his house, he stalked me through the night, but for some stupid reason I felt safer knowing he kept an eye out.

On my bedside, the phone chirped with a notification, and I reached out and grabbed it. There was one message, and it wasn't in the group chat.

> Golden Boy: I'm sorry, pretty girl. I fucked up last night. Don't hate me.

Lifting the phone up to my chest, I replied so fast my fingers flew over the touchscreen.

> Pretty girl: I could never hate you, Golden. You're still my favorite.

He sent back a ton of smiling and heart emojis, and my spirits had lifted by the time I got out of bed and started my day. Twenty minutes later I was showered, dressed in shorts and a shirt, and wandering into the kitchen. Gerald and Florence weren't in the room, but Hunter was seated on one of the stools behind the counter, sipping his coffee and reading through the paper.

"You can get the news in digital now," I said with a smirk as I grabbed a mug and poured myself a coffee too. Hunter nudged the cream and sugar toward me before I could ask.

Like a good stalker, he already knew how I took my coffee.

"I prefer to use my hands," he said, flipping the page. "Really get a feel for what I'm enjoying."

My throat dried up, and I gulped a mouthful of coffee, wincing at the burn of liquid down my throat. Hunter glanced my way briefly, shaking his head before he returned to his paper.

With nothing else to do, I found myself watching him closely. He was already dressed in a light-gray suit, like the one he'd worn the day I met him. The blue of his shirt was a similar color to my eyes, with a darker blue tie open around his neck waiting to be secured.

His hair was tamed, those thick dark waves sitting in the sort of attractive arrangement that you knew was manufactured. It was a nice look on him, but I preferred him a little wilder.

Dark eyes laced in gold met mine, and I swear there was a hint of amusement in their depths. "I'll drive you to the Golden Fin this morning," he said. "Kellan should be able to pick you up when your shift is done."

"If you have a bike I can borrow, I'm more than happy to get myself around as well."

I took another sip of coffee, which was finally cool enough to enjoy. Hunter flicked the paper once more, folding it in front of him. "It's too dangerous for you to *get yourself around*. At least not while you're unbonded. We might have strict rules about the treatment of omegas, but not everyone follows rules. I'm not sure if anyone's told you, but next week is the Summit and Golden Claw is the host city this year. There will be an influx of alphas from other shifter cities here."

I had no idea what the Summit was, but I understood why he'd disclosed this information. Different cities had different rules. Our council and alphas might be discouraged from taking me against my will, but in other cities... not so much.

"I won't take off on my own," I said, and there was not an ounce of sass in my tone. "Thanks for keeping me safe."

They kept me safe without the promise of anything in return, and it was far more than I expected or deserved.

Hunter's voice deepened: "You're part of Reeves Pack, and I protect my pack."

It grew more apparent every time I spoke with him why Hunter was the entitled alpha in this quintet. *Despite* Slade holding more dominance. There was just something about Hunter's protective instincts and capabilities in whatever he handled. Not to mention he was clearly a genius, at least when it came to inventing shifter technologies.

"How old are you all?" It couldn't hurt to have one of my burning questions answered, right?

Hunter's full focus was disconcerting, and I had nothing to hide behind now that my coffee was finished. "Slade is the oldest at thirty-four. I'm thirty-two. Finley's twenty-six, and Kellan's twenty-five. How old are you, Emme?"

My chest warmed as he used my preferred name. "I'm twenty-five. I kind of lied to the council, hoping they'd go easier on me."

Hunter didn't show any signs of being surprised or upset by my mistruth, and I guessed Warrick already told him. "I'd never have let them hurt you, little omega. No matter what they decided on that day."

With that, he got to his feet and deposited his cup in the sink. "Meet me out the front in thirty minutes. I'll leave your uniform for work on your bed."

When he was gone, I remained a puddle of confusion, hating and loving at the same time how safe I already felt in the presence of an alpha.

An alpha with the power to destroy me.

CHAPTER 20

KELLAN

My wolf whimpered in my head as I beat myself up. I'd been trying to take it slow with Emme, who was as skittish as a rabbit caught in the scent of my beast, but it had only taken one moment of listening to her heavy breaths and soft whimpers—not to mention scenting that sweet slick of her arousal—for me to lose all rational thought.

I'd had my hand on her bathroom door about to bust in and claim my omega. It had taken fucking everything to control myself, and then she'd walked out glowing from the hot water, a mere towel separating her naked body from me.

Fuck towels. Fuck them right off. Who the hell even invented them?

It should be my tongue lapping up every drop of moisture from her creamy skin, following the path of freckles dotted across her body... *and I was so fucking gone over her*.

I didn't give a shit what it took, I was going to win the heart of my omega, because the thought of her running again broke me. Yeah, Hunter had warned me that she was ninety percent flight risk, and I told him that if she ran I would follow.

I will follow. No matter where she went, there was nowhere in the world far enough to hide from me. I'd go full-on psycho stalker just like *Daddy Alpha*, but fuck, I shared my soul with a predator, and while we enjoyed the lighter side of life, deep down we were *all* beast.

After a shit night's sleep, I woke to find that Emme had already left with Hunter for Golden Fin, our restaurant which opened for lunch and dinner.

I'd already planned on stopping in to see her since we had a random day off from training. Usually, I'd head into the office and familiarize myself with the current product timeline and dispatch routes. Fin and I wouldn't play hockey forever, and we both had positions in Reeves Industries when we were ready. With that in mind, I made it my mission to stay up to date with the inner workings.

Fin, on the other hand, gave zero shits and knew absolutely nothing about the company. Not that it mattered. We had more money than we could ever spend, and if none of us wanted to work again, we didn't have to. But I, for one, needed to stay busy.

It kept the darkness at bay.

Emme called me a sunshine wolf, and for the most part she was correct. I didn't fuck around with the heavier emotions or darker sides of life, but there would forever be a part of me that craved the chase. The fight and *flight* of the beast. If I'd let my wolf have free rein last night, Emme wouldn't be unbonded this morning—she'd be chained to my fucking bed, and there she would stay until she craved me with the same intensity I craved her.

I'd only lost control of the monster inside me once before, and I wrought destruction in a way I never wanted to experience again. Now I channeled a golden boy, and luckily I enjoyed fulfilling that role even more.

"Asshole!" A heavy palm slammed against my door, and Finley didn't wait for me to say a word before he had opened it. Poking his head inside, he found me sprawled across my bed, brooding. "You wanna hit the ice for a free skate?" He leaned against the frame, expression neutral.

He showed no physical sign of how shitfaced he'd been last night, but there were shadows in his eyes, and for that reason I nodded. "Yep, bro. But I'm going to fucking annihilate you out there for interrupting me and Shortcake. Just give me five to grab my gear."

He ran a hand over his face, and I swore he wiped away a smile. "Sorry about that, Kel. My fucking bad. I need to keep it together a little better, and for that, I need to stay out of the omega's way. Starting with *don't fucking add me back into that group chat.*"

"For sure, brother," I lied, straight to his face.

I'd already added everyone, including Slade, back into the chat this morning. My good morning message remained unanswered though, and I wondered if Emme even remembered to take her phone with her to work. Knowing Hunter, he'd tied it to her hand so she wouldn't forget.

Finley waited while I grabbed my bag, then we headed downstairs to throw on our shoes, and steal a few of the breakfast muffins Gerald left in the fridge. They were a combination of eggs, bacon, and protein powder biscuits, giving us a good shot of energy to start the day.

Finley drove his TRX to the rink, the roads busier than usual as everyone started preparing for the Summit. Over the next week, we'd see thousands of shifters pouring in, most of them staying with friends and family, or in Golden Claw's few short-term accommodations.

Our city would explode with shifters for seven days of trade negotiations, exchanges, peace talks, and security updates. "Did they send through an update on the Summit schedule?" I asked Fin.

In response I got a shrug. He cared about hockey, cars, Kenzo, and us.

Most likely in that order.

You're my favorite. Shortcake saying that would never get old.

I'd never been a favorite before, not even in my family where I was the youngest child, and spoiled rotten, but also considered an annoying shit.

Even in our pack, I was *the annoying pup.*

Emme made me feel like I wasn't a complete fuck up, and for that I'd lie down on burning coals and let her use me as a walkway. If that very specific situation ever should arise...

"Did you learn anything about *her* yesterday?" Finley asked suddenly, sounding tired. "Where did she come from? How has an unbonded omega just been gallivanting around the States without ever getting caught. She's eighteen, right?"

"Twenty-five," I replied distractedly, thinking about how little we really knew. "She lied in her trial in the hopes they would go easier on her."

"And she's a liar. Fucking figures." He muttered it under his breath, but I heard him.

Shooting him a droll stare, I shook my head. "Come on. She was on trial for her life. I'd have lied about every part of me, even the shit they could plainly see, if I thought it would save my life. I don't think you can judge her from that one mistruth."

"What about the fact that she doesn't want anything to do with us, and has rejected the pack's very generous offers without giving any of us a chance? Can I judge her for that?"

I understood why he was upset; it fucking hurt when she

iced us out or got that wild, frantic look in her eyes that betrayed her dream of escaping.

But there was a reason for it.

"She's running from more than just us," I said softly, rubbing my hand over the ache in my chest that popped up whenever I thought of her. "It's trauma, and she has it in spades. Her hyper independence comes from the fact that she's never had anyone to rely on, and I'm guessing the few times she did in her life, it blew up in her face, badly. So... no, I don't know her story yet, but I see the essence of Emme, and her essence is pure. Don't write her off yet."

He was quiet until a long sigh escaped him. "Trauma I understand."

I felt him mull over my gentle plea during the rest of the drive.

The rink was quiet when we entered via the players' entrance. I continued to let Finley have his thoughts as we changed into our training gear. I checked my phone before we headed out onto the ice, but there was still no activity in the group chat. At least Emme had responded to my separate message apologizing this morning.

Otherwise, I'd be driving to the restaurant to beg on my knees until she forgave me.

Shoving the phone into the locker, I followed my pack brother out onto the freshly Zamboni'd ice. The scent in the air reminded me of home, growing up in Thorny Gardens, and the long winter months out on the lake beside our house.

My family was nothing like Fin's, but we did have a similar means of escaping life's woes. That, along with the fact that we were the youngest alphas in the pack meant we'd bonded a little closer.

Hunter was our leader, and Slade would destroy any fucker who touched our pack, but neither of them were particularly warm. Those two dominant assholes understood each other on a whole other level that Fin and I were excluded from.

"Want to race?" I asked after we'd done some warmup laps.

Fin shook his head. "I swear you get worse every day with having to speed through life. You're downright reckless during our Sunday—" Mid-sentence he took off, and cursing, I flew after him, my laughter echoing around the rink.

We were evenly matched for a few circuits, but I'd always been a touch lighter and more agile on the ice. By the time we were done, though, both of us were fucked.

"It's almost like Coach is here," I gasped as I sucked down water like it was my lifeline.

"Exactly like it," a gruff voice said, above where we sprawled across the ice.

I jerked my head up to find Coach sitting in home bench, staring down at us. His arms were crossed over his broad chest, but his expression was soft. For him anyway. "What are you two doing here on your day off? Don't think I'll go any easier on you tomorrow."

"Wouldn't dream of it," Fin groaned and pushed himself up to his skates once more. "We're just working out our demons."

Coach's eyes glazed over, and I was reminded of his loss. One of his quintet fell in the last real pack city battle. A group of rogues had come together to try to take down the shifter councils, and with the help of an ambitious witch they'd almost succeeded.

Fifteen years wasn't enough time to ease the darkness in Coach's eyes—no years would be enough.

"It's cathartic for sure." His voice broke before he cleared his throat. "I thought when I got too old to play I'd lose my mind, but I found my place with our team. The Celtic Wolves saved me, and I'm going to ensure you assholes are the best team to ever grace the cities."

"We appreciate everything you do, Coach," I told him, barely resisting the urge to give him a hug. Coach would rip my fucking head off, even though the grumpy bastard needed a hug more than anyone I knew. Except maybe Slade.

He waved me off. "Get out of here. I'll see you both bright and early tomorrow." The smile that followed was positively sinister, and I swore my balls shrank in response.

He was going to destroy us in training.

Meanwhile, Finley looked as if all his dreams had just come true. My brother had issues, and the fact that he enjoyed our ass-whooping in training told me that therapy wouldn't go astray.

Eh, who was I kidding... I enjoyed it too.

Whatever kept the darkness at bay.

CHAPTER 21

The Golden Fin's uniform consisted of a white button-down and black slacks, so standard fare for a restaurant. Once I was dressed, my hair pulled back in a high bun, Hunter drove me to work in his Bentley.

I spent the first part of the tense ride debating if I should ask him about the bandage on his hand—how serious does an injury have to be to take this many hours to heal? It was still none of my business though, and his expression didn't exactly invite questions, so I shut up.

Hunter appeared unbothered by the silence, his expression calm, while I was a fidgeting mess. "Sit still," he finally ordered, pulling to a stop at a red light. "You're going to wear a hole in my seat."

Clenching my hands into fists at my side, I forced myself to focus on the landmarks of the city around us. "Are we close to the restaurant?"

He turned to me, and the waft of mocha grew stronger, which had me desperately breathing through my mouth to counter his scent. *Which did fuck all.* If anything, now I could almost taste him as well.

"The restaurant is just around the next corner, but we're going to stop at a cafe first and grab you breakfast. I didn't have time to organize anything before we left."

My surprise that he'd even thought of my need for food had me slow to answer. "I'm all good on that front. I often skip breakfast so I can easily work through the lunch rush and eat after."

Hunter responded with a deep, ominous rumble, and proceeded to completely ignore me as he swung his car into a parking spot out the front of Greengrocer Cafe. He was out of the car fast, and before I could decide if I was following or not, he opened my door and held his hand out for me to take.

It wasn't his right hand with the bandage, which I noticed because I had a new obsession. At this point, it was a competition over who was the better stalker.

Hunter was a patient *hunter*, as he waited for me to make the choice to take his offered hand or not. When my stomach rumbled, I decided that it was unbecoming for an omega to play dominance games, and I dropped my palm against his.

Heat enveloped me as zips of energy passed between us. Not so strong that I wanted to yank out of his hold, but enough that my wolf wiggled and whined in my chest.

Hunter's dark eyes turned positively feral, and I heard his wolf in his voice when he said, "We'll run soon."

I managed not to gasp as he used his substantial strength to haul me from the car, and when I was steady on my feet, I met his gaze. "You can hear my wolf's unease?"

He leaned down until our faces were close enough for me to see the pigments of gold in his stormy eyes. "I'm your alpha, little omega. Your wolf belongs to me, and I *feel* her."

I wanted to argue that my wolf—*and me*—belonged to no one, but there was no moisture in my mouth. When I parted my lips to try, a strangled huff was all that emerged.

Hunter kept a firm hold on my hand as he led me toward the café, and it was only when we stepped inside the inviting space with its red brick walls and array of potted plants that I managed to remove myself from his grasp.

His hand immediately pressed to the center of my back, warm and strong, nudging me toward the counter where the scent of toasted sandwiches and coffee had my body betraying me once again by rumbling.

A pretty wolf with golden hair and deep brown eyes hurried right over to us. "Alpha Hunter," she squeaked, her eyes wide and frantic. "We didn't know you'd be in this morning."

It was impossible not to roll my eyes as she all but simpered at his feet, and on top of that Hunter was all charm when he responded. "Just a social visit, Kitty. We're here for two breakfast sandwiches and two take away mochas."

Asshole. "Not my favorite coffee," I muttered, and I swore he smiled in response.

Kitty input his order but didn't take any money from him. Which I found odd, but whatever. Reeves Pack probably had a tab here or something.

I started to wander along the cabinets, checking out their offerings which included breakfast foods and sweets. "Don't leave the café," Hunter called after me. "I'm just going out back into the kitchen."

Wrinkling my nose, I wondered if he was joking but... nope. He was already lifting the bench and striding behind the counter. Was this alpha that much of a control freak that he had to supervise his sandwich being made?

Kitty appeared unfazed as he entered through a swinging door, and I decided to just file that in with all the other weird shit happening around me.

"How do you know Alpha Hunter?" Kitty's tone wasn't quite as friendly without Hunter's presence.

Forcing a smile to my lips, I shrugged. "He kidnapped me off the streets, but his house is nice so I'm going to stay for a while. Let's call it a rapid case of Stockholm Syndrome."

Confusion creased her expression. "But aren't you the omega who was living out in the human world as a rogue?" She examined me from my hair to toes, clearly finding me wanting. "Why in the world would you try to stay away from a pack like Reeves? They're top freaking tier."

"Why in the world would you ask me how I knew them if you were already well aware who I was?"

I fucking hated games. In the shifter world, they were more about winning and less about having fun, and I wasn't here for it.

She snorted like I was the stupid one, but we didn't have time for more conversation as Hunter's scent and dominance washed over us upon his return.

Kitty launched into action, cleaning the counter in front of her like she was about to eat straight off it. "I hope everything was to your liking back there?" she cooed, and I briefly considered how she'd look without her pretty hair. A small spark and *whoosh.* "We know Reeves Pack is generally hands off, but we've been following your protocols."

Ugh. Of course. I kicked myself for not figuring out sooner that this café was a Reeves Industries owned business. Hurricane Hunter deliberately kept that from me, probably in a bid to point out how little I'd bothered to find out about them.

"Everything looks great," Hunter assured her. "You're doing an excellent job as manager, Kitty. We'll discuss bonuses at the next quarterly meeting."

Her smile was as bright as the freakin' sun, and I was fairly certain that if Hunter whipped his dick out, she'd be on her knees in a heartbeat to please the boss.

My wolf surged to the forefront, growls ripping through my chest, and I barely managed to keep them contained. I couldn't do this. Not here... or anywhere.

No matter how badly I wanted to shift and claim this alpha so these eager bitches knew who he belonged to, I never could.

Turning away, I breathed deeply until my wolf was under control, and by the time our food was ready and we left the café, I'd returned to *mostly* not giving a shit.

At the car, Hunter opened my door for me and waited until I had secured my seatbelt before he handed me one of the sandwiches and a coffee. I dropped my travel mug into the cup holder and unwrapped the delicious smelling food.

"Oh fuck," I groaned as I took a bite. Bacon, sausage, egg and relish was a favorite combo of mine. Teamed with the crispy bun and spicy BBQ sauce, and I was in heaven. "This is the best breakfast sandwich I've ever had."

Hunter's gaze locked on my mouth. "We're famous for them." His words were a low rumble, and I forced myself not to make any further happy eating sounds. They were awfully close to happy *other* sounds.

"Is there anything you don't do well?" I asked, taking another bite and licking the crumbs off my lips.

"Nope."

I snorted out laughter in my usual elegant way, thankful at least that my mouth hadn't been full. "Well, modesty is possibly one option."

To my surprise, he chuckled. "Just stating the truth."

Damn, I'd really liked that sound, and found myself wanting to hear it again.

As we got moving, I noticed his sandwich sitting unopened

in the center consol. "Would you like me to unwrap that for you?"

Hunter nodded. "Sure. That'd be great."

Feeling satisfied with what I'd already eaten, I placed the rest of my sandwich in my lap and grabbed Hunter's. I unwrapped one side, folding the paper under the base so it didn't drip all over his fancy suit. When I held it out to him, he parted his lips, flashing a white smile that had heat unfurling through my chest and dripping into my center.

He was dangerously sexy this alpha, even when he performed the simplest of tasks.

"Let me just get through this traffic," he said, glancing back out the windshield and then back to me.

In an attempt to lessen the dangers of his eyes being off the road for too long, I lifted the sandwich to his mouth. Hunter's scent grew stronger, and as our eyes locked over the sandwich hovering between us, energy zapped along my skin until I was in danger of *wearing another hole in his seat.*

I wasn't sure if he would take my offering, but he parted his lips wider, and when those strong, predatory teeth bit into the bread, all the blood in my body moved south.

Oh, fuck me.

He chewed slowly, his gaze still on me, and yet somehow he didn't crash the car into a pole like I would. In a mindless, automatic movement, I lifted the sandwich toward him again, and I swear to fuck the gold in his eyes turned molten. *Burning into me.* "Little omega," he rasped. "You're the anomaly I never saw coming and had no way to prepare for."

An anomaly didn't sound positive, especially for a control freak like Hunter, who must despise anything that threw out his normal routine.

So why didn't he look unhappy about it?

He finished his breakfast in a few big bites, and I ignored

the way my hands shook as I folded the wax paper neatly. I wasn't sure I could finish my own sandwich with the new turmoil inside me, but Hunter glared at my lap until I started to eat once more.

It tasted like cardboard, but I finished every bite, sipping the coffee in between.

It was the best mocha I'd ever tasted, but nothing compared to Hunter's scent encasing me in the car.

Hunter pulled into a parking lot of a huge blue, weatherboard building with *Golden Fin* signage across the top. There was a fishing hook through one end of their logo, and an anchor through the other. The main doors were closed, with only a few other cars in the lot.

"The restaurant opens for lunch and dinner," Hunter said as he shut the car off. "We're positioned right on the wharf, so it's a great spot for family events, dates, and corporate functions."

I'd caught sight of water when he entered the parking lot and had thought it was a great location for a seafood restaurant.

When we hopped out, I took our trash because the Bentley did not deserve to be treated like a wastebasket. Hunter removed it from me, and I was reminded of Kellan refusing to let me carry my own luggage. Neither alpha appeared to think I could carry my own shit, and it was irritating because I'd never relied on anyone to help me before.

The way they treated me threw my entire balance off, and I didn't trust it.

They were trying too hard, overcompensating, and sooner or later their true nature would show.

"Employee entrance," Hunter said, gesturing for me to enter first. "This isn't the fanciest restaurant in Golden Claw because we want to work for *every* budget and reason for dining out."

"That's my favorite style to waitress at," I admitted. "Some of the diners were too rough, and I'm not trained well enough for anything super fancy."

"What diners?" he bit out, grinding to a halt.

"Too many to remember."

Hunter huffed but let it go, guiding me into a small locker room. "They should have one with your name already." He glanced along the dark blue metal doors until he found *Emeline* misspelled and scrawled on a sticker. "You can store your coat and phone in there."

The phone hadn't left my pocket all morning, but I'd at least remembered to charge it.

After my items were stored, Hunter and I ended up in the kitchen, which was a hive of activity. Half a dozen staff ran around in full prep mode, and when they noticed the alpha in their midst, everything grew quiet.

A shifter raced over and bowed his head. "Alpha Hunter, we weren't expecting you for another hour."

He was a beta, a few inches taller than me, with a generically handsome face topped by thick wavy brown hair pulled into a top knot. "Bradley," Hunter greeted him coolly. "I'm here with your newest employee."

Bradley eyed me for a brief second, a welcoming smile on his lips. "You must be Emmeline. We're happy to have you on the team. I'm the floor manager today, so you'll be shadowing me while I give you the rundown."

Hunter's rumble drew his attention with a snap. "Just remember your place, beta," he warned. "No one touches Emme."

Bradley backed up a few steps, hands in front of him. "Of course not. That goes without saying."

Hunter's dominance held him for a few seconds more than was necessary, but his point was well made. "One of us will be back to pick you up at the end of your shift," the alpha told me as he headed for the exit. "Don't leave this building on your own."

I bristled at the command, but again chose my battles wisely. "You've got it, sir."

Hunter's lips twitched at my slightly mocking title, but he didn't break a smile. "Be good, little omega." He turned to leave, pausing just before the door. "Oh, and Bradley..."

The beta snapped to attention, leaning toward his boss. "Her name is spelled with two m's. Don't fucking forget it again."

He was gone before the manager could respond, though I couldn't miss the tightening of Bradley's features. Once Hunter's mammoth energy had faded from the building, the beta relaxed. Relaxed and leveled a cold smile on me.

"Prepare yourself, Emmeline with two fucking m's. I run a tight ship around here, and I won't have you screwing it up because you're the boss' newest pet."

Oh, great. It was dick measuring time. *Thank you, Hunter Reeves.*

Lucky for him, I was sans dick, and felt zero desire to establish myself in the hierarchy. "I won't screw it up," I promised him. "I've worked in restaurants before. Just show me what you need from me. I can handle the rest."

His scoff told me everything he thought about that statement. He spun on one shiny shoe as he called over his shoulder, "Keep up. I'm not waiting for you."

You need the cash. You need the cash.

Maybe if I repeated it enough, I'd be able to drown out the asshole in charge.

I'd only just started, and I could already tell it was going to be a long shift.

CHAPTER 22

The first half of my training passed in a haze of barked orders and snickering laughter when I screwed up. Bradley, the *bastard*, apparently expected me to walk in understanding how to use their ordering system and to know the menu off by heart.

"As I've already told you, I'll take the menu home and study it. There'll be no mistakes next time." I'd been at this all day and was sweaty and pissed off. My reading levels were too poor for me to keep up with Bradley without prior study, which shouldn't have been a problem today as a trainee who was *only fucking shadowing.*

After the lunch rush and a few hours before dinner, Bradley decided that I was done for the day, finishing my shift with a full rundown of everything I'd screwed up. One of the other servers standing nearby—a curvy female around my age— shot me a commiserating smile. At least I wasn't the only one who thought he was a prick.

I was tempted to let Hunter know about how his manager treated his staff, but I wasn't sure if the alpha would take my word for it or call me a whiner unable to hack a day of work.

Bradley faked an excellent personable persona and was an even better gaslighter. He'd easily made me look like an idiot today, even when it was actually his fault, and I refused to give either of them the satisfaction of being the bad guy.

Back in the locker room, I stashed the menus in the pocket of my coat and grabbed my phone to check the chat thread. There were a bunch of notifications, and in my weariness I almost didn't open it up. I wasn't mentally prepared to handle more assholes today.

Slumping on a chair, I decided it would be worse to ignore them, and still needing a ride home, I pressed the app. The first message was from this morning, and I felt bad that I hadn't responded to Kellan sooner.

> Golden Boy: Rise and shine, sweet shifters.
> It's a glorious morning in Casa Reeves.

There were a few hours' break before Hunter chimed in.

> Daddy Alpha: Keep pushing, Kellan, and we can turn that glorious morning around very easily.

> *SLADE HAS LEFT THE CHAT*
> *GROUCHY BEAR HAS LEFT THE CHAT*

I loved to see the ways I grew on them.

> Daddy Alpha: Annoying pup, are you still picking Emme up from work?

> Golden Boy: I've been sitting out the front for two hours. Pretty girl, whenever you're done, let me know. Also, check out Grouchy Bear.

> *IMAGE ATTACHED*

I clicked the image that Kellan had sent through, and chuckled at the sight of Finley sprawled across the ice, his massive arms spread like he was using them to drag himself along.

> Golden Boy: Someone had a big day today. You're going to have to tuck him in tonight, Daddy Alpha.

DADDY ALPHA HAS CHANGED HIS NAME

> Alpha Hunter: If you knew the many ways I can murder you and dispose of your body, you'd shut the hell up, Kellan. Some of the options even involve spiders.

> Golden Boy: Eeekkkk! *sad face emoji* *scared face emoji* I trusted you all with my deepest, darkest fear. I feel betrayed.

> Alpha Hunter: It's my job to ensure no one outside of our pack fucks with you. I never said anything about members inside our ranks.

> Golden Boy: Aye-aye, Captain. I'll be a good boy. Promise.

I might not know Hunter well, but I'd bet a butt load of cash that he'd gritted his teeth through all of these messages. The chat thread ended twenty minutes ago, so I slowly typed out a message.

> Pretty Girl: Just finished work. Thanks for waiting around, Kellan. I'm sorry it took so long.

Within a few seconds he responded.

> Golden Boy: I'd wait forever for you, Shortcake. You don't ever have to thank me for being your alpha. It's a fucking honor.

> Golden Boy: Also, don't leave the restaurant.
> I'll be right in to collect you.

With a sigh, I dropped my head back against a locker and tried to exhale away the tension of the day. Hopefully, once I finished shadowing Bradley, I'd be able to mind my business and do the job without constant harassment.

Today had me questioning my capabilities in ways I never had before.

From this angle I noticed that my name on the locker had been changed to *Emelime*, with the previous *Emeline* crossed out. Fucking Bradley, even though that one was almost funny. There *were* two m's now, and I was sure he'd make it my fault somehow.

I was distracted when the phone beeped in my hand, and I glanced down to read the message.

> Alpha Hunter: Are you okay, Emme?

The stalker struck again.

Glancing around the ceiling, I found the camera in the corner with its red light flashing.

> Pretty Girl: Spying on me again, Alpha
> Stalker?

> Golden Boy: That's Daddy Alpha Stalker
> to you.

> Alpha Hunter: Answer the question, little
> omega.

I *heard* that question even though it was a text. Hunter's voice always lowered into a deeper drawl when he called me *little omega,* and it was starting to drive my beast crazy.

> Pretty Girl: Totally fine. It's just a lot to try and learn everything in a single shift. Hopefully I'll get the hang of it when I'm out on the floor. Bradley is… intense.

Kellan messaged back, even as his scent grew stronger, indicating he was entering the restaurant.

> Golden Boy: Fire him, Daddy Alpha. Now! Or I'll rip his guts out and use his intestines as fish bait out the back.

It wasn't always easy to tell if Kellan was joking or not, but that text sent a shiver down my spine. It was intrigue rather than fear, though, and I was tempted to poke at his beast until it emerged.

Kellan burst into the locker room a second later, at the same time that both of our phones chimed. He hauled me up into his chest, and my gasp was loud and echoing as he wrapped his arms around me in a hug so secure that there was no space between us.

Holy goddess.

The world stopped spinning, gravity ceased, and life as I knew it shifted topsy-turvy. I was held in the firmest, warmest embrace I'd ever experienced. I'd never been held until it felt like all my ragged, broken pieces were dragged together, and through his strength alone he might make me whole.

"Kellan!" I choked out, scraping against his grip, while my breath caught in my lungs. At first, I thought it was a panic attack, which I hadn't experienced since I *found* Mom. But then I realized I couldn't breathe because I choked on unshed tears and unwanted emotions.

"Pretty girl," he rasped, the turmoil in his voice unmistakable as he buried his face in the crook of my neck.

"What's wrong? What happened? I wasn't kidding. I'm going to fucking kill him."

My wolf started to whine, and if he didn't let me go in two seconds, I would embarrass us both by bawling all over him. "Kellan," I whispered through a throat so tight that I barely managed words. "Please."

He didn't react to my weak, pathetic shove. His wolf had taken over as he held me, and with an audible whoosh of air, I finally gave up fighting and sank into his heat, freefalling into the hug. *Just a few minutes.*

A few minutes to experience the beauty in his comfort. Tears flowed silently down my cheeks, and I turned my head to the side, hoping he wouldn't feel their damp heat against his skin. Our phones beeped again and again, before Kellan's started to ring.

Over and over.

No doubt Hunter was glued to the camera wondering what was happening.

Without releasing me, Kellan reached down and answered his phone, hitting the speaker button. "What the fuck is happening with our omega?" Hunter's cold rage poured down the line.

I was busy trying to sniffle without making a sound, but as I lifted my head, I realized the camera was pointed right at my face.

"She's crying, Kellan. Bring her to me. Right. Now."

The line went dead, and Kellan finally got his beast under control, gently releasing me back to my own feet. I frantically swiped at my tears, but they weren't fading as quickly as I'd hoped.

Kellan's thumb brushed across my cheeks as he said, "I've got you, pretty girl. You're never coming back here again, and I wouldn't be surprised if Hunter burned the building down tonight."

"No!" I shook my head violently. "No! Seriously. I'm just hormonal, and I've never—" I swallowed roughly. "I've never really been hugged. It took me by surprise, and just so you know, those tears emerged *without my permission.*" *Traitorous tears.* "But you don't need to do anything about the job. It's a great restaurant, and your staff are great—" minus one "—so I'm not surprised that it's so popular."

He stared at me like he knew I was full of shit but also realized I'd reached my limit of sharing. I was tucked under his arm and guided out of the staff exit toward a massive TRX RAM in the parking lot.

Kellan opened the door for me. "It's Fin's baby. He let me borrow it and caught a ride home with Kenzo."

"I love big trucks," I said as I reached for the handle to pull myself into the cab. "He must feel like the king of the road."

Kellan laughed dryly. "He wishes."

When he was seated in the driver's side, he waited for me to buckle myself in before hitting the start button. As the powerful engine roared to life I asked, "We're going home, right? I don't need to see Hunter."

He lifted one eyebrow in a stare of amused disbelief. "Oh, my poor, deluded omega. We're absolutely going to Hunter. Seeing you is about the only thing that will stop him from levelling the restaurant. And maybe any other structures he runs into on his way home. Trust me, it's in Golden Claw's best interest that you soothe the beast."

A low thrumming of panic was my companion all the way into the city, and when Kellan pulled the truck into a private park out the front of Reeves Industries, I debated my chances of running home from here.

Kellan cupped my chin, his long fingers wrapping around

my cheeks. "You've got this, Emme. You're literally the one shifter who can walk into his rage and come out the other side unharmed. Don't fear your alpha."

If that was the case, why did I need him to hold my hand all the way to the top floor?

When we entered the lobby, Kellan was fawned over by the ladies behind the reception desk, but I was too worried to spare them a glance. Heading straight for the elevators, no one stopped us, and when we stepped inside it was already keyed to the twentieth floor.

Luring me right into the den of a raging beast.

"Breathe," Kellan whispered near my ear. "He's had ten minutes to calm down. I'm sure it'll be fine."

When I glared my strongest, most lethal glare, he just fucking laughed. The fact that none of the alphas in my life feared me was as great a tragedy as *Romeo and Juliet.*

The journey into the skies took no time at all, and despite my fear of these enclosed metal boxes, I spent most of it praying for a breakdown.

When the elevator doors opened, I was surprised to find that the top floor looked deserted. There were no shifters at the reception desk, all the office doors were closed, and if it weren't for the thunderous energy sifting in from the back rooms I'd have thought Hunter had already left.

Kellan flashed his smirk. "Hmmm, maybe we should give him another ten minutes."

"I hate you," I mumbled, my stomach swirling.

"Ouch, that hurts. I thought I was your favorite."

His bottom lip jutted out, and he looked so ridiculous that it eased a fraction of my panic. "It's a constantly rotating list. Best not to rest on your laurels."

He dropped a brief kiss to my cheek, which was a nice

distraction. "Don't have a clue what a laurel is, but I bet I can rest on them with the best."

Of that, I had no doubt.

Further conversation ended when the door to Hunter's office slowly opened. His giant frame filled it a beat later and his dark gaze bored into me.

A silent command wrapped around my wolf, and despite my omega designation, I hurried forward, helpless to stop.

When I glanced back, Kellan remained locked in place near the open elevator.

Our eyes met and he managed a smile. "I'll be right here, pretty girl. Give him hell."

I didn't get a chance to respond before I stood in front of a towering, furious alpha, with his wolf shining in almost golden eyes.

Hunter Reeves was beyond pissed, and I wondered if I'd survive the fallout.

CHAPTER 23

Hunter backed up a few steps, and I followed, as if tethered to his energy. I was helpless to fight the swirling dominance that surrounded him, which should terrify me.

I was still an omega, but there was no will within me to fight his control.

Giving him all the power.

When the door closed behind me, I jumped about a foot in the air, and his hands were there to hold me steady. "Tell me everything that happened today, Emmeline."

Oh fuck. He'd full-named me.

"N-nothing happened."

Hunter broke my brain, and I hated how I always looked like a bumbling fool in front of him. Drawing in a deep breath and near drowning in his addictive scent, I forced a mental image of my mom and her alphas.

Forced myself to remember what they'd taken from her.

It was a sobering memory which gave me the mental fortitude to stiffen my resolve and pull myself together. Stepping out of Hunter's hold, I cleared my throat. "Work was fine. Bradley's an asshole, there's no denying that, but he didn't do anything inappropriate."

Hunter looked unimpressed as he crossed his arms. "Being an asshole is inappropriate."

"For a shifter, it's almost par for the course." Not completely true now that I'd met actual decent shifters in this city.

"Why were you crying, then?" His voice grew deeper, his gaze probing in a way that left me in tatters.

There was no good reason to reveal how vulnerable that hug made me. "Even shifters cry," I said flippantly. "It's not a big deal."

Hunter closed the distance between us, and I'd never felt as small in my life as I did in his shadow. "I'll accept a lot of bratty behavior from you, little omega. But don't ever lie to me."

Goddess save me. His rumbled command had my legs weakening, but I refused to reveal that to the alpha. He could never know how my body capitulated under his control.

Resisting the urge to run from the predator, who'd be on me in seconds, I shored up my fortitude and met his piercing gaze. "Are we done with this conversation?"

Hunter rubbed his right hand across his face, and in my panic over being here I realized I'd forgotten to do my usual stalking of his bandage. Which *was gone*, and in its place he bore a new tattoo.

I felt the scrunch of my eyebrows as I tried to comprehend what I saw.

Four dark letters marked his skin: *MINE*. Below this cursive script was a detailed open jaw of a wolf, fangs visible as if it lunged for an attack. The word and wolf's jaw were angled in a way that followed the curve of his thumb to his pointer finger.

In my fascinated confusion, I'd failed to notice Hunter sliding his hand up and around my throat, fingers flexing against the sides as he collared me. Using that hold, he drew me toward a mirror on the entrance wall, to show me exactly what he'd done.

That *MINE*, while backwards in the mirror, would be clear to everyone else when his hand collared my throat, and with the open mouth of the wolf, positioned like a claiming mate bite, there'd be no doubt who I belonged to.

My legs weakened, and I barely held on to a cry, as my body reacted. Hunter dragged me against him, and my nipples felt as hard as glass rubbing against my shirt. Oh fuck. Fucking fuck. A moan sat on the edge of my tongue, but I kept it from spilling free.

"You told me you needed a collar with my claim on it, little omega," he drawled, applying just enough pressure that I groaned. "I quite enjoy the idea of everyone knowing who you belong to."

I couldn't think. I couldn't breathe.

My pussy fluttered as my senses spasmed, and my head filled with strobe lights. He did nothing except grip my throat, but it felt like he touched me *everywhere*.

This dominant claiming called to the parts of me that desperately craved a pack and mates. It called to the part that found my mates the four hottest alphas in existence, each of them terrifyingly different in their perfection.

Through my tightly pressed lips, a sound escaped, and I knew it was a moan. Unlike before, I couldn't keep it contained, and just as I hoped Hunter wouldn't notice, his eyes darkened, the gold expanding into shimmering starlight.

"Tell me what happened at work." His fingers flexed on my throat.

"No!" I rasped, clawing to keep the sliver of control I still retained. "I'm not your puppet to command, Alpha Hurricane. I'm. Not. Yours."

Liar. Such a fucking liar, but I had to at least try. When death came calling, I could say I did everything in my power to fight fate.

Hunter's laughter was dark and frustrated, and the grip on my throat loosened as he swung me around and pushed me back against a solid surface. *The door.* I was pressed against his office door.

"What makes you think you're not my puppet, little omega?" The hard lines of his body pressed into mine, and I already craved—*and feared*—his strength restraining me. "I think a part of you enjoys losing control like this. You haven't fought my hold around your throat once, and I'd hazard a guess that if I slipped my hand into your panties, I'd find you dripping wet."

It was in my best interest *not* to let Hunter get his hand anywhere near my panties, because then he'd know exactly how accurate his guess was. "I don't... don't want you, Hunter." When in doubt, lie and deflect. "And... you... you promised you wouldn't force the bond."

He leaned down and was gentler than I expected, running his nose along the column of my throat as he scented me. "I will never bite you. Not until you beg me."

The clanging in my head increased and I swore my heart now beat steadily in my vagina, a thrumming pulse that almost brought me to my knees. At least it would have if an alpha wasn't holding me up by my throat.

"Tell me what happened at work?"

It was a game of dominance, and I couldn't let him win. He'd promised not to forcibly bond me, and I sensed this alpha was a man of his word, which meant I could push back without the usual fears.

"Nothing. Happened."

His left hand slipped down the front of my pants, and as

much as I told myself to run, I couldn't move a muscle. "You're racking up punishments, baby," he drawled, and my core tightened around nothing as I fought this devastating need. "You can fight me all you want, but you'll never win."

It almost felt like I was winning as his fingers slipped lower, skirting along the edge of my thong. Even I could scent my arousal in the air. His wolf's energy surged as our breaths mingled. "What happened at work?"

I wanted to sob, in both frustration and desperation. "Nothing. I told you. Bradley was an assho—" I moaned as he slid the lace edge to the side and brushed his callused fingertip along my slit.

"So fucking wet for me," he rumbled sounding far too satisfied. "I bet you taste as sweet as you smell."

He pushed one finger inside and I knew at this point my *game of dominance* was done. He curled his finger, pressing against a spot that sent a bolt of pleasure through me. I cried out and clutched him, gibberish spilling from my mouth.

Hunter: One.

Emmeline: A total fucking puppet.

"Tell me, little omega."

This time my words were a tiny bit clearer. "From the second I started shadowing Bradley, he was an absolute fuckwit. Oh God..." Hunter slid another thick finger inside me, and the stretch reminded me of how long it had been since anyone had touched me like this.

"Tell me exactly what he did, and why Kellan found you crying."

With each command, he curled his fingers and thrummed them against my g-spot. His hand around my throat was the only fucking thing keeping me standing as I cried out, an orgasm already barreling toward me.

I was breathing too heavily to speak, and when he slowed

the thrust of his fingers, I debated punching him. I'd been so close.

In a breathless rush, I told him everything that happened, starting with Bradley insulting and gaslighting me all day. "He made sure that everyone thought I was completely incompetent, even when he was the one to show me the incorrect way to input the meals. He dropped a glass and blamed me and made me clean it up. I gave up defending myself after a while and just let him have his little power play."

Hunter's fingers curled again, and I rocked against him, desperate for relief from the throb in my pussy. "Good girl," he murmured encouragingly, "now keep going for me." I knew he wouldn't give up until I told him *it all*.

"I cried because Kellan hugged me."

My vulnerability was so much harder to lay bare, even with his fingers buried inside me. Sexual need was one thing, but I couldn't allow these alphas to own my deeper emotions.

"I've never been hugged like that before, Hunter. It took me by surprise."

His fingers stilled again, and I wanted to scream. Could you die from being edged like this? *Not* asking for a friend.

"What about your mother?" His tone held a dangerous edge.

I shook my head with so much force I was momentarily dizzy. "She wasn't exactly the affectionate type. Her aim in life was to keep me hidden from the world, which was easier if I was out of her sight too."

Hunter's thumb brushed across my clit and it felt like a bolt of lightning. Burning, pleasure-filled lightning. "Please," I groaned. "Stop torturing me."

He let out a soft laugh against my sensitive skin. "Do you want this, Emme? Do you want me to bury my face in your sweet cunt and eat you like my last meal on Earth? Do you want to finally admit who you belong to?"

Yes. Yes, yes, *YES*.

"No."

I couldn't give him the power he sought over me, no matter how desperate I was, even if his dirty words spoken in husky tones were enough to have an orgasm fluttering.

Jerking my hips into him, I almost screamed when he slowly removed his fingers. He tapped my pussy once and stepped back, leaving me with the burning ghost of his touch on my throat and core.

He lifted his left hand and ran his tongue over the arousal coating his fingers, groaning softly. "Just as I expected, you taste so fucking sweet, Emme."

I was plastered against the door, my lungs screaming for air. "Asshole," I spat, my core throbbing in time to my ragged breaths.

He showed no visible reaction to my insult as he dropped his hand. "You know what to do, little omega. You need to stop fighting fate and admit who you belong to. Then I'll bring you the screaming orgasm you're desperate for." He leaned down again and I held my breath. "Oh, and don't even think about touching yourself in the shower again either. I'll know if you do, and the punishment will be severe."

My knees buckled, and I gripped the doorknob to keep myself standing. Yanking harder on it, it clicked open and I all but fell out into the entranceway.

Dark laughter followed as I scrambled to my feet and raced for the exit. His name had never felt so appropriate as when I escaped his clutches. The *hunter* and his *prey*.

There was no sign of Kellan in the lobby, and even knowing I shouldn't leave on my own, I couldn't stay up here a second longer.

Slamming my hand against the elevator, I closed my eyes and concentrated on calming myself while I waited for it to arrive. I'd completely lost it in there with Hunter, but at least I'd said no when it counted.

I might have let him own my body, but I never verbally handed over the control he desired, which meant I'd be able to do the same when it came to the mating bond.

No matter how hazy my boundaries got around them, I could never forget where I came from, and where I'd be going if I let this desperate need for them win.

CHAPTER 24

Despite my best efforts, by the time I stumbled into the main foyer of the building, my body wasn't remotely calmed. At least a dozen curious employees stared as I fled, and I was surprised when no one stopped me from exiting the building.

It made more sense when I raced down the steps and spotted Kellan chatting to a familiar alpha. Alpha Stalker knew he waited outside for me.

Kellan spotted me not even ten seconds after I hit the street, and he cut off whatever Sorenson was saying to rush to my side. Pausing in front of me, his blue eyes were dark as he examined me.

As he leaned closer, his nostrils flared. "I see you survived."

"That's one way of putting it," I groused.

A knowing smirk crossed his lips. "Judging by your scent and that pretty flush in your cheeks, not all of you is happy. *Naughty Daddy Alpha*. Don't let him fuck you into submission, Shortcake. No one controls you."

"If only that was the truth." I closed my eyes, knowing I

should be embarrassed, but I remained in a state of numbed disbelief. Numbed *horny* disbelief.

"Well, hello there, Emmeline," Sorenson called as he strolled across to join us. "I was just about to head over and pick up Chelsea from her bakery. She'd love to finally meet you, if you want to join us." When he was closer, his nostrils flared as well, as if he could also scent my arousal.

Kellan crossed his arms and leveled the other alpha with a *get fucked* stare. "I will bring her to the cafe. If she arrives home with your scent all over her, you'll have World War Three on your hands. And that's just from me. Hunter will level the planet."

Sorenson threw his head back, deep laughter booming from him. "So dramatic. But rest assured, your little omega smells solidly like your entitled alpha right now. His claim has never been stronger, even without a bite." Probably half the reason for Hunter's actions in his office.

"I'd love to meet her," I said, cutting off further alpha posturing since we didn't have all day. "She's the only omega I've heard about in the pack cities."

Sorenson's expression sobered. "There are a few omegas across the shifter cities, but they don't have quite the same protection we offer here. The council even tried to petition for one who was with an abusive pack, but they couldn't get around quintet law."

Mom's face flashed in my mind, and Kellan wrapped his arm around me as I stumbled. "What happened to her?" Both alphas flinched at the hushed horror in my voice.

I'd already lived through what happened to an omega in an abusive pack, so while I was fairly sure how her story ended, I still had to ask.

Sorenson's gaze was probing as he answered. "As far as we know, she remains with them. Still miserable, but she won't take the necessary steps to leave. They have her so enthralled with their bond that she can't see the abuse."

Wait... "They haven't killed her?"

Kellan's arm around me jerked, like I'd jabbed him in the ribs. "Why would you think they'd kill her?"

In my mind, all I saw were lifeless eyes in the same icy blue as mine. "Just felt like it would escalate to that."

Kellan's pulled me firmly into his side, his scent and warmth comforting as they chased away the ghosts of my past. Sorenson watched our interactions closely, looking concerned, even as he forced a smile. "You know, my offer to join our pack still stands. Hunter is one of my best friends. We grew up together. He knows I'm a strong, caring alpha leader. You have options, Emmeline."

There was a rush of movement, and I was gently shoved to the side as Kellan slammed his fist into Sorenson's face. The crack was so loud it echoed off the buildings and down the street, and when I looked again, Sorenson was dangling two feet off the ground in Kellan's grip.

"You know I like you..." Kellan sounded cheery and casual. "...but it'll take very little convincing for me to murder you right here in front of your office. If you proposition my omega again, I will rip your arms off and beat you to death with them."

His tone remained calm, as if they were discussing his last hockey game and not murder. Despite Sorenson's strengths and muscles, he couldn't break Kellan's hold, no matter how hard he struggled.

Eventually he tapped out in surrender. With a final growl Kellan released him, and the other alpha almost fell to his knees, coughing his guts up.

I waited for a rise of fear over Kellan's violent actions only... *there was nothing.* If anything, his display of strength and dominance had me and my wolf purring like fucking kittens. Kittens who had clearly lost their damn minds.

Sorenson recovered quickly, and when he straightened I was amazed by the complete lack of animosity on his face. "Sorry, Kel. I had to make sure you guys were the right fit for her. Omegas are precious, and I'm glad you already realize that."

Kellan shook his head with a growl. "*Emme* is precious, you dumbfuck. I don't care what her designation is. Now get your stupid ass into your car before I murder you. We'll meet you at the bakery."

Sorenson chuckled all the way to his car, which was a white EV parked in their designated private space. My nose wrinkled as I stared at the compact SUV. "Now that I've seen his car, there's no way in hell I'd ever consider his pack."

Kellan's hand cupped my face, drawing my full attention. "Granted, Soren has woeful taste in cars, but either way, you'd never have considered his pack. One alpha isn't enough to handle you, pretty girl. You need a pack of them. Starting with me."

When I grew up, I wanted Kellan's confidence.

Hiding my smile, I pulled from his grip and headed for the truck. Kellan might not be the alpha I expected, but fuck if he wasn't the exact alpha I needed.

He held my door open for me, and as I made to haul myself up, he placed a hand on my ass and boosted me like I weighed nothing. "Oomph!" Air escaped me because I hadn't expected the boost.

Kellan ignored my surprise, reaching over to buckle me in. When I went to beat his hand away—because *I could put my own seatbelt on*—he leveled a serious gaze on me. "I need this right now. My wolf is going feral, and if we can't claim you so no other alpha ever has the audacity to proposition you again, then I have to give in to some of my baser instincts. I'm sorry, Emme."

The fight died out of me like it was never even there. Kellan had been beyond good to me, despite the ways I'd rejected him. I could give in to him on this.

Ceding control, I relaxed into my seat and let him fuss over me, making sure I was buckled in and safe, before he closed the door. The feeling of his wolf was closer to the surface as he crossed around the front of the pickup and hauled himself into the driver's seat. His scent was stronger as well, and I knew his beast hovered on the edge of his control.

Not that he showed it while driving, smoothly navigating the afternoon traffic, which was heavy enough that I suspected it had to be quitting time for a lot of offices in the downtown area. When he turned into the street lined with restaurants and cafes, I started to worry we wouldn't find a parking spot. There were a lot of shifters already grabbing their dinner after work.

As we approached Chelsea's Sweets, a car pulled out right in front, and Kellan drove straight in. "How does it feel to be one of the goddess' favorites?" I teased.

It was a relief to feel his calmer energy when he turned and smiled. "I knew that long before I scored this epic spot."

The way he stared had heat blooming in my cheeks, and I wished my face didn't feel the need to reveal my inner emotions and thoughts. It was time for a subject change. "I'm guessing you don't plan on waiting in the car while I race in and speak with the omega."

"I won't even dignify that with a response."

He was out and around my side to open my door before I could do it myself, but I managed to get my seatbelt off, which he didn't comment on. Kellan's easygoing nature had returned, the only visible signs of darkness buried deep in his eyes.

We walked into Chelsea's Sweets together, both sucking in a deep breath as the scents of pastry and sugar hit us. "We have to grab some of these for dessert," I said, my mouth watering at the memory of that apple treat.

Kellan approached the empty counter. "I already told Soren to pack us a box. Chelsea's Sweets is the bane of Coach's life, as he tries to keep all of us in shape over the season."

He patted his rock-hard abs, and I attempted not to roll my eyes. "You appear to be in excellent shape, Golden. I don't think you need to worry about a few sweets."

His smile crept up slowly. "You should only make an assessment like that after some hands-on experience."

"Has that line ever worked—" I was cut off by a scrape on the tiled floor, and Sorenson appeared with a woman at his side.

She was tiny, just like my mom had been, and when Sorenson looked down at her, it was as if she was the sun he revolved his world around. "Chelsea, I'd like you to meet Emmeline, our newest city member and an omega."

She pushed her shoulder-length chocolate brown curls off her face, highlighting the faint bite mark on her throat, as her light-green eyes locked on me. When she held her hand out to shake, I noticed the blue veins in her ultra-fair skin. "It's lovely to meet you, Emmeline." She had just the slightest hint of a Southern accent.

I grasped her hand, finding no strength in her limp grip. "Lovely to meet you too. And please, call me Emme."

A smile lit up her elfin features. "I go by Chels. As soon as Soren told me that you were an omega, I've been dying to meet you. Do you have a few minutes to chat while the boys gather up the last of the pastries for you to take home?"

"Absolutely. And I have to tell you how amazing your pastries and sweets are. I'm lowkey obsessed with them."

She practically beamed as she hurried around the counter and hooked her arm through mine. "Well, that's settled, then. You and I are now best friends. Come on, let's leave them to it."

When Kellan hopped behind the counter, Sorenson slapped a hand on his shoulder as their fight from before appeared all but forgotten. "They won't be out of our sight," he said reassuringly. "You don't have to worry."

Kellan didn't look convinced, keeping his gaze on me for an extended moment, until he eventually focused on the pastry cabinets.

Chelsea led me toward a corner booth, sliding in first so I was on the open side. "Okay, tell me everything about your life," she said, relaxing into the pink and teal cushions. "Where did you grow up? Do you know any other omegas? How did you end up here?"

The thought of telling this tiny, pretty omega, with soft hands and even softer eyes about my messed-up life had metaphorical hives breaking out across my skin. "There's not a lot to say. My mom was an omega, but she died over a decade ago, and I've been on my own ever since. Even before that I never really lived in the pack cities. This is all a huge eye-opening experience for me, even as I fear what being near my scent-matched pack might do to me."

Her brow furrowed as she rested her chin on her hands and watched me. "Why do you fear your pack?"

Lowering my voice, I leaned closer. "What's it like being an omega in your pack? Do they treat you well? Is there ever any issue with... power sharing or... similar?"

The crease in her forehead grew deeper as she blinked in clear confusion. "I mean, I'm not bonded in a complete quintet yet, but we're all a scent match." She pressed her hand to the bite mark, and her eyes softened. "My pack treats me like a princess. I'm coddled, protected, and loved. I have freedom but support. It's the best thing that could ever have happened to me."

"You don't share your power?"

Her eyes narrowed as she shook her head firmly. "No. It's impossible for packs to share power with each other. We can feel each other's energy and beasts, we can even communicate mentally on occasion, if the bond is really open, but our power is connected to our lifeforce. Which is ours alone."

I hadn't expected a different response, but I'd still had to ask. "Right. That makes sense. I just heard a rumor that it was possible for omegas to share power."

With that, her suspicious expression calmed. "Maybe because you haven't lived in the cities before. I have a few books on omegas if you'd like to read them, and I believe there are more at the town library. I'm not sure how comprehensive your education was, but my books should be a good place to start."

"Not comprehensive at all. Any information would be helpful for me to understand how it all works."

She gently tapped my hand. "We'll drop the books off to your guardhouse soon. Oh, and it's my birthday next month. I'll be having a huge garden party that I'd love you to be at. I think your pack already RSVP'd, so I'll add you to the list."

I had no idea if I'd still be in Golden Claw then, but there was no harm in confirming today. "Sounds great! I'm looking forward to it."

Kellan caught my eye then as he stepped out from behind the counter with a large white box in his hands. "Ready to go home, pretty girl? Hunter will expect us for dinner."

Already drooling over the contents of the box, I debated if I could convince him just to skip straight to dessert. "Yep, ready to go." Returning my focus to Chelsea, I offered a warm smile. "It was great to meet you, Chels. I'll visit again soon."

"Great to meet you too! I'll get those books to you asap."

As I pushed up to stand, I realized I'd forgotten to ask the most important question. "Have you ever heard of an omega being bonded in an all-alpha pack before?"

Chelsea blinked a few times, tilting her head as if thinking it over. "No, I actually don't believe I have. I mean, it makes sense to some degree because we can withstand strong dominance. Though, it is much harder in a scent-matched pack."

Yep, I'd learned that the hard way today.

Chelsea took in the emotions flitting across my face, and the slightest of frowns marred her delicate features. "Are they treating you well?"

Unable to help myself, I looked for Kellan, who waited by the door. "Far too well," I grumbled.

Her light, airy laughter replaced any concern. "I understand, Emme. I don't envy many shifters, but I think your pack might have us all wishing for a few more alphas. Enjoy them."

There was no part of her worried that my pack would strip my shifter strength from me until my vessel was broken and barren. Nope. She felt safe and loved as an omega.

Had I misconstrued what happened with my mom because I was too young to understand? Or were omegas in an all-alpha quintets so rare that no one knew the dangers? Was there anyone else who knew Mom and her pack, and might have more information? And if so, how did I find them?

CHAPTER 25

"**A**ny chance you plan on gracing us with your presence at work today?"

Hunter was one of the few shifters in the world who continued to exist after speaking to me like that, but it didn't mean I wouldn't beat his ass as a timely reminder of our *true* power structure.

"I found her mother." My statement halted his next smartass remark as he crossed to where I was perched against the island counter, drinking my tea.

"What did you find out about her?"

I let him stew in silence as I took another sip, the earthy herbs of the Wild Bane tea reminding me of home. One of the few reminders which didn't have me ready to raze civilizations to the ground.

"Her name was Morgan Anders. She was born outside of the pack cities to two rogues."

Hunter's face took on a darker hue as his rage simmered in a low burn. "Emme's really never been part of the packs."

"I believe they flittered in and out of them over her younger years, but without any real establishment or records kept."

"What happened to her mother?"

My hands curled, and even though I'd hardly applied pressure, the mug cracked beneath my hold. "Third one this week," Hunter said with a laugh that eased the tension.

Discarding the broken shards in the trash, I wiped away the spilled liquid. "The information about the mother and her offspring is limited. Limited in a way I've never encountered in all my years of hacking systems. But I did find a few members of her mother's old pack. The two that made it through my database are alphas, and they're on the council in Silver City. They're going to have answers, so I might make a trip over there and *have a little chat.*"

Hunter raised an eyebrow. "And do you have a plan where they stay alive?"

"No. Not really."

With a shake of his head, he grabbed a mug and poured himself coffee, most likely needing the caffeine to make it through this conversation. "Why don't we send someone else to question them. I'm sure there are ways to get the information we need without shattering their bodies."

A smirk pulled at my lips. "Possibly, but where's the fun in that?"

My oldest friend was well aware that I was a monster in a human vessel, not the other way around. I'd never thought like the others, but I had learned what was and wasn't acceptable in the world, which allowed me to keep my brothers safe.

"I assure you, no one would miss them."

Information about this pack was limited, but I had unearthed one hospital record for the daughter, with injuries too extreme for shifter healing.

"What about her father? Is it one of her mother's former pack?"

A snarl ripped from me in irritation at the thought of her

and those alphas. "No. There's no record of them being part of that pack until the omega was about four. The father is unknown. While there's very little information on her mother, Emmeline's father is a ghost. I can't find one instance of Morgan making ties with any shifters until she met her pack."

Hunter rubbed his hand over the bridge of his nose, and I was mildly bothered by the exhaustion I saw on his face. "I'll be at work today," I said offhandedly. "We can go over that issue in warehouse five, if you'd like."

His wolf flashed in his eyes, and my beast lazily curled in response. "I need to run this morning or I'm going to be fucking useless as an alpha."

I generally let my beast out in the dead of night when we could hunt and watch over the sleeping city. But I could keep up in my bipedal form if he desired company. "I smelled her on you when you came home last night. I'm not sure there's a distance you can run that's going to help with that problem."

His glare melted into confused frustration as he barked out a harsh laugh. "She's intriguing and exasperating in *all* the fucking ways. I'm off to fire Bradley today too. There's a chance I'll rip his head off while I'm at it too. Not that our omega was going to tell me anything about how he treated her. Every conversation with her is a battle, and even when I make progress, she retreats just as quickly."

I felt a flicker of respect that she had a will strong enough to resist our powerful pack, but a larger part of me wanted to punish her for daring to fight back. She had no true strength here, outside of her *illusion* of control.

Hunter sighed. "She still plans on running."

Cold indifference settled over my features. "I'm aware. Now that I've got her digital identity though, there's no place in the world she could disappear to that I wouldn't find her."

Hunter pinned me with a glare. "Would you find her though?"

I shrugged, unsure of the answer. Maybe I'd be the one to hide her from our lives, before she destroyed everything.

As if to prove my point, Kellan and Finley burst into the kitchen a few seconds later, arguing over who was driving to practice today. "I need to make sure Emme gets to work," Kellan griped, "and if you can't be civil to her in the car, you're going to have to get your own way to the rink."

There was a rumble as the bear slammed the palm of his hand on the island. "She doesn't get to come in here and screw up our routine. You're going to cost us the season with this shit. You know that, right?"

Finley took superstitions to an entirely new level. It was more than just the games; he also incorporated it into training as well.

Kellan, usually annoyingly chipper, turned deadly serious. "I don't give a single fuck about the season. Not in comparison to Emme. I'd quit today if it upset her even in the slightest."

The bear took a staggered step back, his mouth opening and closing. "Are you fucking serious?" he finally choked out, looking like he was about to throw up. "You would destroy your career for the bitch who coldly rejected us?"

This triggered Kellan, who moved super fast, grabbing a fistful of Finley's hair to slam his head against the cabinets behind him. A crack rocketed through the room, and by the time the bear returned the hit, that cabinet door was torn from its hinges.

Hunter sipped his coffee and silently watched as they exchanged blows, each of them getting angrier and angrier. "Don't call her a bitch. I swear to fuck, I will suffocate you in your sleep."

"Where's your fucking loyalty, Kel. You've known her for less than a damn week. We're brothers!"

Kellan's fists moved faster and faster. "That—" *Punch.* "Never—" *Punch.* "Changes." *Punch punch.*

Both were covered in cuts and blood, but we didn't interfere. This shit needed to be worked out of their systems before it infiltrated deeper into our bond.

"We're always brothers," Kellan huffed. "You fucking know that. But she's our scent match and the final piece of our quintet. *She* fucking completes us."

He slowed and let Finley get in one last hit, before they both slumped against the wall. "I will do whatever it takes to keep her in our lives." It was a whispered promise from the youngest, and generally happiest of our pack.

Kellan had a safe and secure upbringing, with a family who adored him. There were only a few specks of darkness in his past, unlike the rest of us who'd drowned in it.

Finley looked like he'd been gutted as he curled in on himself. His eyes were hazy with the demons that plagued him, and I understood all too well. I'd tamed my demons, but they still remained with me through every aspect of my life.

"I'm not sure I can do this," Finley admitted hoarsely. "I thought I could ignore her, but her scent is fucking everywhere except my room."

It wasn't in my territory either. There were never any scents but my own in my room, as even our housekeeper knew not to enter. I had my own means of keeping everything clean.

Hunter placed his dirty cup in the dishwasher. "Fin, you need to pull yourself together. I know having Emme here is new and disturbing to your routine, but you're going to have to figure out how to deal with her. She's not going anywhere."

Finley looked too wiped to argue. "Yeah, okay. I know.

Fuck, I'll figure it out. Just... try to keep her out of every damn room. I'd like to be able to use the gym in peace at least."

So far, the omega had shown no interest in our gym, more content with her ridiculous and sloppy paddling around the pool. I wasn't surprised she couldn't swim, judging on what I'd learned about her past. Even my patchy information was enough to know she'd missed out on a lot during her younger years, and then her older years were spent running and surviving.

I needed to take one of the jets to Silver City and track those alphas down. It shouldn't be hard to *persuade* the information I required from them to further my understanding of the omega.

Hunter was wrong to assume I'd kill them straight up. The dead don't speak. But they absolutely didn't require their hands, which would be an excellent incentive for them to tell me what I needed to know in a timely manner.

I was destroying them either way, but it was in their best interest for me not to take my time. Or get creative.

CHAPTER 26

Listening to Finley and Kellan beat the shit out of each other over me was one of the worst moments I'd experienced. I wanted to race in there and get between them, but knowing it would only make it worse, I hightailed it back to my room and slammed the door closed.

Not that it blocked out all the shouting, but it muffled them enough to stop me from having a full-blown panic attack.

Jittery energy and pain bounced inside me. My wolf scratched against my insides, and I was stripping before I thought it through. The shift was easy, like bending down to touch my toes, and then I was on four legs. I shook off the energy of the change, and like I'd done a million times before, I fell into what used to get me through the lonely years and hard moments. I started to run around my room. *Round and round.*

At least my room here was large enough that I wasn't literally chasing my tail.

I'd heard humans say it was mentally damaging for their dogs to chase their tails, and I could confirm it sucked for wolves too. It stole sanity from our minds, bringing the chasm between beast and person that much closer. Very similar to what happened when rogues went without pack bonds and alpha control.

We regressed back to wild wolves, losing reason and rationality.

We lost our human side.

I stopped hearing shouts on my third loop of the room, but I wasn't ready to shift back yet. I'd be ashamed of my backward spiral into bad habits, but I was too busy trying to survive the mental breakdown.

On my tenth loop of the room I started jumping over the bed, one full leap adding another dimension to the run. I'd learned the hard way to never make a sound, and still bore the scars from that lesson.

With each circuit, my panicked stress eased until eventually my wolf had complete control. My human side blended into the background, calm and protected from emotions beyond my beast's comprehension.

There was a simple joy in racing as fast as I could, losing myself to instinct, and letting the human go. I wouldn't have made it through my childhood without this outlet.

On my twentieth loop, caramel and cinnamon notes wafted through my space, followed by mocha goodness. There was a knock on the door, but I was in no mood to entertain the alphas, so I ignored it and kept running.

I was like that fish from the movie that had to keep swimming. *Just keep running. Just keep running.*

I forgot everything but my task—to outrun my pain and confusion. It wasn't until a set of boots stomped to a halt in my path that I noticed I was no longer alone. I spun to head in the opposite direction, only to find a pair of tanned, bare feet which most definitely belonged to Golden Boy.

Kellan crouched in front of me but had enough sense not to

touch me. His expression remained super calm and his voice was a croon. "Pretty girl, you need to stop running now. Everything is okay. You're not in any danger or trouble." He held out his hand in what felt like a peace offering, and my wolf desired his touch, so she moved forward. His warm palm pressed firmly against the side of my snout, and then there was a second hand on the back of my skull, carrying the scent of mocha.

I let the two of them regulate my wolf with touch alone. The pressure, their scents, and the feeling of not being alone… it was exactly what my wolf searched for in her endless running.

Kellan remained on his knees before me, while Hunter stood sentinel over the top of us, and I'd never felt so safe and comforted in my life. My wolf released her hold, the shift washing over me before I registered it was happening, and then I was naked between them.

Whoops. I growled at my wolf while she preened at her cleverness. She didn't always relinquish control to me easily, but when she did, you knew it was for nefarious reasons.

Neither of the alphas reacted, and I reminded myself that shifters get naked without a second thought. Kellan's eyes remained on my face, and I couldn't see Hunter, but in my half-crouch he would only view my back and the top of my ass.

"Well," I choked out. "This isn't awkward at all. We should totally do this more often."

Kellan's smile was fucking dazzling, the pretty asshole. "Shortcake, this is literally my walking wet dream come to life. Can we just stay like this forever?"

There was a snort from behind and I turned to catch the tendrils of Hunter's smile before his features returned to indifference. "Are you okay, Emme?" he asked as he searched my face for answers.

From his current position, I assumed he could see the scar across my upper back, but he didn't ask about it.

I was too wrung out and exhausted to lie. "I heard their fight."

My voice broke on the last word, and Hunter muttered "Alpha idiots," as he leaned down and scooped me into his arms.

I was too shocked to do more than release a gasping shriek, and by the time my brain caught up, he was already in the bathroom cranking the shower.

He held me with one arm under my ass as if I weighed nothing. When he was happy with the temperature, he stepped in under the spray, *fully clothed* in his perfectly pressed suit.

"Hunter," I huffed. "What in the hell are you doing?"

His hard expression told me not to fuck with him. "Your skin is like ice, little omega. You need heat and the energy of your mates to calm your beast. I know your brain doesn't want a pack, but trust me, your body is telling a different story. You need this right now."

I snapped back in a raspy growl, "And what about when you're not here? How do I deal on my own after you get me used to having support?"

Kellan answered from the open doorway of the bathroom. "Easy. You'll never be alone again. I will follow you to the ends of this world and into the next, Emme. There's no point to this life without you in it."

Panic unfurled deep in my gut, but as Hunter stroked his hand across my shoulders, it calmed me like magic. His touch was a firm massaging sensation, and as it brushed down my arm it finally clicked that he was washing me with my cloth. Cleaning my skin and soothing my panic at the same time.

There was nothing overtly sexual in his actions, and I'd

never felt my wolf as calm as she was after the run and this attention from her scent match. It wasn't just her either. Even when Hunter brushed over my deep scar, lingering on the ropey tissue, it felt soothing.

Kellan's declaration about following me to the end of the world didn't feel quite as shattering now. If anything, there was a new flicker of hope in the deepest, darkest recesses of my mind.

I'd understood my path in life before these alphas. I'd had a plan, boundaries, and yeah, a fucking empty existence.

But it was safe.

Safe and lonely.

Now they had me wondering if it was worth the risk to have these alphas, even if only for a short time until the need for power took them over. I could live many lifetimes in a few perfect moments of being cared for by them.

I was ripped from my contented daydream when the cloth brushed over a hard nipple. I swallowed my groan. Now all I could think about was how frustrated I'd been since yesterday, when Hunter brought me to the edge of an orgasm and sent me off unsatisfied. I'd barely slept last night, as I writhed with the need to touch myself.

His command had worked though, even when it shouldn't have had any effect on me.

The bastard.

Hunter's touch was more clinical today, as he washed me with thorough precision and never quite hit *the spot*. When he appeared satisfied with how clean and calm I was now, he opened the shower screen. Kellan was already waiting for me with a towel in his hands, which he wrapped around my body, before lifting me from the stall and depositing me on the bathmat so my feet never touched the cool tiles.

"What's happening?" I mumbled, unsure if I'd just fallen

into an alternate reality. "This is straight up princess treatment, but I've never needed help to wash and dry myself."

Kellan started to dry me gently, with the same thorough attention to detail that Hunter had shown. "It's not about you *not being able to do this alone*," he told me in his low rumble. "It's the fact that you don't *have to do everything alone*. You might not realize it, but we could feel your panicked run. We could hear your heart slamming in your chest, and your scent... that sweet chocolate was acrid with fear and sadness. What sort of mates would we be if we didn't soothe and care for you in those moments?"

I was stunned into silence, staring at his too gorgeous face. "You're pretty darn good at this," I finally whispered, so out of my depths that I was drowning.

His smile was touched in melancholy. "I've had no practice, I promise. But with you it's all instinct."

Goddess, just kill me now and bury the corpse with a nice view.

How could anyone fight against this sort of heartfelt devotion?

The sound of wet clothes hitting the tiles distracted me as I turned to find Hunter shedding his suit and stepping from the shower. *Butt freaking naked.* I reminded myself to be as respectful as they'd been and keep my gaze on his face, but yeah, that was *never gonna happen.*

One day I'd be a stronger wolf, but until then I was all perv.

My gaze started on his face at least, and I enjoyed watching the damp ends of his dark curls springing to life. Droplets of water beaded across his long, inky lashes, and the stormy depths of his eyes looked darker than ever. Water continued to lovingly caress the hard, handsome planes of his face as I followed their dripping path down broad, muscled shoulders, a heavily defined chest, and *one, two, three...* I gave up counting abs at eight.

This was the first time I'd had a chance to see his ink in all its incredible glory, and while I couldn't make out what was on his back, it clearly wrapped up and around both shoulders, spanning down into black geometrical designs on his arms.

The bulk of the design stopped around his forearms, and there was nothing on his hands except that one claiming tattoo. Which would have held my attention, but I was distracted by finally reaching the hard length jutting proudly between his thickly muscled thighs.

Holy fuck.

I blinked, wondering if I was seeing double... the length. Because I wasn't sure that appendage was made to fit in a vagina.

At least not mine.

Nope.

Well, maybe.

Hunter was huge all over, and his dick did not let the team down. I might not have seen a ton of cocks in my life, but I had no doubt that Hunter's was unusually perfect. Thick and straight, the head was nicely swollen, the length slightly darker than his skin, and the more I stared, the harder it got as pre-cum seeped—

Kellan's laughter broke me from my dick trance, and I jerked my head up with my face now as red as the head of Hunter's—

Stop it. Fucking hell, Emme.

The alphas scored points when neither of them mentioned *the incident*, even if they did both look smug when they left me alone to get dressed for the day. I had a shift this evening at the nightclub, but first I was having lunch with Cora. She'd called last night to invite me out, and with that in mind I dressed in my nicest jeans and a white shirt.

In the bathroom, I brushed my hair out and just applied a little mascara. After the shower incident, my cheeks remained plenty pink with no need for artificial blush.

Not that I had any. My current makeup collection consisted of five items, but I did have plans to grab a few extras after I got my first pay. Kellan had already told me he'd buy anything I wanted or needed, but it felt wrong to take his money or rely on them financially when I couldn't fully commit to the pack.

Not to mention I'd always paid my own way and had no plans to stop today.

No matter how many times a naked Hunter ran tantalizingly through my mind.

CHAPTER 27

Cora picked me up from the front door, and since none of the alphas were home, I offered to bring her inside for a tour. Her stare turned to one of longing as she examined the outside weatherboards on the beautiful house. "You need to check in with your alphas first," she finally said, shaking her head. "They'll scent me as soon as they get home, and I don't want to get you into trouble."

I understood her reasoning, but it also pissed me right off at the thought of needing permission. It was only the fact that this wasn't my house, and I'd claimed nothing with this pack, that stopped me from ranting and raving about it.

But I still found myself saying. "If they want to *pretend* I'm part of their pack, then it's my temporary home. You're my friend, and I'd love to give you a tour of the common areas."

Cora waved me toward her car. "It can wait for another day. Let's lunch. I'm starving."

The way the shifters of this city feared my pack was no joke. No one wanted to cross or upset them. I assumed there were politics at play here that I was unaware of, having not grown up in the cities, so I passed no judgement on Cora for her choices.

"Lunch sounds amazing," I said as I jumped into the passenger side. "I've missed hanging out with you."

She dropped her hand on my thigh and squeezed briefly before she started her car and headed down the street of the family compound. I'd seen a few vehicles enter and exit from the other houses but still hadn't officially met any family.

I wasn't even sure I wanted to, because it hurt to know that if I'd been born with a different designation, they would have been my family too.

Cora chatted all the way to Hawker House Brewery, telling me about pack life. "Warrick's been gone all hours of the day and night with his squad, getting them ready for the Summit. The enforcers provide security while we have so many visiting packs and council members from other cities."

"I never knew what a big deal this Summit was," I said, realizing that if Warrick was this involved, Reeves Pack would be as well. They'd mentioned it once or twice, but not in any sort of detail. "Warrick said one of the alphas from Reeves Pack leads a squad too."

Cora nodded, glancing my way when she stopped for a red light. "Yep, and you might be surprised to learn it's Slade. His anti-social ass doesn't seem the type to lead a group of soldiers or inspire any sort of loyalty, but they would die for him. I swear."

She was right and wrong about suspecting it was Slade. He had the lethal badass vibe I expected from the leader of an enforcer squad, but he also had that whole scary shifter vibe that made everyone stay away from him. "I haven't officially met or talked to him since I moved in. He's..."

"Terrifying, intense, intimidatingly gorgeous?"

I nodded. "Yep. Pretty much all of the above and more."

Her chuckle was relaxed. "Slade is the most dominant shifter in the world, and the last of his kind."

She had *all* of my attention now. "The last of his kind?" I repeated slowly. "I mean, I knew he wasn't any of the obvious shifters…" I started racking my brain to recall any super rare beasts.

Cora's eyes widened. "You should probably sit down for this information, girl."

I rolled my eyes, laughing. "Okay, I get it. He's a big deal. What is he? A cobra or something?" There had been an icy, cold-blooded feel to his energy that would fit a reptile.

Cora drove a few more blocks, dragging out the suspense just long enough for me to start sweating. And then she blew my mind. "He's a dragon. Slade Riverson is a dragon shifter, hence why no one fucks with him. Ever. Ever *ever ever*."

I stared at her, unblinking, while a low hum filled my mind. "Dragon… there… how? That's not possible. *That is absolutely not possible!*"

Cora threw a sympathetic glance my way. "I know. It's not exactly a secret, but if you didn't grow up in Golden Claw, you might think it's only a rumor that one of the ancient ones walk amongst us."

"How old is he?" I sounded breathless. I felt breathless.

Her expression creased into worry, as if she knew I was on the verge of a panic attack. "He's only been walking around on Earth for thirty-four years, even if his egg was much older." His egg was much… *Was she fucking with me?* "Slade's egg was unearthed by shifters in the deep trenches below Mount Blood, over in Europe. Apparently, dragon eggs can lay dormant for years until a burst of heat and energy kickstarts their birth. His was triggered by a volcanic eruption—he was born in his dragon form and shifted to human when he was two years old.

Dragons are the opposite to the rest of us, who are born in our human form and shift when we're older."

"Who found him?" My voice remained echoey and weak.

There was a decent chance I'd pass out after finding out that I'd been *sleeping under the same roof as a dragon*. A dragon I'd rejected, and who quite likely hated me. Or at minimum resented my presence in their lives.

"Hunter's dad, actually. He's this rich old bastard who takes great joy in controlling the shifter world, using his strength and money. He's currently in England, changing laws over there. Hunter has never spoken fondly about him, saying the only decent thing he's ever done was to allow Slade and Hunter to be raised together. They're brothers in every sense of the word except blood."

I told Kellan that I didn't want information unless it came directly from the source, but that had been mostly about protecting myself from knowing these alphas too deeply.

Cora's little story now had shattered the wall thoroughly. All I could think about was seeing Hunter and Slade together. To observe the *brother bond* for myself.

Lunch ended up being a thankful distraction as Cora pulled into the parking lot. She parked in a spot near the front entrance, and by the time we'd been seated in the rustic warehouse brewery, I'd stopped freaking out over her revelations.

I'd truly believed dragons were myths, and now I wondered about unicorns, yetis, and gremlins too. Well, okay, I'd met Alpha Sissily, so the existence of gremlins was all but confirmed.

When the waitress took our order, Cora chose salmon and rice, and I ordered a rare rib fillet steak with mashed potato as a side. Potato was the best of the vegetables, without the audacity of being green. It was also delicious deep fried and could be turned into vodka. It was the true MVP of the vegetable world, and I had a full debate prepared for anyone who disagreed.

"We'll also take a bottle of wine," Cora added at the end, naming a vintage and year that at my last bar job retailed for at least five hundred dollars a bottle.

Kellan had loaned me a hundred dollars for this lunch, which I'd only accepted because I planned on paying him back as soon as I started work. But my loaned cash would not come close to covering the wine.

When we were alone, Cora must have noticed the panic on my face. "It's my treat," she said quickly, reaching out toward me. "It's been so long since I've had a girls' lunch. Sierra is upset she couldn't make it, but they're in full prep mode for the new hockey season. The first game will be on the opening night of the Summit, with *all* the important alphas in attendance."

I hated charity as much as pity, but in the spirit of friendship I searched for a compromise I could live with. "Thank you, it sounds like a great wine. And I'm totally getting the wine next time we catch up, though it probably won't be quite that nice of a bottle."

Cora's stare was assessing as she tilted her head and narrowed her eyes. "Your pack hasn't given you access to their accounts?"

Conversations about finances hadn't come up with the Reeves pack at all, which suited me just fine, because I had no plans of sharing their money. "I can't bond with them," I said, fighting down a surge of exhaustion. Today had been emotionally draining, and part of me wished I'd just cancelled lunch. "In those circumstances, it feels wrong to take their money. It's bad enough that I'm living in their house and eating their food. Not to mention they're driving me everywhere. Anything more, and I'd feel like a selfish asshole."

Cora's expression twisted into sympathy, and when she patted my hand I barely resisted the urge to squirm against how uncomfortable I felt.

"This entire lunch is on me," she said. "I'm so sorry. I didn't even think when I invited you out that you wouldn't have had a chance to start work yet."

Friendship was a new concept for me, and as uncomfortable as parts made me feel, I also knew I'd really lucked out with Cora. "Absolutely not. I can cover my lunch, and I'm so happy to catch up. I needed a little break from all the testosterone. It's not all happy families over at the Reeves pack house."

Cora loved gossip, and I was happy to change the subject to what had happened this morning with Kellan and Finley—and my reaction afterwards. I'd had no real intention of revealing the shower scene, but for some unexplained reason it slipped out.

Heat bloomed in my cheeks and I pressed a hand over my face to hide it. Cora's laughter drew my gaze from between my fingers, and I found myself chuckling awkwardly along with her. "I'm so embarrassed. *Sorry*. I overshared."

Her laughter died off as her mouth popped open. "Oh my goddess, no. This is exactly the juicy goss you share with girlfriends. Not that any of us expected Hunter Reeves to be anything less than exceptional in the dick department, but now I have the proof. What is surprising is his gentleness and caring for you. Hurricane Hunter, as you aptly call him, has never shown a softer side to any female. As far as I'm aware."

Deciding not to touch that statement, I focused on the first part. "Look, his size was shocking, and I'm not sure it's made to fit a regular vagina, if I'm being completely honest."

This set Cora off again, and she told me a bunch of stories about her first time with Warrick, and how they'd almost had to see healers. It initially felt weird to casually chat about such intimate moments, but it was also one of the best conversations I'd ever had with another woman. We got our feelings out and there was no judgment between us.

After that, we moved on to the new house she was working on a layout for. Cora pulled out her phone to show me the mood board she had pinned, asking my opinions on design. I'd never decorated a house in my life, but an opinion was for everyone, so I happily shared mine.

We chatted and sipped the wine, which was as delicious as expected, while the brewery slowly filled around us. By the time our food arrived, almost every table was occupied by packs and friends. The atmosphere was loud and comfortable, and while I noticed a few curious stares coming my way, mostly everyone kept to themselves.

"These portions are huge," I said, pulling my steak closer, my rumbling stomach reminding me that I hadn't eaten yet today.

"This place is one of my favorites." Cora drizzled lemon over her salmon, while I seasoned the meat.

I moaned around my first bite of tender steak, which all but melted in my mouth. It took every iota of my control to not shove my face into the plate and eat like I was in my wolf form. "Okay, this brewery is my favorite now too."

Cora was too busy shoveling salmon and rice into her face to answer, as we both ate in silence. My wolf rolled over in the contentment of sharing food with other shifters, still completely sated after this morning. With the rarity of having shifted twice in a week, I already felt stronger.

I wasn't sure my senses and healing would ever be as strong as other shifters, but it was clear that I could get closer if I stopped keeping my wolf contained.

For a little while at least, I'd let her live her dream of running with the packs.

CHAPTER 28

After Cora dropped me back at Reeves Pack house, I checked the group chat messages.

Golden Boy: I hope your lunch is going well. I miss you.

Golden Boy: We're being kept late at practice, pretty girl. They've got a bunch of press and photos that we can't get out of. But Slade agreed to take you to Luxuria. The club.

I blinked twice, re-read it, and immediately started to panic.

Slade agreed. The freaking dragon shifter agreed to drive me to work! Why? So he could burn me alive and pretend I'd stumbled into a forest fire?

In a daze I continued reading through the messages.

Daddy Alpha: He needs to stop by the stadium and brief his squad first, so can you be ready by 4 P.M, Emme?"

GROUCHY BEAR HAS LEFT THE CONVERSATION
SLADE HAS LEFT THE CONVERSATION

Not the most auspicious start to him driving me to work.

> Pretty Girl: Uh, are you guys sure? I really don't want to make anyone uncomfortable. Is it walking distance maybe? I'm home with enough time for a decent trek.

I hadn't bothered to change my name again, because Kellan woke up every morning and chose violence with this chat, and it was kind of growing on me.

Hunter answered within a few seconds.

> Daddy Alpha: Not a chance, Emmeline. Do not leave the house without an escort. Alphas are already arriving in Golden Claw, which makes it even more unsafe than usual. Slade will do his part to protect the pack, and that includes you.

> Pretty Girl: But am I truly safe with Slade? I haven't actually met him. You know that, right?

It had to be said, especially now that I knew exactly what creature he shared his soul with.

> Slade: You are perfectly safe. I do this favor for my brothers.

Wait. What? He'd left the fucking chat.

> Golden Boy: You left the chat, bro?? How are you still in here? I should have to add you back because I created it.

> *SLADE HAS LEFT THE CONVERSATION*

> Daddy Alpha: If it's electronic, Slade can control it. Don't ask how he does, just accept that he can.

I'd forgotten that terrifying tidbit about him, but at least he'd confirmed, in writing—for what it was worth—that he wasn't planning on murdering me today.

It would have to do.

> Pretty Girl: What should I wear tonight? Is this your typical dress sexy nightclub? Or is there a uniform?

The next two messages delivered at the same time.

> Golden Boy: Sexy!

> Daddy Alpha: Do not dress sexy! I don't have time to be killing anyone.

> Daddy Alpha: There's no uniform, but the staff tend to dress in all black. They'll provide the rest.

Black I could do.

> Golden Boy: See you tonight, Shortcake. I'll be the one tipping big so you can flash me that smile.

My heart fluttered, delicate tiny flutters that I'd never felt before.

It couldn't mean anything good. Probably a heart attack.

Moving to my wardrobe, I pawed through the rows of hanging items, narrowing my eyes as I found extra clothes that hadn't been there this morning. Someone had stealthily added clothes while I was out, sliding them between items.

Kellan was my first thought, but it could just as easily be Hunter. His instincts were to take care of his pack, and he was controlling enough not to care how I felt about his intrusion.

Deciding I'd deal with the culprit later, I pulled out a pair of black slacks that were tight enough to hug my ass—*because tips*—but wouldn't get anyone murdered. I paired them with a black tank that flashed only moderate cleavage.

Dropping both on the bed with new underwear, I raced into the bathroom for a quick shower. When I was clean and dry, I opened the drawer for my hairbrush, only to find it was now filled with brand new makeup.

Enough to replace everything I'd left behind, plus so much more.

What in the…?

Whoever had topped up my clothes had been in here as well, and as heat burned behind my eyes, I let myself have a tiny moment. No one had ever taken care of me before.

Not even my mother.

Without asking, one of the alphas had seen my need and provided for me. Damn them.

There wasn't even anyone here to yell at, and for once I was tempted to just accept the gift and not think about the strings that were no doubt attached.

Were they trying to buy me? Would I end up owing them too much to ever leave?

Or was this a genuine gift?

As I rifled through the drawer, I recognized all the brands —everything was top of the line and expensive. Deciding that whatever I used I would have purchased anyway, and I could pay them back with my wages, I removed a few items.

It took five attempts to get my eyeliner and mascara right, but by the time I'd finished, I was happy with the final results. Dark liner, red lips, and a dusting of powder over my nose. It blended my freckles until they weren't as obvious, since the *Strawberry Shortcake* look wasn't for everyone, and I needed maximum tips.

I pulled my hair into a high ponytail to keep it out of my face, and then got dressed in the black clothes. There was still an hour until Slade needed to leave, so I spent time googling the club and bringing up their menus to familiarize myself.

I'd never been to conventional school, having learned only what Mom bothered to teach me before she met her pack. After that, she gave up completely, though it wasn't all her fault.

Whenever I tried to read, letters jumbled around in words. Half the time they made no sense, but whatever. I'd long ago accepted that I was a dumbass with a kindergarten reading level.

Thankfully, I'd spent years in bars, so most of Luxuria's drinks were already familiar to me, and they only had limited snacks—mostly wings and tacos—which wouldn't give me the issues I had at Golden Fin.

I needed to ask Hunter what had happened with Bradley, and if there was any fallout from his douchery, but it could wait for another day. Maybe if I enjoyed working at their bar, I could keep it as my main job for a while.

At ten to four I wandered downstairs, dressed and already sweating. Not because it was hot, or I was particularly nervous about the job, but because I was about to spend time in an enclosed space with a dragon shifter. *A fucking dragon shifter.*

There was no sign of Slade as I waited by the front door, fiddling with the couple of items I had on me: my phone, the cash left over from lunch today, and a lipstick for touchups through my shift.

The scent of toasted marshmallow wrapped around me first, and he arrived so silently I couldn't be sure he didn't sprout wings and glide down.

Could he partially shift like wolves?

The avalanche of questions in my mind was cut off as Slade, dressed in boots, black combat pants, and a black shirt stretched to capacity over his massive, muscled body, strode past me without a word. I found myself racing behind like a lost duckling.

He led me through a section of the house that I hadn't been to before. We passed the laundry and the drying room, and then he opened a door to reveal a set of stairs.

He didn't glance back once, and I got the sense that this was a test of some description. Neither of us wanted to be here, and he especially didn't want to be doing this and wouldn't be making it easy on me.

Mate. My wolf's whine this time was filled with a thread of insecurity, as if even she was unsure we could handle a mate like Slade. Don't get me wrong, she wanted him, but that need was diluted by fear. *You and me both, sister.* You and me both.

Knowing I couldn't reveal my distress, I followed without fuss, all the while hoping he hadn't decided to lead me into their creepy murder basement. When I reached a large metal door, I pushed against it, the heavy material taking a few seconds to move.

I stepped through to the other side and found myself in heaven on Earth.

A heaven built of cars and bikes. All the beautiful, *beautiful* bikes.

Stumbling toward them, I trailed down the rows of Hondas and Yamahas, grinding to a halt when I reached the very last bike.

Okay, now I hoped that my new mascara's waterproof claim held up, because I was going to cry. Since arriving in Golden Claw, the pendulum of my emotions had been swinging wildly, keeping me constantly on the edge of waterworks, but *come on...* it was my dream bike.

"Hello, sweetheart," I whispered, gazing lovestruck at the Ducati Panigale V4R.

My hand hovered over the shiny black tank, and I debated

how much I truly cared if the alphas killed me after sealing the mate bond.

Provided I got a chance to ride this baby first.

"What are you doing?" I jumped at his low, rumbly voice.

This was the first time Slade had spoken to me, and I was surprised by the faintest hint of an accent that felt as if it originated in Europe. It suited him though, reminding me that he was an ancient, terrifying beast.

"Staring at my dream bike."

Silence followed my statement, and I was surprised to find that I wanted to stare at the dragon even more than the bike. His expression was neutral, those beautiful, unearthly eyes locked on the row of bikes. "Which one is your dream bike?"

My hand shook as I pointed toward her. "The Panigale. I'd sell all non-essential body parts for one."

Silence again outside of a low rumble. It wasn't an angry sound... more curious. "That one is mine." His tone gave nothing away, leaving me unable to tell if he was unhappy or not by my love for this bike.

"Are we riding her today?" I squeaked, barely daring to breathe at the thought.

"No."

Ouch. It was that easy for him to shatter my tiny hope, as he once again became scary shifter. He moved away from the row of bikes, and I gave them all a last longing stare. *Soon, precious ones.*

When I got a chance, I'd have to ask Kellan if any of them were his. Surely there'd be one I could borrow for a quick ride.

As Slade moved deeper into the garage, I experienced the rest of the incredible lineup, barely holding in my gasps at each new revelation. "Range Rover p615, Bugatti Chiron, Ferrari SF90, Bentley Continental GT, Rolls Royce Cullinan... in the fucking Black Badge edition." I kept chanting through them because this was almost as unbelievable as the existence of dragons. "A Rolls Royce Ghost, Lamborghini Revuelto, Bentley Flying Spur—oh, and four Porsche GT3 RS's. Of course."

Their Porsches were no doubt what they used on the track, seeing as they were purpose-built racecars. Goddess, they'd handle like a dream around a track.

Not everything was a supercar, with a few drifters, including a Mazda RX7 rotary and a Skyline R33 with what looked like an RB 26 conversion.

I've died and gone to motor heaven.

Near the center of the massive garage they had their classic cars, including a Chevy Impala, Mustang GT350, Corvette Stingray, and a Shelby Cobra. These alphas were more than just supercar and speed fanatics... they were true car lovers.

Finley's TRX wasn't here, but there were a couple of other pickup trucks, rounding off the bunch.

Slade had been silently watching me die of happiness, and when I reached his side I debated asking to sleep down here tonight. I was distracted though by the bright green car, similar in color to the eyes of the dragon who stood beside it. "Oh my goddess above. You've got a Lamborghini Aventador SVJ? What in the actual fuck...? Holy shit. These are... *holy shit.*"

He examined me like I was a foreign species crawling over his shoe. "How do you know so much about cars?"

Temporarily forgetting that he was an ancient, scary dragon, I scoffed. "Why? Because I'm poor and uneducated?"

He made no attempts to clarify if that was what he'd meant as he stared me down, unbothered by the tension between us. With a sigh, I decided there was no harm in revealing this piece of my past. "Mom lived over a mechanic's shop with her pack. They locked me in my room all the time, but I had a secret escape out the window and down into the garage. I'd watch the cars roll in and out. The owner must have been good at his job, because the shop was a dump but he worked on the fanciest cars I'd ever seen. Sports cars, racecars, muscle cars. If it had four wheels and an engine, it went through his shop at some point."

After catching me sneaking through a few times, the old guy, Mack, had taught me about the cars he'd worked on. A gruff old bastard, but one of the few friends in my past.

I hadn't seen him since the day Mom died.

"I couldn't shake my love for anything with a motor after that. Bikes are my passion, don't get me wrong, but cars hold their own."

Slade shook his head, a gentle movement as if he'd unsettled a thought, and without a word opened his door and slid into the driver's side. When I ducked in under the suicide door, I noticed that he barely fit his massive frame on his side.

All of their low-slung sports had obvious modifications to accommodate alphas, but it was clearly still a squeeze.

When the doors were closed, I breathed in the scent of leather and Slade. A heady combination that had me wanting to squirm on my chair. I didn't though, remembering how much it annoyed Hunter.

Not antagonizing the dragon was the ticket to staying alive longer.

"We could have taken your bike, you know," I said, my words drowned out by the throaty roar of the engine. As the vibrations rumbled beneath my ass, I almost had an orgasm then and there. The feeling of all that horsepower was incomparable.

Slade shook his head, making it clear he'd heard me perfectly well. "I prefer not to be touched unless in fight training. And only because it can't be avoided."

I filed this away with the very limited information I knew about him. "I respect your boundaries," I offered, hoping he understood that I'd do everything in my power to comply with his touch aversion. After all, I had plenty of my own boundaries.

Slade shot me a quick glance and offered the slightest incline of his head. I tried not to think about that tiny acknowledgement as he exited the garage, heading along the driveway down the side of the house.

I'd expected to be terrified in the presence of this dragon, and to some extent I was, but he was also... different... to what I expected. He was icy and contained, broken and terrifying, powerful and reluctant. A plethora of mysteries. And for a brief shining moment I wished to be the shifter who got to unravel them. Only I couldn't ever get that deep with him.

Or any of the alphas.

The fact that Slade was already the most dominant and powerful shifter in the world should be comforting, but if I knew anything about power, it was that you never had enough.

CHAPTER 29

Slade didn't break the silence during the drive, but I wasn't bothered by it.

Mostly I enjoyed my time in his powerful supercar.

Music played in the background, and it was heavily instrumental. I had no idea what genre it was, having only ever listened to pop, rock, and dance music at the clubs, but it was nice. *Soothing.* Between the speed, the thrum of the engine, and the instruments, I felt more relaxed than I'd expected around Slade.

If he wasn't a nearly seven-foot-tall walking wall of muscle, with a face too beautiful to stare directly at, who could turn into a giant dragon, I'd have almost forgotten he was in the car with me.

Almost.

I hadn't noticed how fast he was driving until we were out of the urban center, heading along a narrow back road. The location change didn't worry me, though, after Hunter's message about Slade needing to see his squad. As we raced along the road, I caught sight of a track with stadium seating in the distance. I wanted to ask if that was where the pack raced, but tall, silent, and deadly wasn't exactly inviting conversation.

Pulling out my phone, I found that Kellan had messaged again. I couldn't use any voice-to-text in the car with Slade, so I was slower than usual as I deciphered his words.

> Golden Boy: Emme, what's happening? Is Slade behaving himself? Just don't encroach on his personal space and you'll be fine.

> Daddy Alpha: Don't touch him or anything that belongs to him.

I side-eyed the dragon.

Slade hadn't shown any outward signs of being a threat, at least not right now, appearing content to silently drive like I wasn't even here.

> Pretty Girl: I'm currently sitting in his car. Does that count as touching his belongings?

There was a minute delay before Hunter's reply came through.

> Daddy Alpha: No, brat.

Well, he couldn't blame me for clarifying.

> Pretty Girl: Just quickly, is the racetrack you own on the way to where Slade's squad trains?

They both answered at the same time.

> Golden Boy: Hell yes it is! Can't wait for you to see it tomorrow.

> Daddy Alpha: Yes.

I had nothing more to add, so I fiddled with the phone for a few seconds, and by the time I looked up we'd arrived at our destination. Slade pulled his flashy green car into a spot with his name on it, right beside Warrick's Range Rover. The building itself gave the impression of a state-of-the-art sports stadium, clearly dripping in money.

The large, oval-shaped center was perched in the middle of nowhere, with just trees and patches of cleared land around it. There were dozens of cars already in the lot around us as I exited the vehicle and took a second to enjoy the warmth of the last rays of the afternoon sun. There was a hint of fall in the air, and I couldn't wait to experience Golden Claw during the cooler months.

Cora had told me about their huge pack runs through the snow, and I hoped to be here long enough to experience one.

Slade waited silently for me to stop daydreaming. When I moved closer to him he set off along the path leading to the automatic doors. Air-conditioning blasted us as we stepped inside the foyer, heading past a long desk where a dozen or so shifters were busy on computers or answering phones.

No wonder Warrick made enough money to buy fancy cars; this was clearly a valuable hub in the city. It made sense when you considered the importance of enforcing order and safety amongst large groups of predators, and that these squads were the ones dishing it out. But in my experience, not everyone had their priorities straight. Especially when it came to distributing money.

Heads bowed as the shifters behind the reception called out greetings to *Alpha Slade*. A pungent scent of fear grew stronger as they reacted to the predator in their midst, barely even noticing me at his side.

Clearly, I needed to be more cautious around Slade since I'd all but fallen into a relaxed doze during the car ride. It had been stupid to leave myself that vulnerable.

Jogging to keep up with his long strides, I followed him through a labyrinth of rooms, many of which contained training courses and walls of weapons.

We finally emerged into the center, which was a massive open-aired stadium. Out here there were dozens of shifters, all standing around on the grassed area in large groups.

I noticed Warrick at the same time he saw us, and a welcoming smile broke out across his face. As I started to stride forward, Slade made the mildest—albeit *terrifying*—rumble at my side, and I froze in my tracks.

Fuck. The dragon might not care about me, or want a mate, but that didn't mean he'd tolerate the disrespect of me running toward another alpha.

Swallowing roughly, I moved slower, and Warrick ended up being the one to come to us. "Emme!" he said, wiping a hand over his forehead, his dark skin shiny with perspiration. "How was lunch with Cora today?"

"So freaking good," I replied, unable to help smiling. "The food and company was excellent, and Cora even treated us to a very nice bottle of wine. You found yourself an amazing mate."

"That I did." His lips twitched, and I wondered if he thought my compliment was a dig at my pack.

Not that the dragon gave a shit, having already strode away toward a group of about twenty shifters. "They're Flight Squad," Warrick explained, lowering his voice. "I'm in charge of Beta Force, since they're all betas under my command."

"Can all of Slade's fly?"

"No, but a lot of them can. He has a lethal team at his command."

I watched the dragon closely. Even before he reached his

squad they had fallen into formation. Four lines of five soldiers, representing the biggest and best of what alphas offered.

"All alphas."

Warrick nodded. "Yep. They could have been alpha squad, but Slade prefers not to advertise that to the world. Flight is an ode to his dragon."

I narrowed my eyes on Warrick. "Speaking of, I could have used a little heads-up that one of my pack was a mythical creature."

My face must not have reflected my true annoyance, because he chuckled and almost ruffled my hair before he remembered who was here with us. My wolf rumbled in my chest to remind him that we were a predator too.

"There's no amount of warning that can prepare you for Slade. Plus, you're so skittish, I didn't want to scare you off before you got a chance to know them." He examined me closer, as if searching for injuries. "How is it going with them?"

There was no easy answer to that question. "I'll get back to you when I sort out my feelings on the whole situation."

His worry softened into an expression of sympathy. "We're always here for you, Emme. Cora would add you to our pack in a heartbeat." As he said that, I swore I heard the rumble of the dragon again, but when I looked Slade's way, he was focused on his squad.

"Thank you. I'm grateful to have you guys in my life. Okay, I better let you get back to training." I was about to walk away when a former niggling thought pushed to the forefront, and I had to ask: "When I stayed at your place, did you let Hunter into your territory? Into my room?"

A brief sigh escaped him, and I couldn't be sure, but it felt like guilt flickered in his eyes. "No, but there's no one who can stop Hunter Reeves when he sets his mind to something. He warned me he'd be keeping an eye on you, and while I scented him around the property, I never gave him permission to trespass."

His expression remained open and pleading, and after experiencing a little of Hurricane Hunter myself, I couldn't really blame him. "Thanks for your honesty. I appreciate it."

He bowed his head briefly, and with that respectful gesture, a flare of warmth hit my chest. After we said our goodbyes, I headed for Slade, who was in deep conversation with his squad.

There were eighteen males and two females in Flight Squad, all of them hanging on the dragon's every word. I hovered a few feet away, and was surprised when Slade addressed me directly. "I'm organizing them into sparring groups. You can wait over there."

He pointed toward a bench under one of the few trees out here, and I didn't argue, striding off to wait. By the time I'd seated myself, Flight Squad had separated into pairs, getting right into their sparring.

For the next twenty minutes, I forgot everything else as I watched the most mesmerizing fighting I'd ever seen. They moved in a fast, deadly dance—if I'd gone up against any of them, I'd be dead in seconds.

At first Slade wandered between them, giving instructions and correcting stances, before he eventually moved to spar with a dark-skinned alpha. From this distance I couldn't tell what the other shifter's animal was, but he moved super-fast, striking with lethal force.

Or it would be lethal against anyone who wasn't Slade Riverson.

Slade batted those strikes away like they were wisps of cloud, and when he struck back I winced at the loud snap of connection. The other shifter cursed, stumbling a few steps before righting himself and shaking off the blow.

The pair exchanged more hits, but from this angle none looked to land directly on Slade. He was unparalleled as a fighter, flowing between moves like he was made of liquid. He leapt from one style to another, dodging, blocking, and striking until the other shifter sprawled on the ground, hands up in surrender.

Slade relaxed his stance as his squad applauded, and when I managed to remove my gaze from the dragon, I found all the other squads were also watching the fight. I observed the awed faces, and it was the first time I understood that the respect Slade commanded was about more than him being a dragon. He commanded it because he was a trained and deadly weapon, without ever needing to change forms.

The hit of pride I felt at his accomplishment upset me, even more so because I'd been enthralled during that fight. I hadn't been able to look away from Slade. His body was a finely honed weapon, and the play of his muscles with each rapid strike had felt very close to foreplay. It was bad enough that I'd been a simpering, needy bitch with Hunter and Kellan, but now I had a mini-crush on a freaking dragon.

A dragon who probably wanted to eat me in the *very not fun way*.

It was almost like I, *or my traitorous body*, had a death wish.

I honestly couldn't even blame my wolf for half of my feelings and actions lately.

This lusting after alphas was all on me.

Slade wrapped up his training, and by the time he strode over to me I'd gotten myself together. He didn't say a word, and I found the silence comforting.

Silent and deadly worked for me because he was never going to push the mate bond.

If anything, being around Slade might be the safest of all.

CHAPTER 30

HUNTER

I dialed his number, and it rang twice before he answered. I didn't bother with the usual pause for a greeting, because with Slade it would never come. "Did she make it into the club okay?"

A burst of music in the background caught my attention... *He was still there.*

"Yes. She's already working. No training necessary apparently."

"You stayed?" I knew better than to push him, but this was highly unusual behavior. I needed to monitor where his head was at after spending the afternoon with her.

"She knew every car in our garage." He sounded mildly perturbed. A tone I'd only heard during times he wrestled with a particularly difficult puzzle, whether that be online or within our pack.

"Lots of shifters know car brands," I pointed out.

His rumble was more confused than menacing. "Not just the brands, brother. She knew the make and model. I'd hazard a guess that she could have named the year on most of them if pushed. Of all the omegas, we find one who grew up above a garage and has a genuine love for bikes and cars."

I filed that away with the limited information we knew about Emmeline Anders. "Did you learn anything else about her during your afternoon?"

Like which *dead* motherfucker put that scar on her back. When I'd seen that raised and ropey scar across her tanned skin, I'd been on the verge of losing control of my wolf. It wasn't that it made me look at her differently, or want her less, but the knowledge that someone hurt her had me devolving toward my base instincts. *Protect, hunt, destroy, kill.*

"I've learned very little that's new," Slade grumbled, "but I know enough that with a few more pieces of her puzzle, I'll be able to solve the mystery."

His implication that Emme was nothing more than a mystery to unravel pissed me off, but considering my own intentions toward our omega weren't completely altruistic, I kept my irritation to myself. "Did Kellan arrive?"

Slade's huff was clear down the line. "Ten minutes ago. He's sitting in her section, tipping away our fortune and ensuring no other shifters get too close."

That little bastard had half the city fooled into thinking he was the nice one when he could be just as diabolical and dangerous as the rest of us. The only difference was the smile on his golden face as he stabbed you in the back. It was a relief to know he'd keep an eye on her during her shift.

"That's good. Until further notice, that omega belongs to the Reeves pack, and it'll be a cold day in hell before I let anyone fuck around with my belongings."

There was another huff, but for a change he didn't refute my claim. It spoke volumes that he was still sitting there, attempting to work out the final pieces to her puzzle. Dragons were possessive in nature, and I wondered if Slade had finally found a shifter he couldn't just dismiss and walk away from.

There was a crack down the line as his boots hit the ground. "I'm out of here. This is a waste of my fucking time."

Or not.

Pinching the bridge of my nose, I cursed the fucking morons who thought this thankless job was an honor. Being the entitled alpha was going to be the death of me—not that I'd cede control to anyone else. Not while I still breathed.

"Okay, I'll see you at home in a few hours. I've got to oversee final testing on a new product that hasn't quite gone to plan, and then I have to unravel this shipping screwup between the UK and Australian branches."

Slade hung up and I actually laughed; he was always consistent in being an asshole.

Two hours later I had my new product working as expected, and I'd fired six of our London upper management while promoting one legend who'd managed to pull his head from his ass and help me save about fifty million dollars by getting the shipment to the right fucking location on time.

A quick glance at my Jacob & Co told me it was almost midnight. I was wrecked. It wouldn't be the first night I'd worked until I crashed at my desk, but I wanted to get home and see how Emme's first shift had gone. Bradley, who was on his way out of Golden Claw with two black eyes, and zero chance of ever returning, was hopefully the only shifter I'd need to teach a lesson to during our omega's first days at her job.

Not that it was a hardship to protect her. I was born for the role, and soon Emme would understand exactly what that meant for her. My obsession with the omega grew with each interaction, and one day very soon I'd claim her.

She would beg me for it.

Packing up, I grabbed my phone and briefcase and headed down to the parking garage. I'd driven my Range Rover today, but right now I wished it was a bike. I'd tear through town in half the time if I had my Aprilia or Yamaha.

The gates to the office parking lot opened as soon as I came into sight. Harold was the best damn night watch we'd ever had, and I would pay him double his already high salary if he ever tried to leave. "Night, Alpha Hunter," he called, a hint of his Thai heritage in his accent. "Drive safe."

"Call me if you have any issues," I told him through the half-open window.

He saluted, already back in his booth by the time I drove off. I was too wound up for music tonight, but without background noise all I could do was think.

Think and worry.

The Summit kicked off on Monday, and I'd already fielded five calls today from other council members to confirm requests for visiting dignitaries. If being an entitled alpha didn't kill me, politics would. If I made it through this week without punching anyone... well, it'd be the first Summit I'd managed to keep my cool.

Now that we had an omega to worry about, I doubted I'd last more than the first couple of days. Emmeline was a hot commodity. Two of those five requests were to meet with the newest Golden Claw omega. *Not a fucking chance.*

Her designation was so rare it was still unknown what happened when an omega bonded into a complete quintet. It was this rareness that had everyone wanting to claim one, along with their ability to step outside normal power structures.

Her wolf would fall to no one's call, even if they were as powerful as Slade.

I'd never had a reason to investigate omegas until recently, and I'd been surprised to find a few vague references to them strengthening an alpha in a completed quintet. It was unconfirmed though, and for the first time ever I needed an answer.

Hitting the call button on my phone, I scrolled until I found the right number. Despite the late hour, there was a decent chance my video-game-obsessed best friend would be wide awake and gaming his life away. It'd been weeks since I managed to make a session of *Call of Duty* with Sorenson, but he rarely missed a Saturday night.

"Hunt, buddy. Please tell me you're calling because you're about to log on. We're getting our fucking asses kicked." His voice wavered as if he was ducking and dodging. "You cowardly, flea-bitten pricks! I'm going to rip out your intestines and choke you to death with them."

I chuckled, relaxing for the first time in hours. "Nah, I'm only just leaving the office. Lots of fires to put out today."

That grabbed his attention as he stopped trying to blast his way through the battlefield. "Anything you need help with? You know I'm excellent at fighting fires."

Often literally, since we were both volunteers with the local fire brigade.

"It's all sorted, but thanks."

"Why are you calling, then? Must be serious."

I needed him to confirm what I already suspected. "After you bonded with Chels, did you ever notice her energy boosting your alpha dominance or strength?"

Soren fell silent, and I knew I'd taken him by surprise. "Honestly, no," he finally said. "But we're not a complete quintet, so there's a possibility that could change."

No doubt Soren would have told me if he noticed a boost after they bonded; he wasn't known for keeping secrets. But with him, there was always a chance he just hadn't bothered to pay attention.

Curiosity entered his tone. "Have you had a power increase with Emmeline?"

Annoyance filled me, but I couldn't rip his head off just because he'd guessed the *obvious* reason for my question. "You know we're not bonded. There's been no change, except she's living under our roof to keep her safe."

"And you're no closer to figuring out why she's so against joining your pack? With scent matches, her wolf should be driving her forward. It's fate and instinct."

Normally he'd be right, but Emmeline was an omega. Her ability to fight her base instincts was stronger than ours would ever be.

"We know very little about her. She's afraid of us for some reason, mostly in regard to forming a complete bond. None of us are pushing, of course, but Kellan's working his usual magic by winning her over with charm."

Soren hooted with laughter, and whatever tension had lingered after my question was broken. "He's the only one of you assholes with a chance if that's the play."

He wasn't wrong, but I'd also seen the fragments of Emme's broken soul, and a part of me wondered if she might not need more than Kellan's sunshine to sustain her. She'd craved the submission my wolf demanded. Falling right under my command, even as an omega.

Soren's game picked up in the background, and he was distracted for the rest of the call. "We'll be at the track tomorrow. Oh fuck. You asshole." He cursed out his teammate again. "Then family bonfire night. I'd only miss that if I was dead."

"You'd *be* dead *if* you missed it. It's mandatory."

Soren's good-natured laughter reminded me of the good

and bad years of our childhood. "Yes, Daddy Alpha," he drawled down the line.

A growl ripped from me. "Don't fucking start. It's bad enough that I can't get Kellan to stop calling me that."

All I got in response was more laughter. "You can try this thing where you don't boss everyone around. It does wonders to ease up on the dad vibe."

Dad vibe. The fucking irony when the father figure in my life was one evil sonofabitch. I decided long ago, right after I changed my name, that I'd never carry on his legacy with children. *Daddy Alpha* was as close as I'd ever get to being a father.

"I'll keep that in mind." I kept my tone light, even as my thoughts grew darker. "See you at the track, brother. Don't stay up all night shooting noobs."

"All I've got is noobs," he mumbled. "I'll rage quit soon if these assholes don't pull their weight." The line went dead.

I pulled into my street, and relief hit me when I saw Kellan's Bugatti just up ahead. He wouldn't be here unless Emme was finished and safely home from her shift, which allowed me to stop stressing about her being out of my sight.

The fact that I couldn't just drop everything and follow her around, keeping her safe, bothered me more than it should.

After ensuring the security gates were closed behind me, I followed the other car along our dark street. None of our family members were night owls; the only lights still on were from our house.

Kellan pulled into his spot slowly, and I wasn't worried until he opened Emme's door and leaned down into the vehicle. I made it across the garage in ten steps. "What's wrong?"

Kellan's torso emerged with a sleeping omega in his arms, and unable to help himself he drew her close and breathed deeply. "She's just exhausted, Hunt. I don't think she's sleeping that well, and new jobs are stressful. But she did amazing tonight. There were no incidents, everyone was nice to her. Actually, a few were a little too nice, but I set those dumbasses straight."

My back teeth clanked as I ground them together, an annoyed growl rumbling from my chest. "Give me their names and I'll deal with them."

Kellan's low burst of amusement was fucking annoying. "You can't kill them. Trust me, if there'd been anything inappropriate, I'd have killed them and we'd be figuring out how to ditch a car with five bodies in the trunk."

Five. My wolf howled as rage rose until my vision was red. "Give her to me."

I didn't force my dominance into the command, hoping he'd understand how much I needed to hold her tonight. It'd been one hell of a week.

With a reluctant sigh, he held her out to me, and she looked positively tiny in his arms. "Okay, but only because you look like you're about to bust a nut if you don't hold her."

It was the bane of my existence to be constantly surrounded by smartasses. Not that he was wrong.

Emme didn't stir as he handed her across, and as soon as I wrapped my arms around her, my wolf calmed. Her sweet scent started to mix with mine, and I was thrown back to the day I'd scented her chocolate and honey in the council room.

The connection had been so strong, slamming into me, and I'd almost given into the roaring need to claim her. It had only been the fear on her face which held my bite.

I headed for the stairs but had to slow when Kellan leapt in front of me, his face devoid of his usual joviality. "Don't do anything that will cause me to be angry with you. I will avenge her honor."

My rumbling growl was the only fucking warning he needed to know he'd pushed me as far as I'd allow tonight, but he didn't back away. For that, I respected the hell out of the little shit. "I won't hurt or upset her. Now get out of my way."

He pointed two fingers at his eyes and then at me, before he stepped aside, allowing me to take her upstairs. Emme still hadn't moved, solidly asleep, and it annoyed me that she'd let herself grow so exhausted that she was vulnerable.

I'd never cause her physical harm, but she didn't believe that, so she shouldn't be sleeping this soundly in my arms. Was this about more than exhaustion though? Was there a part of her that instinctively knew she was safe in our pack?

When we reached her room, she let out a breathy sigh and snuggled closer to my chest. Her ear was pressed just above my heart, as if seeking out the beat. With a groan, I shifted her higher and adjusted myself in my suit pants. Being this close to her had my dick trying to punch through the material like I was a fucking teen pup getting laid for the first time.

I had to get her to bed before the slivers of control I desperately clung to shattered.

The roaring need to claim her never went anywhere. If anything, it got worse each day, as I fought a millennia of shifter instinct.

CHAPTER 31

I woke up later than usual on Sunday, feeling refreshed and strangely calm. As I rolled over, coffee and cocoa drifted up from the sheets, and I tried to recall what happened last night. I'd worked at the club, and then Kellan brought me home, and...

A quick feel under the sheets revealed that I was in my underwear, and I might not be able to remember it, but I knew exactly who'd undressed me and put me to bed. *Hunter Reeves.*

I must have fallen asleep in the car, exhaustion and the weird trust I had for these alphas, knocking out my usual security system. I'd have to be dead to the world to not rouse when Hunter removed my pants and tank.

I waited for the anger and sense of violation to strike at his audacity of undressing me without my permission, and it was faintly there, but mostly I was annoyed by my vulnerability around them. The issue here was that my wolf trusted them implicitly, and she was no longer a viable warning system. Not when it came to Reeves Pack.

At least, from what I could tell, he'd done little except strip me of my shoes and clothes—which had stunk from the club, and I wouldn't have wanted to sleep in them anyway—before sliding me under the sheets.

Still, at some point I probably needed to have a quick chat with him about consent.

Pulling myself out of the bed, I padded over to the window and lifted the blinds. A dull light reflected back, and for my first time in Golden Claw, their bright fall weather had been replaced by rain. Heavy and ominous clouds hung low in the sky, the wind blowing fiercely through the mass of trees across their acres of land, and I wondered if they'd still head to the track.

Not to mention, there was no way family bonfire night could go ahead if this weather persisted.

Fighting the urge to crawl back into bed, I almost fell onto the soft surface, until a waft of stale booze drifted off my skin. More than one drink had spilled on me last night, and I couldn't wait another second to shower.

In the bathroom, the bright lights reflected my freckles and clear blue eyes in the mirror. I was surprised to see that any makeup I'd been wearing to work was gone. If Hunter had removed it, it was strangely thoughtful, for that snarly alpha.

Though, it had been Kellan who'd dusted the powder off my nose as soon as he'd arrived at Luxuria. *Your pretty freckles are never to be covered, Shortcake. They're mine to keep.*

He had a way with words that stayed with me long after he'd finished speaking.

Twenty minutes later, I strolled out of the bathroom, scented in a new strawberry lotion I'd found in the drawer, and not even a minute later there was a knock at the door.

"Pretty girl, you awake?"

I was only in a towel, and we did not need a repeat of the last towel incident. "Yep, give me a second to get dressed."

There was a thud, as if Kellan had dropped his head against the door while he mumbled, "I'd rather not."

Biting back a laugh, I hurried into the dressing room to find some clothes. There was no pain in my feet from last night, and overall, it'd been a pretty great first shift. After Slade dropped me off, and half the club fawned over him from a distance, he'd sat in one of the high tables with his laptop and proceeded to work.

Work and stare.

His biting gaze had me stumbling around like a newborn pup who hadn't quite gotten her legs under her yet. The dragon shifter confused me, and when he'd packed up and left a couple of hours into my shift, I couldn't figure out if I was relieved or disappointed to no longer have his green gaze on me.

It wasn't a soft gaze, by any means, more calculating and predatory. But I'd missed it.

Kellan, on the other hand, had been the best addition to my night. He'd shown up after practice and the media call, hair still wet, casually dressed in jeans and a black fitted shirt that showcased every single one of his nicely honed hockey-boy muscles.

His distraction was similar but also *vastly* different to Slade's.

Kellan was comforting in a way that felt like home. Or how I'd always dreamed home would feel. Albeit a home I wanted to strip naked and explore for hours. Kellan was an alpha who made my resolve to run from this pack harder than I'd ever imagined.

During my shift I'd kept drifting by his table, needing to check in. Unlike Slade, he was closely surrounded by other shifters—everyone wanted to be Kellan's friend. He was popular and charming, and he wasn't even buying the drinks to make it so. That had been Christian, another hockey wolf, who was viciously hilarious as he ribbed his best friend all night.

Those two gave each other so much shit, and by the time my shift ended, I felt like part of their friendship group. It had taken a concerted effort to work all my section and not just drop my tray on their table to chat the night away.

Not that the club manager would have said a word, with Kellan being one of the owners, but I also hated for any of them to think I was lazy or unprepared to carry my share of work.

If anything, I'd worked that much harder than usual to do *all the things*, which probably explained why I'd passed out in the car on the way home.

Once I was dressed in jeans and a loose hoodie that smelled a lot like Kellan, I pulled on some socks and padded out of the wardrobe.

"You can come in now," I called as I checked my phone, which had been plugged in to charge by *somebody* as well.

There were no new messages, but I was delighted to find almost four hundred bucks in tips stashed under the device. Kellan and his friends were excellent tippers, and while I felt a little guilty taking their cash, most of it would be going to pay the pack back anyway.

The door crashed open as Kellan bounded in and leapt onto my unmade bed, his massive body spread out to make the queen look positively tiny. "How'd you sleep?" he asked as I tucked my phone into my back pocket and held the money out to him.

"I slept great. And here's some cash to start paying back what I owe."

Kellan narrowed his eyes on my hand as if it were diseased and shook his head. "None of us will ever take your money,

Shortcake. Let's just start from scratch now, but please don't stop me from buying you stuff on occasion."

I felt stupid standing there with money hovering between us, so I quickly stuffed it into the drawer. "Thank you," I said softly, determined not to make this a thing. Though there was one part I had to address: "Speaking of letting you buy me stuff... you wouldn't happen to know where all my new clothes and toiletries came from?"

Kellan's smile was breathtakingly effortless and full of joy. I couldn't remember a time I'd ever smiled that freely before. "It was definitely Florence. I thought I recognized one of my hoodies." Sitting up, he reached out and grabbed a handful of the sweater and rubbed it gently between his fingers.

I was sure my expression was a mask of disbelief. "Are you trying to tell me that not only is Florence buying me items without permission, but she also stole your clothes and put them in my room?"

He laughed hard, and I was thrown off balance when he yanked on the hoodie, pulling me on top of him. "Would you believe me if I said yes?"

I pushed against his chest and he hit me with his puppy eyes, their deep blue color leaning toward that violet hue he got when he was happy. *Or turned on.*

"Not a chance," I huffed, trying not to react to our bodies all tangled together on the bed. *Holy goddess, this was bad, but it also felt so good.* "Please stop buying me things. I really don't need any extras, and I'm never going to be able to pay you back."

Pushing against his chest again, I barely moved an inch in his hold, and then he started to run his hands up and down my spine in soft, gentle touches. "It makes me happy to leave you little gifts." His voice lowered, and I found myself wanting to stay under his soothing touch.

The tension eased from me as I collapsed against him, deciding that I wouldn't take away his joy when it didn't cost me anything to be here with him.

Except for maybe small slivers of my soul, but hey, I could probably live without them.

"Okay, Golden. You can give me small gifts, but I want you to know that you *never* have to buy my love or affection. You will never buy anyone's, you hear me. If they can't appreciate you for all your non-monetary charms, then they don't deserve you."

His hands paused against my skin where he'd slipped them under the hoodie, and I felt tension ripple through him. "Will you freely give it to me?"

Not if I can help it. Though it was starting to feel like it might all be out of my control.

"Just keep being you. It's more than enough."

His shudder this time was stronger, and that soft touch turned firmer as he wrapped his arms around me and pulled me so tightly into his chest that I couldn't breathe.

I didn't want to breathe.

Like the last time he'd hugged me, the sensation tore at my essence and destroyed flimsy repairs to old wounds. I barely managed not to sob.

My throat burned like a motherfucker, my eyes squeezed as tightly as his arms felt.

I wondered if hugs would always feel like this. I also wondered if I'd ever stop craving them with a burn that scorched whatever was left of my tattered soul.

Kellan held on for a long time, and I didn't fight him, falling all the way into the two of us wrapped around each other, while the rain pounded the windows. It was dark, cool and cozy, as if we existed in our own world that no one could touch. Kellan's heart beat strongly under my ear, soothing in its rhythm.

It'll destroy him when you leave.

The thought was so loud, and I had no idea if I'd be able to make that decision in the end because *it would destroy me too.*

That feeling had never been as strong as it was today. After getting to know this pack, leaving them would irrevocably change me.

"Tell me about your life growing up."

His hands tightened as I jolted, panic my immediate reaction to that question. "Why do you want to know?"

He started those gentle strokes along my spine again, as if soothing a wild beast. "Because I want to know you. I have so many questions, but I'm aware that asking them will have you running and screaming. So... just tell me one truth."

One truth. Might as well start with a doozy. "I was a mistake, and my mom never wanted me."

Kellan's grip briefly bit into my skin before he relaxed his hold. His heartbeat was faster though, and that cinnamon caramel sweetness tasted slightly bitter as his anger took over. "She told you that?"

"Yep. She mostly showed me, because, you know, actions speak a million times louder than words. But my mom was thorough enough to also use words to really reiterate the facts."

His fingers moved higher, near my shoulder, tracing over the end of the ropey scar.

I knew what his next question was going to be, but to my surprise he didn't ask; he just kept brushing the scar tissue.

My honorable alpha was sticking to the one truth today.

"She gave me the scar," I freely offered, "before my shifter healing was strong enough to counter it, using a pure silver blade. Her pack helped in her *disciplines*." Silver didn't bother alphas, but the rest of us were weakened by its effects.

Kellan's chest rumbled under my ear, but he just kept up that soothing stroke over my skin. "As bad as it was to find her body," I continued, the words pouring from me, "I was lucky she died when I was young. Her pack wasn't interested in raping children, thank the goddess, but I'd been on the cusp of womanhood when she died." Exactly around the time those four alphas had started to pay much closer attention to me with lingering stares and touches. It had only been a matter of time.

"I need to kill them anyway," Kellan said in the deepest tone I'd ever heard from him, his dominance rising as his scent grew stronger.

Their deaths would only bring me joy and peace, but I'd never want him to risk himself in that pursuit. "I promise, for the most part, they left me alone. There's no need to avenge me."

His hands briefly stilled before moving again. "How alone?"

Entirely, completely, utterly. In every way that mattered. "Let's just say that before I ran, they locked me in my room every day. My only freedom was when they left the apartment and I could escape out the window and hide in the garage downstairs."

Kellan shot up in the bed, keeping his hold on me so I ended up sprawled across his lap. "What about school? What about your wolf? You would have been shifting by then, right?"

I nodded. "Yep, first shift was at ten, like most."

It took him less than five seconds to figure out what that meant. "That's why you ran circles in your room when you panicked. Your instinct wasn't to race outside to the forest, but to hide in the only space that was yours. The only place you were allowed to run as a pup."

Shame coated my insides, hot and bitter, as I tried not to reflect on those dark days.

"Being an omega helped. I—" I couldn't finish as my throat tightened. Being an omega might have helped me through that part of my life, but it was also the reason I could never have my pack. A pack I'd have given anything to claim.

Even the ones who didn't like or want me were a million times better than my mom's old pack. It was unfair really.

A cruel curse of fate.

CHAPTER 32

KELLAN

Emmeline stayed in my arms for far longer than I'd ever expected her to. Her lush curves pressed against the hard length of my body was enough to send me and my beast into a frenzy. I loved how she fit against my larger frame like she'd been made for me. Which she had.

Her curves though... fuck me dead. I'd kept my hands to myself. Barely.

When she'd finally opened up and started to bare her soul, I'd been consumed by my need to know her whole story. It was a pivotal moment in our relationship, and even with my fury toward her mom's old pack, holding her while she shared her past brought me moments of peace.

I'd had no fucking clue it was possible to quiet my wolf in the way Emmeline's presence did. To ease the alpha that wanted to hunt, dominate, and control.

Emmeline soothed the beast.

When she finally wiggled against me, I decided that if I didn't let her go this time, the hard cock pressed between us would start causing issues. Now was not the time or place, especially after her heavy reveals, and I refused to rush the natural progress of our relationship.

It was a forever connection. True fucking mates. Bonded for life.

Going slow might be hard, but the alternative of spooking her into running was unthinkable. These moments of holding her would have to satisfy for now, even if my beast was ready to hunt and chase our mate until she submitted to our claim.

"I'll meet you downstairs," she said softly, gaze lowered. She was beating herself up, and I had no idea if it was about the cuddling or her confessions.

That fucking pack.

Were those alphas still out there? The ones who had scarred my girl, and then overstepped when she'd bloomed into puberty. If I ever found out their location, I would gladly pay them a friendly visit. Definition of *friendly* to be determined.

There was nothing I could say to reassure her that we were nothing like them other than continuing to show up in every way she needed. "Of course, Shortcake. Meet me in the kitchen."

She nodded, and finally lifted her head to hit me with the full force of her depthless blue eyes. Her stare was a fucking shot to my heart. Amongst other places. "I'll meet you there."

Fighting every instinct in my body, I reluctantly left her room, palming my cock which had mostly been rock hard from the moment she'd landed on me. Even the story about that pack hadn't fully deflated the asshole, who desperately wanted to be inside his mate.

With no time to *deal with the issue*, I ordered it to get its shit together, and settle down to a semi-chub. I couldn't function with a baseball bat in my pants.

The house was silent as I padded down the stairs, all of our packmates still in the gym for their morning workouts. I'd gotten up extra early to work out before Emme woke up so I wouldn't miss any time with her today. Yeah, I was whipped, but I gave exactly zero shits about how that made me look.

I'd never be embarrassed to show up for my girl. If you weren't a little obsessed, was she even your mate?

In the kitchen, I got the coffee machine started and threw a dozen of the breakfast sandwiches Gerald prepared last night into the oven. The rain pelted the windows, and while it was disappointing not to make the track, at least Emme was stuck inside with us. I already had a plan to help build connections between the pack, and I couldn't wait to tell my brothers their new plans for the day.

As the scent of freshly ground beans and bacon permeated the air, Emmeline appeared still dressed in jeans and my hoodie. Her curves covered by my clothes created a very Neanderthal reaction in my brain, turning me and my beast feral. The only way that sight would improve, was if she also wore my claiming bite.

One day.

"Coffee?" I said, handing her a perfectly doctored mug. Emme liked her coffee milky and sweet, and I might have added a shot of caramel to remind her of her favorite alpha.

She groaned, and it shot straight to my, once again, rock hard cock. *Fuck.*

"You're a gift, Kellan Jackson. I don't know how I've ever functioned without you."

My chest tightened at how freely she offered her praise. The urge to bundle her up and drag her back to bed for the rest of the day was so strong that I had to grip the side of the counter to stop from moving toward her.

As I battled with my baser nature, she took a seat on a stool and sipped her coffee. Her gaze turned briefly toward the gloomy day outside the windows and then back to me. "Will you still meet at the track today?"

"Nah," I croaked, still not quite pulled together as I busied myself with my own coffee. "The weather is only going to get worse. A bit of rain doesn't bother us, but a full-on storm isn't worth the headaches. Even if it's fucking awesome to take our drift cars around the wet track."

Her cute nose screwed up as she sighed. "That's a shame. I've really been looking forward to it. Oh, actually... I've been meaning to ask if any of the road bikes in the garage are yours? I know the precious, *precious* Panigale is Slade's, but what about the others?"

Her puffy lips parted and her eyes all but rolled back in her head when she mentioned the Panigale. I filed that away under gifts I would be buying my beautiful Shortcake.

The fact that my soulmate loved cars and bikes had me thanking the goddess for her blessings. "I love when you talk dirty to me, baby. Bikes, cars, engines, and racing. It's like a shot of adrenaline straight to my co—" She coughed through a sip of coffee and I couldn't help but chuckle. "Cold heart?"

She quirked an eyebrow. "Right. You were absolutely going to say heart."

"Absolutely. To answer your question, though, none of the bikes are mine. Unfortunately." I was already cursing myself for not having one to give her this morning.

"Why unfortunately?" She looked genuinely curious, and I almost forgot her question as I stared into her perfect face.

I'd seek help for this obsession, except I never wanted it to end.

"Because clearly you want one of the bikes to be mine, and I don't have time to order one and pretend it was mine all along. The ones in the garage are Hunter's and Slade's. Fin and I prefer four wheels."

Her smile turned wistful, and I was *fucking done*. Goddess be damned, this shifter was my beginning and absolute end.

"Four wheels works for me as well. Could I maybe... drive your car? I've been missing the feeling of freedom as I fly along the freeway."

Unable to stay away from her any longer, I leaned over the counter and grasped her free hand. She froze at the initial contact, but just as quickly relaxed and wrapped her fingers around mine.

She was so much more comfortable around me even after a couple of days. *Slow and steady was going to win this race.* "What's mine is yours, pretty girl. You can literally have the clothes off my back and the money in my bank. You want my car... it's yours."

Emme had warned me more than once that there was no buying her affections, and I respected that, but the satisfaction I felt to provide and care for her wasn't a feeling I could give up. It soothed my wolf and alpha side, even if I was forced to sneak everything in and hide it amongst what she already had.

Her eyes softened, shining at me, and I wondered if she knew how expressive her face was when she was happy and overwhelmed. She parted her luscious, full lips into a smile. "You're my favorite, Kel. And you're too good to me."

She'd seen nothing yet, my beautiful destruction.

Falling in love with this omega would destroy the threads of my existence, and at this point I almost welcomed it.

Unable to help myself, I leaned down and pressed a kiss to her cheek, breathing in her sweet scent. My entire body reacted to us being this close, fueled by a desperate need to move a few inches and take her mouth. To *taste* that sweetness as well.

Somehow, I resisted.

"You're my favorite too, pretty girl. Always."

Her eyes widened and she stared at me for so long I

worried that I'd broken her. Her blue eyes were glossy, and if she cried I'd legitimately lose my shit.

She tried so hard to protect herself after her trust and love was repeatedly abused by her fucked-up Mom and that pack. With each new revelation about her past, I better understood the shield she'd clung to ever since showing up here.

But our sweet omega had the softest core I'd ever experienced. She deserved all the love, and I knew if she opened herself to the rest of the pack, she'd find all four of us were the pieces she'd been missing her entire existence.

Emme pulled herself together so fast, it was clear she'd had to do that more than once in her life—pretending to be okay. "If there's no track today..." She cleared her throat. "...and I'm guessing no bonfire, what's in the cards, then?"

Giving her a little space, I turned to check on the sandwiches. "Hunter will insist on some sort of pack togetherness because family bonfire is his idea. He maintains that we're all too busy, so we need to see each other at least once a week. With that in mind, I've got the perfect solution for today."

Emme rubbed a hand over her nose, reminding me of how she'd looked last night with powder over her freckles. Our omega was beautiful no matter what, but I'd had to brush off the makeup. I'd needed a hit of freckles for my addiction, and now, as she sat all cozy and bare-faced, I drank her in like the obsessed lunatic I was.

Emme didn't seem to notice my probing stare. "Do you really think it's a good idea for all of us to hang out today? At least at the bonfire there'd be other family members to act as buffers. Slade and Finley clearly don't want me here, and I'm not keen on forcing my presence."

I could hear the guys finishing up their gym session, and knew they'd be joining us in a second. "I won't force anyone to do anything they're not comfortable with," I said, confident in the knowledge that Hunter would be the one to lay down the law. "But we're all adults. We should be able to hang out for a couple of hours while the storm of the year rages through Golden Claw."

Emme didn't look convinced, but she didn't object again either. Checking on the sandwiches once more, I opened the foil to let them crisp up, by which time Hunter, Finley, and Slade were tromping into the kitchen in search of coffee—tea for the dragon—and food.

I plated up a sandwich for Emme first, sliding it across to her before I got the others ready. There were two for each of us, because we were growing boys and needed our sustenance.

"Thanks, pup," Hunter said with an arrogant smirk.

Bastard loved to torment me, but I gave back as good as I get. "You're welcome, grandpa. Got to look after the elders of the group. Do you need me to chew it up for you first?" A brief rumble escaped him, but it was without any real bite.

Finley slapped me on the arm when I handed him his plate, and when he turned to leave the room, I nudged him back toward the counter. With a sigh, he grumbled his way into one of the stools, farthest from Emme. Hunter sat right at her side, and to no one's surprise Slade chose to eat leaning against the counter near the sink, where no one could accidentally touch him and get murdered.

I loved that dragon like a brother, but he was one unhinged, scary motherfucker.

Especially if you encroached on his personal space.

With my plate in hand, I dropped into the stool on the other side of Emme, scooting close enough to feel her gently flowing energy against my arm. "No track today," Hunter said as he lifted his sandwich. "What's the plan?"

As predicted, there was no way he'd let us get away with

canceling family day. Releasing my cheeriness, I said, "I've got the perfect idea."

"No."

"Not a fucking chance."

Slade and Finley answered at the same time, but it didn't bother me. They could object all they wanted, but this was also a tradition, and we'd gone too long between games.

Hunter dropped his sandwich with a sigh. "Let me guess… family board games day."

Fuck yes it was.

My smug as fuck smile told them everything, and this time I had dual reasons for the event. One: I needed to destroy my pack brothers and bring them down a rung or two. Two: I wanted to make Emme smile after her heavy morning.

This was my new mission in life.

CHAPTER 33

I'd been trying not to laugh ever since Kellan suggested a board game day. For multiple reasons, but mainly it was the look on Slade's face.

His expression indicated that he'd rather have his fingernails removed with pliers than take part in their games, but from what I'd gathered, Hunter was completely inflexible with these mandatory family events. No one skipped unless they were dead or dying. End of story.

After breakfast, Kellan ushered everyone into the games room off the side of the cinema. During my explorations of the house, I'd only ever viewed this room from the doorway.

It was so much larger than I'd thought. There was a pool table, air hockey table, multiple pinball machines, and other old school arcade games, along with three massive screens on the far wall, that looked to be hooked up to every gaming system imaginable.

"Hunter's a closet nerd," Kellan whispered near my ear. "Before the company exploded into this worldwide conglomerate, he used to play *Call of Duty* for days with Soren, and we'd have to pry his fried ass out of the chair to force him to eat and shower."

As hard as I tried, I simply could not picture their entitled alpha as a gamer. The Hunter I knew was the epitome of polished businessman in a suit, always stern, bossy, and responsible. Although, every now and then he showed me a brief glimpse of his more primal side. A side which tattooed his claim and teased me to the edge of sanity.

"I have no doubt he's an amazing gamer." There was very little Hunter couldn't deal with to an expert level. Whatever issue arose, he had it covered, while the rest of us—okay, except Slade—floundered around with our heads up our asses.

Today, for the first time, he was dressed casually in sweats, which gave less gruff bossman and more *Daddy Alpha* vibes.

Crap, now I sounded like Kellan.

All the alphas wore sweats, but at least none of them were gray, meaning I might even be able to concentrate on the games.

Yeah. Probably not.

We ended up near the wall of screens, next to a large table and a shelf of colorful boxes. Kellan perused them with a serious expression, tapping his finger against his lips as he walked up and down before finally grabbing a green box. "Let's start with Scrabble," he said, and I was fairly sure I didn't want to know why he sounded so gleeful.

I also had no idea what Scrabble was.

"Uh, just as an FYI... I've never played a board game before." Might as well tell them now. Once it got started, they'd definitely figure it out.

Four alpha gazes rested on me, and I was hit with a spotlight in shades of green, blue, charcoal, and whiskey. Not to mention the dominance and scents that surrounded me.

It felt like a swift kick to the vagina, and I had no idea if I would survive boardgame day.

Thankfully, two of the four hated me, so they removed their stares just as fast, giving me a reprieve from the overwhelming intensity.

Kellan dropped the game in the middle of the table and reached out to pull me to his side. "I figured, which is why I chose a game with only four players. You can be on my team."

"The others don't need a team?" I asked, looking between them.

Finley remained expressionless, his arms crossed over his chest, stretching his white shirt to the full extent of its capabilities. The massive bear didn't give much away, but his scent was bitter, indicating he was more than a little unhappy to be here.

Today, his eyes were flat, without the chasm of pain I'd seen on that first night.

"Kellan's the only one who needs help," Slade said, his tone so dry I couldn't tell if he was joking or not. "All brawn and no brains."

The dragon shifter sprawled into a large chair on one side of the table, and I noticed Kellan discreetly flipping him off when he wasn't looking. I barely managed not to laugh, because the last thing I wanted was to draw more attention to myself. Or get Kellan murdered.

Slade settled back, the legs of the chair groaning, and if there was ever an advertisement for the strength of furniture, it was this piece holding up to a near seven-foot-tall, buff-as-fuck dragon.

Finley reluctantly took the seat opposite Slade, leaving Kellan and I to sit across from Hunter, who was ignoring us all and unpacking the game.

I studied the board, noticing that it was separated into squares which were different colors, and some even had words written in them. It took a few seconds of silently sounding out, but I managed to figure out they said *Double letter score* and *Double word score*.

Hunter dropped a clinking bag in the middle of the board, and then handed out a small brown piece of plastic to each of the alphas.

"You guys know the rules of choosing the theme," Kellan said, rubbing his hands together. "Emme, think of a number between one and twenty. We'll each try and guess, and whoever is the closest gets to choose the theme."

Against my leg, Kellan pressed seven times, and I barely caught another laugh that would have given us away. "Yep, no worries. I've got my number."

Slade went first, in his raspy, slightly accented drawl that sent shivers down my spine. "Thirteen."

Finley was next with a flat: "One."

Hunter took a second to assess me before he drawled, "Eighteen."

Kellan was last of course. "My guess from the beautiful Shortcake is six."

Pressing my lips together to hide my amusement, I said, "My number was seven, so Kel is the winner."

Finley's calm broke as he groaned and rubbed a hand through his hair, sending the thick brown strands into disarray. "Ah fuck. Here we go. That bastard is always cheating. Every fucking games day. And now he's even roped the omega into it."

Kellan threw his head back and laughed, clutching his flat stomach. "Aw, come on, bro. It's too early to be a sore loser. If you weren't such a grouch, you could also have a mind meld connection with Emme."

Finley opened his mouth with a snarl, but Kellan interrupted him to add, "And the theme for the day is *Star Wars*. May the force be with you."

Hunter was the only one who looked pleased by this announcement, and I was reminded of his secret nerd-isms. "I don't know why it's necessary to have a theme," Slade rumbled with a huff that was heavily scented in ash.

"Got to add some spice to life, S. You know that."

Slade ignored Kellan, reaching out to pick up the clinking bag. He pulled out a square tile, and turned it around to show the letter "H." The others did the same, and when Kellan pulled out a B for his first letter, I swear steam seeped from Finley's ears.

His *Grouchy Bear* persona had never been more obvious and appropriate.

Hunter explained to me that whoever pulled out the letter closest to "A" goes first. I could only assume Kellan had cheated again, and I loved that he was riling them all up this way. Weirdly, I couldn't wait to see how this day ended up, especially since no one generally fucked with alphas. It was about to be a great lesson in humility for them.

"Okay, the aim of this game," Hunter continued explaining it all to me, "is to get the highest point score by using the letters you pick to form words across the board." He pointed toward the center tile. "You start here, and if you don't have a word initially, you can swap out some of your letters for others."

I was following along easily enough, but as soon as he mentioned forming words, I had a mini-panic attack. Even if I were a proficient reader, letters always mixed around the wrong way when I tried to spell, leaving me looking like an idiot.

Thank the goddess I was on Kellan's team and not on my

own. The thought of demonstrating my stupidity to these alphas, half of whom hated me, had bitter shame rising in my body until heat infused my cheeks.

Hunter, who'd been in the middle of explaining how letters held different values, stopped suddenly, and I was once again the center of their attentions.

"What's wrong, Shortcake?" Kellan took my hand, but I was too tense to unfurl my fingers. "Your scent went from sweet to bitter in seconds. What happened?"

My frazzled brain couldn't come up with anything but the truth. "I'm not great with words, sorry. I'm not going to be much use to you." Kellan's eyes softened, and before he could offer sympathy that *I really didn't want*, I added, "I've mentioned it before, but I haven't had much schooling. The best I can do is moral support."

Unable to meet their eyes, I stared at the board as if I were about to memorize it. In reality, I didn't want to see their expressions, which would either be filled with disgust or pity. Each equally as bad.

"Omega!" Hunter's command had my head jerking up to meet his storm-filled gaze. "You don't need to feel shame about what was stolen from you. And you don't have to worry about what you perceive as weaknesses. You were strong for far longer than most wolves would have survived. We see that. We see you. Now... if you feel uncomfortable, we'll choose another game."

Kellan offered his support in a squeeze of my hand, and to my surprise, none of the others looked disgusted by me. If anything, there was a complete lack of judgement from the table. No doubt they felt this way due to our scent bond, but it was my first real glimpse of support via a pack, and it was gloriously addicting.

I wanted more.

I wanted it all. And for a second I pretended it could be mine to keep.

"Thank you. I'm completely fine to watch you all play. Who knows, I might learn some new words, especially since I've never watched *Star Wars*."

I had heard of it at least, so that was something.

As I calmed, Hunter also relaxed, and that press of his dominance faded around us. "Okay, let's proceed."

Each of them drew out seven tiles from the bag, and Kellan placed ours onto that piece of plastic Hunter handed out before. *A stand.* His letters were E, I, J, H, X, Q, and a D.

After he arranged them, he let out a satisfied whoop. "That's a nice start."

He hadn't let go of my hand yet, not even when Finley made a point of glaring at our joined palms, his whiskey eyes finally swirling with emotions.

"Are you starting or not, pup?" Hunter grumbled. "You know I have the timer on, and you're almost out."

Kellan picked up four of the letters and arranged them on the center tile to spell out JEDI. When he was done, he sat back looking smug, while the other three shook their heads. "Oh," Slade deadpanned, "you just happened to pull *Jedi* as your first word? Do you know the statistical probability of that happening?"

My lips were pressed together so hard they were starting to hurt, while Kellan looked adorably smug. "I'd say it's a hundred percent probability based on today."

"Has anyone figured out how he cheats so seamlessly?" Finley demanded, looking around the table to the other alphas. His irate gaze even rested on me for a second.

"It's pure skill," Kellan said around a chuckle. "You know it. I know it. Everyone knows it."

"I know I'm going to put my foot in your fucking a—"

"Twenty-four points," Hunter interrupted, jotting the figure into a little notepad I hadn't noticed until now. "First word gets a double point score."

Kellan flashed me a slow smile, leaning closer to murmur in my ear. "Who do you think will flip out first? Want to place a bet?"

A snort of laughter finally escaped, and every head snapped in our direction, leaving me barely able to resist pressing my face into Kellan's neck to hide.

Thankfully, they moved on to the next turn without comment, and I leaned closer and breathed right into Kellan's ear. "Finley."

Kellan's cheeks had to ache with how hard he grinned, and as he looked between his pack, he murmured, "Hunter."

The entitled alpha heard him and pointed a finger straight in his face. "Don't fucking start or I'll let Fin free on you and you'll be the one wearing the board this time."

"It's our third Scrabble board," Kellan said in a pretend-whisper, like it was a secret.

Slade had the next turn, and he used the D in JEDI for the word DARK.

"Eleven points," Hunter said, jotting his score down as well.

Both Kellan and Slade had chosen more tiles from the bag after their turns, so they always had seven on their plastic stand. After a while, I started to understand how it all worked. They used a combination of the letters on their stands and the free letters on the board to build words, with the aim to get the higher valued letters on the squares that were either double or triple points.

It astonished me how smart all four of them were, as they continuously found ways to create *Star Wars* words with seven random letters, half of which I'd never even heard of, though that might have been due to the theme.

They also argued. A lot.

Mostly about whether a word was acceptable under the rules, and in most cases Hunter had final say. It was enjoyable watching them play, and by the time they finished, Kellan was the winner by about forty points with the word TROOPER.

They moved on to game two, which was fantasy-themed Monopoly.

I'd heard of this game, and didn't refuse when they asked me to join in this time. They gave me first choice of game pieces, and I had to ask, "Who usually picks the wolf?" There was only one wolf, along with a dragon, bear, unicorn, magic wand, cauldron, yeti, and a phoenix.

The alphas all looked at Hunter, and I wasn't surprised. "I'm the entitled leader," he said with a shrug. "I get the wolf."

By instinct, I found myself holding the silver figure out to him. "I don't want to take your piece. I'm happy with the unicorn."

I was fairly sure that wasn't the first time I'd been nice or compromised with these alphas, but they acted like I'd discovered gravity as they fell into silent shock.

Hunter wrapped his palm around my hand, gently closing it over the wolf. "You're the wolf, little omega."

A buzz ran through our joined hands and up my arm, and I couldn't find the strength to pull away until Hunter released me.

While I got myself under control, the others chose their pieces, and all of us started on the GO square. Hunter and Kellan explained roughly how this game worked, and it seemed straightforward enough. I had no idea why there was so much tension in the group as they eyed each other before the first roll of a die.

It started out normally enough, with everyone rolling, moving their figures, and if they landed on a property, buying them up. Kellan picked up a lot quickly, but so did the others, while I had two measly cards in my possession, and a dwindling cash pile.

It turned out that if you didn't own the properties, you had to pay to stay there, which ate through your money fast.

After thirty minutes of intense play, I landed on one of Kellan's properties that he'd just put two houses on, and counting out my money, for the first time I didn't have enough to pay.

"Shit, does that mean I'm out?" I stared sadly at the board. "I'm really fucking bad at this."

"You can stay for free—"

Hunter interrupted Kellan with a growl. "No cheating, even for our little omega. She's out."

Golden's face fell as he reached out a hand for me. "Want to borrow some money, pretty girl? I'm sure we can work out a suitable arrangement for you to pay it back." He waggled his eyebrows, and I snorted out a laugh.

Shaking my head, feeling stupidly happy even as the biggest loser of this game. "Thanks, Kel, but I'm fine to watch you all battle it out."

His lips brushed across my cheek, and as heat coursed through me I completely forgot about Monopoly. My wolf whined, and I felt the other alphas flinch, even though I'd never made an external sound. Kellan pulled away with a low, purring rumble from his chest.

The game continued, and I was stupidly invested in the outcome.

After about an hour, only two remained with a real chance, and when Finley landed on Kellan's property loaded with maximum hotels, he cursed loudly. "I swear to the goddess you've got this shit rigged."

Kellan held his hand out and wiggled his fingers. "Pay up, buddy. You want to stay at Hotel de Kellan, you've got to pay your dues."

Finley slapped the money into his brother's hand. "It was a shithole anyway. I'm leaving you a one star on Yelp."

By now I'd picked up on Kellan cheating once or twice. He was so fast that it was only from my angle beside him that you'd see his sleight of hand. He had it down to a fine art, which was driving Finley bananas.

Kellan spent a full minute slowly counting Finley's rent as if to ensure he hadn't been shortchanged, while the bear grew grouchier and grouchier. When it was Kellan's turn, he rolled a six, which landed him on the final property he needed to own the full side of the board. The most expensive side. Which was the exact straw that broke the bear's back.

Finley lurched to his feet, and as the bear launched himself across the table, Hunter was at my side, yanking me out of the way. An echoing crash rang in my ears, and by the time I looked around Hunter's protective stance, Kellan was sprawled on the ground, and the whole table was on its side, pieces of the board scattered across the wooden floors.

Finley's chest heaved as he stomped his foot right in the middle of the Monopoly board, tearing it in two. "If you keep fucking cheating, I will kill you, Kellan," he raged, before snarling and marching from the room.

The other three were quiet for a beat, and then to my fucking surprise it was Slade who broke the silence with a rumbly laugh. Just one laugh, and it felt like he'd punched me in the gut. His low burst did things to me that I couldn't explain, even as he immediately returned to his regular stoic self.

Kellan dragged himself up off the floor howling and looking pleased that he'd managed to achieve exactly what he'd been aiming for. Chaos and carnage.

Meanwhile, I was still stunned by the dragon shifter. I decided then and there that I wanted to hear Slade laugh one more time.

Just once before everything came to an end.

CHAPTER 34

My phone woke me early the next morning, and I reached out blindly to grab it, answering before I even checked who it was. It wasn't as if many shifters had this number.

"Hello," I mumbled, attempting to pry my eyes open. My room was so dark it felt like the middle of the night.

To my surprise, it was a voice I didn't recognize barking crisply down the line, "Ah, yes. Good morning, Omega Emmeline Anders. It's Beta Jones Shaw here. I'm sorry to disturb you."

Lifting the phone from my ear I squinted at the number and saw it was coming from the Reeves guardhouse. *What in the...?*

"No, you didn't disturb me. Is everything okay?"

"We had a delivery arrive this morning from one Omega Chelsea Thenguard." Jones sounded far too fucking chipper for whatever *ass crack of dawn* time it was.

Chipper and a stickler for the rules as he used every proper title at his disposal. *Omega Chelsea.* It took my sleep-addled brain a few seconds to recall Chelsea saying she'd leave books on omegas with the guardhouse. I cleared my throat. "Amazing, thanks for letting me know. I'll head down to collect the delivery later this morning. If that's okay."

"As soon as possible would be great. There's not a lot of space in our guardhouse. See you soon." The line went dead, and I'd have laughed but I was already half asleep.

Kellan had kept me up watching scary movies half the night, and I desperately needed a few more hours sleep, but as I lay there I couldn't help but ponder over what was in those books. After ten minutes of trying to catch more sleep, I gave up and dragged myself out of bed and into the shower.

When I finished brushing my teeth and washing my face, I dressed in jeans, a different hoodie from yesterday that somehow still smelled like Kellan, and checked the time.

It was just past five, the lingering darkness thanks to the continued rain. The worst of the storm had passed yesterday afternoon, but it wasn't completely done with Golden Claw.

A glance out the window indicated it was between cloudbursts, and I decided now was as good a time as ever to make a break for the guardhouse. Rushing downstairs, there was no sign of the alphas, which wasn't a surprise since this was the time they usually got in a gym session before work or hockey.

Out the front door, cool winds whipped around me as I hurried down the stairs. There was no sign of life in the street, and I found myself curiously staring at each house as I passed by. As much as I'd enjoyed games day yesterday, I was also looking forward to a family bonfire night where I could sit back and observe the dynamics of these four interconnected families.

Living in such proximity to family could either be a dream or a nightmare, depending on your family. I hoped none of them were like my mom. Cora had already mentioned that

Hunter's dad wasn't particularly the nicest, but his name hadn't come up during Kellan's rundown of their compound.

Halfway along the street, I started to worry that I should have let the alphas know I was leaving. Kellan especially, as he liked to see me before he left for training. I patted my pockets for my phone, only to realize I'd forgotten it on the bed when I raced out the door. *Shit!*

Now I really had to get back before they noticed I was gone.

As my lungs started to burn, I realized the street was longer than I'd remembered, and that it might be time for me to incorporate a touch of cardio into my life. My wolf pushed for me to let her out, giving me the distinct impression that I was embarrassing her with my wheezing.

It's too cold to get naked, but we'll run soon. I promise.

The best part about being here in a pack city was not having to keep her suppressed, and I wanted to take advantage of that as much as possible. But now was not the time.

The clouds grew heavier as I raced along, and I wondered if I'd make it back before the sky opened up and poured its rage on me. The heavy breeze had a real feeling of winter about it today, even though we were only in fall.

When the booth finally came into sight, I softly wheezed in and out, trying to pretend that my lungs weren't about to expel from my chest. My wolf whined in embarrassment again. *It's okay. They'll never know.* She huffed, well aware I was full of crap.

One of the guards on duty noticed my approach and opened the gates to let me through to the other side. "Omega Emmeline."

The call came from a tall man with light blond hair, fine lines on his face, and a slim frame. He walked briskly toward me wearing the navy uniform, his with multiple patches on the shoulders, which looked like awards and commendations.

Jones was well decorated, and I wondered what he'd done before he guarded the family compound. Maybe he was, or had been, part of one of the enforcer squads.

"Beta Jones," I replied, hiding my smirk at his formality. "I'm here to pick up the books."

Relief cracked his hard features, his reaction stronger than I expected. "I debated contacting Alpha Hunter to confirm the delivery was acceptable, but it's his workout time, and he prefers not to be disturbed unless it's an emergency."

Before I could think about it, I patted his arm hoping to reassure the agitated shifter. To my surprise, he didn't jump away. A beta as stringent with protocol as Jones would usually do anything to avoid touching another pack's mate.

Especially his boss', but whatever... it was my fuckup anyway.

"Follow me."

I stayed close as he led me into the hut. There was another shifter sitting inside who was less powerful, and his animal had a distinct cat feel. Still a beta, but a weaker beta lion. "Ms. Anders," he said, jumping to his feet. "I'm Harry. It's nice to meet you."

Harry looked even younger than me, his face still round with the flush of youth. He was cute, with curly red hair and hazel eyes. "Nice to meet you too, Harry. Thanks for keeping an eye on this place for the pack. It certainly makes me feel safer to know you guys are out here."

Harry blushed, and Beta Jones patted me on the shoulder firmly, until I glanced down with my eyes widening.

Did this guy have a death wish?

My touch had been a mistake, but this was an extended and firm assault on my shoulder. The alphas were going to flip out when they scented him on me.

I took as big a step back as I could in the small hut, breaking his hold. It occurred to me that I was out here with two strangers and had unintentionally put myself into a dangerous position. I didn't even have my phone to let the alphas know where I was.

"I'd love to grab the books and head back to the house," I said, attempting to keep my voice steady. "The alphas are waiting for me."

There was no reason for them to know that I hadn't told anyone. Even if logically speaking, had an alpha known about this, one of them would be with me.

"Right, they're over here." Jones wandered toward the main desk and leaned down to grab a large hessian bag with black handles. It looked heavy as he hauled it up onto the table, and I was mostly relieved to know it existed and this wasn't all some ruse to lure me from the safety of the pack house.

"One of us can carry this back with you," he said, eyeing the bag. "It's quite heavy."

Bad idea! Abort. I shook my head. "Oh, no. I'm stronger than I look. I'll manage just fine. Thanks though."

He wore a dubious expression, his eyes narrowed on my rather uninspiring biceps as he handed the bag across. The solid weight settled in my hand, but it wasn't unmanageable. At least not if I took breaks hauling it back. Glancing inside, I saw at least a dozen thick books which would take me two lifetimes to read, but I couldn't fault Chelsea for effort.

"This is great, thank y—"

A loud crash shook the booth, and I almost dropped the heavy bag on my foot when I found myself pinned against the wall by Jones.

He pulled a gun out and stood between me and the door.

"Beta Harry, get out there and investigate," Jones snapped,

his stronger dominance leaving Harry no choice but to jump to his bidding.

The younger shifter hesitated briefly, eyeing the way I was pinned. "You shouldn't touch her again, sir. She belongs to Pack Reeves, and we were thoroughly warned by Alpha Hunter."

Jones' voice was harsh. "They'll understand in these circumstances."

Harry's eyes met mine, and I wanted to beg him not to leave me alone with Jones. My creep radar was going nuts, as I tried to figure out what situation I'd wandered into.

Begging wouldn't help though; Harry couldn't disobey a command from a more dominant shifter, not without a fight. I wouldn't get this poor kid killed because I'd screwed up.

"She doesn't like you being that close," he finally said as he raced out the door.

Jones didn't move, so I shoved against him. "He's right. You're too close. Back up."

The only response I got was a growl as his scent grew muskier, indicating his wolf was in control. He leaned closer to my throat, breathing deeply, and I was in full-on panic mode now. "What's an unmated omega doing wandering around on her own anyway?"

Goddess be damned! This was bad. I might not know exactly what was happening, but Jones acted like a wolf who'd lost control of his beast. Omegas could do this to other wolves, completely unintentionally of course, which didn't change the end results.

"They're going to kill you," I growled back at him. "You know that, right?"

He snarled, and he was so close that it echoed in my ears. "Not if they never find you. There's a lot of packs looking for you, Emmeline, and they're all willing to pay *very well* for your time and company. I heard you wanted to escape the alphas. I'm offering you a chance right now."

I forced my terror down and breathed slowly, calming my mind as I ran my gaze over the office in search of a weapon. On the desk I noticed the phone, which had to connect to the pack house. I swept over it quickly not wanting to draw attention to the device.

"I'm not trading one prison for another that might be worse," I told him, trying to keep him distracted and talking. "This isn't about helping me. It's about selling me to the highest bidder."

He didn't even bother to deny it. I had no idea how he had this planned, but he must have been ready and waiting for an opportunity to grab me, and I'd played right into his fucking hands.

Refusing to fall into my fate without a fight, I jerked my leg up and kneed him straight in the balls. When he dropped, I landed another kick to his head, before I dove for the phone. In the same instant I yanked up the receiver and hit the button that said *Reeves Pack*.

Jones recovered near instantly, plowing into me and knocking the phone from my hand as I hit the ground. There'd been no time to hear if anyone had answered, but maybe there was a chance they'd hear the struggle before Jones hung up.

I let loose a guttural scream, shouting for help as Jones came for me again. I dodged his first strike, but the second slammed into my chest, sending pain shooting through my ribs. Pushing back to my feet, I didn't wait around, racing out the hut door while Jones hung up the phone.

The black gates were closed, barring me from the safety of the street, but I still screamed in case anyone was close enough to hear me. Alphas especially had exceptional senses.

Sprinting away from the guardhouse, I worried I was being

herded into another trap, but I didn't have many options. Harry hadn't returned yet, and I prayed to the goddess that he wasn't hurt thanks to this asshole's scheme.

Heavy steps pounded behind me, and unlike my unfit ass, Jones was fast and trained. "Help!" I kept shouting, but there was no indication anyone was out and about in the compound yet.

Knowing I'd never outrun him, I reached out and yanked hard on a low hanging branch, breaking it off and spinning to smash the limb against Jones, who'd been right behind me.

The beta shifter flew back, and I was proud of myself for landing a solid shot. It wasn't enough to do any real damage, but it would give me a couple of minutes head start while he healed.

Changing directions, I raced back to the guard booth and the phone that remained my best chance of survival. I couldn't outrun this shifter, and the compound was far enough from town that I'd never make it to anyone else anyway.

I panic-gasped when the booth came into view, my screams dying off as I gave this new plan my entire focus. When I raced inside, I slammed the door closed and flipped the lock. Propping a chair under the handle, I grabbed the receiver again and hit the house number. It rang in my ear, and I pressed myself against the door, bracing my feet on the nearby table.

"Come on, pick up. Come on, alphas. Come on. Pick up the fucking phone."

A heavy weight slammed against the door, almost shooting me across the room. Bracing myself again, I prepared for the next hit, my legs aching from the first impact.

Come on. Come on. Come on.

It was a continuous chant in my mind as a second hit

splintered the door. Solid as it was, it would only take one or two more hits before Jones made it inside.

This was my last chance.

No one was answering.

The one time I needed my pack, and they were nowhere to be seen.

Jones' scent grew stronger, and I barely choked back a sob as I looked for a weapon. He had a gun, which thankfully he hadn't used yet. I had to assume I was worth more alive than dead, which wouldn't remotely help me out of this situation.

There was nothing in the damn hut except a stapler.

Clutching the phone like a lifeline, I prepared for the final hit, as a roar thundered through the room. It was so strong that the foundation shook, and I had no idea what was coming or if I'd survive the fallout.

Please. Don't let me lose everything. I'm not ready.

CHAPTER 35

The guardhouse rattled so severely that I wondered if an earthquake had struck right when I needed it to, before remembering that would never be my luck. Nope. It was more likely Jones' backup.

Or... it was mine.

Goddess. Please be mine.

For the first time, I had a pack behind me, and even though we weren't on the best of terms, they had made it clear that for the time being I was Reeves' property.

They wouldn't take my attempted abduction lightly.

There were no more hits to the door from Jones, and needing to know what was happening, I removed the chair and unlocked what remained of the reinforced door. When I stepped outside, the shaking intensified, and I slowly rounded the corner of the hut to find the gate was open.

Wait... it wasn't open. It'd been torn from its hinges, the metal lying in tangled heaps with two wolves holding Jones down in the wreckage. Relief hit me hard and fast as my legs weakened. *Hunter and Kellan.*

Their black and tanned coats were sprinkled with blood

and rain as they tore into the beta shifter, and by the time I raced over to them, there was nothing besides a few scraps of blood and bone left.

Two feral wolf gazes lifted from the bloody mess and stared at me, and the sky chose that moment to open up and pour rain on us.

With all the adrenaline racing through me, I barely felt the cold.

Run or stay? I had no idea how far gone these alphas were, devolved to their baser instincts. Would they try to claim me in their primal state? Not that it even mattered—I'd never be able to outrun them. All I could do was face whatever came next.

Hunter stalked forward first, a dark demon with his brother protecting his back. The air shimmered with their dominance, and even an idiot would see that they were hunting me down. I tried to back away, but my feet wouldn't listen. My limbs trembled as I clenched my fists at my sides, ignoring the ache in my face and ribs. Jones had got in a few decent hits, but there was nothing so serious I wouldn't heal in a few hours.

When Hunter reached me, his beast stood near my sternum; terrifyingly deep rumbles rocked his chest. Shivers raced over my body, and every part of my system screamed danger.

What was I supposed to do? Should I lower myself? Not look him in the eyes? I had no idea of the protocol when an alpha alpha'd out, but if he was anything like my mom's pack, I only had seconds before I became the next victim.

Bending, I was about to kneel when Kellan growled, halting me in a weird half-crouch. "I'm really fucking confused," I whimpered, trying not to meet either of their blazing gazes. "What are you going to do? What do I need to do?"

Maybe I should just pass out and hope for the best. It wasn't much of a survival instinct, but at least I didn't have to make a decision about what to do next.

Hunter shifted back to his human form, and alpha energy washed over me in a wave of mocha so strong that it almost pushed me to my knees anyway. Kellan wedged his huge body under my arm to keep me standing, and I hugged his thick, warm fur. His chest rumbles turned softer, almost like a purr, as I used his strength to keep my shaking legs upright.

As I stared at the furious, naked alpha before me, and hugged into the wolf alpha under my arm, I accepted that they weren't going to hurt me. At least not today.

I don't have to fight anymore.

Jones hadn't taken me, and I wasn't in the hands of a sadistic alpha pack who thought it was okay to buy omegas.

Heat burned my eyes, and if Kellan had been a normal wolf I'd have crushed him with my embrace. "Thank you," I murmured over and over into his pelt. "Thank you for coming for me."

Hunter still hadn't said a word, his face wreathed in such fury that he looked like an immortal god risen from the sea to smite the world. This time though, I knew his fury wasn't directed at me.

When he held out his hand, I didn't hesitate to move closer. His touch was surprisingly gentle, the burn of his energy heating my icy fingers as he pulled me closer. "Mate," he finally rumbled, dark eyes blazing into me as his alpha retained control.

Instinct guided me as I said, "I'm okay, Alpha. He didn't hurt me."

Hunter's expression tightened, his free hand gliding over my side, pausing on my aching ribs. "He didn't *seriously* hurt me," I amended. "And you kept me safe by destroying him. The threat is dead."

I had no idea if they'd discovered anything useful from the beta before he was torn to pieces, but now wasn't the time to worry about it.

Kellan's scent wrapped around me as he shifted back and held me in his arms. His touch was gentle, like he feared hurting me, but I was desperate for more.

I wanted them to wrap me up so tightly that the pain and fear vanished. I wanted to be surrounded by their scents and burned in the heat of their dominance. I wanted to fall apart between them.

"Pretty girl, you took twenty fucking decades off my life," Kellan rasped against my skin, sounding absolutely wrecked as he buried his face in the space between my neck and shoulder. "What were you thinking leaving the house without us?"

A deeper snarl ripped from Hunter, who had yet to speak a full sentence. Maybe he was afraid of reaming me a new one when I was vulnerable from an attack, or maybe it was his beast in control, with verbal communication the weakest part of a wolf.

The rain didn't ease up, leaving the three of us completely soaked. Not that the guys had any clothes to worry about—a fact I was trying my best not to think about.

Without warning, Hunter bent and slipped one arm under my legs and the other behind my back, hauling me up into his arms and carrying me wedding style. He set off fast, and unlike my pathetic jog toward the guard house, he didn't huff a single heavy breath as he returned us to the pack house in record time, a grim-faced Kellan by our side.

Inside, Kellan left me with a kiss on the cheek and the promise he'd see me soon, while Hunter took me upstairs. We ended up on the third floor, which I'd been avoiding like my life depended on it. There were only two doors up here, and he bypassed the one with Slade's distinct, smoky scent, striding to the other.

When we entered his room, it was a huge space, dominated in the center by the largest bed I'd ever seen. There was also a sitting area and small office setup in the corner. Everything was decorated in charcoals and blues, and it *felt* like Hunter, especially with his mocha scent permeating the air.

The tight ball of tension I'd been holding in my chest since the attack eased. "Did you find Harry?"

"Dead," Hunter said shortly as we entered his bathroom, also decorated in shades of blue.

My chest clenched as I recalled the cute redheaded beta. *This is my fault.*

My fucking fault.

Fighting the darker emotions that threatened to drag me under, my voice came out flat and broken. "How did they get this organized so quickly? There's no way he could have known I'd come alone or so early, but he was ready for me."

The heat of Hunter's skin flared until it burned against mine, and it was clear that he was still far too out of control for this conversation. If anything, I needed to calm him before he went full feral alpha again.

He yanked on the shower lever with so much force I was surprised it didn't rip from the wall. When the water was warm, he stepped under the stream, and I flinched as the hot stream beat against my chilled skin. After my body adjusted, I tipped my head back and let the cleansing stream wash over me, while waiting for Hunter to set me on my feet. Instead, he took a seat on the large bench running along one side of the stall, keeping me firmly in his lap.

When he dropped his head back against the tiles, I stared at the strong lines of his neck, tracing a path up his bronzed skin until I reached his eyes, which were closed. The tension in his rugged features remained present, but as we sat there in a silence that should be uncomfortable, his anger eased.

"We almost lost you today, Emme."

The husky rumble of his voice had my eyes burning.

"We thought you'd run at first. The phone was on the bed, no note left to explain what happened or where you'd gone."

"I'm sorry," I rasped, feeling like the biggest idiot. "The guardhouse called and woke me up saying that Chelsea had left books for me. I knew she was dropping them off, so I didn't even think anything of it. You were all in the gym, and I figured I could race down and grab them and get back before anyone noticed. I stupidly forgot my phone—I'm still not used to carrying one around—and I honestly never expected your guards would be a danger to me."

Hunter's arms tightened and I was shocked when he lifted me so he could bury his face against my neck, breathing deeply. "We let you down, little omega. I'm the one who is sorry."

I didn't fight my strong need to comfort him, pressing my hand against his cheek and dragging my thumb down the scruff of his facial hair. "I promise, you did not let me down. You were there exactly when I needed you. You saved me and killed that asshole."

His nose traced gently across my throat, and I felt a pulse under my ass as his cock jerked. It was a good thing I remained clothed, because I wasn't sure I'd be able to stop him from taking me right now. I wanted Hunter as badly as he appeared to want me.

His teeth scraped across my skin in this deadly game we played. He only had to shift to his wolf canines and he'd break the skin, claiming me in his bite.

"I need you to tell me everything that happened. In full detail."

I almost missed his question, which felt like a splash of cold water against my heated libido. "Beta Jones called and woke me just before five. He said Chelsea had dropped off some books for me."

I detailed everything, including how he'd touched me, and his abrupt order to Harry. When I explained how my ribs got injured, his chest rumbled hard enough to jolt said ribs before he forced himself to calm once more.

"I smashed him with a branch, which gave me time to get back to the booth. If they got to Harry, he must have had at least one other shifter out there waiting, so I'm extra thankful I doubled back to the guard's hut."

Hunter nodded his agreement against my skin, and I gasped when his lips pressed to my throat, lapping up the water. "I'm never letting you out of my sight again, little omega."

I already knew this was going to heavily impact my future plans to escape this pack. They'd be all over me now, ensuring I was never alone again. But as Hunter's lips moved down the neckline of my soaked hoodie, I found that at this moment I didn't care all that much.

CHAPTER 36

Hunter dragged his hand over my breasts, kneading them through my hoodie, and I groaned at the sensation his rough touch stirred inside me. He cupped my throat, and when I caught a glimpse of the *MINE* with those claiming wolf's teeth, my core clenched hard. The primality of his claim was enough to have me slick and in need of my alpha's touch.

Against my skin, he whispered, "I'm going to strip you bare now, Emme. Then I'm going to taste and mark every inch of your perfect skin to assure my wolf you're here and safe."

He wouldn't get a protest from me.

Desperation guided my actions as I reached out and wrapped my hands as far as I could around his thick biceps. Which wasn't far at all.

"Taste me, Alpha Hunter. Just no claiming bite."

His growl ripped through the room, but he didn't fight my command. "I promise, little omega. No claiming. Everything else is on the table though, so let me know right now if you have any hard limits."

I didn't. Just no claiming.

"Do your worst."

The final sliver of his patience snapped, and within seconds my clothes were torn away, scattering in tatters around the shower stall. His mouth was on my breasts before I caught my breath, licking and biting across the smooth skin until he sucked my right nipple hard. His teeth pressed around my areola firmly enough to leave a mark, but he didn't break the skin.

He moved on to the left and I cried out at the sensation, my hands buried in his hair. He marked my body as he nipped and sucked my skin into his mouth. All the while his hands gripped my ass hard enough to leave bruises.

My body was on fire, Hunter's scent filling me along with his branding touch. The pulsing throb in my core was enough to undo me, and I had to squeeze my thighs together to try to ease the ache. It barely scratched the surface.

Apparently, there was only one touch that would make a difference today: *Hunter's.*

My head filled with a pleasant haze as he dragged me from the shower and, soaking wet, headed in the direction of his bed.

We didn't make it.

He took me down to the carpet, his massive body covering mine as he licked up the side of my neck. The feel of his weight pressing me into the floor, along with the scrape of his five o'clock shadow over my throat, had me hovering on the edge of an orgasm.

Hunter was savage, devouring every inch of skin he got his mouth on. He marked both sides of my throat, and he was the one rumbling when his hand wrapped around my neck, collaring me with his claim. "Mine."

That snarl vibrated all the way to my center, and I was

sobbing as I clenched around emptiness. "More. Hunter. Please... I need more."

He slid his mouth slowly down my chest and onto my stomach as his gaze remained locked on me. "Eyes on me, baby," he commanded, and I was helpless not to obey. "Tell me what you want."

"Hunter." A whine escaped as I clawed at his arms.

"Say it, Emme. You're going to have to *use your words*." His kisses slowed, even as my nails bit into his shoulders.

"Please touch me. Please, for the love of everything holy, make me come."

A low rasping laugh was my response. "You want my mouth on your cunt, baby? You want me to devour that sweet slick dripping down your thighs? You want me to eat you like you're the last shifter on Earth?"

This alpha and his dirty *dirty* mouth. I fucking loved it.

"Yes," I gasped. "Yes. Please eat me like you're desperate for me."

"I am desperate, my sweet omega." His entire body rumbled so hard it vibrated me into the soft carpet, and then his mouth was on my core. As he flattened his tongue and licked me from my ass to my clit, I cried out and held on for fucking life.

He slid his tongue inside me and lapped at my arousal, devouring me like he'd die if he had to stop. He was frenzied, a purring rumble of satisfaction seeping from his chest as I screamed through my first orgasm. The pleasure slammed into me with such force that I lost my breath, and dots danced across the edge of my vision.

"Fuck, baby," Hunter growled. "This perfect, pretty pussy belongs to me." My core clenched violently at those words, extending the orgasm, but Hunter didn't give me a chance to recover.

He slid two thick fingers inside me and curled them up, fucking me hard and fast, while his tongue circled my clit. It was a maddening stroke round and round, and I wanted to thrust in time with his fingers, but his weight kept me pinned until my bruised ribs ached from the force. Not that I cared, I wouldn't have asked Hunter to stop even if one of my ribs popped out of my skin.

Using the hand not fucking me into my next orgasm, Hunter played with my nipples, rough calluses biting into the sensitive tips. I choked out guttural screams as deep spurts of pleasure built with each circle of his tongue.

His free hand moved higher, and when he wrapped that big palm around my throat again, a heavy, heady feeling pushed low in my body. I wasn't sure I'd survive the next orgasm, the building pressure more than I'd ever felt before.

Hunter was playing my body to the edge of sanity, and the fall might destroy me.

His pace eased up, keeping me hovering on the edge as his grip around my throat tightened until darkness streaked my vision.

I hovered and hovered, gasping and crying, until Hunter was once again thrusting hard and fast, curling his fingers, while his teeth pressed against my clit.

I exploded screaming his name. My release drenched my lower half, and for a second I wondered if I'd peed myself, but was too far gone to panic about it. When Hunter groaned and lifted his head, I noticed how shiny his lips, chin and chest were.

"What... what happened?"

He ran his tongue over his lips, closing his eyes with a look of absolute bliss. "You squirted, little omega. You fucking covered me in your sweet cum. Now I'll accept nothing less when I'm eating you."

He dropped his head again to lap at my core, and he was so thorough on my sensitive pussy that I was actually starting to build to an orgasm again.

When I was cleaned to his satisfaction, he kissed across my thighs, marking me with each touch, and at this point I no longer cared if these alphas killed me, I wanted his claiming mark. I wanted to be owned by them if it meant I got to feel this pleasure again, and drown in the complete consumption of my soul.

Hunter slowly slipped his fingers free, and my core clenched in an attempt to keep him inside. "Open," he commanded, and I mindlessly obeyed as he pushed his fingers inside my mouth. "See how fucking good you taste, sweet omega. Now you've got me hooked."

I did taste sweet, a hint of musk and sugar on my tongue, and now I needed to know Hunter's taste.

"My turn," I said, pressing my hands against his chest, and getting *absolutely nowhere* because he was a giant brute of a shifter. "I want to taste you as well."

He dropped his head to kiss across my tits once more, slower this time, without the burst of frantic need from before. He laved one nipple and then the other, over and over, until they were hard, sensitive peaks.

"What do you want to do to me?" he rasped against my marked skin. "Tell me exactly."

Oh goddess. My head spun, but I managed to find the words for him. "I want your cock in my mouth, Alpha. I want to mark and taste you as well. I... I need to."

He pushed off me, his arms braced on either side of my head. "Mark your alpha. Claim me so that no other does."

He flipped our positions fast, and I ended up sprawled on top of him. The scrape of our bodies, my soft curves against his hard muscles, had me craving a life that wasn't for me.

But at least I could hold on to these moments when it all went to shit.

Following Hunter's style, I pressed my lips to his throat, tasting him as my teeth scraped over his skin. He tasted so fucking good, a hint of coffee spilling into my mouth, and I whimpered, barely stopping myself from breaking the skin.

I marked him as he'd done to me, leaving bruises and bites across his skin. His hands draped over my back in firm touches, then he tangled his fingers in the wet strands of my hair, as if he needed an anchor.

I continued down his hard body, licking and kissing over his many abs, and when I reached his thick cock, it was velvet steel spanning halfway up his stomach.

"Goddess," I breathed, taking in the full length and width. "I'm going to choke to death."

For the first time since they'd rescued me, there was a lightness in Hunter as he laughed. "You were made for me, little omega. You can take it."

Wrapping my hand around his thick base, my fingers made it just over halfway as my tongue darted out to lap at the beads of pre-cum on the head of his cock. I moaned at how sweet he tasted. "Hunter, fuck. You taste so good."

He groaned and tightened his hands in my hair. "Baby, I'm not going to be gentle."

That was okay with me. Relaxing my jaw, I sucked on the tip, slowly moving my way along as much of his length as I could take. Which, granted, was not that much.

"Relax your throat," he ordered as I gasped with his thrusts. "Let me in, Emme."

Needing more, I relaxed my muscles, and another inch slid down my throat. I'd never had much of a gag reflex, which could be helpful, but not at his size.

Hunter's hands tightened at the base of my hair. "There's my good girl. You take me so well, baby. That's it," he crooned, and the soft praise traced down my spine like a warm embrace, surprising me with how much I liked it. Hollowing my cheeks, I rocked against him, sucking and licking his length. My eyes watered with his thrusts, and I barely managed to gasp in small breaths around his girth. "That's it, little omega. Oh, fuck. You feel so fucking good."

He rubbed his thumbs across the back of my neck, encouraging me to take more and more as he fucked my mouth. When I was sure I was about to pass out, he eased up, giving me a second to breathe. His pre-cum flooded my mouth, and I was desperate for more.

He started to thrust again. "I want you in my bed for the rest of our lives," he murmured with each pulse. "You're so fucking perfect, Emme. There's never been a shifter as perfect for me, and I already crave you. Actually..."

He released my hair to grip my thighs, and I pulled off his dick as he spun me around until my cunt was in his face, and he was licking and finger fucking me once more.

Returning to his cock, I tried to focus on giving him as much pleasure as he was giving me, but half of my attention was on riding his face into another orgasm.

"Hunter," I gasped around his hard thrusts, which choked me again. There was no stopping for either of us though, and I cried out around his cock as it grew harder, thickening and spilling into my mouth. His release slid down my throat and I took it all while my body shook apart into my own orgasm.

Cleaning him as thoroughly as he'd done for me, I realized that I was in big fucking trouble. One taste of Hunter would never be enough, and I had a feeling it'd be the same with all the other alphas.

If I walked away, I'd be leaving large parts of myself behind.

Parts I wasn't sure I could live without.

CHAPTER 37

FINLEY

My early morning skate cleared my mind, and I was no longer on the verge of shifting into my bear and rampaging through the city like a Japanese anime monster.

After my shower, I changed into sweats, knowing I'd be back here in a few hours for our Summit-opening game. When I grabbed my phone, I blinked at the twenty-five missed calls and as many messages. Swiping my screen, I pulled up Kellan's message thread.

Kel: Fuck! Someone attacked and tried to kidnap our omega. Get home, bro.

There was a twinge in my chest, and a red tinge descended over my vision. *Our omega.* I might not want her, and I might not like her, but to my bear, no one fucking touched what should be ours.

I didn't even bother with the rest of the messages, dialing Kellan's number as I stormed to my car. He answered on the second ring. "What the fuck happened?" I growled, my bear rumbling just below the surface and almost forcing the change.

"She's okay," Kellan said in a rush, and I slowed, taking a few deep breaths. If she was okay, then there was no need to get riled up. The normal day-to-day life of that chick was none of my business, even if I did still peel out of the parking lot too fast for my truck.

"I'll tell you everything when you get home, but just know that she's alive and unharmed. Hunter has her because his wolf was going psycho. I don't know what would have happened if she'd been badly hurt."

"What did she do to cause this? She tried to run, didn't she?" We both knew she'd fucked up somehow. It was her modus operandi after all.

Kellan fell silent and it was clear I'd gone too far during his crisis of almost losing her. "I'm on my way," I added in the heavy air. "See you soon."

He hung up without a word, and I had to reel my animosity in if I didn't want to lose my pack over this fucking omega. When I reached the family compound, the gate was a tangled mess off to the side of the guardhouse. Which was empty.

My speed picked up as I raced down the street, only to slam on the brakes when Kenzo hauled ass from his house and waved me down. I opened my window to my brother's concerned expression. "Is she okay?"

Apparently, I was the last to know about this attack, but at least I had the answers to that particular question. "Yeah, Kellan said she's fine. I don't know any details about the attack, I was just heading to the house for an update."

Kenzo rubbed a hand over his face and through his dark hair. "We all heard the crash and fighting, but by the time anyone made it into the street, Hunter was racing her into the house. For a second, I thought the worst..."

He cared about how this would affect me, but there was no need. As if losing an omega, I didn't even have, would break me more than I already was. "I'm assuming the council and enforcer squads will be here soon." It was standard procedure during an attack.

"Pretty sure they're already at your house. A bunch of cars raced past before, and I wasn't sure if I should get my girls somewhere safe or not. Why the fuck didn't you answer your phone?"

I hadn't even looked to see who else I'd missed calls from. "I was on the ice. I didn't know any of this until I checked my phone after, and I came right here."

He sucked in a deep breath, and then another, until his calmer spirit returned. "Okay, well, get to your house and find out what happened. You can update me later at the game."

I slapped a hand on his shoulder, giving it a squeeze. "Thanks for caring."

Kenzo shook his head like I was an idiot. "Brother, you're family. If you break, I break. And I'm not ready for that, so I need to make sure you remain whole."

My smile was brief and forced. "Pretty sure that ship has already sailed, but I admire your positivity."

He bestowed one of his all-knowing grins on me. "You'll see the truth one day. You might have been broken in the past, but you're kintsugi. *Repaired with gold.* You know that. You just have to accept the truth of who you are now, my friend."

The Japanese art of repairing their items with gold and proclaiming them better than the original had long fascinated me. Probably because in those brief moments when Kenzo called me kintsugi, I almost believed him. Or at least I wanted to believe him.

My brother returned to his house and mates, leaving me to head for home. Half a dozen cars were already parked out the front of our house, and I pulled into my normal spot in the garage, before striding up to the first floor with my gym bag slung over my shoulder.

Everyone was out back by the pool, standing in a large, noisy group of shifters. *Fuck.* It'd take us months to get their scents out of here.

My pack stood a little apart, with Kellan and Hunter on either side of the omega, who was pale and all but expressionless, staring into space, while a dozen or more men argued around her.

Slade was there as well, to the left of Hunter, with five members of his flight squad at his back. None of them touched him because they valued their lives, but clearly this was being taken quite seriously.

Ditching my bag, I strolled over to stand beside Kellan, my appearance interrupting the argument. A lot of the council members were here, including Warrick, Soren, Butler, Gerlason, and even Sissily Buttern.

She was the most dominant female in Golden Claw, and a giant pain in the ass.

For too many years she'd been trying to get her claws into Hunter, in the misguided belief that as the strongest alpha female she needed to command the strongest alpha males. She wanted our pack right or wrong, despite already having two alphas bonded to her.

If I'd had to place money on who was responsible for the attack on the omega, it'd be squarely on Sissily. Emmeline was the final piece to our quintet, and if we bonded, the power she'd command would be a direct challenge to Sissily's perceived spot as the top dog.

"Now that Fin has arrived, we'll go over everything again." Hunter's voice was a snap of command that shut everyone up.

Half the shifters lowered their eyes to the second-most dominant one in the room, while the dragon just smirked.

Not for the first time I was glad to be scent matched into such a strong pack. The four of us were enough, we didn't even need the omega.

I settled in beside Kellan, who avoided looking my way. It bothered me that he was still pissed, but I would make it up to him later. For now, I focused on Hunter as he detailed the series of events from the attack.

"Emme was woken just before five by a call from Beta Jones Shaw, one of our security guards. He told her that Chelsea had left a bag at the guard's hut for her, and since Emme had been expecting books from the omega, she thought nothing of it. We were in the gym, so she hurried down in the hopes of getting back before we finished. It was our guards who called her, and she trusted that they wouldn't hurt her. The fact that a traitor came into our employment will be dealt with swiftly, but for now we need to figure out who else was involved."

Emmeline just stood there, her body tense even as her face remained expressionless. I didn't know anything about the omega, but I'd seen trauma in the mirror before, and it was clear that while Hunter relived her attack, she had retreated into herself.

"Another of our guards, Beta Harry Stilson is dead," Hunter continued, and I felt a pang at the loss of life from such a young shifter. No matter what else happened here, he was the one who deserved justice and retribution. The omega was fucking fine. "His death will not go unpunished," Hunter echoed my thoughts, "even if it takes us months to track every last one of them down."

Kellan nodded. "Yep. We only made it in time to save Emme because he called us after he was ordered away."

With that statement Emmeline gasped, her face crumpling

as she rubbed her hand over her eyes. I hadn't noticed until now, but her hair hung in wet strands around her face, and she was dressed in ratty old sweats. "Harry saved my life," she choked out in a soft voice. She was generally filled with sass and attitude, but today she appeared dull and transparent. "Jones was one more hit from crashing through the door, and I wasn't strong enough to fight him off. I hit him as hard as I could with a tree branch, and he was only down for seconds."

The council started to shout questions, but Slade's rumble silenced them all in an instant. "My team will investigate any shifter who was in the area at the time of the attack," he said. "We have many new alphas and shifters here for the Summit, which will make it difficult to trace those out of place. Everyone is out of place."

Warrick started to pace close to where we stood. "Clearly whoever is behind this attack wanted to take advantage of the confusion of the Summit." A snarl ripped from his chest that made it sound as if he was taking this quite personally. *The fucking alpha she chose over us.* "I promised to keep Emme safe, and I'll be patrolling the streets with my squad for the next week to ensure nothing like this happens again."

Emmeline shot him a grateful smile, and it pissed me right off that she offered such a kindness to an alpha that wasn't even hers. She'd fallen right into their pack like they were her scent matches, while simultaneously rejecting us. There was a reason I believed her to be toxic to our pack dynamic, and she had proven it time and time again.

Hunter wrapped his arm around the omega, and I was surprised when she let herself rest against him. Their scents were intertwined, and upon closer inspection I could see faint remnants of bites and hickeys across her tanned throat.

Kellan had warned me that our entitled alpha had laid his claim after her attack. If his wolf went wild, he wouldn't be sated until she was safe in his arms. No doubt Emmeline took advantage of that situation, lapping up whatever Hunter offered, while walking away with no promises for a future.

They weren't bonded, that much was clear. She wore only superficial marks, which would fade soon enough.

"Is there a reason you haven't bonded her into your pack yet?" Sissily piped up, her voice dripping in condescension. "You'd save us all a lot of trouble if you kept your *omega* safe, and not a free wolf wandering around for all to scent."

If she bonded into our pack, our scents would mix and she'd wear our bites to warn all other shifters that she was off limits. We'd also be able to feel her through the bond and know when she was in trouble. Not that Emmeline gave a single fuck.

Kellan's voice grew uncharacteristically hard. "The fact that she's living in our house should be warning enough, and it needs to be known that we will destroy any shifter who touches our mate."

I hated the threads of sorrow in his voice. I needed Kellan's upbeat nature to keep me from drowning in my past, which was another reason to wish the omega had never ventured into our lives.

Almost everyone ignored Sissily, choosing instead to discuss their next course of action. I forced myself to breathe through my annoyance, hoping this wouldn't impact today's game. That had to go ahead, kicking off the season, and returning us to our normal routines.

"We will bring Harry's body to his family," Alpha Geralson said, his voice breaking. "He was a good kid, and I will be promising them that this will not go unpunished."

The scent of chocolate and honey grew stronger and deeper as Emmeline's sadness seeped through the room, and while technically she didn't do anything wrong, I wasn't about to cut her any slack. She might not have tried to run, but she should have let one of us know she was heading out on her own. She'd been warned of the dangers of being an unmated omega.

I wasn't about victim blaming, but it was hard not to argue that some fault rested with her. She was an omega and knew the dangers. Knew and ignored.

At some point Emme would be forced to choose her future, but it'd be too late for me.

I'd never bond her into the quintet.

Fucking never.

CHAPTER 38

Kellan and Hunter refused to leave my side.

After the other council members left, Slade took his squad out into pack lands to trace scents and investigate, and a company arrived to repair the gates. New guards came on to keep the street safe, but I never lost my personal bodyguards.

It only really hit me hours after how close I came to being taken and sold off. My years in the human world had diluted my instincts to the point that I'd forgotten how serious it was for an unmated omega in the cities. I'd feared my pack, yes, but had grown too complacent about everyone else.

Around lunchtime, I decided I was done moping around. "I'm going for a swim," I declared, and both alphas jerked toward me.

I was on the couch, a giant shifter on either side of me, and while the TV was on, none of us were paying it attention. "I know it's going to feel unsettled until we figure out who's behind the attack. But I can't live like this."

Hunter let out a frustrated growl. "We should have left Jones alive. I knew I fucked up the moment I tore his guts out, but when we scented your fear on him, my wolf wanted him dead."

I squeezed his thigh in what I hoped was a comforting gesture, all the while trying not to linger on his hard muscles. Muscles that reminded me of how absolutely destroyed I'd been under his touch earlier. We hadn't had sex—fuck, we hadn't even kissed—but it was still the most intimate and incredible sexual experience of my life.

Despite my best efforts, I'd fallen into a hard obsession over these alphas, and I wasn't sure I'd ever get out. "I don't blame you for reacting on instinct when that instinct was to save and avenge me. No omega could ask for more from her pack. Don't stress about who was working with him, since I doubt they'll give up. They will be back, and then we can take their asses down."

Kellan dropped his head back on the couch cushions. "The not giving up part is what worries me." My golden boy looked tired, and I wasn't particularly happy about it. "Hence why I'm not leaving your side until this is sorted."

There was another rumble from Hunter. "You have an hour until you need to be at the rink. Otherwise, you're going to miss your first game of the season."

I knew Kellan's response before he opened his mouth. "I honestly don't give a fuck. I love hockey, but I'd quit it today if I had to choose between playing and keeping Emme safe."

"Not a chance," I burst out quickly. "Honestly, I never want you to give up anything you love for me. I promise I'll be at the game watching you play today. Safe and sound and within your sight." Turning to Hunter, I added, "And if you have work to do, don't let me keep you here. I don't need to be babysat, especially not in the pack house."

Hunter released a dark, unamused laugh. "Reeves Industries will survive without me for a day or so. There's nowhere else I'd rather be than at your side, Emme. I'll be with you during the hockey game, and then tonight if you still want to work at Luxuria."

Work. My shift tonight had slipped my mind with everything else going on, but I needed the money. "Thank you both for being here. I'm not trying to sound ungrateful for your support and protection, it's just not what I'm used to."

Kellan wrapped me in his arms, dragging me half into his lap. "You better get used to it, pretty girl. Having one of us attached to you is your new normal."

The heat of his body combined with the heat of Hunter's gaze was an intoxicating experience. After the frenetic way Hunter devoured me upstairs, all I could think about was being sandwiched between these two alphas in a different way.

My fantasies were cut off when Kellan jumped to his feet and hauled me up over his shoulder. He took off through the house, and I was too stunned to offer any form of protest. The pool came into sight, and I barely had time to suck in a breath before he threw us both in, fully clothed.

When we resurfaced, I spluttered through coughing laughter and aching lungs, thinking about how dull my life had been before Kellan was in it.

"You said you wanted to swim." He wore a smug smirk as he kept hold of me in the deeper part of the pool. "And since it's a perfect warmup before a game, I figured I'd join you."

He kicked off toward my favorite spot under the waterfall. "I'm excited to see you play," I said, enjoying the silky water against my heated skin. "Who are you playing?"

"Greenville Red Pandas. We're always against another city's team during the Summit, and the other Golden Claw teams will play as well."

I'd had no idea there were other professional teams here,

but it made sense with the size of this city. "This Summit is on every year."

Kellan nodded, looking delicious with his hair wet and slicked back, water tracing down his tanned skin. "Yep, every year a bunch of alphas get together and start shouting demands, and all of them expect their wishes to be first on the agenda. It's mostly amusing, while simultaneously being annoying as fuck. Hunter usually loses his shit and punches someone, which is nothing on what happens if Slade attends."

"Does he try and kill off all the other entitled alphas."

I'd said it as a joke, but Kellan simply smirked. "Yep, that's exactly what he does."

"Is he really as scary as everyone seems to think he is? Or is it mostly reputation?"

I knew very little about Slade outside of his shifter animal, his hair and eye color, his excellent taste in road bikes, and his unmatched abilities in hand-to-hand combat.

Kellan's expression sobered. "Don't let the humane facade fool you. He's spent years cultivating his human side, but he was born a beast, and deep where it matters, he's got the cold-blooded heart of his kind. If you wrong him, he will destroy you without thought or remorse. Everyone here just knows better now than to wrong him."

A shiver traced down my body, and it had nothing to do with the cool water. "Warning duly noted."

A sense of relief crossed Kellan's face, as if he'd thought I would go out of my way to provoke Slade. I mean, it had entered my mind once or twice, but annoying him was not on my immediate to-do list. There were a couple of more pressing issues to deal with first.

For the next twenty minutes we played and splashed in the pool, with Kellan trying not to laugh at my very sad attempts to swim. "You shouldn't make fun of the orphan kid who had no loving family to teach her shit." I flicked water at him and forced my lips into a pout.

His expression fell as he dove forward, arms out like he wanted to hug me better. I threw my head back and laughed, which had him groaning. "That was just mean, Shortcake. I was about to start groveling on my knees."

The thought of him on his knees was enough to dry up my laughter, and I couldn't tell which one of us was bothered now. "Is... is it time for you to get ready for the game?"

Kellan remained close, his sweet breath washing over me as his palms traced slowly up the sides of my stomach. "Yes, probably," he whispered.

Neither of us moved.

I swallowed roughly against an internal pulse of need, which was so strong that if he'd let me go, I'd have sunk straight to the bottom of the pool. My limbs were unresponsive, mostly because my brain currently was too.

"Emme," he said with a rasp. "Please don't hate me for this."

I had no idea what he was talking about until his lips pressed against mine in a collision of need and desire, the force too great for either of us to resist. Not that it even crossed my mind to try.

With a gasp I wrapped my arms behind his neck, legs winding around his waist to bring our bodies closer. My head spun as his caramel-cinnamon taste exploded across my tongue, and I was craving more. *All.* I craved everything from Kellan.

A guttural sound ripped from his throat, and I felt the energy of his wolf shift closer to the surface, bringing dominance to crash against me. His hands bit into my ass as he held me against him, the hard length of his cock between us, which I was already rocking into.

"The entire house smelled like you and Hunter before," he groaned against my mouth. "Just about drove me fucking crazy. Especially when all I wanted was to feel you against me and know you were okay." I leaned back, needing to see his expression, only to find his eyes blazing with dark, violet energy. "There are no words to explain how I felt when we heard that scuffle and I knew you were at the other end of the compound. I wasn't sure we'd get to you in time. I died a thousand deaths in those moments, Em."

Needing this as much as him, I tilted my head to press my lips to his once more. Behind me, a door opened and footsteps sounded on the tiles. Kellan lifted his gaze in the direction of our intruder but didn't react, and a few seconds later when I smelled lavender, I knew it was Florence.

"I brought you both snacks, and your usual pre-game drink, Alpha Kellan."

Kellan shifted us around in the water so we could both see her drop a rather large tray on the table between the loungers. "I'm very happy to see you're okay, Emme," Florence added as she straightened. "Let me know if there's anything I can get you."

"Thanks, Flo. I'm doing just fine now, but appreciate your concern."

She waved me off. "We all love you here. Of course we'd be concerned. You're a part of the family."

I was pulled closer to Kellan as he hugged me in a tight squeeze. "She's not wrong," he said, his voice filled with so much warmth that I was immediately overwhelmed.

Florence fussed over us for a few more seconds, before hurrying off to finish her mid-day duties, leaving Kellan and I to pick through the tray of fruit, sandwiches, and pastries. Before we finished up, Kellan drank his green concoction that smelled like sadness and lawn clippings, while I ate the two chocolate eclairs, because we all had our roles to play here.

"I'm going to grab my gear now," he said as he pressed a kiss to the corner of my lips, sending butterflies through my stomach. "Meet you here in fifteen?"

"Yes. *Yep*. I'll just have a quick shower and change into fresh clothes."

Kellan's eyes twinkled at my clearly flustered appearance. "I've got the perfect shirt for you to wear today, Shortcake. I'll leave it on your bed."

He remained by my side as we walked up the stairs, dripping pool water over the immaculate floors. When he left me in my room, I headed straight for the shower, needing to wash and dry my hair in minimal time. Rushing through it all, I finished up by slapping on some makeup, happy to see I was less pale than this morning.

It bothered me to notice that most of Hunter's marks had faded from my skin. The visual of them felt like belonging, but alas, nothing was permanent on shifter skin except a mating bite. Oh, and the lovely ropey scar my mom left me with.

In my room, a teal, gold and white jersey sat waiting on the bed, and I slipped it on with my jeans and sneakers. It had the number twenty-two on the back and *Jackson* above it. Of course, Kellan wanted me in his jersey, his name claiming me as thoroughly as Hunter's collar tattoo.

Every part of me should be horrified by these alphas and how they'd wormed their way into my life and emotions, but as caramel and cinnamon scent surrounded me, all I felt was satisfaction.

My fucking wolf wanted to purr her pleasure, and it was only my annoyance keeping it at bay. *It's not forever.*

It couldn't be.

CHAPTER 39

On the inside, the hockey stadium was massive. Not that it didn't look like it from the outside, but it was even bigger than I expected. Bigger and absolutely packed. We'd driven here in Hunter's Range Rover, with a bouncy Kellan in the backseat, adrenaline for his upcoming game rocketing through him.

"Share some of your energy," I joked at one point when he rocked the car as we stopped at lights.

He'd leaned over the center console. "Wish I could, Emme. My parents would have certainly loved it, since I've always been this way. Far too much energy to contain."

Hunter had insisted I take the passenger seat, but I'd practically shared it with Kellan as he hung over me the whole drive anyway.

"He's the only one of us with a normal family," Hunter chimed in. "Hard to believe, I know."

It was equally hard to believe that Hunter Reeves was making lighthearted remarks and jokes. "I'm happy to help you murder any evil family members," I offered, only half kidding. It pissed me right off that these alphas had dealt with a variation of the same cruel, lonely shit as me. Maybe worse, if the depths of pain in Finley's eyes were anything to go by.

Kellan all but purred as he buried his face in my arm. "You say the most romantic things, Shortcake. I don't know what we did before you were in our lives."

Hunter even laughed at that, though he didn't comment further.

When we'd arrived at the stadium, surrounded by cheering shifters clad in mostly teal, gold, and white jerseys, I found true excitement flaring.

"There are more red jerseys than I expected," I said, leaning closer to Hunter after we took our seats.

He'd tried to force me into their corporate box, but I'd wanted to be close to the ice. Our seats were right behind their bench, center of the action.

Hunter took in the rows of red and gold jerseys. "Yeah, a lot of shifters travel consistently for the games. The puck wolves and bears especially."

I'd already learned those titles were reserved for the females who tried to bag hockey players, even if only for one night. The very thought of any of them being near Kellan... or even Finley, had me raging. Not that I had any right to care.

"When do the teams come out on the ice?"

"They'll be out for warmups soon."

I couldn't wait to see what warmups entailed... Was it mostly stretching and skating laps?

Lights flashed around the arena as music pumped, and I loved seeing all the shifters with their plastic cups of beer and plates of nachos settling into seats. Hunter got a lot of lingering stares from shifters not used to seeing him down here with the plebs. Or maybe it was the fact that he was the entitled alpha of the strongest pack in the city and looked freaking gorgeous in his charcoal suit.

This alpha controlled his space without saying a word, and the fact that all the seats around us remained empty felt like a testament to his strength and power.

"Would you like any food?" he asked, glancing over at a group of girls giggling nearby. They were spilling their beer and fries in an attempt to catch a first glimpse of the hockey players.

"Actually, I'd love snacks." Do not ask me where my giddy excitement came from, but like my first cinema experience, I was pumped to watch this game.

Hunter whipped out his phone and shot off a text message. I had no idea who he was messaging to bring us food. Probably one of his many assistants.

When the music grew louder, shifters started jumping up and down in the stands, waving their arms in a weird pattern. It was all fascinating, like I'd stumbled into another world.

A few seconds later, my phone and Hunter's beeped, and I opened it to find Kellan had messaged our group chat.

Golden Boy: *Image Attached*

Hunter ignored his phone and leaned over to stare at my screen. I almost forget to click the image, distracted by his energy licking down my skin. Swallowing roughly, I pressed the message and waited for it to load. A few seconds later, a snort of laughter escaped me.

Kellan had sent a picture of Finley standing in the middle of the locker room.

At first, all I noticed were his muscles... *so many muscles* encased by perfect, dusky skin. Like the other alphas, Finley was stacked, which I saw clearly because he only wore a pair of tight, white boxer briefs. Oh, and socks.

Hunter cleared his throat, and I was surprised by his low laughter. "Fin is going to murder him."

"Why? Because he sent this phot—" *Oh fuck.*

I'd been so focused on his broad shoulders and ripped muscles—yep, I was shallow—that I'd missed two important details in the picture. One: Finley was absolutely furious, his face menacing as he leaned toward Kellan. And two: right on the crotch of his underwear, over the impressive bulge, was my face.

My fucking face.

"What's happening? What's the point of Kellan doing this?"

I was startled to find Hunter looking amused. This alpha rarely, if ever, looked amused. "Finley is extremely superstitious when it comes to hockey," he explained, waving at the image. "Whatever socks and underwear he wears for the first game, he wears for the entire season. No wavering. We're lucky his superstitions don't go as far as not washing said items."

A closer look at the image revealed small bears all over his socks, with a word I couldn't read at the top. "So... Kellan made sure those boxer-briefs were all he had to wear today, and now he's stuck with my face on his dick for the full season?"

I wasn't sure if I should be impressed or mortified. I was pretty much a decent mix of both.

Hunter lost it as a burst of laughter escaped him, and if I'd thought we had attention on us before, it was nothing compared to now. Everyone in the vicinity stared at him like he'd just created snow from his tears. Or like an angel had fallen to Earth and now walked amongst mere mortals. Okay, that was how they usually looked at him, but the awe had certainly amped up with his display of amusement.

"It's really not funny," I grouched, feeling heat in my

cheeks. "Finley and I already have *all* the issues without Kellan piling on."

As his laughter faded, Hunter cupped my face. "Finley needs a shifter like Kellan to keep him from spiraling. Our bear has a lot of trauma in his past, and he'd fall into it without our golden wolf."

That settled my embarrassment, and I decided that if it took my face on his crotch to lighten the mental burden of Finley's life, well... I'd sacrifice for the greater good.

Hunter released me right as our phones chimed again.

Golden Boy: *Image attached* *smiley emoji* *wink face emoji* *heart eyes emoji*

Wondering what I was about to see this time, I opened it to find an image of Finley again, only this time Kellan had taken it without him noticing. And weirdly, he wasn't glaring any longer. If anything, he looked confused and sad as he stared down at his underwear.

"This will all work out," Hunter whispered near my ear. "Let the process take the path it needs."

My throat grew tighter as I nodded. Not that I had any idea what was going to happen in the future, or how anything would work out, but it hurt me when this pack hurt. I hated to see it.

Hunter leaned back in his chair, and my darker thoughts were cut off as he draped his arm behind me. They weren't super roomy chairs to start with, and he had already been half crowded into my side with his bulk, but now I was surrounded.

The heat of his dominance stirred my omega energy, and my wolf preened like a horny bitch. Both of us wanted his mouth on our skin again, which was a terrible idea.

A terribly great idea.

The more I entangled myself with these alphas, the harder

it got to remember the reasons I'd stayed away from here in the first place. I'd spent years running and hiding, and it would all be for nothing if I gave in now.

The stadium brightened and I almost forgot about Hunter's arm as the players emerged. Teal, gold, and white-shirted shifters zoomed out onto the ice, and the crowd screamed and cheered, jumping in their seats. These guys were celebrities, and it hadn't escaped my notice that I wasn't the only one wearing a shirt with Kellan's name and number on it.

In fact, most of what I saw in the stands were twenty-two *Jackson*, thirty-four *Thornton* for Finley, along with fifty-eight *Yamamoto* and eighty-four *Newton*. The players wearing those four numbers remained close on the ice as they skated around and waved to the crowd.

Kellan stopped at the glass where we sat, and without his helmet I could see the absolute joy written across his features. He'd never been more sunshine than he was on the ice.

He pressed his hand to the glass, and I barely resisted the urge to rush down the steps to return the gesture. Kellan tapped his hand to his chest and then blew me a kiss, before he skated off with so much grace it was hard to believe he wasn't flying.

He rejoined Finley and the two other popular-with-the-crowd players.

"That's Kenzo Yamamoto and Christian Newton," Hunter said as I watched their group, realizing number eighty-four was Kellan's friend from the bar. "Kenzo is Finley's chosen brother. They grew up together, and Christian is Kellan's best friend. They also grew up together, but don't have the trauma bond of Fin and Kenz."

Trauma bond. I'd always wondered if the bond part helped with the trauma part. I'd never had any bonds in my life to know. Plenty of trauma though.

I couldn't take my eyes off Finley and Kenzo as they fucked around on the ice, skating between cones, and racing up and down the rink. After a few minutes they dropped to the ground near our seats, and I lurched forward. "Uh, what's happening?"

Hunter chuckled, more relaxed than I'd seen from him before. "Got to warm up their groins."

They were warming up their groins alright as they spread their legs and humped the ice. Kellan lifted his head, threw a smirk my way, and I wished I could say I looked away. I did not.

Thankfully, before I combusted, they moved on to other stretches, drills, and skill work. It was telling how distracting our side was that I barely even noticed the Red Pandas warming up too. Neither team crossed the center of the rink, staying strictly to their side.

After a few minutes of antics on the ice, both sides returned to their locker rooms, and the anticipation grew in the stadium.

Everyone was ready for this game.

The first of the season.

"Are the entitled alphas from the other cities here?" I asked, relaxing against Hunter's arm, despite my best efforts to ignore it.

"Yep," he rumbled, sounding annoyed. "They're in the largest box over there."

He pointed toward a glassed area situated high over the center of the ice. Best seats in the house, except if you wanted to be down here in the action. "Should you be up there with them?"

"An entire game up there would have me wanting to throw myself through the glass just to escape."

I glanced up once more, and I swore I felt eyes on us from

that box. "Well, it's good that you're down here with me, then."

His arm flexed behind me, and my skin tingled from the contact. "Nowhere I'd rather be, little omega."

He'd said the same thing earlier, and as my heart pounded in my chest, I wondered how he could utterly destroy me with a single sentence.

The strobe lights went wild, and I focused on what was about to happen, right as the scent of toasted marshmallow hit me. I turned to find Slade dropping into a chair in our row, not the one directly beside me, but the next one along.

In one of his hands was a giant plate of nachos and in the other a beer.

Slade was who Hunter had been texting about food.

Dragon delivery at our service.

CHAPTER 40

If you'd told me a week ago that I'd be sitting between two of my scent-matched alphas, watching the other two destroy the Red Pandas in ice hockey, I'd have called you crazy.

It turned out to be one of the most enjoyable afternoons I'd had in years.

Maybe ever.

The food and beer didn't hurt either, and somehow Hunter ensured there was always a fresh, cold cup in my hand—despite him and Slade never leaving their seats.

Kellan and Finley were brilliant on the ice. Kellan scored a hat trick, and Finley spent half of his time crushing the other team into the glass. He ended up in the penalty box more than once, as the crowd screamed *eliminator* over and over.

During the game, Hunter explained that Kellan was an offensive player, faster and more inclined to score, while Finley was a defenseman, bulkier and more inclined to crush his opponents into the side of the rink.

Both were talented and skilled, and while Kellan's main job

might have been to score, he wasn't shy about bashing players into the glass either.

"It's a violent sport," I said with a laugh, wincing as a blood-spattered panda hobbled off the ice. The fight wasn't over though. Two players continued to punch each other in the faces, until the Celtic Wolf player lost his helmet.

Slade made a disparaging rumble, as if he watched toddlers wrestle in the yard. He rarely spoke, but his presence never let me truly forget he was nearby. Being surrounded by their scents had my wolf in an absolute frenzy, and no doubt, if I checked my underwear, I'd find them embarrassingly wet.

Hunter leaned forward, more interested than Slade in the fight. "Violence is in our nature, and at least alphas have regenerative powers. Kellan and Finley would be minus a few teeth otherwise."

I shuddered at the thought of how hard they'd have to be hit in the face to lose teeth. *Ouch.* "Finley looks happy out there. Hockey is good for him."

It was a stupid observation considering I'd seen the bear no more than a few times and knew the least about him of all the alphas. I had no idea what he was like when he wasn't scowling at me.

This time Slade's rumble was softer and introspective. "This game saved him. He'd die without it."

The thought of Finley dying had my wolf whimpering, and I wanted to curl in on myself and cry. Refusing to lose control here, I shoved that devastating imagery out of my head as fast as I could. "I'm—" I cleared my throat. "I'm glad he has it, then."

When there was only five minutes left in the game, our team was ahead by four, and the crowd was a cheering, drunk mass. I found myself less invested when Kellan and Finley were off the ice, but I had immensely enjoyed the game as a whole.

The sense of pride I felt watching their skills... They were a lot, and it was no surprise that I'd been squirming in my seat as they destroyed the other team.

This scent match superseded even the strongest bonds I'd ever witnessed, and I was starting to think Mom had lied about being scent matched to her pack. It wouldn't surprise me, since lying was pretty much par for the course with her. There was no one I could ask for the truth, except for Mom's pack, who I assumed were still out there somewhere. Beefed up on her stolen power.

Unfortunately, they were evil assholes who should not be reminded of my existence, so contacting them was not an option.

I side-glanced at Slade, who watched the last minutes of the game, and wondered if his hacking skills could be used to answer my questions. Not that we were at the stage of me asking him for a favor, especially when I couldn't tell him *why* I asked.

Cheers broke through my thoughts, and I glanced around to see that the game was finished. The Celtic Wolves crashed into each other, hugging and shouting in their exuberance. "Great win," Hunter called, and I waited for him to remove his arm from behind me, but he appeared to be in no rush.

Don't snuggle into him. Don't snuggle into him.

The crowds moved around us, and I was amazed when most of them gathered up their trash and took it with them. Humans weren't generally that respectful; I knew that for a fact as the one who was usually left behind to clean up after them.

It felt weird to be proud of being a shifter, after so many years running from my true heritage.

When half the crowds were gone, Hunter stood and held out his tattooed hand for me. I didn't hesitate, dropping my palm against his, and when he pulled me to my feet, he laced our fingers together in a twisting motion. My insides twisted too at the sensation of our interlocked fingers, and I was breathless as he led the way along the stadium seating.

Unlike the crowd, he headed toward the ice, and we ended up on a path inside a long hallway. Slade followed at my back, leaving a few feet between us.

It only occurred to me when the two alphas ducked their heads under a doorway, that Slade had been called in as part of my security for tonight. The alphas were taking turns in keeping me from being *almost* kidnapped again.

"Where are we going?" I asked, noticing a few groups of shifters near a closed door.

Hunter glanced down with an unreadable expression. "Thought you might want to see their victory walk. And that you've got nothing to worry about with the puck shifters."

I paid closer attention to the crowd milling around the door, noticing many of them were scantily clad woman, excitedly chatting or touching up their makeup. Two security guards stood on either side of the closed door, and I had to turn away from the sight of their navy uniforms.

For a few hours, I'd completely forgotten about the shitshow of my life.

Slade, who was perched nearby with his usual personal space in tow, met my gaze, and I found myself asking, "Did you find out anything about the attack? Clues or leads?"

He looked completely relaxed against the red brick wall, but I felt his coiled icy energy as he spoke. "We've got a couple of shifters in the holding cells near the squad training grounds. I'll be heading out to question them as soon as I can hand off guard duty."

"Can I come too?"

That got his attention, as his shrewd gaze snapped toward

me. "Why? What skills in questioning or torture do you possess?"

Glossing over his casual usage of the word *torture*, I shrugged. "I don't have any particular skills, but as the one who was attacked, I want to listen in."

I'd either confused or intrigued him—his expressions were impossible to read—but he definitely felt something. "I don't see what the use would be, but if you want to be there, I have no objections."

Hunter's hand tightened briefly around mine, but he didn't voice any objections either. Silence descended between us, but for once it wasn't uncomfortable. At least not for me. I was too busy watching the puck ladies titter around, most of them in heels so high they were in real danger of breaking their necks if they fell over.

Did they want to reach the heights of the hockey players? An impossible task, really, since they were all massive brutes. Most of the team appeared to be alphas, with just a few genetically blessed betas.

When the door opened, it was almost as loud in here as during the game. The first players out stopped and signed autographs, brushing off the women as they tried to hand them their numbers and business cards. The team all high-fived Hunter as they passed, and nodded respectfully to Slade, while eyeing me curiously.

Kellan and Christian hurried over to us, hair still wet from their showers. They had a similar look, but I preferred my golden boy over Christian's longer brown hair and deep brown eyes.

"Great to see you again, Emme," Christian said, bestowing the hugest smile on me.

I braced myself as he went in for a hug, only to have Kellan yank him back by his hair before he touched me. "No fucking touchy. I told you, asshole."

Christian's smile never faltered, even as he rubbed a hand over the back of his head. "Ouch, you fuck. I'm too young to be bald because you tore out my hair."

Hunter released an annoyed huff and stepped closer to my side, and I barely contained my shock when Slade also closed in ranks. He never touched me, but he was close enough for his scent to mingle with mine. As a warning to the other shifters.

Christian, no longer joking, held both hands up as he backed to a respectful distance. "Kel's my best friend, so anyone important to him is important to me." Multiple alpha rumbles filled the hall, and he hurried to add, "In a purely platonic, brotherly kind of way."

Kellan stood in front of me now, so I had to lean around him to reply. "Ignore the alphas, Christian. They're a little cranky today. I think they all need a nap."

Kellan turned and leaned down to bury his head against my neck, breathing deeply. "Are you the one putting me to bed, pretty girl?" His voice was muffled against my skin. "If so, I could absolutely get behind a nap."

Hunter didn't mind when Kellan wrapped us both up, and I cuddled into our Golden Boy because I'd missed him. "You guys did so well out there," I said against his chest. "I've never seen anyone skate like you do. It's beautiful poetry."

Kellan's huge body stilled, and when he pulled away, his expression was filled with unbridled joy. "Having you watch us play... I can't describe how that made me feel. You make me better, Em. Please tell me you'll be at every game."

"Every game I can." It was the only promise I could make.

His eyes were nearing that violet color I loved so much as he dropped a kiss on my lips. "That'll do for now, pretty girl."

When he stepped back, I noticed the two other players who'd joined our group: Finley and Kenzo.

The bear glared at me, and I got the feeling I was intruding on his usual aftergame ritual. Whatever peace he'd shown on the ice was long gone, and I didn't miss the worried stare Kenzo volleyed between me and his brother.

"I'm Kenzo," he said with a nod, making no move to touch me. "Fin's brother."

Other than a furrowed brow, Finley showed no real emotion to that statement.

I tried not to let it bother me as I smiled in return. "Emme, and it's nice to meet you. You guys played amazing. It was a really exciting game."

Christian whooped, and half the shifters in the room turned to stare. A lot of the ladies glared at me, the sole female in the group of alphas, but it wasn't like I'd deliberately stole all of their hockey players.

"We need to get out of here and party," Christian shouted, pumping his fist. "Though as the last single alpha in our core group, the rest of you have left me with an awfully large responsibility."

Kellan shuddered. "The puck shifters are all yours. They were too much even before I met my omega."

Finley snorted a cruel laugh. "You're not the last single alpha, bro."

If there hadn't been a wall behind me, I'd have staggered back at that blow. As it was, I barely managed to keep the hurt from showing on my face. He'd gone for maximum impact, while staring right at me to catch my reaction. Not that I'd ever give him the satisfaction.

Setting my face in what I hoped looked like boredom, I shrugged. "Should we get out of here and leave them to it?"

Kellan, who'd been glaring at Finley, returned his full focus to me. "Absolutely, Shortcake. We can party up at Luxuria tonight during your shift."

"Perfect," I chirped, ignoring the pang in my chest as I turned my back on Finley. "I'm ready to go."

I didn't wait for a reply, tugging Hunter's hand until he took the lead near the exit. Kellan stepped in and grabbed my other hand, sandwiching me between the alphas, and with Slade at our backs I could almost forget about Finley.

Even if I did spend most of the drive home trying to convince myself it was all for the best.

CHAPTER 41

The week of the Summit passed without further incident.

Hunter had no choice but to head back to the office, with all of his entitled alpha duties and CEO responsibilities. Not that I'd been left alone since the attack, but thankfully today was the last day of their Summit meetings, and I found myself with Slade of all shifters.

Kellan and Finley had training, not that the bear would ever be alone with me, even if my life depended on him. I was probably in more danger with him than out on my own.

"We have two more shifters to question," Slade said as way of greeting when I wandered down to the kitchen for breakfast. "You have ten minutes to get ready."

I glanced down at my skimpy tank and PJ shorts, and then back up at the dragon, who was in his usual enforcer's outfit of black army pants, fitted tee, and combat boots that could kill a shifter with one blow.

"Okay."

Running up the stairs, I hoped that today was the day we unearthed useful information. The other sessions I'd attended had all led us nowhere, except for giving me nightmares about blood-soaked shifters.

I was back downstairs in under eight minutes, dressed in jeans and a light blue shirt that matched my eyes. I'd also thrown on black biker boots, because I had a tiny bit of Slade hero worship going on. It was safer not to question the weird shit that was happening in my head lately. Instead I embraced the chaos.

"Eat," he said, as he stepped aside to reveal a heated breakfast sandwich on the counter, along with a coffee. "You have two minutes."

"Yes, sir."

His pupils flared, and I swung around and hurried to the food.

In my defense, I'd meant that to just be in my head, and I really hoped he wasn't about to fry my ass. I relaxed as soon as the scent of bacon filtered into my system—the guys used these sandwiches as quick breakfasts on the run, but they were my favorite morning snacks.

Wolfing it down, pun intended, I finished by gulping the coffee, which was thankfully only lukewarm. "Done!" I declared, certain I'd made it under his deadline.

I hadn't looked his way since my *sir* slipped out, but I felt his eyes on me. There was nothing quite like the coldly piercing stare of a dragon.

Without acknowledgement, he left the kitchen, and I hurried after him like a puppy. I'd be the one with Kellan's nickname soon if I wasn't careful.

Slade led me down to the garage, and I played my new game of trying to guess which of their amazing vehicle collection he'd take today. When he stopped by the bikes, I felt my eyes grow anime-style wide as I stared at him, and then at the bikes, and then back at him. "Holy shit. Are you fucking with me?"

The minutest of twitches pulled the corner of his lips. "Kellan wanted me to give you a gift."

That was when I noticed one of the bikes had a black, shiny sheet draped over it. Slade nodded, giving me permission to approach, and I almost fell over my own feet as I raced forward. Gripping the edge of the sheet, my heart slammed in my chest, and I'd never been both this excited and nervous at the same time.

I pulled slowly at first, but my eagerness got the better of me. Red came into view and then I was screaming, jumping up and down beside the most beautiful bike I'd ever seen.

It was the match of Slade's Ducati Panigale V4R, but while his was stealth black, mine had been painted a stunning reddish pink, close in color to my hair.

"He had it made custom for you."

I lifted my head as the first hot tear spilled down my cheek, and Slade looked horrified as he took a step back. "You hate it?"

"Goddess, no," I choked out. "This is the most amazing gift I've ever been given. I can't believe Kellan did this for me... I'll never be able to pay him back though." The reality of that dulled my excitement, as I forced myself to acknowledge that I really shouldn't take this gift. It wasn't a few extra clothes or makeup. It was a very expensive piece of machinery.

Slade tilted his head as he took in my expression. "You don't pay for gifts. That's not how they work. It would hurt Kellan's feelings if you refused it."

Hurting that alpha was the last thing I'd ever do, and with that in mind I decided I would borrow the bike but not claim it as my own. A compromise we could both live with. "Okay, I won't throw it in his face," I said to Slade, before sucking in a deep breath. "So... does that mean we're going to ride today?"

My wolf even perked up at the thought of being on a bike again, which told me she had missed it as much as me.

Slade nodded, sending a jolt of excitement through me as my stomach started doing somersaults. "Yes. Jacket and helmet are over there on the rack. Suit up."

Yes, sir! This time I managed to keep my inside thoughts from spilling out.

The leather jacket was black, in a high-quality leather, folded neatly on the rack. When I shook it loose, I chuckled at the *Shortcake* stitched on the back in the same pinkish red as my bike. My full-faced helmet was also pink, and when I slid both on, I felt like a million dollars.

Kellan owned a large chunk of my heart, and he demonstrated repeatedly that his love was the sort that you'd burn worlds for. The longer I knew him, the more I understood there was no real future where I could leave him. Which was terrifying, but for the first time I embraced a sliver of hope that I might find a way to stay with this pack.

Even if it was never perfect, maybe it could be enough.

Slade slid on his black jacket and helmet and then swung a long leg over his Panigale. While I'd suited up, he'd turned mine around for me so all I had to do was get on and enjoy the ride.

"Fuckkk," I groaned, sinking into the seat. It felt like heaven, and I wondered if I'd come in my pants when she started up.

Slade kicked over his bike first, and in the garage it was loud. *Give me more.* My energy bounced as I started mine, the two of us sitting for a beat to drink in perfection.

"There's nothing like it," I choked out, thrumming in the seat. "I swear, this is one of my favorite sounds in the world."

Slade's gaze was extra green when he met mine, right before he dropped his visor. "Mine too."

He took off through the already open garage door, and I followed close behind. Excited tension held me as we started out slow, giving me a chance to get used to the powerful motor, but once we hit that open road, I had plans to explode like a firework.

Out of town, Slade took off and I was right there with him.

My body thrummed as my heart raced with the bike, and I wanted to ask Slade if this was what flying felt like, but we didn't have any comms connecting our helmets.

If this shifter ever opened up to me, I had a hell of lot of questions to ask him. For now, I was content with watching him during the day and having secret naughty dreams at night.

My brief moments of hope should have warned me that everything was going too well. Life rarely ran smoothly for me. Even as Slade swung around to warn me, I never saw the attack coming.

A rocket hit his bike, and the blast smashed into me at the same time. The explosion threw me out into the desert, and I slammed against a tree, my spine cracking under the force. Darkness danced on the edge of my vision while my wolf howled and scraped at my insides.

A dragon roared in the background, but I was too far gone to see what was happening.

Pain dragged me from my semi-unconscious state, and I caught a glimpse of shifters surrounding me. Unfamiliar scents filled the air. I felt a prick in my neck, and warmth flooded my veins, bringing darkness with it once more.

It was a twilight sedation, so I was aware of being carried and thrown into the back of a vehicle. I had no idea of the extent of my injuries, but I'd definitely cracked a part of my body that shouldn't be cracked.

Slade... The drugs kept me from the full force of my panic over what had happened to the dragon shifter. He'd copped the full force of the blast, but I'd heard him roar after, so he wasn't dead. At least not immediately.

Had they murdered him while he was hurt and vulnerable?

Well, as vulnerable as a dragon ever was.

I wanted to scream and rage and destroy every one of these fuckers with my bare hands, but I couldn't even lift a finger, let alone get closer to them.

"Hit her again," someone grumbled, and the voice was vaguely familiar, but I couldn't place where I knew it from.

There was another needle prick, and this time there was no fighting the sedation.

The thought of being unconscious and alone with strangers had me silently screaming all the way into oblivion.

CHAPTER 42

The pounding in my head was the first sensation I became aware of. *Thump thump thump.* Nausea rolled in my gut, and I wasn't sure I'd ever felt my mouth this dry.

What happened? My memory was fuzzy, and as I tried to recall if I'd drank too much last night, the events come back to me in a flash.

Riding with Slade. The attack. Explosion and pain.

A thousand pins stabbed into my head when I lurched up and forced my eyes open. My wolf whimpered as she tried to orient herself, the drugs in our system keeping us groggy.

When my vision finally cleared, I found myself in what looked like an old-fashioned jail cell, my butt firmly planted on the cold, stone floor, while my arms were chained to the wall above my head. The chains kept me upright, and when I attempted to straighten, pain clamped down on my spine. Far superseding the pain in my head and strained arms.

"Don't move, Emmeline."

Slade's low rumble froze me, at least every part of me except my eyes, as I searched for him in the semi-darkness. It was not only dark but freezing in this cell, and as my breaths puffed in front of me, it took a few minutes for my sight to adjust and find the dragon.

Holy goddess babies.

He was in the cell across from me, and unlike me, was chained down with multiple cuffs around his arms, throat, and ankles. All of them glowing with witchy magic. I had no idea how strong dragons were, but to my knowledge no shifter could break through even one of those cuffs, let alone half a dozen.

Who the fuck took us? They had to be both loaded and connected to access magic like this. Shifters and witches weren't on the best of terms, which made this a very unusual display of power.

Granted, they'd have had no chance against a dragon otherwise.

"Slade," I groaned, trying not to vomit as my head pounded. "What happened?"

All I could clearly see was the glow of his green eyes and the menacing expression on his perfect face. "It was an ambush. I took out dozens of them, but they had a veritable army at their disposal. We underestimated their numbers, and it's put us in this position."

"Who—?" I tried to clear my aching throat, but only water would help at this point. "Who is behind the attack?"

Before he could answer there was a clang above our heads, and a second later footsteps echoed down to us. My body still wouldn't respond, even as I attempted to press myself against the wall and move as far from the bars as I could get.

Slade remained silent but deadly, his gaze locked on me.

As the steps grew louder, my stomach churned until I was once again in danger of vomiting all over myself. When the shifter came into view, I stared in blank horror, wondering if I was hallucinating.

"Hello, princess," he rumbled, eyes as dark as midnight staring right into my soul. "We've been looking for you for years."

As I stared back into the depraved gaze of Blaine Rogers, the entitled alpha of my mom's former pack, all I could hear were screams.

It took me a very long time to realize they were mine.

Catch up on what happens next in the Shifter City Fated Mates series in book 2, A Twist of Luck, coming in 2025. You can keep up to date with releases by joining my group: Jaymin Eve's Nerd Herd

AFTERWORD

Thank you! THANK YOU!! I am so grateful to each and every one of you that picked up this book and gave a new series a chance.

I wouldn't be here without you amazing readers, and I can't thank you all enough.

Oh, and by the way... How did you all find the cliffhanger? Loved it, right?

Aw, come on. Don't be like that. I'll make it all better, I promise.

All you have to do is trust me. ;)

Can I say... this series has absolutely destroyed me. Captivated me. I wrote A Curse of Fate in a frenzy because my obsession was next level. The characters wouldn't leave me alone, they invaded my actual soul and forced themselves onto these pages in frantic hours of writing.

I haven't felt like that since the Shadow Beast Shifters series. Utterly Consumed.

This is what I live for as an author, and I hope you felt that same obsession with my characters when you were reading.

I need to thank my husband first and foremost. Trav holds

the household together when I'm a hot mess and can't function. He's my support, my love, my comfort, my home. I also need to thank our beautiful girls. They share their mum with fictional characters, but are always the best part of my day.

Thanks to the amazing Tamara Kokic for painting this incredible cover for me. Your talent knows no bounds, and I'm in constant awe of what you create. Thank you SO much. I can't tell you enough.

Thanks to Lee, from Ocean's Edge Edits for helping me bring the absolute best version of the story to my readers. I appreciate your help and dedication.

Thanks to Gabby for the support, encouragement, hours of discussion of characters, promo material, laughter, and generally being a pretty fucking awesome human. You're the best.

Thank you to my PA Jane! You're such an amazing support and help to me, and I appreciate everything you do. Thank you for being in my corner, and all the promo/book world help you provide.

Thanks to my error's team who helped find any last lingering typo and grammar issues. Thank you to my Nerd Herd for being my calm in the storm, and for always encouraging me to keep writing even when it gets tough out there. I love you guys!!

Thank you to Good Girls PR, bloggers, readers, and reviewers who take the time to share our stories. You're the real MVPs here, and I hope you know how much we all appreciate your support of the book world.

WHAT TO READ NEXT...

I've had a lot of readers contacting me asking for what to read next. Try my complete (MF) romantasy series, the Shadow Beast Shifters. Rejected- Book 1

My father made a terrible mistake. One I'm left paying for.

As a wolf shifter growing up in a strong pack, I should be living my best life. But after my father tried to kill our leader, I'm labelled an outcast, traitor, less than dirt.

When I can't take pack life any longer, I run, but apparently they don't like losing their punching bag. Torin, the leader's son, drags me back before my first shift... a shift that will reveal my true mate. I never could have predicted who mine would be, but the moment my wolf looks upon him, I'm filled with hope for a brighter future.

Afterall, no one ever rejects their true mate, right?

Wrong. Very wrong.

When the wolves attack, my soul screams for vengeance, and somehow I touch the shadow world.

Somehow I bring him to our lands.

The Shadow Beast. Our shifter god. The devil himself.

Turns out being rejected by my mate was only the beginning.

*If you like sexy, dark paranormal romances, with humor, steam, action, a tough heroine and an antihero, this is for you. Rejected is full length (100k) words, is book one of three in Shadow Beast Shifters series, and ends on a cliffhanger. It's recommended for 18+ due to language and sexual situations.

ALSO BY JAYMIN EVE

Fallen Fae Gods (Dark Romantasy dragon shifter/fae 18+) (complete)

Book One: Gilded Wings

Book Two: Crimson Skies

Shadow Beast Shifters (Dark and Sexy wolf shifter/ god Romantasy 18+) (complete)

Book One: Rejected

Book Two: Reclaimed

Book Three: Reborn

Book Four: Deserted

Book Five: Compelled

Book Six: Glamoured

Boys of Bellerose (Dark, RH rock star romance 18+) (complete)

Book One: Poison Roses

Book Two: Dirty Truths

Book Three: Shattered Dreams

Book Four: Beautiful Thorns

Demon Pack (PNR/Urban Fantasy 18+) (Complete)

Book One: Demon Pack

Book Two: Demon Pack Elimination

Book Three: Demon Pack Eternal

Supernatural Prison Trilogy (Complete UF series 17+)

Book One: Dragon Marked

Book Two: Dragon Mystics

Book Three: Dragon Mated

Book Four: Broken Compass

Book Five: Magical Compass

Book Six: Louis

Book Seven: Elemental Compass

Supernatural Academy (Complete Urban Fantasy/PNR 18+)

Year One

Year Two

Year Three

Royals of Arbon Academy (Dark, complete Contemporary Romance 18+)

Book One: Princess Ballot

Book Two: Playboy Princes

Book Three: Poison Throne

Titan's Saga (PNR/UF. Sexy and humorous 18+)

Book One: Releasing the Gods

Book Two: Wrath of the Gods

Book Three: Revenge of the Gods

Dark Legacy (Complete Dark Contemporary high school romance 18+)

Book One: Broken Wings

Book Two: Broken Trust

Book Three: Broken Legacy

Secret Keepers Series (Complete PNR/Urban Fantasy)

Book One: House of Darken

Book Two: House of Imperial

Book Three: House of Leights

Book Four: House of Royale

Storm Princess Saga (Complete High Fantasy 18+)

Book One: The Princess Must Die

Book Two: The Princess Must Strike

Book Three: The Princess Must Reign

Curse of the Gods Series (Complete Reverse Harem Fantasy 18+)

Book One: Trickery

Book Two: Persuasion

Book Three: Seduction

Book Four: Strength

Novella: Neutral

Book Five: Pain

NYC Mecca Series (Complete - UF series)

Book One: Queen Heir

Book Two: Queen Alpha

Book Three: Queen Fae

Book Four: Queen Mecca

A Walker Saga (Complete - YA Fantasy)

Book One: First World

Book Two: Spurn

Book Three: Crais

Book Four: Regali

Book Five: Nephilius

Book Six: Dronish

Book Seven: Earth

Hive Trilogy (Complete UF/PNR series)

Book One: Ash

Book Two: Anarchy

Book Three: Annihilate

Sinclair Stories (Standalone Contemporary Romance 18+)

Songbird

www.ingramcontent.com/pod-product-compliance
Lightning Source LLC
Chambersburg PA
CBHW021216220726

48287CB00015B/1475